Prai
bestse

"A sexy, hot SEAL undercover in more ways than one...Tawny Weber nails this steamy suspense."
—*New York Times* bestselling author Cristin Harber

"Tawny Weber...has created the perfect hero for our time and a sizzling page-turner! What an awesome start to her Team Poseidon series."
—*New York Times* bestselling author Vicki Lewis Thompson

"I love a good SEAL romance and Tawny Weber knocked this one out of the park. Don't miss it!"
—*USA TODAY* bestselling author Karen Fenech

"This hot and sexy adventure takes readers on a thrilling ride of romance, secrets and SEALs."
—*RT Book Reviews*

"Reminiscent of Suzanne Brockmann's Troubleshooters series, Weber's latest will appeal to her fans as well as other military-romance readers. Diego personifies the honor and strength of a SEAL warrior in a good read with an engaging heroine and child."
—*Booklist*

"*Call to Honor* is a tightly plotted story with a few startling turns of events, the characters are all credible and...the pace never falters."
—*Fresh Fiction*

**Also available from
Tawny Weber
and HQN Books**

Team Poseidon

*Call to Honor
Call to Engage
Call to Redemption*

To see the complete list of titles available from
Tawny Weber, please visit tawnyweber.com.

TAWNY WEBER

CALL TO ENGAGE

HQN™

HQN™

ISBN-13: 978-0-373-80196-1

Call to Engage

Copyright © 2017 by Tawny Weber

Recycling programs for this product may not exist in your area.

To my daughters, with love and thanks.
You changed my life.

CHAPTER ONE

THE SHADOWS WERE closing in. Dark and silent, they smothered the light. Sucked up every ounce of air, ripping it from the very atoms of his body.

Then there was the pain.

Vicious. Cutting. Fire deep in the bones, exploding outward. Tearing inward. Flesh shredding as flames engulfed his body.

Cries of terror rang out, circling his head. He tried to move, tried to force himself to ignore the agony. He had to rescue the caller. Had to. The screams continued. Sharp at first, calling for help. Then weaker. Then nothing. Just the crackling roar of fire, the hideous thunder of a heart struggling to keep its beat.

Just as the struggle became too much, a hand reached into the fire. Cool, liberating, extricating him from hell. Long, slender fingers soothed the misery, eased the terror.

Even as he grasped salvation, desperate for respite, a part of him—a remote particle of his brain—recognized the hand. He knew the scar that bisected the index finger had come from a broken bottle. The ring, a twist of gold and silver with tiny copper beads, had been bought at a county fair.

For a heartbeat he was free of the pain. But even as

he escaped the fire, the hand disappeared. Leaving him in the aftermath.

The pain.

Soul-ripping pain.

The bitter taste of failure.

Trapped in the heavy silence, the reminder circled, spiraling tighter. Closing in.

The pained cries from his teammate. His brother. His friend.

Everything went black. Soulless and empty as reality clenched around him in a tight fist, forcing him to face the inescapable. That instead of rescuing his teammate, instead of doing the job he'd been trained to do, he'd let the man die in a miserable inferno.

He would pay for that forever.

If only here in the silence.

"Yo, Rembrandt."

Lieutenant Elijah Prescott woke drenched in sweat that felt like ice on his skin, his mind—his heart—still gripped by the sharp teeth of the dream. His breath came in guttural pants. His body flashed hot, then cold, then hot again as his pulse whipped furiously through his battered system.

Still spiraling through a hideous slide show of mental images, he pried his eyelids open and hoped like hell it really had been just a dream. *No. Memories*, he realized as he blinked in the dim light.

Half dreams, half memories. It didn't matter.

He pushed himself upright, rubbing both hands over his face to scrub away the sticky layer of dried sweat.

"Rembrandt?"

"Yeah?" Face still buried in his hands, Elijah turned

his head toward the voice in the shadowy dark of his doorway.

"Supposed to report for duty in less than an hour," Lansky said, the shrug clear in his tone. "Figured you might not have heard your alarm."

Was that the shrieking siren that had been blaring through his dream? His alarm clock? He glanced at the numbers glowing red and noted that it was already 5:08 a.m.

"Thanks, " he said. *For the wake-up, and for letting it go at that.*

Waiting until Lansky melted back into the darkness, Elijah dropped his face back into his hands and breathed, shaking off the nasty dregs of the nightmare.

They had fifty-two minutes until they reported for duty. There'd been a time that he could go from waking to duty in ten. Three if he was stationed in a hot zone.

That was then.

Now?

Now he was rolling out of bed feeling like a goddamn eighty-year-old arthritic on a wet, cold night.

Or, worse, an invalid.

Elijah gave his face one last scrub before shoving to his feet. Ignoring the pain ripping down his side, tearing into his thigh, he stretched.

Katas, chaturangas.

His body was a machine.

He dropped to the floor for his customary one hundred push-ups.

His body was well honed and built for power.

By the time he'd finished his morning trifecta with

sit-ups and pull-ups, he was ready to admit that his well-honed, powerful body hurt like hell.

Bare skin covered in a layer of sweat and boxers, he ignored the trembling muscles and moved back to his bed. A part of him wanted to drop down, face-first, into the pillow, wanted to burrow under the covers and find the sweet oblivion of dreamless sleep.

Instead, with the military precision honed by a dozen years served in the Navy, he tucked and stretched the bedding into place with a couple of practiced moves. He didn't have to think about what to wear, just grabbed the neatly pressed digies—blue camo multipocketed pants and tee—on their mutual hanger, snapped up boxers and socks and headed for the shower. He didn't bother with the lights. He had vision like a cat, and the dark was easier on the burning behind his eyes.

He stepped into the shower, letting the brutally hot water pound away the ache of a restless night. Letting it wash away the nagging pain he couldn't explain. Or, rather, chose to ignore. Elijah rubbed his thigh, running soap over the glossy, puckered flesh as if it didn't bother him. But the water, comforting a second before, felt like shards of glass. Instead of stepping out from under the water, he turned up the heat.

He refused to be a wimp.

It took him under ten minutes to shower, shave, dress and get ready for the day. He'd spent a couple of years serving on a submarine, so he could have done it in three, but he kept finding himself frowning at the wall, trying to recall what he'd dreamed that had left such a hollow feeling in his gut.

Following the scent of coffee through the living area

of the apartment-style barracks he shared with Lansky and into the postage-stamp-size kitchen, Elijah took the mug his new roomie held out and gulped the caffeinated elixir with a grunt of appreciation.

By the time he'd drained it, Lansky had eggs scrambled into a tortilla, covered with a couple of slices of bacon and a tidy sprinkling of cheese.

"Living with you is going to be one sweet pleasure," Elijah stated, nodding his thanks as he eyed his teammate. Both SEALs, he'd served with Jared Lansky for a decade now. Elijah had never realized the guy could cook like this. Goes to show you could know someone for years, train and serve and bleed with them, drink until sick together, but they could still surprise you.

Elijah used to like surprises.

"I figured you could use a hot breakfast today," Lansky said, his words light and friendly. But there was a deep well of concern in the man's eyes. "First day back and all that."

Elijah's shoulders jerked, his spine stiffening. He knew the concern was heartfelt, brother to brother. Just as he knew it was justified. But damned if he wanted it. Concern like that, it was a heartbeat from pity. And he'd had enough of that in the past few months to last a lifetime.

Enough to put doubts in the corners of his mind. Doubts that tried to creep out in his dreams. Doubts that, if left unchecked, could destroy him.

"All I need is a great breakfast to kick today's ass," he said, biting into the burrito and grinning as the heat and spice hit his tongue. "This is damned good."

"You need anything else? Fruit or oatmeal or something?"

Oatmeal? Elijah had to swallow quickly to avoid choking on the second half of the burrito.

"Dude, you think I'm so pathetic that you need to stick me with oatmeal?"

"Sorry. It was my mom's go-to for big mornings. You know, first day of school, finals week, the day I enlisted, the day of my dad's funeral." Looking embarrassed—something Lansky never was—the other man gave a good-natured shrug. "Guess it's one of those crazy kid things that we never lose, ya know?"

"Yeah. I know."

And he appreciated it. The offer. That Lansky cared enough to make it. And the guy's insight. The idea of oatmeal itself? That he didn't appreciate so much.

"Pretty sure this burrito and coffee are all I need to handle going back on duty."

He'd handle it.

He would. He had to.

Because he was a SEAL.

Being a SEAL, it's all he had. It's all he was. He'd protect that, hold that, to his dying breath.

While Lansky scooped up another burrito for each of them, Elijah poured coffee and pondered how he'd gone from the classic skinny kid growing up in a small town outside Napa to become a supposedly badass SEAL.

He'd spent his childhood in Yountville, a dreamer more interested in drawing pictures and scoring with girls than taking on bad guys. When he'd learned that bad guys—or rather, the hard-ass jocks who'd run the school like gangs ran the streets—didn't check interest before they kicked ass, he'd figured he'd better reconsider his thinking.

He'd joined the service fresh out of high school, eager to serve, sure he could make a difference. That choice had taken him the world over, had shown him man's highs and lows and had netted him a fistful of commendations. Trained first in linguistics, then in cryptology, he'd put his skill with words and his talent with puzzles to good use.

He'd learned to fight. He'd developed strategic skills. He'd found himself.

But true credit for making him the man he was came down to his being a SEAL. A SEAL and, more to the point, a member of the elite group of SEALs that formed Poseidon.

Twelve men had come out of BUD/S together ten years back, and thanks to Admiral Cree, all twelve served among SEAL Team 7's various platoons. That meant they were able to continue training together, studying together, excelling together.

And when called up, to serve together. They were an elite force of warriors, all focused on one purpose: to be the best of the best. They trained longer, they pushed further, they fought harder than anyone else. They focused on strategy; they specialized in everything.

They were, Elijah knew, the reason he was the man he was, and they were the reason he was alive today. They'd pulled him from the flaming bowels of hell, he admitted to himself as he and Lansky finished their breakfast.

"I cook—you clean. Since I hate dishpan hands, I figure this works fine," the other man said with an easy smile at odds with his bloodshot eyes. As the sun rose, washing color into the jut of space deemed the kitchen, Elijah studied his roommate. You'd think Lansky'd been the one having the crap dreams from the drawn-out lines on his narrow face.

"Works for me. Don't wanna do anything to hurt your pretty looks." Elijah gave him another once-over. The guy resembled one of those cherubs his mother had painted on little china dishes, only all grown up. Blond hair, blue eyes and a sweet-cheeked innocence combined with a body sculpted by military training were just a few of the many tools Lansky put to use in his never-ending quest to bag as many chicks as he could.

And speaking of...

"I didn't figure I'd see you this morning," Elijah said, dumping the pans into the sink with a squirt of soap before adding hot water. "Thought you had plans last night that'd keep you in someone else's bed until reveille. What happened? You strike out?"

"I never strike out, my man. I simply move on."

Didn't look like he'd moved on. Looked more like he'd spent the night suffering, brooding and hating life.

But as members of Poseidon, Elijah and Lansky had worked enough missions together, and yeah, cruised enough bars, that he knew the other man's style. Lansky would give a friend—hell, an enemy—the shirt off his back if he needed it, but he didn't share diddly unless he wanted to. And the man hated giving up to the point where stubborn tiptoed toward stupidity.

Come to think of it, they probably had all those things in common.

"What's her name?"

Lansky's scowl deepened as he refilled his own mug; the way the rich brown liquid sloshed against the white crockery made it clear this wasn't a breakfast conversation he wanted to have.

"Her, who? It'd be a waste to limit myself to just one woman, Rembrandt. You know that."

"Right."

That was Lansky's usual MO. Love 'em and leave 'em smiling was his motto. But if Elijah wasn't mistaken, that motto had taken a nosedive since the other man had met a sexy brunette a few months back. With the skill of a man who enjoyed beauty in all its forms, Elijah brought the face to mind. A lush brunette with the face of a Greek goddess and the body to match.

Although Lansky had gotten to know her a lot better—along the lines of biblical knowing—they'd both met Andrianna Stamos months ago on a covert op run by Poseidon in search of a rogue SEAL. One who'd dirtied the team, who'd betrayed his country, who'd jeopardized a critical mission. A man who'd hidden treason behind a friendly smile and lied his way up the ranks about who he was, about what he'd done, about everything from deserting his child to where he'd hidden the riches reaped from treason.

They hadn't found Brandon Ramsey. Still didn't know if he was dead or alive. All they knew for sure was that he'd stolen classified information under the guise of an explosion.

Elijah rubbed his fingers over the puckered scars discernible even through the fabric of his slacks and hid his grimace with his cup.

"You ever had it hot for a woman who didn't want

jack to do with you?" Lansky asked with a shrug. "You know, the kind of woman you can't shake from your mind?"

The swallow of coffee turned to vinegar in Elijah's mouth.

Damn.

The memory of big brown eyes and the sexiest smile ever to curve a Cupid's-bow mouth flashed through his mind. Just as quickly as that memory appeared, it was followed by those eyes filled with tears, brimming with accusation, and that mouth trembling as it said goodbye.

The vicious, cutting pain hit all the harder because it was unexpected. He knew exactly how it felt to have a woman rip his heart out of his chest and crush it to dust while he watched, helpless on the sidelines. Recovery in the burn ward was easier, and it hurt a hell of a lot less.

Elijah dumped what was left of his coffee in the sink. Looked like the scars on his leg weren't the only ones being poked at this morning.

"Yeah. I know what it's like. Rejection is fucked, my friend. Rejection when the heart's involved? Fucked beyond words." Wanting to put it from his mind, he started on another dish.

"Pretty much the worst," Lansky muttered, his tone making it clear he was looking for assurance that he was wrong. But Elijah didn't have any to give him. Not when it came to heartache and women.

"I'm pretty sure I'd rather take on a dirty bomb and a cell of urban terrorists single-handed than give a woman my heart again," Elijah confessed, naming two of the threats the team hated most. Urban environments usually meant higher collateral damage, bigger rebuilding costs and, worse, playing nice with locals. "I figure there's a better chance of beating the terrorists. Women? That's a no-win game."

"That is not a comfort," Lansky said with a bitter laugh, holding out his empty cup for Elijah to add to KP.

"Even at the best of times, relationships are never easy, " Elijah shot back. He didn't know if it mattered if the relationship had lasted two weeks, two years or two decades. The other party ending it sucked hard.

"Good thing we're not in the business of easy," he added as he stacked the dishes in the cupboard, hoping to make up for the dismal morning pep talk.

"So why do we play?"

"Best game in town."

"True that," Lansky agreed, grabbing his cap from the closet before tossing Elijah his own.

They both gave one last, automatic look around before stepping outside. They lived on base in the apartment, and while an inspection might be unlikely, it could still happen. But it was habit more than concern that had both men tidying on their way out the door.

Even as he welcomed the cool air of a Southern California morning, Elijah's gut tightened. Excitement, he figured. He'd been on inactive duty for way too long. This was his first day back in the trenches, his first op since the mission gone wrong.

He was ready, he vowed, ignoring the twinge in his thigh as they made their way down the stairs.

More than ready, dammit.

As if reading his mind, Lansky slid a glance sideways and asked, "You looking forward to getting back to it?"

"Yep. Nothing like a few hours of ass-breaking PT, target shooting and some dive practice to let me know I'm alive." He grinned.

"You know, most guys go for kinky sex as proof of life. Gotta wonder at one who's looking forward to physical training, which'll consist of a crapload of push-ups, pull-ups and sit-ups, followed by a sweaty run and ice-cold swim."

"Did all that yesterday, and every day last week," Elijah said with a shrug. At Lansky's look, he admitted, "I had to make sure I could."

"Of course you could. You're a SEAL, man. More than that, you're Poseidon."

The men who served as SEALs were diverse, their reasons and motivations as varied as they were. But their goal, as one, was to be the best and to serve their country, the Navy, their team.

Poseidon, on the other hand, was a group of twelve men whose numbers and names never varied. Their team was built on years of trust. The men knew one another inside out, knew what made the others tick, how each man's tick meshed with their own. Their goal was bigger than to simply be the best. Their goal was stronger than one man's hopes. They trained beyond what the others did; they studied further than the rest. Every man on the Poseidon team held multiple ratings—including Special Ops Combat Medic—each qualified to handle everything from EODs to aviation to intelligence.

They did it because they knew that's what it'd take to achieve their mission of absolute cohesion. They did it because their leader asked them to.

"Just remember... We are Poseidon, king of the sea.

Better than best is what we be. We rule by day, we rule by night. We kick every ass that's in our sight."

"My favorite cadence. By the time I was done with the workouts, I was grunting it," Elijah confessed with a laugh as they continued toward a series of low-slung buildings. There were more bodies here, uniforms crisp and faces fresh as the base made ready for the day.

He'd missed this, Elijah realized. The never-changing change that was life on a military base.

"You know you could have tapped me to work out with you. I don't mind the extra PT, and there's no reason you had to go it alone."

Just like that. Chest burning with words he couldn't say, Elijah's laugh faded. "I appreciate it, man."

Then, because he could see Lansky was just as uncomfortable as he at the sentiment in the air, he shrugged. "Wouldn't have mattered if I did, though. You were on leave last week and nowhere to be seen. What'd you do? Fall off the face of the earth? Torres said he tried to reach you a couple of times to no avail."

Something flashed over Lansky's face—a different kind of discomfort—before the guy offered his own shrug. "I had things to do, my friend."

"Female things?"

"Always." With that and a shake of his head to indicate he didn't want to talk about it, Lansky changed the subject. "Hell of a long break between missions. You looking forward to getting back in the game?"

"Ready and able." To serve, and to prove himself.

Elijah had never been big on caring what other people thought about him. He'd lived his life pretty much on his terms. They were easygoing, go-with-the-flow terms that fit with the credo his father had handed down.

If he lived life to the fullest, he could live with his regrets. If he listened to his heart, he could overcome any doubts. If he walked the honest line, he could always hold his head high.

He had to admit, he'd racked up a few regrets in his thirty years. He'd lived through pain, heartbreak and a loss he didn't expect to ever recover from. He'd listened to his heart, and, yeah, it had ended up crushed like a week-old cookie left in someone's pocket. But had no doubt that he'd done his best.

He knew a few people—CIA, Naval Investigation, even other SEALs—wondered if Brandon Ramsey had tried to blow Elijah to hell in a clean-sweep effort to eliminate his cohorts. But the people who mattered knew better.

At least that was what he told himself.

He'd taken a hit and he'd gone down in the line of duty. But now he was back in shape. He was back on duty. And, dammit, he'd get his reputation back on track.

He wanted to believe that.

He needed to believe that.

But it wasn't easy. Not when he had to take a slower pace than the usual double-time to cross the base. Not when he saw the looks cast his way. The speculation in people's eyes. Without comment, Lansky matched his steps, chatting instead about random crap like box scores and the hot blonde working the PX. When they stepped into the sparse briefing room five minutes later, Elijah breathed the familiar in deeply.

Shoving both hands into the front pockets of his digies, he ignored the sudden tightness across his shoulders, the raw feeling in his gut.

It was time to report for duty.

There was no room for any of that other crap.

CHAPTER TWO

"You boys are late."

Neither Elijah nor Lansky bothered checking the time. They knew it was T minus five. If they were late, Savino would already be there. And instead of milling about the room, the men would be in their seats.

Captain Milt Jarrett was the military version of a worrywart, though. It was his job to keep them on track, to keep things tidy and—something beyond Elijah's ken—to keep their missions on budget.

"My fault. I was whining about heartbreak," Lansky said, pulling a face. "You know how that is, right, Jarrett? The way I hear it, every woman you've been with has dumped you."

Jarrett laughed along with the rest of the room. Lansky just grinned. Since the ribbing had put him at ease, Elijah started to pull his hands from his pockets and noticed a slip of paper in one. *Weird.* He hadn't been in uniform in months. He pulled it out to see what he'd left there that'd made it through laundry detail while Jarrett returned fire.

"The way I heard it, Lansky, you don't have a heart to break. Bummer, that. The rest of you, if you've finished gossiping and aren't planning to do each other's nails, maybe we can get down to business," Captain

Jarrett called as he strode to the front of the room. He had an equal-opportunity scowl, spreading it among everyone whether they'd been late or not, were simply standing or already seated at their desks.

The men still on their feet began moving at a leisurely pace toward the remaining empty seats. Nobody rushed. Jarrett had asshole tendencies that rubbed most of the team wrong. The only thing saving the guy was his rank and the fact that he was a brilliant strategist.

Elijah noted that his accustomed seat to the right front of the podium was available. Whether by design or luck, he didn't know, but he made his way over, sinking gratefully into the questionable comfort of the wooden chair. As Lansky started chatting with Diego Torres, another teammate, Elijah unfolded the paper to see what'd been left in his pocket. Scrawled in black ink over the torn corner of college-ruled notepaper was a handwritten note.

A real friend listens until he hears the truth.

Shit.

What was with this morning and painful reminders? If Elijah was a man who believed in omens—and he constantly told himself that he definitely was not—he'd be having some serious worries.

Because he recognized the handwriting as that of a former—and supposedly dead—teammate. One who'd caused intense pain to a lot of people, himself included. Jaw clenched against the memories, Elijah started to crush the paper in his fist, then thought better of it. How the hell had it gotten into his pocket? He'd roomed with

Ramsey before the mission that had sent Elijah to the burn ward and Ramsey into an ash can. But he'd never seen that paper before, and he and Ramsey had never been note-sharing, or pants-sharing, kind of guys.

Pulling his sketch pad out of his satchel, Elijah tucked the paper into the back of the pad and snagged a pencil. Then, in his usual way of working through something that puzzled him, he ran his fingers over the thick blank page, letting his mind clear and his pencil fly.

The sounds, the chatter, the varied scents of colognes and soap all faded into the background as he sketched. Impressions, memories, imagined scenarios.

"Dude, I missed breakfast," Diego muttered next to him. "That's a whole lot of ugly to offer up to an empty stomach."

Elijah glanced at his tablemate, then back at the sketch pad and grimaced. It was a page full of Ramsey. Full face, side view, body shots, action images. In some he'd drawn the guy to look like a movie star, in others like the devil himself. Which was the true face of the man? Did any of them show the lies? The hideous betrayal?

Elijah would have to look closer later. For now...

"Sorry." He flipped to a blank page.

Yeah. Brandon Ramsey had given the entire team a gut ache, but Diego had special reason to hate the guy. Before he could explain the drawings, the room went silent.

"Gentlemen."

Commander Nic Savino's single word was quiet, his steps easy as he strode into the room. Tall and lean despite the powerful breadth of his shoulders, Savino was a man who demanded attention without ever having to force the issue. Elijah had seen him bloody; he'd seen him drunk. He'd seen him pissed, and he'd seen him thrilled. What he'd never seen was Savino out of control.

Savino didn't command the entire SEAL Team 7, but he was in charge of this unit. And he was the leader of Poseidon.

As soon as he reached the front of the room, Savino slanted Jarrett a nod. With automatic deference, the other man stepped away from the podium and took his own seat. The captain booted up his computer, the information on it flashing on the screen behind the podium with the familiar trident insignia.

"If everyone's ready?" Savino's dark eyes scanned the room. Knowing he was taking in every detail, Elijah wouldn't be surprised to find out the guy was checking their souls along with inspecting the team. "We have a mission."

As one the men came to attention, each using his own method of recording data. To Elijah's right, Lansky whipped out a computer tablet and gave it a snap to release its keyboard. To his left, Torres pulled out an encrypted recording device and, being a big believer in backup, a notebook. Elijah's own notebook was actually a sketch pad. It was filled with drawings, encrypted notes and, if he did say so himself, clever doodles.

As he listened to his commander outline the objective, detail the plan and delineate strategy, Elijah drew. He sketched his impressions from the buildings Savino showed on the view screen. He added a helicopter in the sky, then as he considered, a few bodies in the water. Savino hadn't mentioned a water approach yet, but given that the water was there, he would.

That's how Savino preferred to work his missions. He outlined, he detailed and he delineated. Then he opened the floor for input. It was one of the many reasons the man was a great leader. He inspired trust and elicited loyalty because he offered his team exactly that.

So it was a piss-off that that trust had been betrayed by one of their own. That the team had landed under investigation because a decorated SEAL played dirty, faking his own death after stealing top secret intel to sell to enemy militants.

Elijah jabbed the paper hard enough to snap his pencil lead. He drew air through his teeth, but it didn't much cool the fury of his thoughts, so he tried a couple more.

A few months back, Savino had led a small covert team in an attempt to locate and detail the traitor. They'd apprehended his coconspirator, but as far as Elijah knew, the target was still in the wind.

Fucker.

"Yo," Lansky murmured, rapping Elijah on the arm with a fresh pencil. He lifted it and one brow, warning Elijah to pull his head out and focus.

With a grimace and a nod of thanks, Elijah took the pencil and a deep breath. Using every iota of training garnered in his years of service and the determined focus that'd gotten him out of the hospital and back on duty eight months ahead of schedule, he gave all his concentration to the briefing.

Though his specialty was cryptology, or deciphering code, Elijah had still taken part in dozens of similar missions in his ten years as a SEAL, so the basics were ingrained and as familiar as his own name.

However, hostage extraction was always a delicate undertaking, and he'd been out of the game for a few months, so he took special care in his notes. He crafted suggestions, backup scenarios. After eyeing the schematics of the embassy they'd be infiltrating, he sketched alternate escape routes.

Chances were he'd be on the copter, monitoring communications. He knew the wisdom of such an assignment. He'd been sidelined for a while; others had earned the privilege of boots on the ground. And his specialty was, after all, communications.

Still, he chafed at the restriction.

He wanted—needed—action.

He had to prove he had what it took. That he was still a SEAL in top form. One of the elite. *The best, dammit.* He needed to prove it to the team. To Savino.

And, yeah, to himself.

Elijah's pencil flew over the page, lead scratching out a list of reasons to offer his commander to convince the man that Elijah should be part of the ground team. Then Savino began assigning roles.

"Lansky, Torres, Prescott, Loudon, Masters, Rengel. You're on the extraction. Lansky and Masters will enter here and here." He tapped the blueprint of the embassy with his stylus so the screen lit with red dots. Then he tapped again to light four green dots near the delivery docks. "Prescott, Torres, Rengel and Loudon, you'll come in from the water."

He finished with, "Danby, Ward, Powers, you're in the air with Jarrett."

He was on the ground? Not in the air? *Hell, yeah*, his mind celebrated. His first mission back on active duty since he'd damn near exploded into a few hundred painful pieces, and he wasn't holed up in the back seat. Nope, he'd be right there in the thick of the action. Right there, where it was all going down, he thought, rubbing a hand over his thigh.

Elijah's other hand gripped his pencil so tightly that he flattened the wood, destroying it with a resounding crack. Yeah, he'd smile. Just as soon as his gut unclenched.

"Any questions?"

A few men shook their heads. Others silently gathered their notes. A couple simply waited.

"Torres, Lansky, Loudon, Prescott and Ward, remain. Everyone else, dismissed," Savino barked, releasing all the men except the members of Poseidon.

Nic Savino glanced at the clock, confirming that he was right on schedule. He patiently waited for the room to clear of everyone but his elite team. Even as some men moved out, others moved in until there were thirteen of them in all.

He glanced at Jarrett, who clung to the chair as if he knew they all wanted him gone. He looked like a grumpy bulldog guarding his favorite bone.

"Comfy, Captain?" Savino asked, his words calm and his expression pleasant.

"Orders are orders, Savino," Jarrett said, rising to speak in Savino's ear. The man kept his words pitched low, as if trying to keep them from the rest of the room. Ridiculous, since Poseidon heard everything.

From the expression on the men's faces, they definitely heard. And didn't like. Savino could relate.

But, as Jarrett said, orders were orders. And Admiral Cree had decreed that until Ramsey was in the brig and Poseidon in the clear, they'd have company. So Savino gestured to the chair and suggested the man sit back down. After all, it wasn't Jarrett's fault that the team was under supervision.

Savino was a man who epitomized control. Some would say it was his trademark. He'd used it, and rigid focus, to form a team of special operatives, skilled assets, into even more. Poseidon was the elite among the elite. Unlike DEVGRU, the Navy's Special Warfare Development Group, Poseidon wasn't open for applications. It was composed of men he'd handpicked ten years before. Men who had, over the course of a decade, trained together, fought together, bled together, until they were, essentially, one.

And now that one was threatened.

"Gentlemen, in case you didn't notice, we've earned ourselves a babysitter." The room buzzed with mutters and complaints. Savino waited for it to ebb before inclining his head in agreement. "Captain Jarrett will be monitoring missions for the next little while. The team and Poseidon have been officially cleared of wrongdoing in the Ramsey situation, but there are some in Naval Investigation who don't accept the official stand."

"I'm not here to interfere or horn in on the workings of Poseidon," Jarrett said, addressing the entire room.

"I'll do whatever I can to help clear the team, to get you guys back to business as usual."

Wanting to believe that, Savino nodded. Then, skilled at moving past pain—even when it was a pain in his ass—he got back to the duty at hand.

"To bring everyone up to speed, I'll recap the details of our current situation. These details are for Poseidon ears only," he said as the men prepared to take mental notes. Everyone put away their papers, pens and electronics. They'd work from memory on this one.

"As you all know, we encountered an incident last February on a routine mission. During the extraction of a kidnapped scientist, a militant base exploded, the fire severely injuring a SEAL." He inclined his head toward Prescott, who, according to the doctors, was lucky to be alive. "The explosion was said to destroy the formula for a potential chemical weapon and killed numerous militants, including the jihad leader and, to all appearances, one of our own."

The words *to all appearances* caused a stir. Nobody spoke; nobody even moved. But the room came to attention.

"Under CIA orders and pursuant to NI protocols an investigation was launched on SEAL Team 7 and, more specifically, on Poseidon."

Savino laid it all out. The chemical formula had been coded with a time stamp that'd put its theft at the exact time of their mission, implicating the team when its sale was discovered.

"Sir," Loudon interrupted. "Why would Naval Investigation be looking at us for the theft? It'd make more sense to look to the militants themselves for the theft and sale of that formula."

"It would, if not for the fact that the sale was to a tribe that group has been at war with for centuries." Savino named the tribe, which elicited grimaces from most of his men. Because there was ugly, and there was *ugly*. And this group of militants had one goal and one goal only: world annihilation.

"To date, five more incidents have been traced back to SEAL missions in which weapons, information or technology was sold. Of those, three missions were led by Poseidon."

The tension was so tight it was as if the room had turned into a vise. Savino didn't need to look around to see the men's reactions. He could feel them. Hell, he had them.

Fury, betrayal and just a hint of worry.

Only a stupid man thought he was invincible. Only an arrogant man thought his mantle of right protected him from persecution. Even Jarrett grimaced, his jowls tight as he shook his head in disgust.

"I don't have to tell you the ramifications of an NI investigation." Savino slid a sideways glance at Jarrett. Babysitters were only the beginning, he knew. "The damage that it can cause to a career, or in this case, to the very existence of Poseidon."

Giving up his spot behind the podium, Savino paced in front of it as he continued the briefing.

"Funds for the chemical weapons sale were traced to an account under Ramsey's name as well as a civilian. The account is still in active use despite his supposed death. Further investigation cleared the civilian."

His gaze cut to Torres, who'd led that investigation and was now engaged to marry the civilian. "But it resulted in the kidnapping of Ramsey's son. A team retrieved the child and detained Petty Officer Dane Adams, who while implicating himself and Ramsey, indicates that there are others still involved."

Who?

Savino's fists clenched behind his back as he paced, wondering for the hundredth time since this had begun what the hell NI had on Poseidon that made them so sure his team was dirty. He'd dug deep himself, but he hadn't come up with a damned thing.

"While we do not have confirmation that Ramsey is still alive, NI assumes that he is." Savino paused, taking the time to look from man to man, meeting each of their eyes, deepening their connection.

"I want him found. I want him taken down and made answerable for his crimes. Crimes against his country, against his uniform and, yes, against this team. He tried to set up one of our own. He tried to take down Poseidon." He leaned back against the podium now, his usually unreadable face a study of icy fury. "Somehow, he got past us. He not only carried out treasonous actions under our very noses, but he thinks that he got away with them. We need to correct that, gentlemen."

"What's the plan?" Torres asked. Rightfully, as far as Savino was concerned, since he was the one who'd been specifically framed to take the fall a few months back.

"In addition to continuing with your current assignment, each of you will be taking on additional tasks. These tasks are Code Red, gentlemen." Meaning they didn't disclose them, not even to one another. They reported directly to Savino, and everything was done in person. No emails, no phone calls, no handwritten notes. "Poseidon has one goal now, gentlemen. To take down Ramsey and whoever else is involved. As of now, Operation Fuck Up is in effect."

ONE THING ABOUT SEALs, they were hell on multitasking. Operation Fuck Up might be in effect, but members of Poseidon and SEAL Team 7 had other missions to carry out. So while time was devoted to tracking their treasonous teammate, the rest of their focus was on the current assignment.

When breaking into another country's embassy on foreign soil, *stealth* was the keyword. When breaking in with the objective of covertly extracting a man slated for execution, a sticky layer of diplomacy was wrapped around the stealth. The priority was retrieving the hostage. Secondary was doing so without taking lives.

Using the moonless sky to their advantage, six men rappelled down from the roof. Infrared confirmed the hostage was held on the eighth floor, two guards in the room with him, four more stationed outside the door. Bars on the windows, men stationed at the end of each hallway and on the exits.

So they went in through one of the empty offices two doors down from where the hostage was being held. Working in concert, their moves as coordinated as they were automatic, the team used a silent explosive on the window bars, sliding inside as quietly as smoke.

They stunned the guards outside the door just as quietly, tucking them into the empty office, neatly bound and gagged. Elijah and Torres took their place outside the door while the other four slid into the hostage's room.

Eyes sharp, senses on full alert, even as he kept watch, Elijah wanted to grin. Stupid reaction, but, man, it felt good to be back on track. To do what he was trained to do.

Not that he'd worried about it. Much. But he was glad to see it wasn't an issue. Sure, his leg was a little tight, the puckered skin protesting over screaming muscles. But that wasn't slowing him down.

As if proving his point, the signal came from inside the room. He moved with easy stealth down the hall to the left, Torres to the right, then returned the all clear.

Powers's voice came through the comm in Elijah's helmet, giving them the green light that he'd shut down operation of the security cameras on the rest of their floor.

Ready to rock and roll.

They moved exactly as planned. Two on point, two escorting the hostage—a Humpty Dumpty–looking guy in a three-piece suit and little round glasses—Elijah and Torres at the rear. The guy wasn't in any shape to take out the window, but they just had to get him down one hall and over to the next to make their escape route.

Elijah scanned, his gaze always moving, his ears on full alert as he tapped into their surroundings, listening, watching as they proceeded down the antiques-filled hall, their booted feet silent on the glossy marble floor.

Quite a step-up given that his last mission had taken place in a desert cave.

Then it all went to hell.

Elijah saw it going down a second before it actually

did. The ambassador slipped, his slick dress shoes losing traction on the marble floor. Despite Lansky's hold on him, the man still flailed out, his hand slapping the wall. Just a tap.

And he screamed like a scared little girl. He might as well have sounded a Klaxon.

The team angled to the right, taking the secondary, longer route just before they heard the sound of boots quick-marching down the hall. A shout of alarm went up, voices called out, running footsteps of what sounded like an entire platoon ricocheted off the walls.

The team tightened their circle around the hostage, stepping up their pace to an easy run. Torres and Elijah automatically slowed, covering the rear as Loudon signaled a warning to the men in the air.

The voices came closer. *This way*, Elijah translated the Arabic shouts. "They know where we are," he warned the others calmly. "Company's coming."

Then company was there.

The bullets didn't dent his calm. Not until one of them ripped through an ornately framed painting on the wall next to him.

"The sonovabitch shot a Monet," he swore. "What the fuck is wrong with some people?"

"Guess they aren't much for flowers," Torres returned, grinning even as he ran. "Too bad we don't have time to educate them on art appreciation."

As he marveled at the sacrilege, hoping like hell it had been a reproduction, Elijah moved. A small metal canister flew from his hand, landing smack-dab between the feet of the lead guard with a loud clang. A heartbeat later, the end of the hall exploded in smoke.

A quick glance assured him that Lansky and Loudon had the hostage covered. As sweat poured off the man's pale, bald head, they angled him into the air duct. As soon as the ornate, man-size grill was back in place, Masters and Rengel cocked their heads to the left, indicating they'd lead the guards that way while Elijah and Torres waited ten seconds, then took the right to distract the guards on the other side.

"I've been ordered to remind you of the preference that your ammo stays in your rifle," Powers said through the comm, his tight voice making it clear just how he felt about being ordered to share Jarrett's preferences.

Hard to blame him. Elijah couldn't say he much like hearing it, either. Obviously the guards weren't so particular because they just kept on shooting.

"Out and on our way," came through the comm as Lansky let them know they'd safely cleared the building with the hostage and were en route to the pickup site.

With the hostage secured, Elijah and Torres moved fast, angling out the doors and into a small garden they knew led to the sea. Torres shifted to the left, heading for the cliffs to secure the lines for their escape while Elijah provided cover.

Something exploded with a jarring crash, sending pieces of a statue flying every which way. Fire flashed, hot and blinding. The roar, engulfed him, pulling Elijah into its unspeakable hell. He hit the ground, his leg eaten away by pain as the cries of the dying filled his head. He waited for the flames to eat at his body, to tear at his soul.

"Prescott!"

The dead faces came riding on the flames. Elijah gripped his weapon, finger on the trigger as he tried to aim, tried to stop them from taking his teammate. From killing them both.

"Prescott, snap out of it."

Strong arms gripped his shoulders with a jarring shake. The flames were gone. The fire out. The dead still circled, though, round and round in his head.

Chest heaving, sweat burning his eyes, Elijah tried to bring the man in front of him into focus.

"Rembrandt? You okay?"

Elijah blinked again.

"Yeah." He tried to breathe past the constriction in his chest, but the air barely wheezed through. He managed to nod. "Yeah. I'm okay."

"Guess they weren't big on flowers outside, either," Torres joked, gesturing with his chin to gutted landscape. Trees were splintered, statuary rubble, bushes leveled.

Elijah caught sight of the hole on Torres's flak jacket. "You're hit." *Alive, not burned to a crisp*, was Elijah's next thought. Then fury rode a wild wave of guilt inside him, overriding that thought with reality. His job had been to cover Torres. Because Elijah had let his personal nightmare distract him, he'd blown his job.

"Nah, bullet grazed my body armor. C'mon, rendezvous in thirty seconds."

Elijah wanted to protest. He wanted to check Torres, to make sure there was no real damage. He wanted to howl at the fucking moon, then go back and kill the already-dead man who'd detonated the bomb.

But instincts and training, or maybe it was Torres's

steady gaze, did the trick of getting Elijah on his feet and, limping only a little, back on track.

Twenty minutes later, they were in the helicopter with the hostage secured. Loudon, the medic, sedated the ambassador before he shook to pieces. Jarrett entertained them during takeoff with his version of wringing his hands over their inability to tiptoe their way out of the embassy. The guy looked as if he was going to cry when he mentioned reparation and damage costs.

Elijah, along with the rest of the team, ignored him. After all, it wasn't like it was coming out of his pocket.

"Rembrandt?"

He lifted tired eyes to Torres.

"You okay?"

Was he okay? He wanted to say no. He wanted to know what the hell was wrong with him, why he couldn't shake the monkey off his back. He wanted to beat the hell against the walls of the helicopter until he punched his way through the metal and out to freedom.

As he glanced down the line of men leaning against the bulwark of the bird, he saw the same concern reflected in their eyes that was gleaming in Torres's. Concern for him? a little voice wondered. Or about him?

Elijah gave up, simply closing his eyes and letting his head drop back against the steel wall. It didn't shut out those questions, didn't erase the doubt he saw on the squad's faces. But after a few seconds focusing on steadying his breath, lowering his heart rate, he could shove that aside.

He drew a picture in his head, a landscape. The sun setting over water that stretched as far as the eye could see. Add a sandy beach in the back, some trees and scrub for texture and interest. And maybe a rickety hut off to the side, the driftwood walls leaning in on themselves. *Yeah*. He sighed as peace washed through him. A hut, with a hammock lashed between two palms.

The sun would be hot and the beach quiet but for the sound of the surf beating its song. Deserted. Away from everyone and everything.

Except the woman.

He didn't picture her face. He wouldn't let himself. But a part of him recognized her. Knew her body, knew the ring of twisted metal she wore on her finger. A part of him knew she was it.

Salvation.

What he didn't know was whether she'd grant it to him or not. Whether she'd deem his life worth saving.

Or if she'd simply walk away, leaving him to drown in fiery misery.

CHAPTER THREE

To AVA MONROE, life was all about the simple choices.

Cardio or strength training.

Yoga pants or fleece.

A jog or a bike ride.

An egg white omelet or a fresh fruit protein shake.

She'd worked hard to simplify, to bring it down to choices as clean and easy as those.

She liked it that way.

Liked, too, that she'd structured her life so that she was answerable pretty much only to herself. She lived alone, with a month-to-month rent. She worked for herself. And she trained for herself—for her own goals, her own purposes.

It kept her responsibilities to a minimum.

And it meant that she didn't need or depend on anyone else's approval.

That concept had become her mantra when she'd escaped her old life in Mendocino to start over in Napa three years ago. Not only did Napa offer gorgeous views of green and gold, elegant wineries and ageless architecture; Northern California was familiar enough that she'd felt safe. Best of all, it was far enough away from Ava's smothering parents that she could breathe easily, yet not so far away that they'd pack up their high-society life and follow her.

Not that she didn't love her family. But she'd never again be the princess they expected, and she'd learned the hard way proximity didn't mean dependability.

So Ava had simplified. And her life was great. So great that even she was surprised at how many people valued her skills enough to pay good money to attend a kick-ass workout class at seven in the morning.

Focusing on those people, Ava let the heavy beat of old-fashioned rock and roll pound through her system as she guided a group through a warm-up. She thought they'd use the gym's smallest workout room for this session, assuming there would be a limited interest in a six-week Hard Rocking Bods course. But ten minutes before they'd kicked off the initial session, she'd had to move it to the largest room and offer sign-ups for a second course at a yet-to-be-determined time.

"Let's step it up, folks," she called out as she assessed the progress of thirty people finishing their warm-up. "Knees high, backs straight. Double time."

"How much longer?" gasped one already sweating guy with an enviable tan, tight body and pathetic muscle tone.

"Warm-up? Another two minutes." She flashed a wicked smile. "Then the fun starts."

The groans filling the room warmed her heart. She figured if they weren't moaning, she wasn't doing her job. And that job was to build the best bodies. Through exercise classes, through training, through bodywork and massage.

It didn't matter what shape they were in when she

started, she had no doubt that if the person was willing, they'd end up with a better body in the end.

Ava firmly believed that with hard work, if you just gave it long enough, anything could change. She was proof positive of that.

Heavy on results, light on believing in anything that relied on others. The complete opposite of how she'd once lived—with her eye always on that fabled happily-ever-after so dependent on Prince Charming. Now she took one day at a time.

Today included hitch kicks, butt lifts and, oh yes, the dreaded burpees.

"Okay, people, let's rock and roll." Already warmed after her morning run and a round of intense circuit training, she took her students through their first set. "Grab your medium weight and begin with bicep curls. Squat on the curl, side kick on the release."

After a brief demonstration, including modifications, she gestured for them to join in and began the count. Twelve reps, rest, three times.

By the time they'd hit the three-quarters mark, the heavy beat of rock and roll couldn't disguise the heavy breathing and pained grunts of exertion sounding through the room. No matter how cool the air-conditioning was set, it didn't prevent the sweat streaming off the bodies doing that panting and grunting.

Ava prized every bitch, moan and aching groan as a sign of success. Her own breath might be a little short, but her voice was clear as she called out instructions.

"Come on, ladies, lift those butts," she called out, fully aware that half her class was men. But she'd learned that some things better motivated women—

encouragement, commiseration, results. And some things motivated men—insults and questioning their virility. "Nobody walks out of here comfortably. I want you moaning, groaning, huffing and puffing. I want those muscles screaming because you pushed them to the max. Lift, release. Lift, release."

She finished with a series of stretches.

"Arch, higher, higher, people. Stretch those muscles. Release the burn, let it go. You don't want those babies locking up. At least not before you all make it to your cars."

That snared a round of breathless laughter. Ava rode it out pulling them through the rest of the cooldown, ending with a little light meditation and a few body affirmations.

"Breathe, people. Pull that cooling air into your belly. Let it fill your body with soothing light. Repeat after me. I'm strong. I'm capable. I kicked butt today. I'll kick butt tomorrow."

And with that, she pushed to her feet. Ignoring the sweat that drizzled down her collarbone into the wicking fabric of her turquoise tank, she clapped her hands.

"Great job. You all kicked butt today."

As always, Ava moved through the room making contact with students. A form correct here, a congratulations there. There were enough newbies in the class that she didn't know everyone's name, but thanks to years of what she called extreme socialite training, she was able to make everyone feel as if they were a friend.

"Ava, you're the best."

"So are you, Terri. You're really mastering those burpees." She patted the red-faced woman's arm, smiling as she noted the developing muscle tone. "By the end of this course, I'll bet you're in that pair of jeans you bought."

Like a lot of people who hit the gym, Terri had come with a goal to lose weight for an event—in her case, a high school reunion. Once she'd hit that goal, Ava encouraged her to reach for another one, so the woman was now fixated on fitting into a size-nine jeans.

Some people worked out for the love of it. But Ava knew the other 95 percent of the world needed incentive. She figured tapping into that was as much a part of her job as modifying a workout to fit a variety of needs.

"Thanks to you and this class, I bet I'm in them two months ahead of schedule," Terri said, patting her hip as she headed out the door.

"You are the kick-ass woman, aren't you," rumbled a voice as big as the man framed in the doorway. As always, Ava smiled a little as she noted that Mack had to duck to get through without banging his shaved head. You'd think the guy would have built taller doors given that it was his gym.

"There's a reason the phrase *no pain, no gain* is popular," she pointed out, taking the towel he offered. Mack Prescott was a man the size of a bulldozer with a face to match, with the personality on par with a bear. Grumbly and gruff with most, but cuddly sweet with some.

"If the whining moans from your students are anything to go by, they're gaining more than they bargained for."

"Too much?"

"They sing your praises right along with those moans," Mack said with a shrug as he moved through the room. She could see him doing a mental check of the inventory, assessing the state of the mats, the chill of the A/C and the quality of the speakers still beating with music. "You've got a way about you, Ava—that's for sure."

"I plan to make the world stronger, one hard body at a time." Ava dabbed the towel at her throat, sopping up the beads of sweat still pooling there. "Resistance makes strength, my friend. You know that as well as I do."

"I do, indeed. From the looks of it, all those resisting students are going to be in a whole lot of pain later," Mack observed with a smirk. "Pretty smart, actually. First you pummel them in workout class so they're so sore their muscles are crying. Then you lure them in for a massage so you can pummel them on the table, work the knots out of those muscles so they're ready for your next workout class."

"Perfect, right?" Ava laughed. "I even have Chloe handing out massage flyers at the door."

She was only half joking. Chloe James, the receptionist for the gym, was perched at her desk right outside the door. And she did have flyers advertising Ava's massage services. But she wasn't waving them in the air.

Ava slanted a look through the glass walls and smiled.

Probably because the bubbly woman was otherwise occupied.

"Have you thought about my little proposition?" Mack asked as he straddled one of the workout benches lining the wall.

"You know, the propositions I get usually involve booty calls, naked workouts and offers to show off a guy's most impressive *muscle*."

Mack snorted.

"Sorry, sweets. You're not my type."

And that was the sad, sad truth for womankind. Ava had lost count of the number of complaints she'd heard over Mack's preference for hard bodies of the male variety.

"Only one of the reasons I love you, Mack," she said, at ease with him as she was with few men. "Another is your impeccable taste, of course."

"You mean in wanting you to come on board as a partner? I'm serious about it, Ava. I need someone I can trust, and you're my top pick."

But she didn't know if she ever wanted to be a man's top pick at anything. Or if she wanted the responsibilities and stresses of being part owner of anything, even a business she loved. So she simply shrugged.

"I haven't given it much thought yet," she said.

"Well, I told you I'd give you until the end of the week before I asked anyone else—so take as much time as you need." He got to his feet with a grace at odds with his size and offered a smile so reminiscent of his cousin's that her heart squeezed for a second.

"I don't think—"

"Don't answer yet," he interrupted. "Just think about it. If it's the money, we can figure that out. If it's the workload, we'll hash that out. If it's because you don't want to make another commitment to a Prescott, well, that would make you a wimp. And we both know you're not a wimp."

Ava angled her chin, pretending she wasn't insulted at the idea of returning to wimpiness after so many years of wallowing under the weight of her wimp crown. But she couldn't ignore the tight knot in her gut at his reference to Elijah. She spent so much of her life acting as if Elijah didn't exist that being reminded of him twice in as many seconds was a little much.

"I'm a good trainer, and excellent massage therapist. But I don't I know that I want to be a businesswoman," she said stiffly. Then, with a roll of her eyes at his sharp expression—God, the man could nag without saying a word—she lifted one hand in surrender. "But I'll think about it, and we'll talk next week."

"Atta girl. You've done good, Ava." Laying one beefy hand on her shoulder, Mack gave it a quick squeeze. "You should put some of that energy into your personal life now. You know, give one of those propositions a chance. Go on a date or something."

She almost laughed. But knowing it'd be hysterical laughter tinged with horror, Ava managed to keep her response to a shake of her head.

The answer to that'd be a no.

Actually, that'd be a hell, no. Or even a hell, no, never, no way, not a chance.

But she didn't say any of that aloud. Not because she wanted to encourage Mack, but because she didn't want to hurt his feelings. The poor guy had strong family loyalties, and her reasons for the multiple forms of *no* would slam right up against that devotion.

So Ava cleared her expression and gave him her best upbeat smile.

"I'm much too busy for dating, my friend. And from

the sound of this plan of yours, just considering it will keep me even busier."

"Maybe I should rescind the offer."

"No way," Ava objected, punching him in the arm. Since she knew it would be like ramming her knuckles into solid steel, she pulled the punch so it was more a graze of skin on skin. Still, her forearm sang at the impact. "Not if it means I have to rescind my no-dating rule."

"Maybe I should make that a part of the deal. You know, all gym owners are required to have an active social life."

Her social life was as active as she wanted. It revolved around work, fitness, hanging out with a few friends and... *Hmm*. Ava stopped to consider, but she couldn't think of anything else. Which was absolutely perfect.

"That kind of talk will be factored into my considerations," she warned.

"Forget I said it," Mack shot over his shoulder as he headed out the door.

Ava was still laughing as she started cleaning the room for the next class. But she wasn't changing her mind. Dating led to relationships. Relationships meant commitment. Commitment guaranteed heartache. She'd done her time, had her share. She was finished.

It was only after accepting that that she'd created the perfect life. It wasn't the life her parents had outlined for her, it wasn't the one her large, opinionated extended family expected of her. It wasn't even close to the one she'd envisioned for herself when she'd been a country-club princess/society bride with no higher goal than planning the perfect party, obsessing over whether the whites were white enough and making sure all her husband's needs were met.

But her life now? It worked for her. Why mess with something that was going well?

On the other hand, she loved Mack's gym. It had an excellent reputation, a savvy owner, an ever-growing clientele and the perfect location for what she wanted to build. With all the traveling he was doing now for fitness competitions and training, she could see his need to take on a partner.

And she'd be good at it. She understood their clientele, she could step into almost any role. Personal training, massage, teaching classes, scheduling, bookkeeping, even advertising. She'd helped with all of that over the last couple of years, so she definitely had the experience.

What she didn't have was money. At least, not readily available. Lips pursed, Ava finished wiping down the last mat. She had plenty in trust. But she couldn't access the funds until her thirtieth birthday unless her parents okayed it.

Something to think about, she decided as she moved around the room gathering abandoned towels and empty water bottles.

Of bigger importance than finding the funds was the idea of working for someone besides Mack. The large bodybuilder was the perfect boss. He let Ava choose her own hours, design her own classes, come and go as she pleased. But if he brought in a new partner, that could change.

Ava strode out of the classroom into the gym's reception area. At the chest-high desk, perched on a stool and writing in her planner sat Chloe. Probably the only woman in the world who could pull off the cat-eyed makeup with flaxen-blond dreadlocks, her tie-dye tee proclaimed her belief that Love Is the Ultimate Trip.

Part-time receptionist, all-round party girl and, much to the surprise of both, one of Ava's best friends.

"You whipped some butts, girlfriend. I've rarely seen such a sweaty, bedraggled bunch limping out of that classroom as those students today," Chloe said, her expression somewhere between impressed and amused. "And look at you, fresh as a daisy."

"Maybe not quite daisy fresh," Ava denied with a grin, gratefully unbraiding her hair and running her fingers through the long tresses. "I definitely need to hit the showers before my next class."

"Half those students were hobbling," Chloe said, giving Ava a quick up-and-down inspection. Sure, Ava's workout bra was soaked and the tank she wore over it spotted with sweat. But her face was pain-free, her gait easy and her smile bright.

"Bet they loved it, though," Ava shot back with a smile, angling her head to look at the latest page of art in Chloe's planner. The double-page spread was decorated with colorful butterflies and a flourish of sharp-edged flowers bordering her weekly to-do list.

More than once Ava had suggested that her friend keep track of all her goals, appointments and scheduling on her phone or computer, but Chloe argued that the left brain was engaged by the act of handwriting. She sometimes threw in things like creativity fostering energy or a pretty planner lowering stress, but the bottom line was, Chloe detested technology. Still, her method worked great for her.

Chloe's obsessions with planning every second of her life had started a few months back when her boy-friend had snuck out of her bed to run after his dream of being an archeologist. Or, considering that he didn't have a degree, any plans to go back to school or any money, to dig in the dirt.

She'd accepted Ava's shoulder at the time, but as soon as she was through crying on it, Chloe was sure her man would be back. Ava had talked herself blue in the face, but the woman wouldn't budge.

Chloe had complete faith that Bones would be back.

To make ends meet, in addition to working part-time at the gym, Chloe worked the counter of the health-food store up the street, led bike tours through Napa Valley and ran her own dog-walking business.

"Does this mean you're double booked tomorrow morning?" Ava asked with a frown, pointing to the sketch of a cute pair of Yorkies.

"My bike tour finishes at the Wine Train, so Mrs. Burns is dropping off Dinky and Winky for their walk and picking them up later."

Ava's brows arched. Apparently filling every mo-ment of every day wasn't enough to keep Chloe too busy to think about Bones—or Derek Herringbone to some people. Now she was double booking herself.

It was crazy. The curvy blonde had a way with peo-ple that Ava envied. Her combination of pinup girl looks, good-natured flirting and friendliness put every-one at ease. She had guys lining up to date her, but she said her heart belonged to Bones. So instead of dating, she played matchmaker to any guy who asked her out.

"I'd try to talk you into joining me on the bike tour since you could use the fresh air and the vines are gorgeous this time of year. But you have a pile of new massage appointments that I'm sure you'll use as an excuse to avoid socializing," Chloe said with a friendly eye roll as she handed Ava a clipboard.

"I socialize enough," Ava replied, flipping through the list of names and client information, along with her appointment schedule. It would all be better logged into a computer with a central booking system, but like Chloe, Mack was a technophobe who preferred paper.

Silly, Ava thought. It was one thing she'd definitely want to change if she ever did partner up.

"Two of these are new," she said, reading one of the names listed on the next day's schedule. "Did they fill out an input form?"

"Nope. Mack added them to your schedule and said it was all good," Chloe replied, flicking her fingers to dismiss things like client identity, health backgrounds and pertinent information.

Ava wrinkled her nose but didn't object. She appreciated Mack's support and all the clients he sent her way. She'd have to buy him one of those big green, filled-with-so-much-healthy-stuff-they-tasted-gross drinks as a thank-you.

He'd brush it off, she knew. A few years back, Mack had taken it upon himself to look out for her. Or as he put it, to watch her ass. He liked to think she couldn't manage her life without him. Ava's smile flickered, since she wasn't sure he hadn't been right.

Then.

Now, though, she was stronger. She'd learned to stand on her own feet, to defend herself and, yes, to watch her own ass if necessary. But Mack wasn't ready to give up his role as her overprotective caretaker. He was stubborn that way.

"If you won't join the tour, how about a hike through Glass Beach this weekend? I'm free Saturday morning."

"Just us, or are you educating a bunch of strangers on the beauty of the Napa River and the history and ecosystem of the wetlands?"

"Just us," Chloe promised before her smile winked out. "Unless Bones makes it home for the weekend."

"Have you heard from him?" Ava asked cautiously.

"No. But I'm sure I will any day now." Frowning at Ava's doubtful look, Chloe shook her head. "We've been together since we were fourteen. You don't spend a decade with a person and not know them. This is just a phase. Something he has to get out of his system. Believe me—he will be back."

"Okay. Just, you know, don't get your hopes up too high," Ava warned before heading for the locker room.

She knew there was no point in saying more than that. Any lecture she offered would fall on deaf ears. But she knew for a fact that men didn't change. But women did, as Ava had proven. All it'd taken was a hideous bout of depression, a couple of exercise classes and a pulled muscle to completely change her life.

Spinning had led to kettlebells, which led to yoga, then to weight lifting. Next thing she knew, she was teaching kickboxing, certified in Pilates and attending weeklong training camps in exercise instruction. One of those camps had hooked her on the benefits of massage for training the body, inspiring her to get licensed. Now, after another year of training, she'd added a rehabilitation massage certification to her roster.

Not bad for a woman who, until the age of twenty, had been convinced that the sum total of her ambitions were to hold the crown of socialite princess, to be a perfect wife and to always look pretty.

Thank God she'd escaped that life. It would have been pure hell.

ESCAPE COULD ONLY last for so long.

Experience and familiarity got Elijah through the team debriefing without a problem, but by the time they got to his individual round, he was feeling raw.

But, again, experience and familiarity got him through.

Still, he was damned glad to hear, "Dismissed, Prescott."

Gut churning and his throat hot from keeping his voice at an even keel, Elijah nodded to the two Naval Intelligence officers and Admiral Cree. He offered his salute, turned on his heel and strode out. And he didn't breathe fully until he'd cleared the room.

"You okay? Damn, Prescott, you look rough."

Ignoring that, Elijah nodded to the ensign manning the desk and continued into the hallway. He wasn't surprised when Jarrett joined him, matching his pace as they passed both military and civilian personnel until they'd reached the end of the hall.

"Debriefing can be rough, but I've never seen you come out looking this worn. Seriously," Jarrett said, sounding concerned, "are you okay?"

"I'm fine." Like Jarrett, Elijah stopped at the double doors. The sun filtered through the small windows, dust motes dancing between them. "I finished debriefing. I'm cleared."

"Hey, I just wanted to give you a heads-up." Jarrett made a show of glancing to the left, then to the right before leaning closer. "Watch your six."

"Why? Someone coming down on my ass?"

"I'm hearing a lot of buzz. Worry, doubts, that sort of thing. Some are saying Poseidon is, and I quote, a 'fancy-ass clique rallying around a loser in the name of protecting their own.'" Jarrett rolled his eyes as if to say it was ridiculous. But if it was ridiculous, why bother with the warning? "Just wanted you to know."

Elijah met Jarrett's frown with a look of calm. Not because that's how he was feeling—hell, no. The warning, on top of a brutal debriefing, had his gut twisted with a miserable sort of fury. But there was no point confirming the gossip that he was a mess. "I'm good," he lied.

"I know you're clean, Prescott. I just want to make sure you watch your back. People get ugly when they're under suspicion." Jarrett snapped his teeth together, his eyes worried. "You don't need more dirt thrown your way. Not after everything you've been through. So if you need anything, I'm here for you."

His own jaw tight enough to snap his teeth off, Elijah nodded. "Yes, sir. But Commander Savino is my commanding officer, and I report to him." Elijah pulled his cap out of his back pocket and tugged it onto his head. "If there are any issues, I'm sure I'll hear it from him."

"If he's brought into it," Jarrett said quietly, stepping forward until the tips of his boots knocked against Elijah's. "Someone wants Poseidon brought down. How long can Savino stop that? People higher up are watching. It's making everyone nervous. They're wondering who's involved, who's clean and who's not."

"Are they looking at me?" Elijah asked.

"They're looking at everyone. You roomed with Ramsey. You've had some shit going on, and your psych eval says you have reason to resent the Navy. Some people worry about serving with a guy with your issues. And then there's the question of who really sold the chemical formula. Do you think everyone believes it was some dead guy?" Jarrett shook his head, as if disgusted by the chatter. "Just watch your back."

Elijah refused to reply. All he could do was nod. Then, shoulders stiff, he watched the captain shove through the doors and saunter away. He wished like hell he could claim the man was full of crap. But Elijah had seen the looks.

The warning was legit.

TWO DAYS LATER, Elijah strode down the hallway toward Savino's office. He didn't know if he was making the right choice. He just knew he couldn't make a different one.

So when he strode through the door, his chin was high, his eyes direct and his expression clear.

His commander was at his desk, papers stacked in two neat piles on the dingy metal surface. Elijah wouldn't mind the rank, but damned if he'd want the paperwork that went with it.

"Reporting as ordered, sir."

"You want to explain this?" Savino invited, lifting one of the papers from the stack on the left.

His face blank, Elijah looked from his commander to the paper the man held and back again. It seemed pretty self-explanatory to him. But he knew Savino wasn't asking him to clarify the request for leave. He wanted to know why. He wanted details; he wanted insights. As always, he wanted every damned thing.

Savino was a hard-ass. He was a tough commander, a man with a wicked sense of humor held under tight control and razor-sharp lines in the sand when it came to right and wrong. He was the first man to reach out his hand and the last to walk away.

He was a friend.

They'd trained together. They'd sat watch in a cave over a village beset by terrorists together. They'd gotten drunk together. They'd been through a million experiences in the near-decade they'd known each other.

So Elijah couldn't hold back. "I'm not one hundred percent. I thought I was, pushed the medics to release me and ignored their concerns," he said quietly. Then, in case Savino suspected he meant the head shrink as well as the physicians, he drummed his fingertips over his thigh. "I'd rather take a few weeks' leave before I do irreparable damage."

He knew that excuse would hold. His medical records said as much. But Savino knew him too well. So the question was, would he accept face value or would he push for the truth?

"And this has nothing to do with the heap of crap chickenshit gossips are trying to pile on you?"

Had he thought that wouldn't get back to Savino?

Elijah almost smiled. "Someone wants to take down Poseidon," he said, sidestepping. "They're using the convenience of gossip to accelerate that mission."

"That doesn't answer my question. Do you believe that anyone on the team doesn't trust you? Do you believe anyone thinks you're dirty?"

Yeah. He did believe that. "I believe there are some that might have questions," he said carefully instead. "Since our job is not to follow blindly but to think outside the box, I don't blame them for wondering."

Savino frowned, but simply folded his hands on his desk instead of saying anything.

"At the very least, they've got to wonder why I hadn't seen anything. Why I didn't realize that Ramsey was dirty, that he was a psychotic traitor with a taste for greed and a hard-on to take down Poseidon." Elijah rubbed his hand over his face, feeling stained, as if he'd never be clean. "I served with him and Adams. I partied with them. I roomed with them for eight fucking months. How could I miss something that ugly?"

"By that train of thought, you'd think I should have realized it, too," Savino countered quietly, looking tired. "I served with Ramsey myself. I trained him, commanded him. Hell, Rembrandt, I signed his fucking DEVGRU recommendation."

Knowing Savino's use of the word *fucking* was permission to fall out, Elijah dropped to the empty chair in front of the desk, his boots clunking against the metal.

"I can't get past it," Elijah admitted. "The weight of it. The feeling of failure."

"You're going to have to. You've got enough weighing you down already. Don't haul someone else's crap, too."

Made sense. Elijah knew it made sense. He'd told himself the same thing already, hadn't he? But he'd seen the expressions on some people's faces. He'd read the question in their eyes, the wondering. Was he in league with Ramsey? Was that how he'd survived the explosion? Did they think he'd missed that sniper last week because he'd meant to? That he'd fallen back on the command not to fire, had used it as an excuse to let his partner take a bullet? The questions swirled, ugly and sharp, scraping at his composure, tearing at his resolve.

"I need a break. I need to get away from it all," Elijah murmured, finally meeting Savino's eyes. "I thought I was ready to come back. I'm not."

"I could order a psych eval, another round of physical therapy," Savino said. "That's what I should do. For your own good and for the good of the team."

"You could. But I'm hoping you won't. I just need a break. A real break. Away."

A dumb-ass move, his brain warned.

Walking away now would only add fuel to Jarrett's insinuations. To those who thought him guilty, it'd look like a retreat. Even to himself—who knew he was clean—it would feel like he was running.

"You'd be smarter to stay on base, take light duty until you're ready to face fire again," Savino advised, reading Elijah's mind with his usual savvy.

"Yeah. I know." He'd been going on eight months without leave when he'd been blown to hell. After that had been a couple of months in and out of the base hospital, a month easing back into training. For the last year he'd lived and breathed the Navy, SEAL Team 7, Poseidon.

Once he'd thrived on immersing himself in this world. Now?

He didn't know if he could live or breathe it any longer. He didn't know how much longer he could before he simply cracked. And what would be revealed through the fractured pieces could break him beyond repair.

Savino must have seen some hint of that on his face because he rubbed a hand over his hair and sighed. "Okay. Yeah. I'll green-light leave. But three weeks. No more." Not a man to waste time, he snagged the request for leave again and scrawled his signature.

But he didn't hand it over. "I'm temporarily relieving you from active duty, but as long as Operation Fuck Up is in effect, you're still serving Poseidon. Clear?"

In other words, until they'd determined once and for all if Ramsey was dead or not, every member of Poseidon was on alert. "Is there something you want me working on while I'm away?"

Savino tapped his fingers on the desk once. Twice. After a third rat-a-tat-tat, he opened a drawer and pulled out a sheet of paper. "Codes, log-ins to access certain files that need to be decrypted. You going to have access to a secured computer where you're going?"

"I'll make sure of it," Elijah promised, knowing as he reached for the paper that Savino was giving him more than an assignment.

He was handing over his trust. A show of faith that damn near changed Elijah's mind about getting away.

Damn near. But not quite.

"Where will you go?"

Elijah hesitated, then shrugged. "Not sure yet. Just… Away."

"You need somewhere to chill? My place in Monterey is sitting there empty."

God. Elijah gritted his teeth against the wave of guilt pounding over him. "Thanks, but I think your castle is a little out of my league." Trying on a grin, Elijah rolled his eyes at the idea of a middle-class guy like him chugging beer in that glass tower of a place that Savino called his home away from base.

"I expect you back here in three weeks. Excuses won't be tolerated."

"Yes, sir." *No problem.* He could figure out the rest of his life in three weeks. Elijah headed for the door.

"Rembrandt?"

Hand on the knob and escape just a twist away, Elijah looked over his shoulder.

"You need anything, you let me know." Savino's brow creased for a moment, the shield dropping to show his concern. "Anything. We're a team. We're here for you."

Not trusting his voice, Elijah nodded on his way out the door. Maybe that was the problem. They were a team. They were there for him. But did they trust him to be there for them?

Did he—could he—trust himself? No.

That was the bottom line.

Elijah couldn't trust himself—or ask anyone else to—when his entire world was crashing down around him. His life—starting with his mind—was simply falling apart.

Until he figured it out, until he fixed whatever in the hell was going on, he simply had to accept the hard truth.

His life sucked.

CHAPTER FOUR

JEREMY PRESCOTT HAD been a man of great responsibility, deep pride and a quirky sense of humor. When he'd died, he'd left behind a devastated family, a tidy nest egg and a few special bequests to his only son, Elijah. Among them were sage bits of advice, mostly in the form of clichés handed down with a wink and a smile; the responsibility for an emotionally fragile widow with a propensity for drama outmatched only by her gift for nagging; and a cherry '53 Corvette.

Chevrolet's first attempt at what would become an icon. The red body was a rough testament to fiberglass, the white leather interior almost flawless with some wear and tear along the edges of the driver's seat. Granted, at ten years old, Elijah had been too young to drive—hell, his feet had barely reached the pedals—but nobody challenged his right to the car. For a while, especially when he'd been deployed overseas, he'd kept the vehicle garaged at his mother's. But two years ago a friend had convinced him to live a little, to bring it down to Coronado, take it out for a ride once in a while.

Given the cost of gas, he'd often joked that cruising the car was his guilty pleasure. The pleasure was dimming as he was cruising past hour seven on the drive from Coronado to his hometown of Yountville. Nestled

in the heart of the gorgeous Napa Valley, the charming
town was known for its fine dining, with restaurants
like the French Laundry pulling in locals and tourists
alike. Less well-known was the meddling prowess of the
Prescott women. Elijah's mother and sisters specialized
in forming, sharing and debating their opinions on the
lives of others. He loved them all, but damn, the idea
of facing that after a long drive while his body ached
was a lot to take.

So when he came up on the exit to Napa, he debated
for all of two seconds whether to continue another handful of miles to his mom's before pulling off the freeway
and heading to his cousin's instead. He'd rather bunk on
Mack's couch, eat wheat germ and drink lemongrass.
Parking the 'Vette in the gravel lot behind a three-story
building, he leaned one arm on the steering wheel and
contemplated the gym his cousin had built.

Scarred gray stucco walls were framed in crisp
white. Through the wall of plate glass fronting the
building chrome flashed, highlighting row after row
of cardio equipment. Treadmills, ellipticals, rowers and
spin bikes were filled with bodies.

He knew they were positioned there to give the ex-
ercisers a view as much as they were to advertise the
gym, and he wondered if Mack still seeded the machines with ringers. A handful of men and women who
sweated for free and made it look as if they'd built those
perfectly sculpted bodies on those machines, luring in
the gullible to think that three twenty-minute sessions
each week would give them the same.

Mack Prescott was a canny businessman.

When Elijah stepped into the gym, he could see

that canniness was paying off. Hard rock pumped out a heavy beat and instead of the sweat he was used to at the base gym, the air was fresh with something that smelled like clean air.

About thirty of the forty cardio machines were occupied, with the same number of people on strength equipment or using free weights. There were two more rooms enclosed in glass, one filled with women in spandex and the other empty.

Even through the milling, sweating and grunting bodies—and the temptation of those spandex-draped babes, Elijah only had eyes for one person. He grinned when he saw the guy manning the desk next to what appeared to be locker rooms.

At six-two and SEAL fit, Elijah wasn't a small man. Standing tall at six-four and a comfortable 230 of muscle, Mack Prescott lived by the motto that fitness was king. And it ruled his body with an iron fist. Bald as an eight ball and just as crazy, Mack had spent his early twenties on the fitness circuit, competing and collecting trophies that paid ode to his ripped body. Seven years ago, he'd decided to turn his expertise to training others and opened a gym. Something Elijah appreciated on so many levels.

A wide grin spread over his homely face when Mack saw Elijah weaving his way through the gym rats.

"Well, if it ain't my favorite sailor. Elijah, how the hell are you doing, man?" Not waiting for an answer, Mack grabbed Elijah close and smothered him tight enough to make a man grateful for good deodorant. "You just passing through?"

"I'm on leave," Elijah mumbled into Mack's armpit. "Needed some time to rest and recoup."

As if testing that assessment, Mack gripped Elijah's shoulders and pushed him out arm's distance for an inspection. If his scowl was any indication, he didn't much like what he saw.

"You said the injury was minor," Mack growled, accusation clear in the deep rumble.

"It was." Compared to death. But Elijah didn't figure sharing his yardstick was going to do much to wipe that look of worry from his cousin's eyes. He shrugged. "I was cleared for active duty. That means a US of A doctor said I was in good enough shape to serve my country. That should be good enough for you."

From the slow shake of his head, Mack wasn't buying it. But while his eyes took another inventory up and down Elijah's frame, the bigger man didn't argue. He tilted his head toward the car visible through the windows fronting the gym.

"You staying with your mom?"

"Only if I have to."

"She know you're here?"

"You telling her?"

Elijah's two sisters were still in Yountville with his mom, while most of Mack's family was scattered over the Napa Valley. So unless one of them had recently gottten into the fitness craze, there was no reason for any of them to notice he was here.

"Should I keep your company a secret?"

Elijah puffed out a breath. He could evade. He could even lie. He was trained to do both. But he was tired. So damned tired. "I could use a break, some downtime," he murmured, rubbing a hand over his hair with a worn sigh.

"How long you got?"

"Three weeks, thereabouts." *Or forever.* "Long enough to rest up, get in fighting shape and show you up in the gym and the bar." A worthy challenge, actually, and one Elijah figured would be fun.

Apparently Mack agreed. "Now that's what I'm talking about," he said, slapping Elijah on the back and damned near sending his face through the chest-high service desk. "You'll stay at my place."

"Thanks, man." That was just what he'd hoped for. "I won't be any trouble."

As if he'd heard something Elijah hadn't intended to let slip, Mack's eyes narrowed. He didn't say anything, though. Just gave a long hum, then inclined his head toward the elevator.

"You've had a long drive. Bet that leg is stiff. We'll go up this way—save the stairs for tomorrow. Better yet, I'll set you up for a massage in the morning. I've got a couple of solid massage and rehab therapists attached to the place now."

As if his body knew it was finally home—or as close to a home as Elijah had—it gave up all pretense of energy and drooped like a used condom. In a fog of exhaustion, he followed his cousin through the gym, vaguely aware of Mack pointing out his new weight-lifting equipment before they settled into a glass tube for the ride to the third floor.

"That's the dojo," Mack said as they slid past the second floor, a study of white on white with rich wood accents. Diamond tuck padded walls were visible beyond two groups of students following the instructors and a dozen or so others practicing kicks and punches solos.

One stood out. Slender yet curvy in the white gi, a woman with dark hair pulled back in a ponytail performed a series of running jump kicks. There was something familiar about the move, but Elijah couldn't pinpoint it. His eyes narrowed. But before he could focus, the elevator's ascent blocked his view.

"Guest room is all yours for as long as you want it. I'm busy tomorrow, but I'll book you a massage first thing. Then we'll spend some time getting that leg back into shape," his cousin promised as he opened the door to his third-floor apartment and waved Elijah inside.

"You've redecorated," Elijah noted, looking around.

Mack's living space reflected the man. Big, intense and comfortable. A television covered a wall opposite a deep purple leather sectional. There was art, most of it nudes, and a chrome-and-glass table plus leather chairs straight out of the 1970s. Instead of the slew of trophies that had once crowded the far wall, there were now a trio of abstracts that, if Elijah tilted his head to one side, appeared to be a ménage à trois.

"Sit, be comfortable. I'll get us a beer, and you can catch me up. Start with your sex life," Mack instructed, heading for the kitchen as Elijah dropped onto the couch, sinking into the soft leather.

"Nothing there to catch up on. Between the hospital time, recovery and my regular duties I've been pretty busy."

To say nothing of the random flashback onslaught, the nightly retrospectives through the terrors of his subconscious and the nagging feeling that after sacrificing everything that mattered for his career, that career was spinning wildly out of control.

"Too busy for sex?" Mack had a pitying expression when he returned with a tray carrying two chilled pilsners of beer, a bowl of mixed nuts and a plate of what looked like a cross between potato chips and green beans. "Sounds like your leg isn't the only thing we need to work on while you're here."

Call it exhaustion. Call it instinct that had the little hairs on the back of his neck standing on end. Whatever it was, Elijah vowed then and there to step carefully. Because that matchmaking gleam in Mack's eyes could mean only one thing.

Trouble.

And the last thing Elijah needed right now was more trouble. Even if it came in the form of a naked woman. He didn't care how hot she was. He didn't care how willing. He didn't even care if she came wrapped in a bow holding a list of kinky preferences.

"No work necessary. I'm here to rest and recuperate, nothing more," he said, taking his beer. As he swallowed down a healthy gulp and shifted the conversation into safer realms, Elijah changed that vow.

Not about avoiding trouble or needing to rest. That vow was rock solid. But the naked woman part? No point making any hasty decisions on that subject until he saw what Mack came up with.

Because, after all, who could resist a bow?

MY LIFE ROCKS.
My life is right on track.

My life kicks serious butt, and I love every minute of it.

Ava repeated the affirmations on each exhalation, the soothing tones of bells and chimes ringing softly in time with the words. The gentle scents of sandalwood, vetiver and neroli wrapped around her bare shoulders, as soft as the raw-silk fabric of the lush, oversize pillow she sat on.

As the music slowly faded, so did her words. But her breath stayed even, slow and easy. After a few seconds of silence, she scanned her body for any tension, but she found no tightness, no stress. She felt great.

She let herself grin as she opened her eyes. She knew from experience to give herself a few moments to find her balance before pushing to her feet.

It never failed to make her smile that she felt as if she were opening her eyes to a rainbow. Colors glinted from every corner. The walls were a soothing teal, the low-slung couch sapphire blue. Drapes framed the floor-to-ceiling window in shimmering shades of emerald and amethyst. Pillows in a myriad of shapes, sizes and colors scattered like jewels over the couch, pouring onto the floor. A couple of topaz beanbags rounded out the seating around the low, surfboard-shaped ebony table.

On the far side of the room, partitioned off by a curtain of beads, was a hanging bed covered in white, with more pillows strewn over the surface so it looked like a fluffy cloud amid all the rest of the color. She had a few antique pieces here and there, a tiny kitchenette opposite the bed, with the only door other than the front one opening to a dollhouse-size bath.

The studio was unquestionably small. Cozy, she

liked to call the space. It was actually the attic level of a renovated three-story Victorian. The polished wood floors creaked, and the plaster walls tended to let in the cold in the winter and the heat of summer.

Ava loved it.

Her mother hated it. It'd taken Ava a year or so to decide whether she loved it out of spite, a bit of rebellion against a domineering mother who considered her own opinions pure gold. Eventually, though, Ava had come to accept that the space simply suited her, and the whys didn't matter. She considered that a sign of maturity.

Rising with a lithe move, Ava stretched her arms high overhead. Grasping each hand around the opposite wrist, she twisted from one side, then the other, pulling air all the way into her toes and greeting the sun rising outside her window.

She prepared for her day with Mack's offer playing through her now-clear mind. It was tempting—so tempting—to say nope, she didn't want commitments and responsibilities cluttering up her life. But the fact that she was automatically angling for the easy route told her that she shouldn't.

She needed to consider the partnership seriously. Beyond the money, what it would cost? Was it worth the risk? How big of a difference would it make in her life, and could she be just as happy without it?

Ava gathered her gear for the day. Her duffel, with street clothes and a change of workout gear. Her iPhone, earbuds, charger, wallet. A new bottle of shampoo to replace the almost-empty one in her locker. Car keys, although she walked to work in good weather.

She capped the protein smoothie in her insulated

mug and added it to the duffel, then crossed to the door. Hanging there on the wall by the heavy polished oak was a oval silver beveled frame, not more than three inches tall.

It didn't hold a photo, but instead a swatch of pale blue fabric and a tiny lock of hair, shades deeper than her own nutmeg brown.

Ava kept most of her previous life exactly where it belonged—in the past. She'd locked away the memories, buried the emotions, let go of the reminders.

Except for this.

Her talisman. To remind her that while things might be simple now, she'd once held a life that made every complication worthwhile.

Dominic Prescott.

Her darling baby.

There was no buffer that could dim the pain of waking up one morning, surprised that the four-month-old had slept through the night. Riding high on her first full night's sleep since his birth, breasts full to aching, she'd all but danced into the nursery to nurse her baby.

But he wouldn't wake. He wasn't breathing. He'd never opened those gorgeous eyes again. Other than the hysteria, Ava didn't remember much after that. Not her husband finally coming home after three frantic days of trying to reach him. Not the doctor's pronouncement. Not the funeral. Not the multiple people who'd tried to comfort her through a pain that couldn't be assuaged.

SIDS. Sudden infant death syndrome. A clean, tidy term for the end of her world. A hideous loss that had blown her already-fractured marriage all to hell.

The only way she'd been able to survive was to leave

it all behind. The perfect home she hadn't chosen. The smothering attention of her controlling parents. Her charming prince of a husband who'd been too busy battling the world's dragons to give a damn.

It had taken months of therapy to pull her out of the depths of depression enough to function, and another year to work through the guilt and hatred and self-blame. But, eventually, she'd accepted that her old life was over. Gone in a blaze of misery.

From those ashes, her new life had formed. The only thing she allowed herself to bring was her love for Dominic. Her sweet boy.

Ava pressed her fingers to her lips, transferred the kiss to the frame.

Then, chin high, she pulled her bright mood around her once again, grabbed the bag of granola she'd made the night before and headed out the door.

Five minutes later she stepped through a rustic grapevine arch into the lush bounty of greens and golds. Not as big as the Napa Community Garden, this plot served Chloe's small neighborhood.

"Good morning," Ava called when she spotted the blonde crouched low between rows of flowering tomato vines.

"We're having fresh strawberries for breakfast," Chloe declared in lieu of a greeting. She rose with a smile, tipping the basket to show off the bright red fruit. "And a couple of nectarines, a sprig of grapes and, mmm, the first pears of the season."

Her stomach growling in appreciation, Ava gestured to the rest of the bounty. "And the cabbage, beets and cucumbers?"

"Juice bar," Chloe declared, stuffing the vegetables into a cotton bag. "I'm trying a couple of new recipes. Want to be my tester?"

Ava eyed the sad-looking spears of asparagus and, remembering how long it had taken to rinse away the bitter coating of the last recipe she'd tested, shook her head. "Not even a little bit."

Ava pulled the granola out of her tote while she waited for Chloe to gather the rest of her ingredients, her bullet journal and a fist-size ring of keys.

Nibbling on the oat-and-almond mixture as her friend turned off the hose, Ava checked the time on her cell phone. Six forty. Leave it to Chloe to be right on schedule.

Granola in the summer, bran muffins in the winter, fruit year-round. Thanks to the near perfection of Northern California's weather, they shared this routine of breakfast to-go and a morning walk to the gym whenever their schedules meshed.

Chatting about everything and nothing between bites, the two women strolled along the riverside promenade that fronted downtown Napa on their way to the gym.

"The guy would have been irritating if it wasn't so funny watching him try to stay on the yoga ball during planks," Ava said as she wound up her story about a know-it-all first timer who'd tried to take over her core class the night before. "He finally quit trying to instruct the rest of the class on proper form the third time he went down on his head."

"Bet all that giggling gave everyone some extra core work, too." Chloe laughed. "But, hey, speaking of irritating? That creepy guy, Rob? The one who drives that gas-guzzling monster truck and calls every woman he meets a doll? I heard he's given up trying to hire you as a personal trainer. He's decided to go the massage route instead. He's one of those guys that think getting naked on your table will turn the tide. Like you're gonna see a woody and jump on. You know, to ride it like a pogo stick."

Ava wrinkled her nose. "And yet I manage to resist."

"Speaking of pogo sticks…" The blonde gave Ava a playful look. "I have the perfect guy for you. He's a banker, which is like, totally uptight sounding. But he's not, really. He used to jam with Bones in this jazz band, and he's pretty fit. Not gym fit, but he plays B-ball with the guys every weekend so he's not a slob, ya know?"

"Nope." Ava breathed in the cool morning air, reveling in the simplicity of it all.

"Don't say no. Just listen—he's a nice guy. He drives a BMW, has good personal hygiene and likes Bourne movies. He mows his mom's lawn even."

"Nope." Wondering if she could get an extra yoga session in before her afternoon classes, Ava tried to remember her massage schedule. She knew she had morning clients but wasn't sure if she had someone booked at eight or at nine. She wished Mack would move to a computerized system. Then she could sync it to her phone, change it on the go. It might be worth considering the partnership offer for that reason alone.

"Ava, you're not listening," Chloe complained as they left the riverfront promenade, crossing the street toward a row of redbrick shops.

When they passed the bakery, Ava breathed in the

yeasty scent of fresh-baked bread and promised herself she'd stop on the way home for a small round of sourdough.

"I listened. You want me to date a lawn-mowing, mother-loving, BMW-driving banker. Why, I'm not sure, so if you mentioned that part you're right—I wasn't listening."

"Because he's hot. He's nice. And you need to date. If you don't, you're going to dry up inside. You know the rule about muscles. Use them or lose them." Chloe added an arch look at Ava's hips just in case she missed the point about which muscles were in question.

"I've got a Bikram yoga class this evening. Don't worry—I've got it covered." She offered a sassy smile. "Moist, hot air and a lot of Kegals. See, that way nothing dries out or withers away."

"You're killing me." Chloe sighed before stepping into the small health-food store. She came out again, adding a bag of flaxseed and tube of honey to the vegetables in her bag, and picked up the conversation as if it had never stopped. "So, are you going out with this guy or not?"

"Not. I'd rather spend the time figuring out what I want to do about Mack's proposition."

"Proposition? Do tell," Chloe insisted, leaning closer with a naughty smile.

"Not that kind of proposition." Ava rolled her eyes at Chloe's lash-fluttering attempt at innocence. "As if you don't know what I'm talking about."

"Well, I'll admit to hearing a thing or two about Mack's plans to take on a partner." With her usual exuberance, Chloe waved to shopkeepers and tourists alike as they picked up their pace. "With his travel schedule heating up and all those competition guys wanting him as a trainer, he's gone as much as he's here. So having someone he trusts on board would take a lot of worries off his big ol' shoulders."

"Uh-huh." Giving Chloe a narrow look, Ava waggled her fingers in a *tell-all* gesture. "Spill it. What else have you heard?"

"Rumor is that you're top of the list, but I think he'd consider Joe Peters or Con Barton if you turn him down."

Oh. He had names lined up? Ava's teeth snapped together at the realization that she didn't have a lot of thinking room with those guys on the list. They were both solid trainers, and Con used to own a gym back east before following his wife to California.

"Hmm," was all she said.

Chloe pursed red lips and considered Ava carefully. "I think you'd be a great boss, if that matters. Are you considering it? I mean, seriously considering. Not just pacifying Mack by thinking about it but planning to say no."

Good question. "I don't know." Ava tapped her fingers on her thigh a few times, watching the river as a pair of kayakers found their rhythm. "It's a big commitment, and it'd mean I have to get serious about things like schedules and time frames and budgeting my energy."

"Is that a bad thing?"

"I don't know," Ava said again. "I guess that's what I have to figure out. I teach enough classes and have enough massage clients to cover my bills, and I can pick up extra classes here and there if I feel like it. Commitment is a big step. Right now I can just go with the flow."

Of course, she kept throwing commitments into the flow, things like class competitions, black belt testing and new massage classes to increase the range of treatments she could offer clients. But those were all on her terms. It would be different if the schedule were etched in stone. Or at least carved in wood.

Wouldn't it?

"Only dead fish go with the flow," Chloe pointed out, her face perfectly serious.

Ava had to laugh. Leave it to Chloe to sum it up perfectly. "Well, I guess I'm still swimming, so I might as well consider it."

By the time they strode into the gym, Ava realized she wasn't just considering it. She was *seriously* considering it. She loved this place, she thought as they worked their way through the early gym rats toward the locker room. She really did. She appreciated the scent of exertion, the pounding music accompanied by swearing grunts and easy chatter.

"Are you sure you don't want to meet the banker?" Chloe asked, eating the last of the strawberries while Ava stashed her bag in her locker. "He really is cute."

"Nope. My schedule is full," Ava replied. "Tonight I'm trying that new Bikram yoga class. Right now I'm heading to the supply closet for a dozen nunchakus for weapons training in this afternoon's taekwondo class. And at some point I have Mack's proposition to consider, remember?"

Chloe shook her head, her dreadlocks sweeping over

the hemp straps of her beige tunic. "I tell you about the hottest guy you could ever meet, and you turn down a date because you claim you're going to be busy stretching yourself into a pretzel in an oven filled with sweaty people. Then you receive a career-changing offer and you're going to count out a bunch of sticks on chains so you can teach pajama-clad Bruce Lee wannabes?"

"Don't be silly," Ava shot back with a delighted smile. "I'm going to put my gi on first."

WHETHER IT WAS twelve hours down, or simply getting his first dreamless night in months, Elijah woke feeling great.

Rested. Refreshed. Alive.

One way or another, Mack had always been there for him. He'd taught Elijah to drive in his Honda, had stood by him when Elijah had pissed off the family with his choice to join the Navy and had given him the sex talk at the tender age of twelve. Of course, Mack's version had been more along the lines of birds and birds than birds and bees, but Elijah had been a smart kid. He'd made the translation without too much trouble. Mack had helped guide Elijah after his dad had died, then a dozen years later had gotten him through the darkest time in his life.

Elijah didn't expect his cousin to fix his problems now; he was a big boy. He'd fix them himself. But it would be nice fixing them here.

With that in mind and ready to get started, Elijah rolled out of bed. He snagged his jeans from the floor, fishing out his cell phone to check the time: 8:05 a.m.

Elijah tugged on his pants, then strode out of the

room in search of hot coffee and his cousin. He found neither. But as he wandered the apartment, he did find a note propped against the coffeepot.

Sorry! Got called away to step in as referee for a big match. Gotta follow the money. You chill here, take it easy, rest up. We'll talk when I get back. I know I got things to explain. Get your massage—you're booked for 8:30. I'll be back in a few hours. In the meantime, coffee is ready to go, just push the red button.

Elijah read it twice, but no amount of cryptology training was making Mack-speak any clearer. So he took the last part to heart, pushed the red button and noted he had enough time for coffee and a shower.

He was still feeling good when he stepped out of the apartment. Damned good.

It wasn't pride that made Elijah take the stairs down to the Fit Wellness Clinic. It was a desperate attempt to work the stiffness out of his leg before someone started pummeling it.

Located in the same building, the clinic was as unisex and comfortable as the rest of the gym, with wide glass doors opening to the street and a juice bar along one wall. The narrow hallway leading to the treatment rooms was guarded by a display counter showcasing fitness gear, energy bars and insulated bottles. Sitting behind the counter was a pretty blonde who looked like she'd gotten lost somewhere between deciding if she wanted to be a hippie or a sex symbol. Her dreadlocks were tied back from her face with a wide magenta hairband, her shirt appeared to be made from hemp and her lips were painted bloodred.

Elijah approached her with a wary smile. "Hi. I'm booked for an eight-thirty massage."

"You must be Bruce Banner." Her smile was appreciative. "Mack said you were a big boy."

"Is that what Mack said?" Not as big as the Hulk, though. Figuring there was no point trying to explain his cousin's joke, Elijah shrugged.

"You're in room one. Go ahead and go on in. Strip down naked and get comfy on the table." She inclined her head toward the first door on the left. "You let me know if you need any help."

"You the one who's going to come work the kinks out?" he asked.

"I wish. But you're down for an injury rehabilitation massage, and we only have one person qualified for that." Her sigh said that person wasn't her. "Your therapist will be with you in a few minutes."

Therapist. Elijah grimaced. He'd had enough of that. But he didn't figure anyone rubbing his burn-scarred flesh was going to ask what was going through his head. They'd be too busy holding back their gasps of horror.

He stepped into the massage room, letting the door close behind him as he checked it out. The therapists must have free rein on their decorating choices, because this was not a room done by Mack.

The colors were soothing, cream and tan with splashes of black and red to keep it from being boring. There was an Asian feel to the art and statuary, with delicate coins on a red string hanging in one corner and chimes in another. But the star of it all was the massage table. Bigger than most, it looked sturdy enough to hold an elephant and was set at its lowest height, telling Elijah that the massage therapist was probably a woman.

Cool, he grinned.

He wouldn't mind being rubbed down by female hands. Something that his recovery had put on the no-fly list for the last few months.

He stripped down, neatly folding his clothes and stacking them on the chair. Comfortable with his nudity, he reached for the ceiling, stretching out muscles still tight from yesterday's drive, then climbed under the sheet.

Maybe that was his problem, Elijah considered as he propped his chin on his fists and began systematically relaxing his muscles. He started with his toes, breathing deep, relaxing each digit before moving on to his ankles and calves.

Maybe all he needed was a good lay. A hot ride to clear his pipes, knock loose the kinks and get him back in fighting condition.

His eyes drifted closed as he felt a few of the tighter knots loosen in his thigh. Seemed like his body was all for that idea.

About the time he'd breathed relaxation into his shoulders, he heard the door open. A familiar scent tickled his awareness, teased his senses with both desire and dread.

"Sorry I'm running late, Mr. Banner. Bruce, is it?" There was humor in the friendly words and a hint of doubt. "I hope my delay didn't upset you."

Elijah didn't have to turn his head to know who had

just walked in. Like her scent, he'd know her voice anywhere.

Fuck.

He was going to kick Mack's ass sideways.

He forced his expression to clear before he turned on the massage bed, propping himself on one elbow and offering as close to a friendly smile as he could manage.

"Hello, Ava."

CHAPTER FIVE

"Elijah?"

Elijah Prescott?

Her emotions ricocheting between denial and delight, Ava tried to think straight. Her fingers itched to reach out, to touch that gorgeous face, to caress that warm skin. To see if he was real.

But all she could do was stare.

Then, in her next breath, her initial surge of joy-filled pleasure died a fast, ugly death as memories flashed in a painful cacophony of images. White lace and teddy bears. Gold rings and baby bottles. Basic black and a tiny coffin.

"What the hell are you doing here?" she snapped, stepping away from the table as if breathing his air would suck her back into the past.

"I *thought* I was getting a massage, but clearly I was mistaken," Elijah remarked in that deep, easy voice of his. Once that unflappable calm had comforted her, had made her feel safe and secure and even, yes, on occasion, had turned her on.

Now it made her want to storm over to that massage table and kick him.

Hard.

"Why are you here?" she asked again. "Here. In Napa. In the spa. On my massage bed?"

"Yours?"

Those sharp bottle-green eyes angled around the room. Not a flounce, flourish or bit of fluff to be seen. She didn't need his arched brow to tell her that he didn't think she fit this setting.

Good. The woman he'd known *didn't* fit here. Ava took comfort in that. But comfort wasn't much of a cushion against the shock of seeing Elijah Prescott again.

Her gaze shifted from the intensity of his face to check out the rest of him. A mistake, she realized when her eyes roamed the corded muscles of his shoulders and arms. It was bad enough that she could barely form a coherent sentence or think straight. The last thing she could afford to add to that was lust.

She tried to look away, but her eyes wouldn't cooperate. God, the man was built. Not gym fit, but weapon fit. She'd forgotten that there was a difference, and in ignoring the former had blocked out how deliciously tempting was the latter.

"I'm in Napa visiting my cousin. I'm in the *fitness clinic*," he continued, "because Mack insisted I get a massage. Now how about you fill me in on the details of how this came to be your massage bed?"

It wasn't the demand in his voice or the absolute assurance in his expression that she'd do exactly as ordered that snapped Ava out of her stupefied fog. It was realizing that she was about to obey. Chin high, she pulled on her best bitch face and threw out a snotty—albeit pretty lame—insult.

"Well, well, what do you know? You're one of those guys who can't handle a woman giving them a massage," Ava taunted. "Like, what? Just because you're some big, hard-bodied sailor boy, a woman can't be a professional and do her job? Are you a misogynist, Elijah? Is that what's wrong?"

The words were as empty of truth as they were ugly. But they had the desired effect.

"I'm fucking naked," he snapped, shoving into a sitting position and making her mouth water when the sheet slipped down his chest to pool in his lap. "That's what's wrong."

"I've seen you naked before. Quite a few times, as a matter of fact." She rounded her heavily lashed eyes as innocently as she could. "I have pictures if you need a reminder."

"I'm aware of the past, and remember every naked moment, thanks all the same," he said dismissively. Then his frown deepened. "What pictures?"

"Wouldn't you like to know?" Ava laughed, a real laugh this time. For a man who'd never had any issue walking around in his altogether, he sure had a puritanical streak about some things.

"I'm taking that as my cue to get dressed," he said. At her questioning glance, he added, "I assume I'm not getting that massage. Unless you want to set aside your touted professionalism and use this opportunity to get your hands on my body again, of course."

His brows arched and his smile slid into wicked as he gave her a long look up and down. Ava pretended that look didn't send tiny thrills of desire sparking through her system. God, she was doing a lot of pretending today.

"No, thanks. The last thing I want to do is touch you," she lied, trying to make the words sound uninterested instead of breathless and filled with regret.

Elijah didn't seem to care either way. He simply stared with an intensity that seemed to see right through her secrets and into her soul.

"What?" she finally asked, forcing herself not to brush self-consciously at her hair or tug her simple black tee to make sure it was in place.

"You look…different," he said, his tone not indicating whether that was good or bad.

Ava's spine stiffened, her jaw jutting out as she filled in the unsaid blanks. Yes, she'd lost most of her curves when she'd dropped fifteen pounds. She heard that lament often enough from her mother, the woeful despair that men preferred curves to angles, softness to muscle.

And, yes, she'd let her hair grow out without the golden highlights she'd sported for so many years. Monthly salon visits were too much time and money, so the world had to settle for seeing her natural dark brown hair in all its waving glory. Her face was free of makeup but for a layer of tinted moisturizer, and her nails were short and unpolished.

She knew she didn't look the same as she had four years ago. *So what?*

The last thing she wanted was a man gazing at her with interest, with desire. As far as Ava was concerned, that part of her life was over, and she was glad for it. Mostly.

She bit her lip, watching the play of muscles as Elijah shifted position. His green eyes flashed with irritation; his own gilded-brown hair was just long enough to show a hint of curl. His full lips were pressed tightly together, but she knew they could be seductively soft or hard with demand, depending on his mood.

His lap was covered by the sheet, but she took a moment to consider what the fabric hid. Oh so many kinds of heaven, she knew. Then her gaze shifted to where the sheet had fallen away.

Her breath caught, pain gutting her of all thought but for horror. It wasn't the sculpted perfection of his abs or the corded muscles of his thighs that Ava's eyes were glued to.

It was the scars, rigid and red, scored in ugly lines over his right leg. From hip to knee with a scattering of scars dotting his calf. Her heart wept at the sight. What had he done? She tried to swallow past the scream knotted in her throat. Those were burns. She'd never worked on a burn-recovery client, but she'd seen enough during her stint at the hospital to recognize them. How deep did scars like that go?

She wanted to ask. Her hand ached to reach out, to run her fingers along the puckered tissue and ease the tight pain.

Her mother had predicted that Elijah's job would kill or maim him. From their first date, Celeste Monroe had warned her that Elijah would never put her ahead of his daredevil ways, his need for glory. She'd dismissed Ava's argument that the SEALs operated on the down low and never sought credit, that Elijah was highly trained and skilled, and that he was trained in linguistics—basically, talking, and how much trouble could a guy get into talking?

According to Celeste, the wrong words could get him blown to bits. Damn Elijah all to hell for proving her mother right. Again.

She tore her gaze off his leg to meet his eyes instead. "Ouch," she said, pulling a face.

"Ouch?" he repeated with a half laugh.

"You expected me to, what? Get hysterical at the sight of your mangled flesh? To throw myself on your body, wailing over your injury?" she asked, putting as much sarcasm as she could into the words since her stomach was quivering to do just that.

"Actually, I didn't think about it," he said with jerk of his shoulder. "But if I had, yeah. I'd have expected wails and tears and hysteria. As I recall, you were pretty good at freaking out."

"Unlike you, who nothing ever fazes," she countered, gripping her arms tightly over her chest. Using her chin, she gestured toward his thigh. "I'm sure when that happened, you simply got up, dusted yourself off and finished your supersecret mission."

"That's what I'm trained to do."

Of course it was. Ava had once figured Elijah was the perfect combination of Lancelot, Michelangelo and Superman.

But she'd been wrong about so many things.

"And you? Suddenly you're trained to rub naked people's bodies for a living now?"

"That'd fall under the category of none of your business," she snapped. She hated people judging her. Her life, her choices. She'd grown up with it, had spent her life guided by it, had once accepted that as simply the way things were. But no longer.

Apparently Elijah hadn't gotten that memo.

"Your old man lets you do this?" he scoffed with a look that was much too condescending for a man naked but for a pale cream sheet. Granted, his body was freaking awesome. But that was beside the point.

"My *father*," she emphasized, "has no say in my life and no authority over my choices."

"I meant your—what do you call him? Boyfriend is pretty high school, isn't it?" The bitterness in his words matched the expression in his eyes. "Booty call is tacky. So what's the term? Man friend?"

Ava had to swallow hard to breathe past the knot in her throat, but she hoped she managed to look nonchalant. "I hear significant other a lot, or partner." Partner. Something she'd never been. She let the bitterness show through her smile for just a second before shrugging. "Personally, I think lover sounds perfect."

Not that she had one. But there was something satisfying about watching fury flash in Elijah's gorgeous eyes.

Tossing the sheet aside, he didn't give her much time to appreciate the view before he yanked on his jeans. She indulged in a brief sigh of regret when he grabbed his shirt and yanked the gray cotton over his head.

"Is that what you call yours?" he asked as he shoved his feet into running shoes. "I hear he's got everything you were looking for, Ava. Money, status and, more important, Daddy's stamp of approval."

She took a deep breath to reminded herself how far she'd come from the naive young woman whose life revolved around the idea of making everyone happy. Everyone but herself.

Well, never again.

"I answer to no man. Not my father, not my friends." She turned toward the door, then shot a look over her shoulder as she fluttered her lashes and offered the sweetest smile in her arsenal. "Not even my ex-husband."

SERIOUSLY?

Elijah slammed his fist into the punching bag later that afternoon, the impact singing up his arm in sharp retort. Five years of visiting Mack, of hanging at his gym, and not a single Ava sighting.

Right cross to the bag. Knife hand strike. Jab. Left, right, jab. Roundhouse kick. Jump kick.

Four years after the divorce was final, he'd gotten his shit together. Living the life he was supposed to live, the one he'd planned to have since he was a kid.

Reverse side kick. Elbow strike. Fist-heel uppercut.

But now, when his world was fucked, his mind a mess and his convictions wavering—that's when his ex had to show up in his life? To walk into a massage room—what the fuck was Ava doing giving massages anyway?—while he was naked except for a sheet and some scars? Seriously?

Sweat dripped, burning his eyes, sliding down his face as he executed a jump spin kick, slamming the heel of his foot into the top of his target. The heavy bag went flying as the hook ripped from the ceiling, showering drywall dust over the sweat-dotted floor. The bag hit the opposite wall with a loud thud.

Ignoring the stares and muttered remarks, Elijah stood, fists on his hips as he sucked in air. He shook his head. The timing was unbelievable.

"You didn't mention that you were going to rip my gym apart," Mack said from the doorway. His words were light, carrying a hint of laughter. But beneath it there was a layer of concern. For him? Or for the equipment? Elijah didn't actually give much of a damn right now.

Ignoring the bag on the floor, the sand scattered through the drywall dust and the shocked expressions, Elijah crossed the room.

"I tried going for a drive, but it didn't have the same impact."

Elijah gave his cousin a long look.

"You didn't tell me Ava was working here. Or that she's a massage therapist now. Or that you'd be pulling a stupid stunt like booking me an appointment with her." Thinking about that sent a red haze of fury through Elijah's head. He didn't hesitate. He simply gave in to the anger. It wasn't until he saw his cousin's head snap back that he realized he'd given in with his fist.

His hand reverberated all the way to his shoulder, his breath a hiss of rage. Instead of flexing his fingers to shake off the pain, he curled them tight. Held it inside.

That's where it belonged.

The pain. The guilt. The memories.

"I guess I deserved that," Mack murmured, wiping the blood off his lip with his knuckles. His words were calm. But he watched Elijah with narrowed eyes. Preparing, most likely, to counter the next swing.

But Elijah simply turned away. He unbound his

hands, tossing the wraps in the laundry bin as he passed the hallway toward the showers. People scrambled to get out of his way as he strode through. He didn't head toward the locker rooms. He slammed both hands into the back door, sending it flying open, and took the outside stairs to the apartment above.

He headed straight for the shower, keeping the water cold to counter his temper. He focused on emptying his mind. On letting his emotions level out. He didn't track how long he stood under the pounding spray. He simply let the water pour over him until he was calm enough to shut it down.

He was calmer, he decided as he scraped the razor over his whiskers. Wasn't he calmer? Sure he was. All that rage, washed away. Good to know cold showers worked for more than wasting a good hard-on.

Smirking, he remembered when just the thought of Ava had inspired a woody. Not this time, though. Maybe it had been shock. There had been plenty of that rocking through him at the sight of his ex-wife walking in, ready to rub those long, talented fingers of hers over his body.

Maybe he'd simply been too worn out, too sore, with all the stiffness in his body dedicated to his leg after yesterday's lengthy drive.

Or maybe, just maybe, he'd finally gotten over her.

His lips slid into a half grin. He liked that one. All things considered, he had enough to deal with without facing ghosts from heartbreak past. His smile dimmed.

He'd fallen for her sweet face once, had loved every inch of her curvy figure. He'd adored her sense of playful fun, her quirky humor. Even her vulnerable need to please her family had appealed to him. But most of all, the woman had been gorgeous. It wasn't her looks that had hooked him into marriage, though.

Ava had been pure sweetness.

It had been her sweetness that had melted all his good intentions, his willpower and his better judgment. He'd known the stats on military marriages. They were pure crap. But given that he was a man determined to succeed, he'd figured they'd overcome the odds.

His grin faded completely at the memory of the price he'd paid for that loss of judgment. The cost of losing to those odds.

He'd lost Ava.

He'd lost his son.

He'd lost his heart.

Elijah turned his back on the mirror and the memory. It wasn't as easy to turn away from his body's reaction.

It wasn't as if he'd lived like a monk the last five years. He was a man. He liked sex. A lot of sex. But he knew better now than to believe that sex—even a lot—could, would or should turn into anything more.

Unlike sex with Ava, which had come with a million strings and emotional ties. But that was then. He didn't get that vulnerable vibe from her now.

She had an edge that she hadn't carried years ago. She might still have that lush mouth with its full upper lip and sexy overbite, but the smart-ass comments coming out of it were new.

Put it aside, he ordered himself. Thinking about her, comparing then and now? It was a lesson in misery.

Elijah strode into his temporary quarters, pulling clean clothes from his duffel and tossing them on the bed. He frowned, noting the red light flashing on his cell phone. Only messages left by the team would trigger that alarm.

He snapped up the phone, keyed in his code, then another one, then hit messages. Text only.

Innocent until proven guilty?

Elijah scowled.

Who'd sent it?

He scrolled backward, then forward again, but there was no sender designation. Not cool, considering it was a secured line.

Elijah frowned at the message again. He read it backward, every other word, jumped letters, replaced others. Off the top of his head, it didn't fit any currently used encryption sequence, but that didn't mean it wasn't code for something. The words themselves were rather obvious, and it didn't take a genius to infer they referred to Operation Fuck Up.

Was it from Ramsey? Did he have accomplices other than Adams? Was it someone using the operation as a distraction for something else? Or was it bait?

Savino assumed that Ramsey was alive. Torres and Lansky were sure he was. They were probably right.

Elijah had bunked with both Ramsey and Adams. Shouldn't he have sensed it if they were so twisted that they'd betray their country, their team, their friends?

He remembered Poseidon's support. Nobody there had questioned his innocence. But he'd seen the look in some of the others' eyes. The doubts. The questions. The suspicion.

Had someone put that suspicion into play? Was there

a mission—sanctioned or not—to smoke out the truth of Elijah's involvement? Anger curled in his gut but didn't take root. It couldn't. How could he be pissed at the men for questioning his ignorance when he was trained to see patterns, to analyze anomalies, to decipher mysteries?

How could he claim innocence when he didn't feel innocent?

But his personal crap wasn't the issue. The issue was that someone had concocted an elaborate setup to either find out what he knew or simply fuck with him for not seeing the truth before it damaged the team's reputation.

Savino had said that despite orders to the contrary, he suspected someone in NI was still investigating. And they all knew Ramsey was slithering around out there somewhere, jacking off until the team caught his lying, traitorous ass and extracted payment for his actions. In other words, Operation Fuck Up was in play.

Elijah rubbed his thigh, working the rippled flesh, the scars feeling like jagged glass beneath his fingers. Fire flashed through his head. Overwhelming pain, the horrific misery of the flames eating his flesh, devouring his body.

Ramsey.

Elijah had a thing or two to say to him. He just had to find him first. Elijah's leg twinged, pain stabbed. His chest tightened, lungs squeezed so hard he could barely breath. *No, dammit. Goddammit all to hell.*

He put every iota of his focus onto his clenched fists. The pressure of his fingers against his palms. His pulse, blood constricted under flesh pulled taut. His nails, short and even, gouging skin.

Focus, dammit.

Slowly, so damned slowly, his breath evened out. Eventually, the roaring in his ears quieted to a hum. Finally, he could think. He could breathe. He could open his eyes and be in the moment.

It took a couple of tries before Elijah could unclench his hand, flexing and straightening until the blood flowed again. Then, only when the numbness was gone, did he use it to wipe at the sweat dripping down his face.

Enough of this shit.

He'd lived through it once. He was sick of living through it over and over again. *Done*, he promised himself. All he had to do was focus. Stay focused. Stay in the moment.

But first…

He grabbed the phone. Fingers flying over the small screen, he typed, Working on decrypting. Need a trace.

He hit Forward.

Savino would get whatever there was to get. They'd complete the mission. And it would be done. All done. It would. Or he would.

Worrying about the future was as useless as living in the past, he reminded himself. *Get dressed—get out.*

He wasn't surprised when his phone rang before he'd got both legs into his jeans. "Yeah?" he answered, putting the phone on speaker while he finished dressing.

"How's wine country?" asked Savino.

"Not as soothing as one might think."

"Maybe you should've tried Monterey."

Elijah waited until he'd pulled his gray Henley over his head before responding. "Maybe I should have."

"How's the family? Had a big family dinner welcoming you home yet?"

Small talk? That wasn't good. Elijah frowned but played along. "Mack's doing good. I'm staying at his place. Haven't seen anyone else in the family yet."

"Nobody?"

Giving it a scowl, Elijah grabbed the phone and took it off speaker. "You keeping tabs or something?"

"On you? Of course not."

"No reason for you to keep tabs on my cousin. The guy's a tough sucker, but he's not a threat to team or country."

"Nope. If I remember right, he's got one helluva left jab, though."

Elijah wasn't interested in discussing Mack's history in mixed martial arts. "Why would you keep tabs on Ava?"

"Not tabs. More like periodically satisfying my curiosity."

"About my ex-wife?"

"You were hospitalized, Rembrandt. You might not remember, but that first week, your prognosis was crap. It's called being prepared. And, like I said, my curiosity was tapped when I realized Cupcake was a yoga-wielding ninja."

Elijah would have smirked at Savino's nickname for Ava and puzzled over the yoga-wielding ninja comment. But he was busy trying to imagine the woman he'd seen this morning standing teary eyed over his hospital bed. Nope, the image didn't fit.

Once he could have easily pictured it. Once Ava had loved him enough to care about his welfare, to worry about his safety. Truth be told, she'd worried so much it had been a bit of a pain in the ass. But at least she'd been invested. *Yeah. Those were the good ol' days.*

"You're staying at your cousin's. Did you run into her?"

Elijah's jaw clenched. "Yeah. We ran into each other."

"Damn." In that single word, Savino conveyed concern, friendship and support. "Sorry."

"For not warning me? It wouldn't have mattered."

He'd had to get off base, had to get away from all the questions he couldn't answer. Where else was he to go but home? Besides, sooner or later, he had to fill his family in on the details of his hospitalization. Civilian-friendly details.

Maybe.

He was still considering skipping over sharing that little tidbit.

"Warning or not, you're in a precarious situation," Savino said. "You should be on full alert."

"You think this message is that dangerous?"

"I think seeing your ex again after a long bout of hospital-induced abstinence is that dangerous," Savino replied. "Unless you had some good times with a nurse you failed to mention."

Hardly. Elijah snorted. He'd been in a Navy hospital, surrounded by male nurses and one very masculine female who'd looked like she could bench-press him.

"I can handle my sex life, Dad," Elijah shot back.

"Bet you can." Savino laughed. Then his tone dropped into concern. "Still, given the emotional implications, and your latest communiqué, you might consider returning to base."

Not an order, Elijah noticed. More of a friendly suggestion. He knew he should consider it. Operation Fuck Up was definitely in play. Someone was baiting him. The best place to deal with that was with the brotherhood.

Elijah dropped to the bed, dug his elbows into his knees and rested his head in one hand. He was on leave, dammit. He was sore. He was tired. He was burned out, and now, thanks to seeing Ava again and some of the memories that had stirred up, he was fucking horny.

Savino could be dedicated and resourceful.

Elijah was used up.

"You get anything out of that communiqué?" he asked quietly.

"In the two minutes since you sent it? I'm good but not that good."

"Is Lansky working on it?"

"He is that good, but he's out of touch right now."

Elijah frowned. There was something in Savino's tone, but he couldn't pinpoint it. Since the man didn't elaborate and Elijah knew he couldn't be prodded, he set it aside to consider later.

"I'll keep you in the loop," Savino promised. "In the meantime, do you need anything?"

"A stiff drink would be good."

"That going to help you decode that message?"

"Might." Elijah reached into his duffel for his sketch pad, flipping through it to check his notes. "I've probably got everything I need here, but I'll let you know if there's anything else."

"Anything at all," Savino reiterated before the line went dead.

The guy is such a sentimental fool, Elijah thought with a soft laugh. His grin fell away as he tossed aside his notebook. The guy wasn't big on emotional declarations, but damned if he wasn't always there with an ear, advice or a good kick in the ass.

Elijah wasn't interested in any of that at the moment. He just wanted a break. He glanced at his phone, then at the sun setting outside the window. A break wasn't in the cards right now.

He had too many things to do. None of which included a pity party.

He had no concerns about his notes being deciphered by anyone given that they were randomly integrated and carefully hidden in a series of elaborate drawings throughout the notebook. But training had ground deep that old saw about better safe than sorry, so he kneeled and locked the thick book in the small safe Mack had installed behind a false drawer at the bottom of the dresser.

As he rose, Elijah knew he had company. He didn't have to look around to see who it was. He knew that, too.

But he didn't want to talk. So he ignored his cousin and, keeping his back turned to the door, wove his belt through its loops. Strapped on his watch. Rubbed his hands over his drying hair. Shoved his wallet in his back pocket, his keys in his front.

Then, only because he was out of things to do, he took a long breath and turned. And ignored the twinge of guilt at the sight of the mottled, purpling bruise already forming on Mack's beefy jaw.

"Where you going?"

"Dunno."

Bruised jaw jutting in consideration, Mack stared for a moment, then nodded. "Want company?"

"Yours?" Elijah snorted. "Definitely not."

"Holding a grudge?"

Shit. Elijah pressed his thumb and forefinger against his eyes as if the pressure would ease the aching in his head. "Look, it's already five. If I leave now, I can be at my mother's in time for dinner and drama. You can consider that my restitution for the fist if you want. But unless you want another one, leave this alone until I'm through being pissed."

His cheeks puffed out, Mack considered, then nodded again. "You sure you don't want company? I can talk about the guy who dumped me last week and give Aunt Marilyn something to go on about besides your dangerous career."

"Thanks. But I figure listening to the lecture is the cost of hiding my injuries from them. If you diluted it, I might feel I have to do a second dinner—or worse, a family weekend—before I've made the proper compensation."

With a half laugh, Mack leaned against the door frame. "Dude, you have the strictest sense of right and wrong of anyone I've ever known."

"It is what it is." Elijah shrugged.

Mack moved aside when he approached, following Elijah into the living room.

"Sorry I took my frustration out on your face," he offered.

"Sorry I didn't give you a heads-up about Ava." Mack grimaced, his expression folding into lines of regret. "Want an explanation? A—what do you call it? Situation accounting?"

"Sitrep. Situation report." *Hell, no*, Elijah thought. "Don't worry about it."

"Want to skip dinner with Aunt Marilyn and spend the evening with my latest hottie and me? We're doing dinner at Mandarin's, then hitting Decadence for dessert."

"Thanks. But I'm more an apple-pie guy. I'm not into booze-filled chocolate pudding with a fancy name." Elijah snagged his jacket out of the hall closet and shrugged into the soft leather. "Besides, I thought you said you got dumped last week."

"That was last week, cuz."

"Then I'd be a total ass to horn in on your making time with a new hottie. I've got an assignment to work on, so I'll probably be holed up in my room when you get back." Hoping it would soothe the last of the rough edges away, he slapped his cousin on the back. "Don't bother keeping your screams of ecstasy down. My headphones are sound suppressing."

"Gonna have to be damned good to drown out the sound of groaning to *Boléro*."

Sex, sex, sex. Everybody was talking sex.

Elijah took the stairs.

He had the image of Ava, the reminder of their heat, in one corner of his mind. Now he had Nic concerned that he'd gone so long without sharing orgasms with a woman that he'd do something stupid. Why not throw in the idea of his cousin and some big, buff guy getting their jollies while *Boléro* played in the background.

Boléro? Seriously? Elijah grimaced. Mack needed

to get some better tunes. Then again, it was better than his previous soundtrack—"On the Good Ship Lollipop."

And Elijah? He was facing celibacy and radio silence, with only the memory of his hot ex-wife and her sexy new body to keep him entertained.

Maybe he should reconsider Nic's advice and get the hell back on base.

CHAPTER SIX

AVA KNOCKED BACK her third shot of tequila, the liquor hitting her throat like fire and burning its way down just as hot as the first two.

"Freaking-A." Her glossy lips rounded in shock, Chloe could only shake her head as Ava slammed the shot glass on the table. "I've never seen you drink like this."

"I never *have* drank like this." Ava breathed hoarsely through the flames. The last time she'd seen Elijah, she'd buried her feelings in food. She figured it was only fair that she give booze a try this round. She'd bet she got numb faster, forgot easier and wouldn't have to do as many hours on the treadmill to offset the results. "I decided it was time to try something new."

"Uh-huh. How about we give food a try?" Chloe gave the laminated bar menu a grimace. "It doesn't look like they serve a single organic or fresh dish—we can call fried food the new thing."

"Oh no. No way." Ava gave an adamant shake of her head, then had to pause when the bar decided to take a fast spin in the opposite direction. She really wasn't used to drinking. "I ate fried food last time. Fried mac-and-cheese balls. And batter-fried shrimp. And fries.

French fries, cheese fries, chili fries and sweet potato fries."

She'd eaten enough potatoes to depopulate every potato field in the state of Idaho. Ava swallowed a couple of times to get past the memory. Then, for good measure, she sucked in a couple of deep breaths until the craving for sour cream and onion potato chips passed before continuing.

"Let's see, besides my worship of fries, there was chocolate. Mmm, chocolate, in all forms. Cherry-chocolate cake. Double-chocolate cupcakes. Chocolate cream pie. Triple-dipped—"

"Stop," Chloe interrupted. Her blue eyes pained and her expression tight, she shook her head. "I'm begging you, stop. Don't say another word. I already have to work out five days a week or I balloon up. I just bought my first pair of designer jeans, Ava. They were on sale. I can't return them, and muffin tops are only acceptable if they're sprinkled with sugar."

"See, that's why we're avoiding food. I gained forty pounds last time."

"Last time." Her usually mellow expression impatient, Chloe waited a beat, then lifted both hands. "What last time? We came in here so you could explain over a drink, and so far I've watched you slam three and you haven't explained a single thing."

Explain. Yeah. She'd promised to do that, hadn't she? Ava swallowed hard, wishing she could blame the churning in her gut on the booze. Doing shots was a new thing for her, but this sick feeling was very familiar.

"So I went through this rough time a while back," she said slowly, dancing around the explanation until she was sure she could get through the telling of it. "Because of it, I gained lots of weight. Which is what led me to start exercising. That's what put me on the fitness path and led to teaching. That's when I became interested in massage and decided to get my certification. Which is how I came to work at Mack's gym, where we met. And you know everything from there."

Ava offered her most angelic smile and even added a flutter of her lashes for effect. She sighed when all she got in return was a shake of Chloe's head.

"You said something about a guy when you called," Chloe prodded, her fingers tapping on the varnish of the dark wood table. Frowning, she shook her head again. "I've never known you to get worked up over a guy. Actually I've never known you to have anything to do with guys." The hint of impatience faded as sympathy took over Chloe's face. "Is that what's wrong? You finally found a guy that you're interested in? Who is he? Where'd you meet? Is he interested?"

Talk about making her head spin. Ava pressed one hand to her temple to try to slow her swirling thoughts and wondered if she should order another tequila. It would either slow the swirling or dull the pain already stabbing through her heart.

"Yes, there is a guy. You might have seen him this morning, since he was my eight-thirty massage appointment. But I'm not interested in him," she declared, waving one hand through the air as if she could erase the very thought. "He's Mack's cousin, actually. I knew him once. The last time I saw him, I was an emotional mess. Seeing him again just reminded me of that."

That and so much more. Ava took a shaky breath, then another sip of water hoping it'd cool her throat.

"Was he part of the mess?" Chloe guessed quietly.

"Everyone and everything in my life at that point was a part of the mess." Her words were surprisingly bitter. Maybe it was shock over seeing Elijah again, or maybe the alcohol had opened doors usually secured so tight. Whatever it was, the memories were flooding through her, hard and intense.

So many memories.

So many losses.

So much pain.

"But it's no big deal," she tried to dismiss with a jerk of her shoulder. "I suppose I overreacted."

"That's it?"

"Sure." Ava tried to smile but her cheeks were a little numb so she wasn't sure if she pulled it off or not. "I shouldn't have bothered you. It's really not a big deal."

"Okay." Chloe nodded, her sky blue eyes as serious as Ava had ever seen them and her face set in lines of disappointment. "So it's no big deal that you ran out of the treatment room, or that you've blown a day's calories on alcohol, or that you're now drunker than I've ever seen you. It's no big deal."

Ava couldn't stop her face from sliding into a pout.

"I thought we were friends. The kind of friends who are there for each other," Chloe continued, pouring more water into Ava's glass. "You were there for me when I freaked out because after thirty years of unmarried bliss, my parents decided to get all traditional and tie the knot. You talked me off the ledge earlier this year when I was so upset about Bones taking a relationship sabbatical that I fell off the vegetarian wagon and started scarfing down breakfast sausages like there was no tomorrow."

Ava grimaced.

"You've been there to listen to my relationship rhapsodies and my plans for happily-ever-after. You've mopped my tears, held my hand and, yes, brought me chocolate." Chloe pulled out all the stops then with a deep sigh and woebegone expression. "I didn't realize it was a one-way deal."

Oh, God. Ava wanted to drop her head to the table and cry. The guilt. Ava was an expert on guilt. She'd been raised on it. Her parents had employed guilt and bribery in equal measure, using them to train Ava like a puppy to do their bidding. She'd been so well trained that she hadn't even recognized it until Elijah had forced her to. She'd spent the last few years weaning herself off her parents' influence, learning to recognize the signs, to sidestep the effects.

And here she was, wallowing in it again. Wave after wave of it washed over her, the nasty-tasting dregs swirling and mixing with the tequila so she felt like she was drowning.

God. Ava heaved a deep sigh. She rubbed two fingers against her temple—at least she thought she did. Her face was pretty numb. Maybe that was a good thing. She couldn't avoid thinking about the situation since it had been slapped, naked, in her face. But if she had to offer details, offering them might be easier anesthetized.

"Elijah." Just saying it made her heart spasm. Ava pressed her lips together until she was sure they wouldn't tremble. "His name is Elijah."

This time instead of stopping her from lifting her shot glass toward the waitress to signal for another round, Chloe simply lifted the appetizer menu and pointed to order food along with the tequila shot.

"He and Mack really are cousins. You probably remember me telling you I met Mack when I was in high school and he was one of the coaches at cheer camp." Her lips curved at the memory of the burly bodybuilder trying to teach a bunch of giggling teenagers the benefits of muscle tone. "I didn't embrace strength training then, but he did help me build up enough upper-body strength to do a handstand, so I snagged the head cheerleader spot. I was so impressed, I used to come all the way from Mendocino to Napa a few times a year for a personal training session."

"I didn't realize you drove, what? Three hours? Just for one training session?"

"Sure. Every few months he'd create a new workout program for me, take me through it a few times, then video it so I had a visual reference for the workouts I was supposed to do on my own between sessions. I usually flaked, though. Oh, I'd put in the time the week after each session, and the week before the next. But in between?" Rolling her eyes, Ava shook her head. "Flake city."

"And you met this guy, Elijah, through Mack because of those sessions?"

"Mmm-hmm." She gave a nostalgic sigh of pleasure as she remembered the first time she'd seen him. She'd been home from UC Santa Barbara the summer after her freshman year, thinking she was so mature and worldly. A quarter of the way to an ineffectual degree in art history, she'd spent her days quoting poetry, passing judgment on the state of social justice and bemoaning the lack of good shopping in Mendocino. Her evenings were mostly spent at the country club or at any number of similar appropriate upscale events where parent-approved potential husbands gathered.

One fine weekend in July she'd driven to Napa to shop, to lunch and, as a lark, to stop in for the grand opening celebration of Mack's gym. It had been filled wall-to-wall with people, including the burly trainer's large extended family.

And Elijah.

As soon as their eyes had met over the row of tread-mills, he'd stridden over to say hello.

And she'd fallen in love. Just like that.

"It was through Mack that I met Elijah. We were…" *Best friends. Husband and wife. Soul mates.* "A couple for a while. Then we weren't. It wasn't an easy breakup."

And wasn't that a gem of an understatement. Ava let it ride while the waitress brought her drink and a platter of cheesy nachos piled high with black beans, vegetables and sour cream.

Chloe waited for the server to leave before she asked, "How long were you together?"

"Two years. Or three. Maybe four, depending on how you count."

While Chloe puzzled that and began eating, Ava licked the flesh between her thumb and forefinger. She sprinkled a dash of salt and licked again, then tossed the glistening gold tequila down her throat. Fast was best, she figured, shuddering just a little before biting a wedge of lime between her teeth and sucking back the tart relief.

"How many ways are there to count?" Chloe asked as soon as Ava smacked the glass down on the table.

Oh, so many. Regretting the deep breath as soon as she took it, Ava ignored the burning in her throat and shrugged. "First meet to last sight, four years. First date to breakup, three years. Commitment to end, two years." She let her head fall back on the padded seat, closing her eyes and losing herself in the room's heady spins. The scent of fake cheese goo rippled through her system, stirring either hunger or nausea. She was too miserable to tell which. "Given that he was gone more than he was with me, we could even count actual time together."

Feeling Chloe's curiosity, Ava opened blurry eyes and mumbled, "Fourteen months, twenty-three days."

"Okay." A loaded chip halfway to her mouth, the blonde nodded. "Okay. So I guess that means yours was pretty serious."

Ava couldn't stop the watery laugh. *Serious? Oh yeah. As death.* "Until it wasn't," was all she said as she lifted a chip. Since she couldn't think of anything else to do with it, she took a bite. And realized she actually was hungry.

She and Chloe spent the next few minutes focused on the nachos. Ava wasn't drunk enough to believe the conversation was over. But she knew the secret to getting through a tough workout was carefully timed breathers. *Power up to power through.*

"How long ago were you and this guy a serious thing?" Chloe asked when they were left with mostly naked chips and a sprinkling of diced tomatoes scattered over the thick white platter.

Done, full and now sure the nausea in her stomach was from nerves, Ava leaned back again. *How long ago? A lifetime.* "Today was the first time I've seen Elijah in four years. So…" She lifted her empty glass. "Long enough that I shouldn't be sliding through stupid over him."

"Nope." Chloe shook her head hard enough that the silver chains hanging from her ears jangled. "I think when it's that serious, there's no way to avoid the stupid."

Ava managed to find the smile she knew Chloe was angling for, but she couldn't hold it for long.

"It must suck to see an ex and he looks good. I like to imagine the guy losing the will to live, or at least to groom himself, without me. It'd make me feel better thinking he's miserable with a beer gut hanging over his belt and his comb-over fluttering in the breeze." Popping the chip into her mouth, Chloe gave an exaggerated eye roll. "But your guy? Yowza, Ava. He's hotter than hot. Did he improve with age? I mean, I can't imagine better than what I saw today. Granted, I didn't get the naked view like you did, but what I did see was prime."

"It's been almost eight years since I first set eyes on him, and he was just as gorgeous at twenty-three."

"And that body? He looked pretty ripped. Is that new?"

"Elijah's body has always been amazing." Her mouth suddenly dry, Ava took a sip of water. When that wasn't enough to combat the heat, she gulped down the rest. "He's naturally lean, cuts and bulks pretty easily. And he's seriously dedicated to keeping in shape. Part of that's personality, part of it's his job."

"What does he do that demands a body like that? Fitness instructor? Cop? Underwear model?"

"He's…um…" For a lot of reasons, she'd never been able to talk about what Elijah did, about what he was. But the guilt waves were still riding high, so she forced it. "He's in the Navy."

"The Navy? Like, out on submarines and big boats and things?" Chloe looked impressed.

Impressed enough that Ava wanted to leave it at that. But if she were going to spill the whole truth, she might as well keep it at nothing but. "He's a SEAL."

"Oh my God, wow." Chloe's brows veed high as she gave a soft whistle. "Talk about dangerous. Was that why you guys split up?"

It could have been. God, she wished it had been.

"There were a lot of factors," she finally said, carefully blocking the key ones from her mind. From her heart. "But the high-risk career and the fact that he was gone so often were definitely issues."

"That'd be hard. I can't imagine what it's like when the guy's gone half the time. And I'm like, the queen of paranoid. No way could I handle a guy with a dangerous job like protecting the world."

Protecting the world. It sounded so cool. Romantic and heroic and even glamorous in a way.

Her mind flashed to the image of Elijah's leg, the deep burns etched into his muscular thigh. There was one on his face that hadn't been there before, too. He saw his body as a weapon. One he willingly used. And damaged.

"At first, I thought it was sexy. God, that body. You think he looks good clothed?" Now able to view her past through the nice, comfortable cushion of tequila, Ava gave a low whistle and waved her hand in front of her face. "Nude, the man is incredible. Perfection from head to toe."

For a woman—girl—used to country-club fit, a man like Elijah had been an epiphany.

"Beyond that body, which is worth a few days of worship," she acknowledged, "he's got this single-minded sort of intensity that's easy to miss because he comes across as being totally mellow. He doesn't talk about what he does. He doesn't brag like you'd expect. You know, big, tough guy out there fighting the bad guys, making the world a safer place. I admired him."

A part of her still did.

"So what happened?"

"So we started dating." She sighed. "Then we got married. Then we got divorced."

"Oh. Ouch." Looking as if the words were going explode out her ears if she didn't say them, Chloe asked, "So you lived on a military base? Like, surrounded by hard bodies who do push-ups all the time and exercise and look incredible?"

"No. My parents bought us a condo in Mendocino when we got married."

Having heard plenty about Ava's parents and their control issues, Chloe didn't question that. Ava would almost rather she had, since she went right for the jugular instead. "So you lived up here and he was in Southern California? How can you be married and live apart all the time?"

Good question.

This time Ava grabbed the pitcher herself to refill her glass. She gulped the water down, but it didn't do much to wash away the bitterness coating her tongue. How many times had she sat down to dinner alone? Slid between the cold sheets of her empty bed? How many nights had she lain awake, desperately wishing for her husband? For a sounding board, advice, help or even just a damn hug. But, as Elijah had so often pointed out, she'd known what she was getting when she'd married a SEAL.

"Military, especially SEALs, are deployed a lot. They're gone anyway, so why not live where I was comfortable," she finally said, using the excuse she'd offered so often that it should have been written into their marriage vows.

As far as her parents had been concerned, it was. Hence, their insistence on buying the newlyweds a condo near their house. After all, they'd argued, why should Ava move to Coronado when Elijah would be gone part of the time? And Ava had been so afraid of leaving home, so afraid to trust the new life Elijah had offered, that she'd cozied up in that condo and refused to move south.

"Wait," Chloe said. "But what about sex? You can't have sex if you're not together. I mean, you can. Phone sex. And computer sex. And text sex. I guess you could have plenty. But real sex? What about that?"

"We had plenty," Ava said, rolling her eyes. But the idea of sex and Elijah was making the room heat up— not her, she was fine, *thankyouverymuch*, so she ordered another drink. "We had enough sex when we were together to average out to twice-a-day sex if we'd been together seven days a week."

"Holy moly." Looking awed, Chloe snagged the tequila as soon as it hit the table and knocked it back herself while Ava gaped at her. "That's like—" she tapped her fingers as if trying to calculate "—more math than I can do."

Wondering if steam was rising off the top of her head from the heat of the memories, Ava settled for ice water.

"So, um, I guess it didn't work out?" Chloe finally asked. "I mean, obviously it didn't, or he wouldn't be your ex. He'd be your now. As in, you'd be doing him now. So what happened?"

Ava lifted her pain-drenched gaze from her empty glass to meet Chloe's. "Do you have any idea what it's like knowing that a kiss goodbye could be the last kiss? That a farewell hug might be the final touch you'll share with the man you love?"

"I can't imagine it," Chloe admitted as she wiggled her fingers at the waitress to get her attention before pointing at something on the menu. "Is that why you split up? Because you couldn't handle the danger?"

"Maybe. Partially," she said. "My family hated what he did. Oh, they were okay with him. It's impossible not to like Elijah. But they kept trying to get him to change careers. Trying to get me to get him to change careers. Added to my own fears, it was a lot of pressure."

"Was he open to it?"

"Elijah open to leaving the SEALs?" Ava laughed. A real laugh, completely sarcasm-free. "No. He'd never leave. No matter what I did, or how I asked, he wouldn't consider it."

"You're a great trainer, Ava. You see the potential in everyone who walks through the door, and you find a way to motivate them to reach high and grab at that potential." Chloe gave a sweep of her hand down the front of her own body as if it were the perfect example. "But you usually wait for them to walk through the door, wanting to be changed. What's up with deciding to change this guy's life for him?"

"Pressure, I suppose." Ava shrugged. Pressure, and a baby.

"But you tried? What'd you do?"

"Well…I hinted and teased and danced around the idea of him leaving the military. You know, talking about spending more time together, randomly pointing out jobs he'd be great at, that sort of thing. Maybe eventually I would have gotten through."

"What changed?"

Pain crushed her chest in its fist, clenched so tight she couldn't breathe. "Life," Ava managed.

By the time the trio of ice-cream-covered cookies arrived, Ava had shared everything.

Everything except Dominic.

Her precious Dominic. Her dark hair, his father's bottle-green eyes and a smile that made the whole world brighter.

"One more question," Chloe said as she handed over one of the two spoons.

"Just one?"

"A guy that good, one that hot, sounds like he'd be a hard act to follow."

"True that."

"So that's why you don't date?" At Ava's nod, Chloe

asked, "Does that mean you haven't been with a guy since him?"

Had sex with another man? Horrified, Ava shuddered. Despite everything, the idea still seemed like betrayal. And maybe that's why she was totally freaked out over seeing Elijah again. Maybe that's why just the sight of the man had got her so hot and bothered that she was still vibrating ten hours later.

"Maybe I was just too picky. You know, so busy grasping tight to my yardstick that nobody could get close enough to measure up."

"Well—"

"That's stupid. Talk about living in the past, right?" Ava interrupted, tapping her finger against her lip. "My mistake was forgetting that you can never start again where you left off. It's like working your ass off to get in shape, then taking a break. You know, the sort of break that packs on twenty pounds and turns the muscles into mush. When you finally get the discipline together to get back in shape, it's always a mistake to think you can start at the same level you ended. The muscles aren't trained, you can't lift as much, can't go as far."

"I don't think it's—"

"I've been going about this all wrong," Ava announced, scanning the room with blurry eyes. "I need to ease in, to work back up to the big leagues."

"Ava, don't be crazy." Following her gaze, Chloe's expression turned frantic. Reaching across the table, she grabbed Ava's arm. "You're in an emotionally vulnerable place. You're not thinking straight. And you've had too many drinks."

"Pshaw." Ava slid her arm out from Chloe's grip and

her body out of the booth. She took a second to steady herself, then aimed her fingers like a shotgun at her friend. "Locked and loaded, baby."

"Ava…"

Ava didn't look back.

She was too busy scoping out the men scattered around the dance floor. Automatically dismissing any who were with a date, she narrowed her choice down to three potentials. Admittedly, her criteria wasn't rigid— all she was seeking was someone who looked clean and didn't remind her of Elijah.

A tiny voice warned her that she wasn't dressed her best, wasn't carefully made up or wearing heels. That her hair was in a loose ponytail instead of curled and coifed. Her jeans were worn white at the seams, her tee simple red cotton without frills or adornment. Her only jewelry was a pair of half-carat diamond studs and a slender gold necklace.

A lady didn't appeal to the correct type of man unless she presented her most attractive self.

But Ava wasn't interested in attracting a potential mate. She was trolling for a man. With that in mind, she headed for the closest one.

Ten minutes later, she'd written the first off for having lousy moves on and off the dance floor and had moved on to the second. This one sang along as Nickelback promised she was never gonna be alone and made Ava long for a little isolation.

She peered over the guy's shoulder—not a difficult feat since he was barely taller than her own five-seven— looking for target number three. Because number two couldn't carry a tune and had definite rhythm issues.

And in her opinion, no woman should settle for bad rhythm.

"Cutting in."

Ava knew that voice. Hoping she was hearing things, she didn't bother looking up.

"Back off, buddy," rumbled the dancer.

"I said, cutting in."

Ava glanced up in time to see her dance partner turn his head. As he caught sight of the interruption—the six feet four inches of muscle-bound threat—the rhythmless crooner's eyes widened, his Adam's apple bobbing as he choked back his words. Then he tossed Ava at the newcomer as if she carried the plague.

"Sure, yeah. Sure thing, buddy. Here ya go. Cut in. Have a good dance."

"I'm going to kill Chloe." Ava gritted her teeth, turned on her heel and headed back toward her table.

"Hey, don't you want to finish the dance?" Mack rumbled as he followed her off the floor.

"Right. Like I want to have one of those size thirteens stomping on my feet," Ava snapped, wishing she wasn't glad for Mack's bulldozer-size presence as he cleared their way through the crowd. Given how wobbly she felt, one good bump would send her flat onto her butt.

"So what's the deal?" Ava asked as soon as they reached the table. Chloe was nowhere to be seen, but there was a pitcher of ice water sitting next to Ava's glass. Since she couldn't think of any reason not to, she slid into the booth and poured herself a cold drink. "Did Chloe run away after ratting me out? What'd she do? Call you as soon as I left the table? Is she tattling that

I'm in violation of training by drinking tequila? And, worse, eating junk food? Am I in trouble?"

"I'd say you're troubled more than in trouble. And I'm not your trainer anymore—remember? You're the trainer now."

Dammit. "I'm sorry," she murmured as he took a seat across from her.

"Don't gotta be sorry to me. You're the one who's gonna feel like shit when you're sweating out the booze in tomorrow's class. Have fun explaining that to your students."

Ava cringed when she finally looked up. Her eyes narrowed. Was that a bruise on his jaw? It was rare for anyone to land a hit on Mack.

"Were you fighting?"

"Nope," he said. "And that's enough about me. Why don't we talk about you. As in, why are you in a bar knocking back tequila when a glass of white wine usually puts you to sleep?"

"Don't forget the nachos," Ava muttered, rubbing one hand over her stomach.

"Of course not. Can't forget those."

"How, exactly, did you expect me to react?" she asked quietly. "Why didn't you warn me?"

"Not the first time Elijah's been home since you two divorced. Didn't have to warn you then—why's this time different?"

Ava had always heard about the other times Elijah had come back *after* the fact. Or she'd had enough warning ahead of time to make sure she was far, far away during the visit. "You pulled a fast one this time, sneaking in that massage."

"What? Like you didn't realize it was a setup when you saw the name in the appointment book? Who else would qualify as the Hulk?"

Ava knew Mack had been calling Elijah that name since he was a kid, his way of encouraging his younger cousin to work out, to bulk up. She'd simply forgotten.

"I wanna go home," she said with a sigh, letting her head fall back against the plastic-covered cushion of the booth. "If I go to sleep, this will all be a dream. Then I can wake up and pretend it didn't happen. Like so much of my life. Just pretend it didn't happen."

"Let's go. I'll drive."

"Don't know where my purse is. Or my keys." Ava forced her eyes open and tried to look under the table.

"Chloe took your stuff with her when she split." Like magic, Mack was at her side, helping her slide from the booth.

"She's so sweet. I should be gay like you. Then I could be with someone sweet like Chloe. Except she likes guys. Remember that Bones guy. What kind of name is Bones anyway?"

She liked Elijah's name better. Unlike the man, the name was soft. It flowed from the tongue.

Oh, the tongue. She wanted to use hers on Elijah. Did he still taste as good as he had before? Would he still like it if she scraped her teeth down his thigh, then licked her way back up?

His thigh. Ava groaned, jagged pain stabbing at her at the memory of his mangled thigh.

"C'mon, girlie." Mack slung one arm around her waist, taking on her weight so he was all but carrying her from the building. As he maneuvered through the packed crowd, Ava moved her feet.

Step, step, step. But her shoes didn't touch the ground.

"I'm floating," she giggled.

"Babe, you're flying."

Flying. Wheeee. Ava liked that. Flying high, up above the swirling misery that liked to peek out from its hiding places, reminding her that as much as she liked to pretend differently, her past really was a part of her.

Fly, she thought, closing her eyes and leaning into Mack.

Just fly.

Away from all of the problems.

Apart from all of the pain.

CHAPTER SEVEN

ELIJAH PULLED UP in front of Mack's place and, with the engine still idling, let his head drop back against the seat.

He sighed.

The best lasagna in the world, served up with guilt and garlic bread in equal heaping portions.

Why hadn't he waited a few days? A week, even. Because he was a sucker for pain; that was why.

After seeing Ava, he'd figured things couldn't get any worse. So, in the spirit of getting it all over and done with at once, he'd driven to Yountville to have dinner with the family.

His mom, and her overwhelming worry, so sure that every time she saw him would be the last because he'd die in service to his country. This visit, she'd showed him the frame she'd had made to hold the flag she expected to receive some day commemorating his death.

His sisters with their undisguised pity over his failed marriage and son's death. It wasn't that he hadn't appreciated their sympathy at the time, but dammit, it had been five years and they were still giving him commiserating pats on the shoulder and rushing around to hide pictures of Elijah's wedding and son.

As if they thought he didn't remember what his son

looked like? That stuffing a photo in a drawer would dim the memory of losing him?

As if he needed to see that glass-framed photo of himself all spiffed up in his dress blues standing next to a white-gowned Ava—who'd looked like a fairy-tale princess right down to the tiara—to remember the feelings he'd had the day he'd married her?

The love.

The pride.

The overwhelming awe that a girl like Ava Monroe was his. His wife, and already pregnant with their baby. He'd been so fucking happy.

Until he wasn't.

Elijah's head fell back against the headrest as he drew a harsh breath against the memory of Ava's expression that horrible morning he'd burst through the door.

The gut-wrenching despair. The heartbreaking misery.

And beneath it all, the blame.

Stomach churning with the familiar dregs of guilt, Elijah rubbed his fingers over his eyes. This was what visiting his family got him. He should have stayed home and eaten a sandwich. *Just goes to show, whenever you think things are as fucked-up as they can get, they get worse. A lot worse.*

As hard as it was to see the loss and pain in his mom's eyes, the sympathy in his sisters', it had been worse seeing all that and more in Ava's again.

A part of him wanted to put the car back in gear and head south. He could be in San Diego by morning. Back on base, where life made sense. Where emotions took a tidy back seat to duty.

Where all he had to face were a few whispers gathering behind his back until the roar mowed him down. The curious looks and obvious doubt from team members who couldn't believe he hadn't seen Ramsey's guile. And, of course, the subtle pressure to get himself a little psychiatric help.

Elijah had been in some crappy positions in his life, but this one pretty much took the cake and smeared it with frosting and sprinkles.

He had one hand on the gear knob and his foot on the clutch when his phone rang. Three beeps and a buzz.

Poseidon.

Saved by the team, he decided with a bitter laugh, shutting off the engine.

"Prescott," he answered.

"Rembrandt. Draw any pretty pictures lately?"

"Yo, MacGyver." He exited the car. "You got a sitrep for me?"

"Situation normal, my friend," Lansky said. "The team is in the house, under the Kahuna's watchful eye. Operation Fuck Up is plodding along with nothing new to report."

So Savino hadn't filled Lansky in on the message. Because he hadn't talked to him yet? Or was there another reason?

"You're on base?"

"Affirmative. Just came from a powwow with El Gato and the Kahuna," Lansky said, referring to Torres and Savino by their call signs. "Looks like they're digging into Ramsey's previous service record, digging into the details, seeing what they can turn up."

"And they didn't give you a shovel?" *Odd.* That sort

of digging, anything that involved a keyboard and the internet, was right up Lansky's alley.

"Nope. Savino's got me diving deep into another assignment. But I'm still poking around on my own time. Might as well, right? Something has to pop on this guy sooner or later."

"You finding anything at all?" Like proof, one way or the other, of Ramsey's status.

"Nothing useful so far. It'd help if the guy sent a message or something, you know? Drop a taunting note to say, 'Gotcha, suckers.' That's his style. Cocky and obnoxious."

Remembering the multiple notes he'd found cropping up in strange places, the hair on the back of Elijah's neck stood a little taller. His gut, once a foolproof radar, clenched.

No way MacGyver had a clue about the notes. Which meant that Savino wasn't telling him because he thought there was a legit reason.

Any legit reasons for a call like that meant bad things for the team.

"No big. I'll keep digging you keep relaxing," Lansky said, oblivious to the weight of Elijah's thoughts. "I'll touch base if I find anything juicy."

Yeah.

One way or another, Elijah knew he'd be hearing something. He just didn't know if he wanted to. Not ready to be alone with his heavy thoughts, he asked, "Speaking of juicy, how's it going with the Greek goddess? You back in her graces yet?"

"Greek goddess? You mean Andrianna?" Lansky asked in a lousy pretense of not knowing who Elijah meant. "Things are looking up there, buddy. She's coming around enough that she took my last call."

"She take it long enough to say more than kiss off?"

"Nope."

"You ready to give up?"

"Nope."

Elijah couldn't criticize him. He'd been where the guy was. He knew, too, how badly women like that could screw a guy up. He hesitated, then heard himself doing the unthinkable.

Offering advice.

"Look, man, maybe you should rethink chasing this chick. Even under the best of circumstances, SEALs are a bad bet. Our lives revolve around our work. Our work is dangerous. It's secretive. And it's too damned important to take the back seat to emotional drama."

"Torres seems to be making it work. Ward, too," Lansky muttered, pointing out the two team members who'd recently gotten engaged.

"Dude, they haven't tied the knot yet." As the only member of Poseidon to have actually gotten married, Elijah figured he had a little more expertise in this particular arena. "And both of them are with women who are okay with what they do."

As if that mattered. Ava had known he was a SEAL when they'd hooked up. She'd said she was okay with it, but it hadn't taken more than a couple of months of marriage before she'd launched a campaign to change him into her version of the perfect husband, starting with ditching his career. She'd even pitched the idea of him going to work for her dad at his bank. He could be a big executive, she'd claimed. As if an expense account and company car were comparable to his dog tags and M4 rifle.

"What do you do when the woman isn't cool with your job, though?" Lansky wondered quietly, his words echoing Elijah's thoughts.

"I guess it depends on how you feel about your job. Is it still your priority? Can you live it, and live without the woman? Can you walk away from it, and live with yourself?"

He hadn't been able to before. Not even to save his marriage. Could he now?

Lansky was silent, probably wondering the same thing. Finally, the other man's soft laugh came through the phone.

"What the hell else would I do? Go all geek and work for some tech company? Can you see me trying to play by corporate rules?"

God, no.

"We are totally not the nine-to-five type," Elijah said, trying to laugh it off.

"Ain't that the truth? We spend our life living on the edge, training to survive there with precision balance. Can you imagine us trying to fit into the civilian world? How the hell do we adjust?"

"Maybe we're not suited for the civilian world." *Which left what?* Elijah wondered.

"What are we suited for, then?"

"What we are." But Elijah wasn't sure if that was true any longer.

"We're SEALs, my friend," Lansky reminded him in a jovial tone too upbeat to be real. "We never quit."

"We're SEALs, my friend," Elijah shot back. "We thrive on adversity."

"No shit. Guess I'd better make some decisions, huh?"

"The sooner you do, the sooner you deal with the fallout."

"Which would be?"

"Fall one way, the two of you hook up and you have to adjust your entire life. Figure out how to deal with juggling the demands of your commitment to team and country versus the commitment of a relationship where you can never be fully present. Fall the other way, you start getting over her."

Elijah let himself into the building to the silence of Lansky processing those words. It wasn't years of knowing the guy that had him anticipating the next question. It was simply knowing it was the same question he himself would have asked.

"How do you get over her?"

"Hopefully, with a little time and distance. Unless she really matters."

"Then what?"

Elijah remembered his body's reaction to seeing Ava again after four years. Instant awareness, like she was Pavlov and he was panting for a dog treat. Now his mind was tangled with memories and his heart aching for what might have been. Their split might have been yesterday, the pain was so sharp and strong. Four years, or forty, he knew it would be just as intense.

"Then you never get over her."

"Dude, you suck."

"Glad I could help," Elijah said, this time with a real

laugh before hitting the off button. It was small of him, but there was something about misery and company getting cozy together that came into play right now.

He was still grinning as he used the spare key to enter Mack's apartment. A quick glance made it clear his cousin was out. Mack had left the light on over the stove. In its golden glow, he could see a note propped on the counter. Elijah crossed the shadowed room.

He knew his cousin kept his meds in the counter over the stove instead of the bathroom. Why, was a mystery. But given that the kitchen was closer, Elijah figured it wasn't his place to ask the question.

Snickering a little at the variety of protein powders and supplements mixed in with muscle creams and a precarious pile of essential oils, he spied the aspirin behind the coconut oil. But as he reached for it, he knocked over the tower of small apothecary bottles, sending them flying. One tilted, its delicate fluid dripping out the cupboard and onto the counter.

Shit. He snagged the bottle and stoppered it, then grabbed a couple of paper towels to sop up the oil before it dripped its way to the floor.

The scent of eucalyptus filled the air, soothing the muscles knotted across Elijah's shoulders with every breath. Still wanting drugs for the rest, Elijah grabbed the aspirin. He shook out a half dozen and, using his hand as a cup, swallowed them down with water from the sink.

The aspirin downed and hopefully working its magic, he snapped up the note Mack had left propped against a plate of pie. Apple from the looks of it. Elijah's favorite. And, he read, there was ice cream in the freezer. Elijah kept reading.

Figured dinner was as far as you could handle with the family en masse. So eat up, buddy. Dessert will wipe that nasty taste out of your mouth.

Damn. His cousin would make someone a fine wife someday. Tucking his phone into his pocket, Elijah ignored the pie. He'd skipped out of his mom's before dessert, but as usual lately, he didn't have much of an appetite. Weighing the consequences of ignoring Mack's gesture versus choking down something sweet on an already tense stomach, Elijah decided to save the pie for breakfast.

Now? Bed.

More than ready to drop his head on a pillow and put an end to the day, Elijah turned toward the hall.

A shadow moved from behind.

Attack! Adrenaline exploded through his system, sending his body into instant defense mode. He dropped to a crouch, breath slowing as his brain automatically slipped into alpha. A vivid contrast to the tension ratcheting through his muscles, tense and painful.

The threat loomed to the right, dark and menacing. Whether its intent was to kill or incapacitate didn't matter. He'd be damned if he was going down again.

His leg swept out, foot kicking high overhead in a roundhouse sweep as he rose in a jump, his right hand thrusting heel first.

The target shattered on impact, pieces exploding as if a bomb had blown them apart. As the head flew one way, the body toppled the other. Elijah dived forward, wrapping himself around the torso to mitigate the assault. Unprepared for its lack of heft, he went down on his back, the body cradled in his arms.

The very hard, very cold, very ceramic body.

A statue.

His breath came in pants. His head swam with the images of bodies—real ones——exploding, blood and flesh splattering everywhere. Covering him in hideous pain. In the misery of failure. Elijah's head dropped to the floor. His teeth clenched, gritting tight as if he could grind the painful memories away before they overwhelmed him. But the wave was too strong.

He was back in Iraq. Under fire. First from the enemy, shots ricocheting off the walls of the computer lab, taking bodies and equipment to the ground.

Zig to the left, cover Loudon's advance. Zag to the right, wait for Ramsey. Release the hostage's shackles, scan for electronics. Elijah got to work on disabling the explosives secured to the scientist's chest while Ramsey started on the computer. Three minutes, perfect timing.

Hand the scientist off to Lee while Loudon and Ward covered the doors, deflecting hostiles. Elijah moved to assist Ramsey in infiltrating the computer system.

"Hostage in hand," Ward said through the comm built into their helmets. "Heading to rendezvous point now."

"Electronics?"

"T minus thirty seconds," came Ramsey's reply.

T minus thirty seconds. A confirmation that Ramsey had installed the electronic virus and it was scheduled to take down the system in thirty seconds.

Covering the door, Elijah watched to make sure the hostage was clear. The team was moving.

He signaled Ramsey with the one-minute mark.

Ramsey nodded. His fingers flew over the keyboard, his movements easy and practiced. The wall of screens flashed, indicating the intel was secured and the virus finished. How'd that get done so far ahead of schedule? Shortcuts were well and good, but they had orders and a method to this mission. One they'd all practiced and timed to the millisecond.

Elijah frowned.

Ramsey was probably showing off, trying to out- shine Torres. Elijah made a mental note to have a chat with the guy later. He seriously needed to get his ego in check. Torres was team leader, and this mission was running like clockwork. Ramsey needed to respect that.

Elijah signaled that it was time to move. Ramsey nodded.

Exiting the building with practiced stealth, Torres pro- vided cover while Elijah waited for Ramsey to catch up.

Where the hell was the guy? He'd been right there, two steps behind just a second ago.

"Yo, Ramsey. Move out, man."

What was with the delay?

Elijah doubled back to make sure Ramsey was clear. The guy wasn't paying attention, though. He'd signaled the all clear, so why was he still screwing with the com- puter?

Elijah started to ask. He moved to check it out.

Ramsey looked his way. Seemed to hesitate.

Then the world was shot to hell. The explosion had taken out half the building.

Elijah ran, trying to reach his teammate.

Flames roared, a tidal wave of fire pouring over him. Tearing him apart. Eating him alive.

He was dead.

He had to be.

There was no way to hurt this badly and live.

No fucking way.

ELIJAH GROANED.

Not real.

It isn't happening.

It's not real.

Not right now. Not this time. Not again.

Turning it into a mantra, Elijah repeated the words over and over. He used them to focus. First to even out his breath, then to slow it. To calm it. Training brought him Zen; Zen brought his pulse rate down.

Get a fucking grip, he ordered himself.

His body so tight his muscles were cramping all to hell and back, Elijah forced himself to release the statue, lifting one finger at a time. By the time he'd managed his palms, he had the hyperventilating under control. His heart rate took a little longer, but as soon as he had it leveled, he pushed to his feet.

And stared at the mess on the floor.

Oh yeah. He stuffed his fists into his pockets and sighed at the sight. He'd killed it all right.

Busted the head right off one of his cousin's life-size sculptures. Glossy ceramic pieces were scattered to hell and back over the floor, one eye poised by Elijah's right foot, staring accusingly.

Ignoring the temptation to stomp that eye into dust,

Elijah forced his screaming muscles to loosen and, avoiding scattered pieces as if tiptoeing through a mine-field, made his way back to the kitchen for a broom and dustpan.

He used the cleanup time to empty his mind. Let all thoughts go. To level out, steady his system. Years of living on the edge had taught him the importance of letting it go. Savino considered that element of training as important as hand-to-hand or weapons, so they trained and trained hard. Elijah had long ago mastered the ability to center, to find that Zen-like place in the mind where nothing could touch him.

Used to be, he was good at it.

But even as he breathed, emptied, images flashed.

Fire.

Ramsey's face.

Betrayal.

The sound of the broom handle splintering under his fingers pulled Elijah back from the edge. *Shit*.

He gave up centering and settled for getting all the ceramic dust into the dustpan.

The mess cleaned, Elijah contemplated what was left of the statue through exhausted eyes. He'd caught the bastard before it went down, so the body was intact. Other than the rough edges where the head had broken off, it didn't look too bad. Headless, the eye was drawn to the impressive array of glossy muscles.

And the penis was still there, standing erect and happy. Knowing his cousin, that would be enough until Elijah could replace the damned thing.

Too weary to care, his body aching from the vicious adrenaline crash, Elijah slowly made his way down the hall, eyes peeled left and right for any more threatening statuary.

In his room, he nudged the door shut and dropped clothing as he walked, too tired to care that leaving his gear on the floor went against his natural—and Navy—instincts. He gave his boots a half-hearted kick so he wouldn't trip over them in the morning, then crawled, naked, between the cool sheets. Eyes closed, he waited for exhaustion to carry him to sleep.

Instead it carried the image of Ava's face into his head. As he fell into dreams, he took her with him. His subconscious, well used to visits from the only woman Elijah had ever loved, made minute adjustments to her image, bringing it up to date.

Her face was thinner, the sharp cheekbones emphasizing those huge eyes. Her body had lost some of its lushness, the curves slighter, tighter. Oh, they were still there. Her breasts were full, rising high over a slim torso and legs he'd spent hours dreaming of. He bet they would feel just as good wrapped around his waist. Better, maybe, given the muscle tone.

As Elijah held tight to Ava's image, angling himself over her welcoming softness, fire crept out of the corners of his mind, flickering and finessing its way through his dreams.

Not even the memory of love was enough to hold back horror.

PAIN PIERCED AVA'S SKULL, sharp and nagging. She tried to turn her head, but apparently the spike jammed into it went all the way through to whatever she was lying on, because she couldn't move.

With the care of the infirm, she lifted one hand to feel around, to ensure that that really was her head throbbing there on her neck.

Oh yeah. All hers. What the hell had she done? Worse, who had she done it with?

She couldn't remember.

All she could think of was the memory of desire. Of wishes and needs and wants like she hadn't experienced in years. She blamed Elijah, of course. But she hadn't slept with him. Ava knew what it felt like to be satisfied by Elijah. Even in her dreams, the memory of his touch inspired orgasmic pleasure that lasted well into waking.

No amount of alcohol could dim that feeling. And she didn't feel satisfied. Just miserable.

God, she wouldn't have gotten drunk enough to sleep with a stranger, would she?

She tried to turn, just a little, so she could see where she was. And almost slipped off the slick fabric. She jerked back into place before she could hit the floor. Her stomach recoiled at the sudden movement.

She clamped her lips tight and sucked in a long, slow yoga breath through her nose. When that seemed to help, she tried two more. Once she was sure she wasn't going to be sick, she risked patting herself down.

Beneath a cloud-soft blanket she could feel her clothes. She was pretty sure they were the same clothes she'd been wearing when she'd dived into her evening love affair with tequila.

Okay. Worst-case scenario cleared. Her virtue, such as it was, was intact. So now, since she knew what she hadn't done, it was time to figure out what she had done.

Ava took a deep breath and rolled into a sitting posi-

tion. The blanket dropped into her lap, then lifted again
as she anchored her elbows onto her knees so she could
use her hands to hold her head in place.

Never again.

No more tequila.

It took her a few minutes to realize the sounds she
heard were her own whimpers. Where the hell was she?

Ava carefully lifted her head off her hands until she
could look around. She peered through eyes that felt
like fire, trying to see through the dark and the pain.
Big purple chair. Glossy statues of well-hung naked
men. The scent of—she sniffed, gagged, then breathed
through her teeth—eucalyptus and citrus.

Mack's.

Her breath came in a relieved sigh this time.

She was safe.

His uncomfortably slick couch, the scent of that useless muscle therapy cream he'd taken to using after a
match, Mack's art. She squinted across the murky darkness of the room.

Was that statue missing a head?

Foggy with confusion, Ava rubbed her fingers over
her eyes. Mack must have come by the bar. To join in
the copious drinking? Or simply to fetch his drunken
massage therapist?

She couldn't remember much past the third tequila
shot. She had a bed here. She always used Mack's spare
room when she needed a place to crash. Why wasn't
she in that? There was probably a reason. It was right
there on the tip of her brain, but her head was spinning
too fast to think.

Knowing Mack would rise with the sun, Ava pushed

to her feet. A pillow over her head wouldn't save her from his morning routine, but a closed door might. As slow as an infirm ninety-year-old with a bum hip wearing too-tight stilettos, she made her way toward the bathroom.

She spent a few minutes debating getting sick, but she finally settled for the aspirin and water, pouring some down her throat and more over her face.

It felt so good, she stripped down to step into the shower. One hand holding her hair back, she let the water pour over her, hoping that if it wouldn't wash away the drunken fog, it would at least rinse off the bar stench.

She wasn't sure how long she stood there. It might have been minutes, could have been hours. Eventually, finally, she slapped off the water.

She didn't bother drying off. Just wrapped herself in one of Mack's blanket-size bath towels. The ends of her damp hair sticking to her wet shoulders, she remembered to scoop up her clothes before padding to the bedroom.

The water and meds had worked their magic, so the miserable pain was down to a dull throb. *Time to sleep off the rest. Oh yeah, sleep.*

Three steps down the dark hallway and a slow, oh so slow, twist of the doorknob and she was almost there. The haven of bed.

She eased the door shut in case the sound would trigger the now-dull pain in her head and let her clothes drop as she crossed the room.

The faint, filmy light drifting in from the window

like slender moonbeams glinted off a large, man-size lump in the bed.

Whoa.

She froze, then grimaced as her stomach churned. She slammed her hand over her mouth. She felt like one of the three bears when they discovered Goldilocks. There was someone sleeping in her bed.

And that someone was moaning.

Ava squinted but still couldn't make out who was in the bed. Risking her stomach, she leaned forward just a little.

Not enough moonlight. But the moans were groans now. Her squint turned into a scowl. Who was that?

Ava stepped forward. Her bare toes caught the edge of—was that a boot? *Boot? Dammit.*

That was her last thought before she pitched forward, face-first onto the bed.

And the man sleeping in it.

CHAPTER EIGHT

NOT EVEN A thick coating of alcohol could keep her brain from recognizing who she'd landed on. She'd know his body morning, noon or night. Sober or wasted, it mattered not.

She knew Elijah's body as well as she knew her own.

Now two people were moaning.

But one of them was moaning with pain because she'd rammed into a body with the texture of cement. The other was moaning over having a woman dive onto his belly, waking him from a deep sleep with her knee in his gut.

Better than a nightmare, Ava supposed. But given the plethora of other reactions shimmying through her—everything from needy curiosity to heated desire—she knew she'd better move before she did something she'd regret come the morning light.

But her body was pressed against his, and he felt so good. Hard, so hard and warm. Her fingers dug into the rigid silk of Elijah's bicep, marveling at how firm he was, even when relaxed. She swallowed with a click as she felt something much more interesting than a bicep hardening beneath her belly.

Knowing that only a blanket separated her from heaven sent a wave of edgy passion washing over her.

God, she wanted him. Wanted, so badly, to feel the ecstasy that she knew Elijah could inspire. Memories of
the intensity of the orgasms she'd felt with him filled
her mind, made her body tremble.

It was the idea of coming *before* morning light that
finally spurred her to roll away. But she couldn't move.
His hands were gripping too tight, holding her in place.

"Ava?"

"Let me go," she ordered through clenched teeth. But
no matter how she twisted and turned, she couldn't get
loose of the hold he had on her arms.

The strength in his hold was a vivid reminder of how
powerful he was. In bed, and everywhere else. Like in
the shower. Or on the kitchen table. Or against a wall.
Or under her in the back seat of her car. Or…

Stop, Ava ordered herself.

*Quit obsessing over something you aren't ever going
to have again, will never do again*. Otherwise, she
knew, she just might forget all the reasons they were
horrible for each other and try to seduce him.

It worked once, the little voice in her mind whispered. The same voice that seemed to be controlling
her body as it pressed tighter to the hardness of his.

"Let go, Elijah," she snapped.

"Babe, you're the one that climbed into bed with me."
His voice was rough, his words impatient. "I'm not sure
what you're here for, but if it's not sex, you might want
to quit wiggling like that."

Ava froze. She didn't wiggle this time. She shoved.

As hard as she could, pushing against his shoulder,
her knee digging into his leg as she tried to gain traction enough to put distance between them.

It was only when he winced—an infinitesimal move that she felt more than saw—that she stopped. Worry slipped, unwelcome, through the shimmering need. Was it his leg? Was it hurting him? Or was it something else?

She'd heard the groans. It had sounded like he was in pain. He still was, she realized, able to see him better now that her eyes had adjusted. A sheen of sweat covered him like a fine mist, glowing in the moonlight. Deep lines creased his face.

"Are you okay?" she couldn't help but ask.

"Hard to be okay when a hot woman climbs into your bed, stirs you up, then knees you in the groin—don't you think?"

As her body hummed at the compliment, and at the idea of stirring a little more, Ava forced herself to focus. "You were upset."

"I was asleep," he pointed out with a scowl visible even in the dim light. But even as he growled the words, his hands were sliding over her hips where the towel had gaped open, drawing her back against him. Nestling her tighter between his thighs.

Her pulse danced as the heat raced through her system, bringing to life feelings she'd long believed gone. More to the point, feelings she'd *wanted* gone.

Her skin tingled at his touch. She breathed him in, the scent that always made her think of fresh ocean air and midnight. Her body wanted to snuggle into Elijah's. To slide her thigh between his, wrap her legs around his hard muscles and press herself to the length of him. As familiar as breath, as natural as a sigh, she could slide against him. She could either press her lips to his and turn the smoldering flames into an inferno, or nuzzle her head under his chin and cuddle into the haven she'd once called love.

"So what's the deal? You just realized that you missed me?" he asked, his gaze roaming over her face in a caress as gentle as the slide of his fingers on her waist.

She didn't need light to see the heat kindling in his eyes. She knew it was there. She knew exactly what it looked like, exactly how it used to make her feel. It didn't make her feel anything now, she promised herself. But, just in case, she shifted. Angled her hips away so they weren't actually nestled against the growing length of his erection.

If she didn't feel it, she could pretend she was ignoring it.

Distract and distance, she thought. *Get away before you do something stupid.*

"What's the matter with you? You were…" "Moaning" didn't sound right. At least not when she was snuggled up so tight against him. "Upset. You sounded like you were having a bad dream or something."

His expression didn't change but she felt his minuscule flinch.

"So you, what? Came in here and threw yourself on me to stop a supposed nightmare?" His smile spread, the image of sleepy sex, over a face that she saw in her own dreams. One hand still clamped to her hip, he pulled her against him again as he slid the other up her side. His fingers were like brands as they rested just below her breast, sinking into her skin. Reminding her where she belonged. "Worried about me, babe?"

"No. I didn't. I don't." Ava cringed, closing her eyes as if she could pretend this away. Wait, that was how she used to act. *Not anymore, dammit.* She forced her eyes open, lifted her chin and, wishing like crazy that her head wasn't still swimming in tequila, started again. "I didn't know you were even here."

"You just happened to climb, naked, into bed with me?"

"I fell into bed wearing a towel," she corrected him coldly. But a snippy tone was a lousy shield. Especially as she realized that he, too, was naked beneath the flimsy sheet.

"A towel and a lot of damp skin," Elijah noted, his voice husky as he skimmed his free hand up her arm until he reached her throat; then his fingers twisted and twined through her hair.

Warning bells clanged, loud and strong. Her body tightened, her muscles bunching in preparation for action. Which type of action was debatable since her body desperately wanted to toss the towel and sheet to the floor and explore the spark, damp and needy, between them. Her mind, so much smarter than her body, screamed for flight.

"You'd better go," Elijah suggested. His words were quiet, his eyes intent on her face. "And you'd better do it in the next thirty seconds. Or you're liable to regret what happens next."

"What's going to happen?" And what, her body wondered, was one more regret?

"Go," he said tightly. "Get out of here before it's too late."

Maybe it was the tequila. Maybe it was years of pent-up frustration. Or maybe it was simply the shock of having Elijah in her life again, of having him back in her life in any form at all.

Whatever it was, Ava snapped. She couldn't even logically connect his words to her outburst. But burst out she did.

"I hate it when you do that. I'm not some fragile innocent in need of protection. I don't need special handling, dammit." As if her head wasn't about to spin right off her shoulders, she slapped her hand between them to push away from his chest. "I run my own life. I make my own decisions. I'm an independent, intelligent adult woman, dammit. Treat me like one."

"Is that what you want? To be treated like a woman? An independent, adult woman?"

Before she could blink, Ava found herself on her back, sandwiched between the warm mattress and Elijah's body. His hard, muscled, so-so-tempting body.

Uh-oh.

Ava felt like a woman. A very adult, very passionate, very independent woman. Needs, long dormant, so carefully ignored for years, screamed. Her fingers dug into the hard flesh of Elijah's shoulders, and she reveled in the strength there. She breathed in his scent, her eyes tracing the need etched on his face. She recognized the narrow intensity of his gaze, knew he wanted her.

God, she wanted to be wanted by him again.

Knowing she was playing with fire, not caring, Ava held that gaze as she ran the tip of her tongue along her upper lip.

His eyes darkened, holding hers prisoner as he lowered his head. His mouth brushed hers. Soft. Sweet. A gentle rub of lips over lips.

Her heart melting a little, Ava sighed. *Mmm, so good.*

Then Elijah changed the angle. Just the slightest shift. A suggestion of teeth scraping the sensitive flesh of her lower lip. The teasing sweep of his tongue along the seam of her lips.

Ava's sigh turned to a moan. As if seeing that as a signal, Elijah shifted again.

His mouth took hers.

Teeth nipping her bottom lip then sucking hard before his tongue thrust. Hot, intense, demanding. For a second—an infinitesimal second—Ava froze. What was she doing? This was insane. The man was her ex-husband. *Ex. Over. Past and done.*

He was the best lover she'd ever had. A lover every woman dreamed of. Generous. Demanding. Delicious and tempting.

His tongue slid over hers.

God.

Oh, oh, God.

Ava moaned again at the intense pleasure coursing through her body. It shouldn't be new. She'd had Elijah before. She'd had him hundreds of times, dozens of ways.

But she'd never felt like this before. Never experienced anything so intense, so powerful.

She wanted to know what it was. She wanted more. She needed—desperately—to dive all the way in and dive deep.

Before she could, Elijah pulled away.

While Ava blinked in shock, he rolled away, dropping onto the mattress with a groan as he threw his arm over his eyes. His fist was clenched so tightly that the knuckles were white, as if he were holding every iota of control there between his fingers and was desperate not to let it go.

She was tempted to reach out and, one by one, pull those fingers free.

"Sorry," he muttered into the dark.

Ava's breath came in ragged pants, her pulse racing so fast she could barely think over the pounding in her head.

Sorry? Had he apologized? *No way.* She must have heard him wrong.

"You should go. Now."

Ava tried to find the strength to move, but all she could manage was a sweep of her eyelashes as she slid her gaze toward the man lying next to her.

"Fine," he finally ground out when she didn't say anything. "I'll go."

Go? He'd leave her? He'd walk out while she lay here panting and aching and desperate for satisfaction? She wished she could believe otherwise.

But he'd left her before. She didn't have a single doubt that he'd leave her now. He'd get out of this bed and walk away. Leaving her wanting.

Leaving her alone.

Ava knew she'd regret it. With full, shining clarity she had not a single doubt that this was a huge mistake. But she didn't care.

"Take me," she ordered.

Some things were worth regretting.

ELIJAH WAS A man with a strong sense of right and wrong. He was a man with exquisite control. He'd

learned long ago that the best way to meet and overcome any obstacle was to stay flexible.

But waking to Ava's body pressed against his, the
feel of her hair sliding like silk over his skin, the sweet
citrus scent of her skin had pushed that control to the
edge.

Being pulled out of dreams—or wherever he'd been
in sleep—to the face he so often saw and craved when
he closed his eyes at night, when he dropped his guard
and gave over to his subconscious rule?

And then being ordered to treat her as a woman?

His control had snapped like a brittle rubber band.

He did what he'd denied wanting to do since seeing
her yesterday. He crushed his mouth over hers.

Damn, she tasted good. Heat and spice and sweetness, all blended together on a frothy wave of passion.
His tongue swept over those full lips, revisiting the delight he'd once taken for granted.

As if the touch of his tongue was the trigger she'd
been waiting for, Ava exploded. Her fingers dug into
his flesh with erotic demand. Her body pressed against
his, passion sparking between them everywhere they
touched. Her mouth devoured, tongue tangling with his
in a demanding dance of power.

He gave over to it, letting her call this first volley.
Her hands were hot as they skimmed his shoulders,
down his arms, over his back. When they fisted into
his lower back, he arched against her, pressing the rock-
hard length of his throbbing erection against her hips.

She dug her heels into the bed, knees high as she
ground herself against him. Elijah shifted. If he was
doing this, he was doing it right. He tossed the towel

aside, and he angled himself higher so he could study her body.

Hello, baby.

He knew it was her. He recognized the shape of her nipples, the rich berry color. He'd memorized the birthmark, a tiny crescent of gold, on the curve of her hip.

But her body was different.

Hard, strong, muscled and sleek.

Gentle as a whisper, his fingers slid over her skin. She felt like warm silk. He leaned closer, sipping at the budding tip of her nipple, sliding his tongue around the hard, round nub.

Mmm, yeah. Delicious.

He kept his moves delicate, worshipful, even. But he could feel the demand in her body. The need building, spiraling, tightening.

Good.

He wanted her crazed with it. He wanted her desperate for it. He nibbled, sucked, teeth scraping over her nipples, fingers teasing, flicking and pinching her into a frenzy before moving on.

His thumb moved over her belly button, his fingers tangled in the hair between her thighs. Then he found her.

Wet and hot and so, so tempting.

"No regrets," he said, both as a reminder and to check her willingness to go on.

Her response was to press her hips higher, to clamp her thighs around his hand. He dipped his fingers deeper, swirled, then pulled back, despite the grip of her legs. She'd gained some muscle, but she was still no match for him.

"Elijah," she begged.

He dipped again, using his thumb this time to work the wet bud as his fingers danced inside. Ava moaned; her body shook.

His own pleasure washed over him in an emotional wave as she came. God, he loved watching her come.

"No regrets," he repeated.

Too focused on the orgasm still trembling through her body, Ava could only shake her head.

"Ava," Elijah insisted, the word a hoarse demand.

"No," she breathed, opening her eyes to meet his. Then she smiled. A wanton smile that pierced his heart. "No regrets. Not sorry. Not, not, not. Give me more, Elijah. Give me everything."

Damned if he didn't want to.

He knew the feel of her skin under his fingertips, the gentle field of goose bumps that shimmered along her chest as she arched high to offer her breasts to his mouth.

He knew those nipples, ripe and rosy aureoles tipped with berry-size peaks, pouting in wait of his lips. He knew if he blew on them, they'd tighten. If he licked them, she'd moan. If he bit, she'd explode.

He pressed his palms down her sides, tracing the indention of her waist, measuring the slender width of her hips. His thumb skimmed the birthmark just there along her bikini line, its size the exact fit to his fingerprint.

He would have sworn that even though it had been four years, he still knew Ava's body. But he would have been wrong. The woman was pure muscle. Her body a work of sculpted art.

He'd worshipped her many times before. He'd dreamed

of her. Once he'd known her body inside and out. He'd been so familiar with every lush curve, every soft bend of flesh, that he'd been able to draw her in his mind from memory each night they were separated.

"You like?" she asked, her voice husky. Elijah met her eyes, noting the sultry passion of her heavy-lidded gaze.

"I like. A lot."

"Show me."

In the past, she'd shyly seduced with teasing looks, timid touches and sweet suggestions.

Now she demanded.

He liked that, too.

Ava's hand skimmed between their bodies, her fingers sliding around the throbbing length of his erection before she wrapped her fingers tight and gave him a good squeeze.

Oh yeah, Elijah thought as his breath jammed in his chest. He liked. A lot.

And he wanted more.

Following her lead, he shifted, reached between them to slide his fingers between her thighs. His knuckles skimmed the rigid muscles of her leg, reveling in the power there. He'd never realized how damned sexy strength was.

Then, as his fingers dipped into her wet heat, he forgot about comparing present to past. He didn't notice the changes. He simply felt. Her.

And she felt fucking incredible.

So wet.

So hot.

He slipped his forefinger along the silken folds, reveling in the way her body trembled, in the sound of her breath as it shook with small whimpers of pleasure.

He took her up again, waiting until she came with a low moan before sliding into her trembling depths.

Holy hell, she felt amazing.

Ava's body gripped his, her orgasm milking his erection. Squeezing. Condensing every drop of pleasure until his cock was full, throbbing with passion so intense it ached.

Elijah plunged.

Ava's fingers dug into his hips, her short nails cutting into his skin.

He drove deeper.

She slammed her hips up, high and strong, meeting each thrust with a slap of flesh. With a moan of pleasure. Her breath came in pants, matching his as they climbed higher and higher together.

Her thighs tightened on his hips, heels of her feet digging into the small of his back as if she wanted more— needed more. Knowing exactly what she needed, Elijah balanced on one hand, his thrusts uninterrupted as he skimmed the other between their bodies.

Down the flat delight of her belly, between her legs. He found the tiny bead of wet flesh, working it as he felt himself thrusting in, sliding out. Her body tightened around him. Her moans turned to keening cries of pleasure.

Her eyes, misted and mysterious with pleasure, stared into his as Ava arched, her breasts high, hips grinding against him. She came in a fast, intense explosion of pleasure, gripping him tight, as if desperate to ensure he came with her.

His pace didn't slow as Elijah drove her up again. He dipped his head, taking one berry-fresh nipple into his mouth to suck. The taste of her was all he needed, everything he needed.

He burst.

Pleasure exploded like fireworks, shattering his control, blasting him to pieces. Ava went along for another ride, her cries of passion echoing through his head as he emptied himself in her.

Incredible.

That was the only word in his head as the aftershocks trembled through their bodies.

Incredible.

And then he came down.

Not in a nice, slow, gentle descent, either.

Nope, he crashed like a plane plummeting from the sky to ram into a mountainside.

He'd just had sex.

With Ava.

His ex-wife. The only woman he'd ever loved. The only one he'd ever wanted to love. The one who'd broken his heart into tiny little pieces and tossed them aside.

Shit.

His body still slick with sweat, the scent of Ava wrapped around him like a second skin, Elijah wondered if she realized that while extracting her promise of no regrets, he hadn't offered the same.

After all, Elijah knew just how pointless promises could be. Especially the ones between him and Ava.

His body spent, his mind worn, he couldn't find anything left to offer up on the altar of past regrets, though.

He wrapped his arm tighter around her shoulders. Ava responded by snuggling closer, her thigh nestled between his as she shifted her chin into the indention where his shoulder met his chest. Her breath fluttered over his throat, soft and easy in sleep.

Regret?

Oh yeah, he knew he'd regret this in the morning. Hell—he glanced out the window, gauging the time from the angle of the moon—it was nearing dawn and the regret was already winding through him. Shoving aside pleasure, easing out satisfaction.

Closing his eyes against it, he drifted into sleep with her hand entwined with his, the twisted band of her ring rubbing gently between his fingers.

And he knew it for the talisman it was, the hope that lifted him from his nightmares.

If only for tonight.

Because nobody knew better than Elijah that tonight was all they had.

CHAPTER NINE

"Ava?" Chloe's brows hit her hairline. "Wow, what're you doing here? I didn't think I'd see you at all today, let alone first thing in the morning."

Crap.

Ava froze in the act of sneaking in through the gym's side door. Looked like she'd used up all her stealth skills sneaking out of Elijah's bed, out of Mack's apartment and back to her place to shower and change.

She'd wanted a nice, sweaty, mind-numbing bout with the weight machines before her first class. No, actually she'd wanted a platter covered in country-fried steak, biscuits and gravy with a mountain of breakfast potatoes.

But after a lecture on how far she'd come, she'd settled for the workout.

What she hadn't wanted was conversation. But she knew Chloe. So Ava took one second to put on the best version of a happy face as she could manage and turned to smile at her friend.

"Hey. I'm on tap to teach in an hour, and figured I'd get in a workout ahead of time." Hoping that'd be enough to release her from further conversation, Ava started toward the locker room.

Dreadlocks flying behind her, Chloe hurried around

the counter and grabbed Ava's arm. "Wait, slow down."
Frowning, she gave Ava a thorough inspection. Then
she wrapped Ava in surprisingly strong arms and
hugged her tight.

It took everything Ava had not to curl into the woman's
arms and bawl. Thankfully she kept it to a quick squeeze,
then stepped back.

"How're you doing? You feeling okay?" Chloe asked
quietly, her eyes drenched in sympathy.

Ava wanted to laugh through the tears clogging her
throat. *Okay? Hell, no.*

She exercised for a living and specialized in relieving muscle pressure. Yet thanks to last night's little bed-
time bout, she was walking like a bowlegged cowboy
fresh off the range.

"I'm fine," she lied. "Just a headache is all."

*A six-foot-two-inch, finely muscled headache, as a
matter of fact.* Ava managed a smile. "I guess I'm really not a tequila shot kind of gal after all."

"Well, it takes a special type to handle that many
shots and not feel the results." Chloe's gaze angled to
the right, but Ava didn't need to see the wide-eyed look
to know who'd just walked into the gym. The scent of
Mack's cologne filled the air like a spring forest, but
it was the shift in energy that tipped her off to Elijah's
presence.

She steeled herself. Stomach tight, nerves quivering like a bowstring, she tried to keep her breath even.
The last thing she wanted this morning was to pass out
at Elijah's feet.

She waited for the confrontation. But instead of feeling his presence behind her, she saw Chloe's eyes fill

with concern. At the same time, the sound of voices raised in greeting sounded behind her.

Chloe bit her lip and glanced at Ava. "Are you sure you're okay?"

No. "I don't want to see him right now."

"He's been cornered by a few of Mack's buddies," Chloe said in a low whisper. "Go head for the back."

Ava knew that would be a total chicken move. A quick glance over her shoulder showed her that Elijah was surrounded by groupies in the form of men who probably thought SEALs were the epitome of manliness. Her thighs quivered at the sight of him, her body reacting instantly just knowing he was nearby.

Chicken move or not, Ava started toward the back, automatically checking the class board on her way. At this point, she didn't care if she sprouted pinfeathers. She needed the distance.

Whoa. Wait a minute.

The large whiteboard indicated the week's class schedule, noting times, instructors and which classroom each event was held.

"What happened to my kickboxing class?" Feathers forgotten, Ava shifted out of Elijah's line of sight and scowled at the board. "Why did it get moved?"

"I moved it." Looming over her shoulder like a thick-necked bull, Con Barton tapped the board. "You had a group of eight booked in the biggest classroom."

After a quick look to be sure that Elijah was still surrounded by his groupies, Ava faced the other instructor.

She knew he tried to intimidate, using his bulk and height to get into people's personal space. So she lifted her chin, squared her shoulders and met his gaze head-on.

"Because we need the room. The workout includes a lot of running and jumping." Then she moved forward until he stepped back. "The larger room wasn't booked, and it doesn't look like it's needed now. So why would you move my class?"

"Rules are you book the room based on the class size," Con said, his bulldog jaw jutting stubbornly. "Someone might've needed that space."

"Generic rules bend to specifics," Ava shot back, all of that irritation that had been churning through her system focusing on the big man with his stupid rule book. "Do you need the space yourself?"

"No."

"Has someone requested it?"

"No?"

"So what's the problem?"

"Your class size doesn't justify that room."

"My workout does," she said between her teeth. What was the guy's problem? She exchanged looks with Chloe, who shook her head in disgust.

Ava's smile faded at Con's next words.

"Why don't we take this up with Mack? He can decide."

"You want to bother him with something this trivial?"

"I think we need a solid ruling. As long as Mack doesn't play favorites, that is."

Seriously? Ava ground her teeth together to bite back the frustration. Con was one of the possibilities Mack was considering as a partner. If she couldn't get the funds together, this Neanderthal could be her boss someday.

That was nastier than a hangover, morning-after regrets and caffeine deprivation combined.

"Maybe you should quit running to Mack when you don't get your way," Ava suggested.

"Maybe you should quit playing diva," Con snapped.

"Maybe you should back off."

Now? Elijah was interfering now? Ava cringed, more than ready to lay her throbbing head on the desk and groan.

"Maybe you should mind your own business." Con turned to glare at the interruption. His stance changed as soon as he got a look at Elijah, shifting from combative to conciliatory in a blink. "We're just nailing down a few gym details here, man. Is there something you need?"

Ava slid a sidelong look at Elijah. Noting that his eyes had turned to ice, she stepped between him and Con.

"I need Ava."

Those words filled her with equal measures of delight and terror. Years ago she would have given anything to hear Elijah say he needed her. Now?

No. A million times no.

"Oh." Con's eyes slid from Elijah to her, then back again. He repeated, "Oooh."

Resisting the urge to give a quick uppercut to that smirking jaw, Ava made introductions. "Con, this is Mack's cousin Elijah. The two of you probably have a lot in common."

Leaving it at that, she slid out from between the men with the same relief she figured she'd feel sliding out from between a pair of rabid dogs.

"Sorry about that," she heard Con apologize. She

missed Elijah's response, but caught Chloe's little hand flutter, as if the air were getting too hot to handle.

If only she knew.

Ava quickened her steps in hopes of disappearing with the same ease she'd had sneaking out of his bed that morning. But no such luck.

"Yo. Hang on," Elijah called just as she rounded the cardio machines on her way to the back of the gym.

"I didn't need rescuing," she snapped, pretending her stomach wasn't swirling like a carnival ride.

"Who said I was coming to the rescue? I just wanted to get rid of the guy so we could have a little privacy."

Privacy? Ava gulped, her nerves jangling like bowstrings. That's when she noticed at least a dozen pair of eyes aimed their way, including Chloe, who appeared to be taking notes.

"You growled at him like you were my guard dog and I was a juicy bone," she said, tossed back in time to the multitude of instances when he'd done the same. "You always do that, Elijah. Act like I can't take care of myself. I'm a big girl. Believe me, I've handled worse than a goon with a scheduling fetish."

"Fine. We can add that to our list of things to discuss."

"Fine. We'll talk about it later. I'm busy right now," she claimed, pulling her arm free and heading for the locker room. Away from Elijah and, more important, away from prying eyes.

As soon as she stepped through the door to privacy, he cornered her. "According to that handy-dandy chart you all were fighting over, you don't have any classes booked or private training scheduled today.

The bombshell said your massage schedule was clear. Which leaves fear." Elijah's smile turned wicked as he leaned closer, one arm blocking her exit while his body warmed hers with heated memories. "Are you afraid to talk to me, Ava?"

"I'm not afraid of anything," she lied.

"No? Being alone with me doesn't make you nervous?" He angled one leg between hers, his thigh riding high enough to send a tingling spiral of desire through her system. His breath was warm on her face, a delicious caress that made her desperate for more.

"I'm not nervous," she said, this time the lie coming out so breathless and shaky that she would have been better off keeping her mouth shut.

"No?" he said again, those green eyes darkening when they locked on her lips. "My mistake. I figured it had to be fear or nerves that sent you sneaking out of my bed this morning. Why else would you slink away without a word?"

He lowered his head so his mouth was just inches from hers. So close that if she lifted her chin, she'd taste him.

"Why else wouldn't you wake me for another round?"

Why, indeed?

Before Ava could think of a lie, any lie, her phone buzzed against her hip.

"I have to take this," she croaked, her eyes locked on his mouth. Oh, the pleasure that mouth offered. Her breath caught in her chest, heart pounding as she watched it coming closer and closer. Another few inches and she'd taste heaven.

Oh man, she wanted to taste heaven.

Using every bit of willpower she had left, she ripped her eyes off him to look at her phone. She had to blink a few times before she could manage to focus.

Seeing the name, Ava automatically pressed a finger to her right eye to stop the automatic twitch. Could this morning get any worse?

"I have to go," she muttered, slipping her hand between their bodies to tuck the phone back into her pocket.

"Whatever it is, it can wait," he said. "You were going to prove you aren't afraid, remember?"

"It's my mother." Like a switch, his eyes chilled. "I have to go. Have to take her call."

"Of course you do." It wasn't exactly a sneer that covered his face, but it was close enough. With good reason, given the number of occasions her parents had demanded her time, her allegiance, in the course of their marriage. Toward the end, it had just been one more issue among hundreds that Ava and Elijah had fought over.

Ava found herself wanting to apologize. To make excuses. But as it had so often in the past, shame reframed her words. Whether it was triggered by fear or simply a reaction to the text, the next thing she knew, she heard her mother's accusations falling from her lips.

"Gee, Elijah, which is worse? My mother caring enough to want my attention? Or me, sitting around worrying about my husband's safety while I wonder if he'll even be alive for his next birthday?"

"You forgot the part about me selling my soul to Uncle Sam for a pittance and an ego boost," he said, finishing the familiar refrain. "Looks like some things never change."

Elijah moved to one side, sweeping his arm out to indicate her path of escape.

Sick at herself, furious at how easily she turned ugly to keep from dealing with things, Ava hesitated for just a second. Then, not knowing any other way to deal with it, she scurried away.

She didn't care if he thought she was a chicken. For the first time in her life, one of her mother's nagging texts filled with emotional demands was a welcome escape.

Damn, she was desperate.

DESPERATION WAS STRONG enough to send Ava home, digging into her closet, then on the road toward Mendocino. Her fingers tapping the steering wheel in time to the beat of Aerosmith's "Just Push Play," she maneuvered her way through the early afternoon traffic with a grim expression.

A visit home was rarely an occasion for joy, but for multiple reasons, she didn't have a choice.

First, the confrontation with Con had been a rude wake-up call as to what things would be like if he was in charge. Rules, regimentation, rigidity.

The only way to stop that from happening was to go into partnership with Mack. And if she wanted to buy into the gym, she needed money.

She had diddly-squat for money.

At least she had diddly-squat for *available* money.

She did have a more than ample trust fund that she couldn't access until she was thirty. Unless she got her parents to approve a withdrawal. *Hence, this visit*, she thought as she pulled the Silverado into the country-club parking lot.

Having not seen her only child in seven months, her mother preferred that they lunch at the club instead of meeting somewhere private and comfortable. Fine with Ava. The club would put tidy limits on things. Not the drama—there was no limiting Celeste's drama. But the club closed between lunch and dinner, so the drama couldn't last more than three hours.

Ava circled the parking lot a second time. Why the hell were parking spaces made only for compact cars? How was she supposed to fit a full-size truck in a spot the size of a motorcycle? She huffed, then finally angled herself into a spot with the most distance between neighboring cars.

She had a delicate bead of sweat snaking down her temple and a dull headache brewing by the time she turned off the ignition. What was she doing here? She obviously didn't fit. She wanted to drop her head on the steering wheel and cry. That or drive right back to Napa. But crying was pointless, and running wouldn't get her what she wanted.

So, calling on the lessons she'd learned over the last few years, Ava powered through. She angled the rear-view mirror to check her makeup. Subtle with a hint of elegance. She'd taken the time to curl her hair, so it fell in long, loose spirals over her shoulders. The glint of gold at her ears and her grandmother's diamond drop necklace around her throat not only bespoke wealth but were subtle reminders of where the trust money came from. Not that subtle would work on her mother, but

Ava figured she had to use anything and everything at her disposal.

Ready as she'd ever be, she opened the door. It took some clever maneuvering to squeeze out the door and sidle along the truck bed. Especially in heels and a dress. Once free, Ava could only grimace and shake her head when she got a good look.

Like her, it simply didn't fit. The rear of the truck was hanging out between the two compacts like a roll of fat squeezed between the waistband of too-tight jeans and the hem of a skinny knit top. When something didn't fit, it wasn't comfortable and definitely wasn't pretty.

But it was worth it if it got you where you wanted. She figured sometimes that was what it took to get through. And she was an expert on getting through.

With that in mind and the afternoon sun beating down hot enough to straighten her curls, she took a fortifying breath, smoothed her hair one more time, then wended her way through the BMWs, Mercedes and Jags toward the club. Her heels clicked on the polished cement as she hurried past the tweed-clad golfers and glowing people in their crisp whites on the tennis courts. Once she would have recognized—and been recognized by—most everyone she saw. Now they were all strangers.

She nodded her thanks to the doorman when he opened the heavy oak-and-glass door, the brass trimmings blinding her for just a second before she stepped inside the restaurant. The plush luxury was so claustrophobic that Ava had to take a second to breathe before moving through the gilded tables filled with pretty people toward her mother.

Unlike Ava, Celeste Vargas Monroe was in her element. Her mother's hair was a short sweep of rich chestnut framing the pampered perfection of golden skin. The daughter of an Argentinian vintner, she'd been raised with only one goal. To marry well.

A goal she'd tried to pass on to her daughter, an ultimate frustration for both.

Stress tightening her neck, her shoulders stiff with it, Ava took one deep breath, plastered on her best smile and stepped forward.

"Hello, Mama." Ava brushed her lips over the plump softness of her mother's cheek. "You look lovely, as always."

"There you are, darling. What took you so long? I've been here for ages. A lady should always be early, Ava. You know that," Celeste chided in lieu of a greeting.

Ava didn't have to check her watch to know that she was only three minutes late. But she did mentally kick herself. She was here to charm her mother, not irritate her.

"I'm sorry to keep you waiting," Ava said as cheerfully as she could manage, sliding into her chair. "It's too bad Daddy couldn't join us."

"He's in meetings all day. But he'll finish in time to meet us for drinks at six. You'll stay for dinner, of course. Better yet, stay for the night."

"I'd love to," Ava lied. "But I have to get back this afternoon."

"Nonsense." Celeste waved that away while signaling the sommelier to fill Ava's glass. "We'll spend the afternoon shopping. It's past time to freshen your wardrobe. That dress must be at least three years old."

Six, actually. But there was no point mentioning that, or the fact that she'd dug the Versace sundress out of a suitcase she called "Past Lives" and kept hidden in the back of her closet for occasions exactly like this.

"Good fashion is timeless," she said instead. "And as fun as all that sounds, I can only stay for lunch."

"Nonsense."

"I have a commitment this evening."

"Do you have a date?" For the first time since Ava had sat down, Celeste looked excited. She reached across the table to lay one pampered hand over Ava's. "Darling, that's wonderful. Now tell me everything. Who are his family? What does he do? When will we meet him? Soon, I hope. Before you become too attached."

Listen to that. There were so many things her mother left unspoken, yet the words still screamed through Ava's head. The reminder that her parents hadn't considered Elijah's name, wealth or occupation worthy of their only child. The accusation that she'd kept her relationship with him secret from them until she'd gotten pregnant, stealing their opportunity to refuse when Elijah asked for her hand in marriage.

Struggling not to squirm in her chair, Ava clenched her hands tight in her laps and summoned a smile.

"I don't have a date tonight. Actually, I'm not dating anyone." One night of sex with her ex didn't count. "I have a class tonight."

Wrinkling her nose, Celeste said, "You mean you're

making a bunch of flabby housewives huff and puff and sweat."

"Not everyone stays in shape through the wonders of plastic surgery," Ava pointed out.

"Surgery, exercise, what's the difference?" Waving that away with a flick of her fingers, Celeste took a ladylike sip of wine. "It's a tragic waste, Ava. With your upbringing, your family connections, you're qualified for so much more."

All her upbringing and connections qualified her for was to be a pampered princess. And an unhappy one at that. But pointing that out—again—wasn't going to help achieve her objective.

"I wish you'd understand how much I enjoy what I'm doing," she said instead. "Mother, in the last year alone I've earned my accreditation in clinical and rehabilitation massage as well as my certification as a Pilates and yoga instructor. I'm also a second-degree black belt."

"And your point would be?"

"That I love what I'm doing. That I'm good at it. And that I'm continually expanding my skills and qualifications, which makes what I offer more and more in demand." *There*. She leaned back in her chair, glad to have finished that pitch after practicing it so many times on the drive.

"Oh, darling, that's just a distraction. None of that can make you happy. Not like taking your place in society would. It's time you found the right partner and focused your priorities. A home, a family. A future." Celeste patted her hand again. "That's what will make you happy."

The room dimmed. The sound of the other diners,

of cutlery on china and the soft background music all faded, drowned out by the roaring in Ava's head.

"You mean being a wife and a mother?" Hoping it would keep her from screaming, Ava gulped down her wine. She took her time setting the glass back in the precise same place on the white linen tablecloth before meeting her mother's gaze. "We both know it takes more than that to be happy, Mother."

"It needs to be the right marriage, darling."

"The right..." Ava didn't have enough air to finish the sentence. "You think that Elijah and I...that I lost Dominic because..."

"Because it wasn't right," Celeste finished. To her credit, the words were sympathetic and her eyes were bright before she blinked away the tears. "If it was right, it would have been easy, darling. You shouldn't have to stress or struggle or sacrifice to make a marriage work."

Ava opened her mouth, but nothing came out. She had no words. She could only stare in stunned silence.

Her mother believed that. It wasn't simply another one of her patronizing attempts at manipulation. Ava racked her brain, but in that moment, she couldn't remember a single time her mother had stood up to her father. She'd never argued, she'd never disagreed, she'd never expressed disappointment.

No wonder they'd always called Ava their little princess. She'd grown up in a fairy tale.

Had she done the same thing? Had her marriage stood a chance against that sort of emotional sabotage? Ava clenched her fist around the napkin in her lap. How had Elijah?

"Ladies, may I serve your lunch?"

172 CALL TO ENGAGE

Thank God. Distraction. Ava wanted to leap up, grab the waiter's narrow face and give him a big, smacking kiss of gratitude. She settled on a smile and a murmured thanks as he set a gold-rimmed plate on the charger in front of her.

As soon as the waiter left, Celeste grabbed control of the conversation. Social news, gossip and sugarcoated criticisms filled the next half hour. By the time they'd reached coffee—God forbid someone mention dessert around Celeste Monroe—Ava's head throbbed and her stomach growled. How far could a girl get on a four-inch square of salmon and three broccoli sprigs? Her nerves were shot.

She wanted to leave. She wanted to go home, curl up in her rainbow-tinted bedroom and hide.

But she hadn't gotten to the point of her visit.

"Mother, there's something I need to ask you," she burst out, interrupting Celeste's ode to why Ava should try her hairdresser. "It's about my trust fund."

"Darling, we're not going to discuss money at lunch. That's so tacky."

"Tacky or not, I have a favor to ask you and Daddy. I'd like you to release part of it. Not the trust itself," she rushed to add when she saw the immediate refusal on her mother's face. "Just the interest. It'd be more than enough for me to invest."

"You're planning to invest?" One perfectly arched brow rose. "In what?"

Oh boy, here we go.

"In Mack's gym. I'd like to buy in as partner." Before her mother could get out the *no* hovering on her lips, Ava hurried on with her carefully rehearsed explanation of how well the gym was doing, how happy Ava was there and why she thought she'd be a strong partner for Mack.

"So you see, it'd be a smart investment," she finished, trying to smile despite the refusal she felt was coming. "I have an outline of what it would entail, and what the benefits would be."

Her mother shook her head before Ava could reach into her purse. "Oh please, Ava, don't be ridiculous." Celeste dismissed her with a wave of her hand. "This is just another silly impulse of yours."

"Another? This is a business I've been involved with for three years, one I've devoted a lot of time and energy to learning. I hold multiple certifications denoting my skill at it. I've even written up a business plan to show to Daddy so he can see that I'm serious about it. How is that a silly impulse?"

"It's obviously something you think will make you happy in the moment, but in the long run it'll only cause problems. Your father and I don't approve of your spending your days in gyms or massage parlors, Ava. We indulged you before because we love you, darling. But we won't do it again."

"Before?" She'd never asked for money before.

"Before, when you ran off and married Elijah. And look at how that turned out. A mistake of epic proportions, complete with heartbreak and misery."

"And Dominic?" Ava asked, her voice breaking on the words.

She knew her parents had loved Dominic. They'd been doting grandparents. But once he was gone, Dominic had ceased to exist in Roger and Celeste's world.

"That matter isn't open for discussion, Ava." To emphasize her point, Celeste rose from her chair. "Now, if you'll excuse me for a moment, I need to say hello to Meredith and Sharon."

And with that, lunch was finished. Knowing that if she stayed, she'd say something she'd regret, Ava grabbed her bag and left.

She wasn't going to call this a wasted trip, she decided as she drove home, even if she didn't like the things she'd learned. And she'd take out a loan if she had to. Because she was definitely buying into Mack's gym.

Nobody would ever say that Ava Monroe walked away from a challenge again.

CHAPTER TEN

WHEN A MAN awoke sexually satisfied and alone, it was usually cause to count his blessings. But for Elijah, it had only served as an irritation.

He just wasn't sure if he was pissed about the sexual buzz still rippling through his body or if it was the fact that she'd snuck out of his bed like a booty call gone bad.

Oh, oh, maybe it was the fact that she was still dancing to her parents' tune. That thought sent a shaft of fury straight down his spine. Elijah knew from experience that his feelings about her family didn't matter. Actually, his feelings in all things having to do with his ex didn't matter.

Something to remind himself of a few million times, until it sank in.

Frustrated, irritated and suffering from the occasional pang of hunger, Elijah strode into Mack's apartment a little after three without a clue what to do with the rest of his day.

This leave was turning into quite the challenge.

He hit the kitchen, grabbed pizza from the box he'd stashed in the fridge as emergency rations and paced the kitchen while it heated.

Too distracted to draw, not interested in TV, he took

the pizza into his room. He eyed the bed, but didn't give in to the temptation to crawl under the covers. He wasn't in the mood to be dogged by dreams, for one. And two, he'd be damned if he was going to fall into the habit of napping just because he was on leave.

It would feel good, but habits like that could be damned hard to break when he went back on duty.

Unless he didn't. Go back, that was.

Elijah shoved to his feet as if movement could shake off the unwanted thought. He'd unpack, he decided with a deep breath. Unpack, settle in and clear his head.

Then he'd figure out what the hell he was going to do with himself for the next three weeks before reporting for duty. Because he'd damn well be reporting for duty again.

He kept his thoughts calm, his mind on the task at hand. Clothes out of the duffel, into the drawer. Neatly folded, all perfectly aligned. Toiletries stacked on the dresser, ready to take into the bathroom. One pair of shoes, his spare boots, tucked in the closet.

That frantic energy still pulsing, he decided to empty his backpack, too. In the second pocket he found a photo.

Weird.

He looked at it. Frowned, shook his head. Him and Ramsey?

Tents were pitched behind them on a lush carpet of grass, trees dotting the background and the sun shining high enough to cast shadows over their faces. But shadows or not, that was definitely him and Ramsey standing, arms around each other like they were buddies or something. He flipped it over. Written on the back was a note.

Got your back.

What the hell?
Elijah rubbed his thumb and forefinger over his eyes, trying to remember the last time he'd used this backpack. Not for missions, not on duty. Maybe the camping trip he and a few members of the team had taken a year or so ago? He tried to bring it to mind.

They'd hit the Sierras, a three-day hike into the mountains before they'd made camp. Elijah, along with Diego, Ty, Jared and Nic, had spent a week partying among green trees that speared high into the heavens, listening to the roaring power of the river. They'd spent their days climbing, their nights gathered around the campfire, bullshitting one another with tall tales of their prowess at fighting, their exceptional talents at holding their booze and their infamous skills with wild women.

Their laughter had lightened the load each of them carried, their sharing had deepened the bond among them. Those, as Nic liked to say, were the times that gave light to the shadows they too often lived in.

Shadows so strong that Elijah felt engulfed. The misty-gray whispers reminding him of the horrors he'd lived, the pain he'd endured, the misery he'd inflicted. His fists clenched, teeth gritted. He closed his eyes against the heaviness, told himself to ignore it. To push it aside. He wasn't giving in to the lure of the dark.

But the dark engulfed him anyway.

It wrapped around him, grasping fingers of misery holding tight, smothering the light.

He wanted to crawl into that bed, to lose himself in sleep. But his sleep was haunted, torment filling his mind when his guard was down.

Training took over.

Deep breaths.

First one. Then another. Then more.

Long, deep breaths pulled through the nose, down the throat, past the chest and into the belly. Cleansing breaths to drive away the dark, to release the pain, to energize the body.

Only when he was clear again did he look at the photo once more. He pushed his mind back further. He'd camped with Poseidon several times but rarely with other teammates. A number of team missions involved tents and campfires, of course, but most were in desert regions. He couldn't recall a single one where they'd pitched tents in verdant green.

And none with Ramsey.

Which meant that the photo was doctored.

Someone was sending a message, playing games, digging for intel. Fucking with him.

Whatever it was, Elijah had to know.

He dumped the contents of the backpack, started tearing through it all piece by piece. Then he turned the pack itself inside out, inspecting the lining, each scrap of fabric.

Nothing.

He grabbed his duffel, did the same. Every item of clothing was methodically inspected. He ran his fingers along hemlines, dug into pockets, even shook the damn fabric in case something would fly free.

Nothing.

No. He refused to accept nothing.

His clearheaded calm starting to fray, he went through it all again, holding each piece up to the light. First sunlight through the window, then a bare bulb. It was only when he found himself considering how to get his hands on a laser that he stopped and took a breath.

And looked around the room.

Holy shit.

Talk about a mess. The room appeared to belong to a teenager. Clothes, toiletries, personal belongings, they were strewn everywhere. His reheated pizza, long forgotten, congealed on a plate on the nightstand. All that was missing were a few science experiments under the bed and he'd believe he'd gone back in time.

Back in time.

His eyes landed on the cardboard box shoved in the corner, folded flaps covered with a pair of jeans and rolled-up socks. He'd forgotten to take it to his mom's to store.

Crawling across the clothes-strewn carpet, he ripped the flaps open and dug in. He went through all the notebooks, every sketch pad, each page one by one. Then he went through them again.

And again.

He ended up with five stacked on the floor next to him, pages marked with strips of paper.

Numbers.

Someone had worked numbers into various drawings. Had tried to incorporate them so they were hidden, so they looked like part of the image. But the pencil stroke was just a little harder, the lines just a little wider.

Four letters. Twenty-one digits.

IBAN. A Swiss bank account.

Sonovabitch.

He grabbed his cell, dialed Savino.

Nothing.

Not bothering with a message, he tried Torres. After getting Diego's voice mail, he tried Lansky. Nothing.

Holding back the feeling of being cut off from his team, Elijah forced himself to dial Savino again. This time, he left a message for his commander. Priority One, SOS.

Only then did Elijah let himself lie back on the bed. One arm over his eyes to block the light, he forced himself to relax inch by inch.

Okay. Maybe he wasn't going insane.

Maybe.

But damned if he liked whatever was going on in his head.

Because for a man who'd spent his life courting control, his was all shot to hell.

Some men were innately suited to desks, office work and delving into the mysteries of the world through technology.

Nic Savino wasn't one of them.

But he wasn't about to let his lack of natural skill stop him. Like every other block in his life, Nic worked around it, plowed through it, climbed over it. Or, if necessary, flat out ignored it until he turned it his way.

Damned if his current block wasn't causing a serious pain in his ass, though.

Betrayal. Suspicion. Treason.

Quite the wicked triad.

Nic reread Prescott's forwarded message. He hadn't bothered running through cryptology. Prescott would handle it, and if his man couldn't pull anything from it, nobody could. Even facing a new version of his own personal hell, Prescott was the best.

Good enough to misdirect the investigation if he wanted.

That was what NI would say.

And Nic was sure—damned sure—despite their assurance that the case was closed and Poseidon cleared of all suspicion—that they were still watching. Still investigating.

Too many whispers, and a couple of low rumbles, had reached his ears. Naval Investigation was many things, but subtle wasn't one of them. Someone was pushing to keep the eagle eye on Poseidon. Someone was focused on taking the team down.

Nic planned to take them down first.

With that in mind, he dived back into the drudgery and eyestrain of the internet. He delved into the history of each of his men, tracing their family connections, looking for anything that sparked.

When a knock hit his door an hour later, the only thing he'd managed to spark was a headache.

"Enter," he barked when the knock repeated.

"Yo," Diego greeted him as he stepped into the office. As per protocol, he shut the door behind him, engaging the lock. It didn't matter if they were talking mission details, training or sports, Nic insisted on privacy.

While Nic worked out in his head how to approach the situation, Diego kicked back in a chair opposite him.

"You heard from Lansky lately?"

"Not a word." Never one to sit still for long, Diego tapped his fingers on the desk while considering Nic's expression. "You worried about MacGyver?"

"Not worried." *Per se.* Nic leaned back in his chair, considering the latest developments. "Just wondering how he's doing. He hasn't been around much."

"Neither have I." Diego's brow furrowed into a considering expression. "What with moving Harper here to San Diego and all the craziness with getting a place off base, I've been pretty tied up. I haven't seen much of anyone except on duty."

"How's that going? The lifestyle changes, I mean."

Nic wanted to laugh at the expression of baffled discomfort on Diego's face. Wanted to but didn't. He'd never seen the guy look so confused.

"I'm down with the relationship stuff—that's oddly easy," Diego said slowly, as if he was considering each word before using it. "I never thought about it before, but wouldn't have figured a woman could fit into my life, into my lifestyle, the way Harper did."

"Yeah, we haven't seen a lot of successful relationships on the team. I always figured that was due to our high standards, though." Nic grinned. "Not that we're difficult to live with."

"Of course not. We're pussycats."

Nic snickered at Diego's reference to his call sign, El Gato.

"How's almost married life going for you? You and Harper having fun playing house?"

Diego's fiancée had recently moved from Santa Barbara, settling herself, her son and her business into a cozy little place in Coronado.

"Getting used to it. Weird to shift from living on base for the last dozen years to living in an actual house. I think I'm actually supposed to use a lawn mower."

Laughing at the pained look on his friend's face, Nic leaned back in the chair as if he were relaxing.

"How about Nathan?" he asked, referring to Harper's seven-year-old son.

The boy was Ramsey's son, as well, but the man had skipped out when Harper was pregnant, never seeing or supporting her or the kid.

She and Nathan had been unwittingly caught in Ramsey's games, with the guy tracking their movements and keeping tabs until—as far as Nic could tell—he'd deemed Nathan old enough to steal custody away from Harper. Not out of any sentiment, but because the boy was a Ramsey, a trophy to present to the family patriarch. The dirty SEAL had also used their names to hide funds he'd garnered selling top secret information.

"Nathan's doing okay. The kid's rubber, totally bounced back like nothing ever happened."

That said a great deal about the child's resilience, Nic thought. The boy had been kidnapped, stolen from camp in an attempt by Ramsey's wingman to lure his friend out of hiding. Dane Adams was in the brig awaiting trial, but so far had offered nothing helpful in tracking Ramsey down.

"He's a good kid," Nic said. "Have you given him a tour of the base yet? Of the ships?"

While Diego described the things he'd done with his new son, Nic calculated his timing.

He'd wanted to give Harper and Nathan a chance to settle into their new home. To find their footing. And more important, to get used to him and the team.

They'd been used before by Ramsey. Now Nic was going to use them again. He didn't like it. But he'd use them all the same.

"So what's with all the small talk?" Diego wondered after describing the kid's reaction to a submarine. Tilting his head toward Nic, the other man arched one brow. "You going to ask about Harper's decorating plans next or just get to the point?"

Nic gave a soft laugh. Nobody ever said Diego was big on subtle social niceties.

"There's activity in Operation Fuck Up."

"Specifically?"

"Money is moving, files being accessed. Very few people know of the existence of either."

"Very few meaning Poseidon and Ramsey and/or his partner."

Nic inclined his head.

"We have to find out who is involved. We have to know if it's one of our own, if it's one of Poseidon."

"Or if it's Ramsey himself. You keep ignoring that possibility, Nic."

"Not ignoring it. It's simply low on the probability list."

"Why?" His eyes boring deep, Diego pinned Nic

with a look. "What happened that has you looking so hard at your own men?"

Nic's expression didn't change.

"Like I said, money is moving and files are being accessed." The only sign of agitation Nic allowed himself was to give his desk a few taps with his pen. "Money in accounts with limited access, files that only the team should know about."

A man who chose action and movement whenever possible, Diego pushed to his feet and started pacing the office. Given that it was the size of a walk-in closet, Nic knew his steps weren't shaking off much in the way of frustration.

"What else? There's got to be more." Diego shot him an exasperated expression when Nic paused to consider how much to divulge. "You've told me this much— that means you know I'm loyal. To you, to the team, to my rank. So why don't you give me something to work with."

Good point. Nic's only concern was whether or not Torres's sense of loyalty might get in the way of his ability to carry out his duty. Trust was integral to the work they did, but in this instance, trust was the hardest thing to give.

So Nic went with his instincts. He opened one of the thick folders on his desk and handed Diego the sheaf of papers containing the printed texts Prescott had forwarded, along with the tracking codes.

After a glance, Diego took his seat again and focused on reading. He let out a silent whistle when he got to the balance of the Swiss bank account accessed through the code Prescott had sent earlier that day.

"This was sent to Rembrandt?" Diego confirmed, glancing up once before flipping back to the beginning to read the pages again. "He's being used?"

"Maybe."

"You can't think he's involved." The words were firm, as solid and determined as the look on Diego's face. That was one of the man's strongest traits, his loyalty to any and all he deemed worthy. "Rembrandt wouldn't betray the team. He wouldn't betray us."

Nic wanted to believe that. He wanted to believe that every man in the brotherhood, every member of Poseidon, every SEAL was loyal to his oath. He didn't want to question that any man he served with might not be worthy of the trust he'd been charged with.

But his wants weren't a priority. Reality and truth were. And the reality was that people lied, even good people. Bad people lied better. The truth was that teams were made up of men, and every man had his own agenda. Sometimes that agenda aligned with the mission.

Sometimes it didn't.

Right now Nic's mission was to find out who was on which side, and to eliminate the conflict before it caused any further harm. So he chose his words with care. "This message indicates someone is playing a game. What isn't clear is how many levels have already been played, and who is in the lead."

"I read it as someone fucking with Rembrandt." His expression set, Diego tossed the paper on the desk. "If he was dirty, why would he forward the message? Why would he have taken fire? Why would he have stepped up and helped take down Adams a few months ago?"

All good questions. Ones Nic was glad were being asked. "Could be that forwarding the message has a purpose. Could be that the fire was revenge, an accident or carefully planned. Could be that Adams was in the way." Nic shrugged. "Could be that's all bullshit and he's being used. Again. But the question has to be asked."

"Ask all you want. I said it before, I believe it now. Nobody on Poseidon is dirty."

Nic simply inclined his head again.

His face a study of fury, Diego looked like he was going to explode. It took only a few seconds for his expression to clear, which was no more than Nic expected. The man had one hell of a temper, but his control was legendary.

"So what's the plan?"

"The plan is to set a trap." Nic leaned back in his chair, forcing his body to appear at ease in hope that Diego would follow suit. "A very risky, multifaceted trap."

"What's my assignment?"

Nic knew some leaders made a point of offering their team the choice to opt out when a mission came with the guarantee of great personal cost. But Nic didn't work that way. He expected 100 percent from his men, whether the cost was minimal or extreme.

But this mission, this trap…the cost would go beyond Diego. So Nic leaned forward, resting his elbows on his desk and folding his hands together over the stacked folders. He met his man's eyes with a level look and inclined his head.

"As I said, this is a multifaceted trap. One that carries great risk to everyone involved. So before I lay it out,

I'll tell you that this comes with a get-out-of-serving-free card. After hearing the mission outline, you'll have twenty-four hours to decide whether you're in or not."

Diego's head jerked as if he'd just taken a hit to the chin. But the man stayed silent, coming to visible attention for the briefing.

As Nic laid it out, he could see Diego's struggle; the resistance was visible in his furious gaze, in the fists clenched at his sides. But he didn't say a word until Savino was finished. His eyes never left his commander's.

"Anyone else would merit a fist to the face and an offer to help shove that plan where the sun don't shine. But given that it came from you, and knowing what's at stake, I'll refrain."

"I appreciate it."

Diego shoved to his feet, towering over Nic's desk like a bomb waiting to explode.

"Like I said before, there's no way anyone in Poseidon is involved. It'd be impossible."

"Sometimes we have to consider the impossible." Nic waited a beat. "I'll need your commitment within twenty-four hours. No less."

"Yes, sir." With an expression of fury on his face, Diego yanked open the door and stormed out. Nic didn't take it personally. He understood the man's objections. He shared them.

But he couldn't—wouldn't—let them stand in his way.

"Too much at stake," he muttered, opening another file and spreading the photos inside across the surface of his desk.

A dozen men stared back at him. He knew each of their faces as well as he knew his own. He'd served with most of them for the bulk of his naval career. He was closer to the men in Poseidon, but still had long-term ties to the others.

SEALs: Torres, Prescott, Loudon, Ward. Lansky, Rengel and Lee. Petty Officer Dane Adams, Captain Milt Jarrett, Ensign Doug Roberts, Lieutenant Commander Burton Cho. And, of course, Lieutenant Brandon Ramsey himself.

Along with each photo was a personnel dossier. There was nothing in any of them that Nic didn't already know, but he'd decided it was time to refamiliarize himself with a few details. Before he was halfway through the stack of dossiers, his phone rang.

"Savino."

"Cree," barked the Admiral with enough force to be heard without the phone.

"Sir." Even though he was alone in his office, Nic stood, coming to attention.

"Status?"

"Operation Fuck Up phase two is in play."

"Estimated time frame?"

How long was it going to take to find a dead man and destroy his accomplices? "Three weeks."

"You have one."

He didn't bother to swear when the line went dead. Frustration was pointless. Nic had been ordered to do a lot of things in his career that sat uncomfortably. But he did them. Because that was his job.

He lifted the photos of Prescott, Lansky, Jarrett and Loudon from his desk and stared at them with troubled eyes.

Sometimes his job was fucked beyond words.

CHAPTER ELEVEN

CHARCOAL PENCIL FLYING over paper in quick, sure strokes, Elijah let his mind relax. The dark gray images forming on their blanket of white were the only way he knew to find answers, and the questions pounded through his brain.

Water, the waves chopping like a sharp ax. Vicious and mean with edgy teeth, ready to engulf the tiny boat adrift in the sea. A ship, as solid and sturdy as any home a man could know. Flames danced around the ship like imps of fury, their painful touch burning away the facade of safety.

The clouds, dark and furious, were filled with staring eyes. Some dripped with pain, some held regret and doubt, others shot accusation like bolts of lightning.

They screamed betrayal without a word, stabbing, jabbing, ripping at the figure in the boat.

Damn.

Sweat sliding down his forehead, dripping into his eyes, Elijah threw the sketch pad onto the table. It landed with a heavy thud, but it didn't slide across the slick glass, out of sight. It just sat there, the image angled toward him in a stark reminder that it didn't matter what he did—it wasn't going away.

Elijah stared at the drawing with eyes that burned.

He'd drawn it. It had come from his subconscious. And it didn't take a psychologist to decipher the message. Chest so tight it burned almost as hot as his eyes, he glared at the image.

Yeah. He knew what it was saying.

What he didn't know was what the hell to do about it.

"Yo. You okay?"

Shit.

His hand was at his hip reaching for a weapon before Elijah took his next breath. He stopped himself just before he slid into a crouch, fists ready to fly. Instead he froze. Forcibly, physically made himself stay still. He could feel his muscles twitching, desperate for action.

He shot a look over his shoulder. The sight of his cousin, standing in place as if they were playing freeze tag—one foot lifted to step and a finger pressed to his lips—sloughed off the top layer of tension. He made a show of rolling his eyes.

"Is that your way of asking permission to enter your own kitchen?"

"You seemed so deep in thought I figured I'd better check." At Elijah's go-ahead signal, Mack lumbered into the room with all the grace of a grizzly, immediately making the space feel half its previous size. The guy was dressed for exercise in a sleeveless tee proclaiming Mack's Gym to be the best and black sweats cut off at the knees. His hair was damp, his muscles rippling, evidence that he'd had at least one workout already. "I'm between coaching sessions. Figured we could have lunch together."

"It's lunchtime?" Frowning, Elijah checked the sleek clock in the corner. How'd it get to be twelve thirty?

He frowned at the sketch pad. He'd been drawing for three hours?

"You eat yet?"

Elijah gestured with his chin toward the half-empty bowl of cereal on the table.

"You ate that dry?"

"You don't have milk."

"Hellooo." Pulling open the fridge, Mack held out a carton and gave it a gentle shake. "What do you call this?"

Elijah didn't bother to look.

"Milk comes from cows. Goats in a pinch. Not almonds."

"This is healthier. Less calories, lower fat, no additives."

"Mack, I spend half my life working out, the other half in death-defying situations. You think I'm going to spend what's left of my time worrying about fat and calories?"

Then again... Elijah glanced at the bowl of dry twigs he'd been eating by the handful like snack mix. Maybe juiced almonds would have helped.

"So you aren't overly concerned with cholesterol," Mack observed when he parked himself and his own bowl of white liquid and cereal across from Elijah. "What are you concerned with?"

Before Elijah could claim nothing, Mack slid the sketch closer. His eyes widened.

"I've always admired your talent and your imagination. Not sure I do now, though. Not if you've got this knocking around in your head."

"I've got all sorts of things in my head." Elijah shrugged. "Mostly questions."

Mack ate a few shovel-size bites of cereal as he inspected the drawing.

"If I were a deep kind of guy who got things like symbolism and imagery, I'd think this was some scary shit. Like, you're-questioning-your-life scary shit." Mack took another bite and considered. "Actually, if this was in my head, I'd be questioning my life, too."

Absently grabbing a handful of cereal twigs, Elijah watched Mack flip through a few more pages, a few more images, all variations on the theme.

"I'm questioning a lot of things," he finally admitted. The twigs were too dry to swallow; he grabbed his bottle of water and chugged.

"All these boats make me think some of them are Navy things."

His expression set, Elijah gave a single nod.

"You're thinking of leaving the Navy?"

God. Elijah's gut clenched. It sounded worse when someone else said it.

"You'd really leave the Navy?" Mack's rugged features folded into surprise. "Elijah, you're a SEAL. You've wanted that since you were a kid. I can't believe you'd walk away from it."

"I've served for twelve years. Four tours, a decade as a SEAL. I reached the pinnacle. I put it all on the line for my career every single day I served. Nothing came before my service." Elijah met his cousin's eyes. "And in the end? I don't know if it makes any difference. I don't know if it'd ever be enough. And I don't know if I have anything left to give."

Mack wrapped his hands together and leaned forward. The guy was big enough that the move put him halfway across the table, pretty much in Elijah's face.

"Sometimes after a match, I figure I'm done. It doesn't matter if I won or lost, I'm empty. Bottomed out. I think, you know, there's a whole lot of life out there. Most of it doesn't involve getting repeatedly hit in the face or kicked in the nuts. Maybe I should try living it that way, instead."

"You saying you agree that I should leave the Navy?"

"Hell, no." Mack scowled. "I'm saying I get it. On a much smaller level, I get it. But you don't see my ass giving up, do you?"

Vision blurring red at the edges, Elijah opened his mouth to scream at Mack, to pour out the hideous truths of what he'd been through. The explosion. The fire. The hospital.

Betrayal.

Guilt.

Suspicion.

But training, as much a part of him as the color of his eyes, kicked in before he could release more than a puff of air. And just like that, he shut it down.

"I'm simply considering choices," he finally said.

"You might want to factor the price you've paid into those considerations. I'm not talking about the secret stuff, the mission stuff. I mean what it cost you, personally."

Ava. "Pretty sure the cost's the same whether I stick around or not." Elijah shrugged. "I'm still divorced. Dominic is still gone. My being a SEAL doesn't make it any easier to pay freight on that."

Mack gave him a long, considering look, then shook his head.

"I just can't see it. What're you going to do? Settle into some boring-ass job as an electrician or maybe put your drawing skills to use sketching caricatures at the local mall?"

Elijah laughed, only partially in horror. Beat the hell out of Lansky's suggestions.

"I guess I haven't thought that far ahead," he admitted, rubbing his hands over his face to try to scrub away the confusion. "Maybe it's seeing Ava that has me jacked up, has me questioning my choices and, yeah, the costs. It's a huge reminder, you know."

Mack nodded. "Look, I'm good with advice. I tell grown men what to do on a regular basis. I advise, I coach, I kick ass." Mack's smile was edged in arrogance. But there was a sadness beneath it as he continued. "But when it comes to relationships, dude, let's get real. I suck at them."

"What happened to your Decadence date?"

"Turns out he's got a penchant for the golden arches, Two Buck Chuck and the Three Stooges."

Elijah grimaced. The fast food and cheap wine were bad enough. But he knew slapstick movies were Mack's line in the sand. Poor guy simply couldn't understand the humor of a good poke to the eyeballs.

"I guess neither of us is having much in the way of luck when it comes to relationships," Elijah responded, pulling the sketch pad toward himself and flipping to a fresh page.

"Not sure as I'd say that. At least you know what a good relationship is. You had that connection—a strong enough connection to want to spend your life with someone who wanted to spend hers with you."

Had he? Or had Ava just married him because she was pregnant? Sure, she'd seemed like she'd loved him at first. And other than the nagging about his career, he'd thought they were happy together.

Until they'd lost Dominic.

Elijah's gut clenched with a vicious, stabbing pain before he could shove that thought back behind lock and key where it belonged.

"Like I said, a lot of good it did me."

"Pouting seems to be serving you pretty well."

Elijah's laugh was something along the lines of a puff of air as he added a teddy bear to the arms of his quick sketch of his cousin. He'd drawn Mack as a he-man, so muscular he should be ringing the tilt bells as he pressed a Volkswagen Bug overhead with one hand, cuddling the bear with the other. A couple of flourishes in the form of an empty chocolate box and bouquet of wilting flowers and it was done.

He tore the sheet off and tossed it onto the table between them. Mack glanced at the paper and burst into a guttural belly laugh.

"You are such an asshole," he said, still laughing as he took a closer look.

"What? I didn't get your best side?"

His eyes on the drawing, Mack's smile dropped away with a sigh. "You're in a rough place, buddy. You've got some big decisions to make. I can't tell you what to do. I can't even tell you what I'd do if I were in your position."

"Maybe you take the role of a family member who

worries about my safety, wonders if I'll be alive for your next birthday and maybe figures I've sold my soul to Uncle Sam for a pittance and an ego boost?" The words tasted as bitter as they sounded.

"Ouch." Mack shook his head. "Ava lay all that on you? I didn't think you two had said more than kiss ass in that massage room."

Unable to draw his way out of his tangled thoughts, Elijah tossed his pencil down and shrugged.

"Look. I don't know what happened that put you in the hospital, and I'm not asking. No point since you can't tell me. As a *concerned family member*, I'm okay with that because I know how important your career is to you. I've seen the years you've devoted to your training, to perfecting your craft. I know you had reasons for doing that. And I always figured those reasons were solid."

"I did, too."

Mack nodded. "A handful of years ago, you had it all. Then you lost it. But not all of it." Mack sighed. "Dude, giving up your career is one thing if it's what you want to do. But walking away because you're screwed up over something that happened, or because you're mixing up your Ava issues with your career ones? If that's the case, you need to take a little time and think it through."

"That's why I'm here, cousin. To think it through."

"Then I strongly suggest you try to compartmentalize. Deal with your career, deal with your hospitalization, deal with your history with Ava. But deal with each issue separately."

Elijah let his head fall back along with the chair so he was balanced on the two back legs.

Compartmentalize. Yeah. He could do that.

He couldn't make a career decision with his head buried in the gray fog of pain that was dogging him. He had to clear the fog somehow, had to find his way through the pain.

Once he did, he'd know what to do. About his career.

But Ava?

"She slept with me the other night," he admitted quietly. "First time we see each other in four years, she basically tells me to kiss her ass. Next thing I know, she's in my bed and we're rolling around naked."

"You know, most guys would consider rolling around naked a good thing."

"I woke alone. When I ran her down, instead of a 'Damn, you were good,' she laid a guilt trip on me."

"Maybe you need to work on your skills? Learn a few new moves, take up some kink? Might garner a better morning-after reaction."

Elijah snickered as he slowly lowered his head. "I'll take that under advisement."

"And the rest?"

And the rest? He frowned. He didn't see that there was any going back with Ava. They weren't the same people anymore.

He'd always had his shit together. Now he had stress issues.

Ava had always been a cupcake, soft and sweet. Now she was a hard-ass.

She'd spent most of their marriage trying to get him to give up his career. Now he was questioning it, and she didn't care.

And Mack's suggestion of kink? Years ago, they'd

rocked every variation of the missionary position because that was all she'd been comfortable with.

But now? Now he'd bet Ava might actually go for some kink. She'd like it. Maybe a little bondage, a few toys, some public displays of orgasm.

Sex wasn't enough to base a relationship on. But all things considered, it might be powerful enough to tidy up the past and tie up those loose emotional ends. Once and for all.

"You happen to know where Ava is at the moment?"

He had to give Mack credit. His cousin managed to keep his smile to an infinitesimal quirk of his lips. "She's teaching an advanced kickboxing class for the next thirty minutes."

"Downstairs?"

"Second-floor ring."

Elijah took a deep breath, then shrugged.

"Guess I'd better gear up for class. I've never done any kickboxing, though. You think she'll let me play?"

"A chance to kick your ass in the ring? She'll welcome you with open arms."

ELIJAH CHANGED INTO loose gray sweatpants and a US Navy tee with the sleeves ripped off. He didn't bother wrapping his hands or grabbing gear, just headed toward the gym.

He used the inside staircase, taking his time and checking out the view while he settled his thoughts. He still couldn't answer any of the questions pounding through them, but he figured settled was good enough.

It's all mind over matter, he'd been taught as a SEAL. If he didn't mind, it didn't matter.

If nothing else, his little chat with Mack had been a reminder of that. It'd also helped him put a few things in perspective.

He was a SEAL. He'd put a lot of his life into being a SEAL. No matter what choices he made in the future, he'd always be a SEAL.

So he'd damned well better act like one.

Right now he had a mission. To assess and ascertain the relationship between he and Ava. A week ago, he would have called it over and done with. Their night together could be written off as sex for the sake of sex. It could be chalked up to old times' sake. Or it could be seen as a signal of something bigger.

He'd been trained to recognize potential threats and secure the situation until a determination could be made. In this case, the determination of whether the emotional ties between he and Ava were truly dead or not.

They'd never said goodbye.

After Dominic had died, she'd refused to talk to him. After they'd buried their baby, she'd refused to see him. After she'd served him with divorce papers, she'd refused to listen to him.

He supposed that was the sort of thing that a shrink would say required closure. And while hot sex was a great means of communication, he didn't figure it actually counted as any form of closure, no matter how many orgasms they'd shared.

So this was it.

Elijah rounded the last flight of stairs and headed for what Mack called the sparring gym.

This was his shot at closure. And with it, the means

to figure out what he wanted in life, where he'd gone wrong. And more important, what the hell he was going to do next.

He paused just inside the doorway to assess the conditions. The heavy beat of rock pounded, low and steady, through speakers lining the ceiling. Gray carpet and pale blue walls were an oddly soothing contrast to the grunts and groans of boxers filling three of the four rings in each corner of the second-floor gym. Along one wall were a row of black freestanding floor bags; red leather punching bags hung on the opposite wall.

In between stood Ava.

Damn, she looked good. She'd always looked good to him. He'd appreciated her curves, the welcoming softness of her body when they'd first met. He'd been awed by her during pregnancy, watching the magical growth of her body as she nurtured their son. And he'd appreciated the serene, Madonna-like luxuriousness of her body after Dominic's birth.

But Ava now? Rippling muscles and gleaming strength were wrapped in spandex and a loose-fitting tee, and, yeah, she looked good. So damned good.

Her hair was pulled back to leave her bare face un-framed. Her arms rippled as she demonstrated a punch combination. Then she arched to the side, executing an impressive high kick that made Elijah's heart beat just a little faster as he considered how that body had felt beneath his.

It was a thought that couldn't be understated: she looked damned good. After a long, appreciative glance, he shifted his gaze to consider the people with her.

Sixteen people, all in pretty decent shape, took turns

either punching or kicking the bags in concert with the moves Ava called out.

"Jab. Left hook. Sidekick. Uppercut. Roundhouse," she ordered. "Mia, put your shoulder into it. Jack, kick with the flat of your foot, not your toes. Good job— there you go."

She moved along the line, correcting, adjusting and praising in equal measures. He'd trained with a wide variety of instructors, enough to recognize Ava's skill. Elijah wasn't sure if he was more impressed or surprised.

He was still trying to decide when Ava caught sight of him. In the middle of demonstrating a kick-punch-kick combination, her eyes widened. The hitch in her kick was infinitesimal, small enough that he doubted her students caught it. Color washed over her cheeks, sweeping down her throat to disappear into the collar of an oversize red tee that draped temptingly off one shoulder.

Elijah grinned as she straightened, giving him a narrow-eyed look that clearly said, *Get lost*.

He could have gone. Saved their little confrontation for another time. After all, she was working, and he was a firm believer in the sanctity of work time.

But she added a little shooing motion with her fingers. Like he was a bug. Amusement fading, Elijah squared his hips, planted his feet and crossed his arms over his chest. He really didn't like being shooed.

"Class, it looks like this is our lucky day," Ava said after a frustrated sigh. "We have a celebrity in our midst."

Elijah narrowed his eyes. She knew how he felt about advertising what he did, about taking credit for his role in Special Forces. Even when they'd been married, half of her family hadn't realized what he did for a living beyond that he was in the Navy. Now she was going to proclaim him a SEAL in a room full of strangers. She wouldn't. Ava tossed the hair she'd braided into a long rope behind her back and gave him a chilly smile. "This is Mack's cousin. He's a SEAL."

Body tensing, adrenaline surging, Elijah gritted his teeth. She did. God*dammit*. She definitely wasn't the same woman he'd married.

"Now you've all heard of SEALs, haven't you? They're supposed to be pretty strong. Well trained, the best combat warriors of our times. Famous for their fighting skills."

Where was she going with this? The sharp look in her eyes assured him that she had somewhere in mind. Somewhere he wouldn't like.

He ignored the murmurs as the room reacted. He simply watched. And waited. Ava didn't keep him waiting long.

"You've probably all heard about the SEAL fitness requirements. The Grinder Finder. SEAL Fit. SEAL Intensive. Some of the most challenging workout programs created, all based on what we civilians imagine the SEALs PT looks like."

She moved as she spoke, circling her students and gesturing to emphasize her words. Her gaze locked on Elijah's as she grabbed the ropes of one of the empty rings and flipped herself over the top in an impressively smooth jump.

"Because of the covert nature of everything SEALs do, we can't know for sure that their workouts—and

the results thereof—are actually worthy of such pres-
tige." Her smile sharpened. "We can assume they are.
Or we can use this opportunity to run a little SEAL
fitness test."

The murmur rose to a buzz as the energy in the room
spiked.

Elijah shook his head. He wasn't going to play.

Ava simply arched one brow as she drew the long
braid of her hair into a knot at the base of her neck.

"Now, the fitness of the SEALs is legendary. But
what some of you might not realize is that most of them
are unable to refuse a dare."

Even as Elijah gave another infinitesimal shake of his
head, he scanned the room to assess which of the guys
she planned to pit him against. There were fourteen
in total, but only two looked as if they could go more
than a half minute in the ring. Never one to underesti-
mate an opponent, he started to give them a thorough
study. He'd barely made it past assessing muscle tone
and reach when Ava spoke again.

"I think it's time for a little kickboxing demonstration. So." She shot Elijah a smile wicked enough to stir
quite a few workout thoughts. But all of them required
privacy and less clothing. "I dare our guest to step into
the ring and help me demonstrate technique."

He was tempted to remind her that she was already
well aware of his technique. Then he realized she was
serious.

"You want me to fight with you?" It wasn't easy to
hold back his laughter.

"I want you to partner with me as I demonstrate
the kickboxing technique I've been teaching," she cor-

rected, the flash in her eyes making it clear she heard the laughter even if he didn't set it free.

"Am I giving you a handicap?"

"You wearing a cup?" she asked.

"Good point."

He didn't doubt for a second that she'd try to damage the goods she'd enjoyed so thoroughly two nights ago.

"I did mention that it was a dare, didn't I?" Ava's smile was more than wicked now. It was filled with laughter.

Elijah remembered a time he'd do anything when she smiled at him like that. Looked like that hadn't changed. And, of course, there was the dare.

He puffed out a breath. She probably did deserve a few shots. He decided to let her put on a show. He'd go easy, give her a chance to demonstrate a few defensive techniques. Angling between the ropes, he stepped into the ring. And waited.

Ava didn't keep him waiting long. She did make him suffer once she was there, though.

First, she took her time stripping off the baggy T-shirt, leaving her in body-hugging purple leggings that stopped just below her knees and a black halter-style sports bra that left her rippling abs bare.

Damn, she was hot. Taut, tight and tempting. He'd recently explored every inch of that gorgeous body, but he could see now that he hadn't given it the reverence it was due.

Elijah wondered if he was supposed to strip, too, but he figured they could hold off on that until they had a little privacy.

She was way more focused on the people gathering around the ring than she was on him. She didn't even look his way as she outlined fight strategy, tactics for taking on opponents larger than oneself and the importance of limbering up before a match.

Then she started limbering.

There was buzzing again, but it was all in his head this time. But his eyes weren't glazed over enough to miss the sideways look she shot his way. Then he caught that half smile of hers as she bent in half, pressing her forehead to her knee.

She was playing him.

Ava straightened, bracketing her hand around one wrist and stretching both arms high overhead. The move threw her body into sharp relief, the long lines of it etching the image of pure temptation in his mind.

Psyching him out before the match, figuring he couldn't see past the layers of lust she was weaving to sidestep a punch. As she dropped her clasped hands straight down behind her back, the move arching her breasts upward and her hips forward, Elijah's mouth went dry. He had to give her credit.

The psyching out was a damned good plan.

But he was a SEAL.

He was trained by the best to be the best. Through thick, through thin. In battle, in war. He specialized in strategy. He had to admire the skill in which she employed lust as a weapon. And since this was a match, not a battle, he'd meet her on even ground, with equal weaponry.

He'd shoot that lust right back at her. He'd use it

against her. He'd wrap her up in it until she was moaning and sweating and begging for mercy.

He'd done it two nights ago.

He could do it now.

CHAPTER TWELVE

"READY?" HE ASKED when she finally wound down with her classroom instructions.

"Are you?" Ava countered with a smile, skimming her fingers down her hips in a subtle invitation before lifting her hands into fighting position.

"Yep. Let's go." Feet planted on the mat, he started to lift his hands, then made a show of shaking his head. "Wait. Hang on."

He stripped his shirt away, his gaze locked on hers as he tossed the tattered cotton over the rope. He liked the way her eyes widened, pupils dilating as she blew out a long, slow breath. From the way her pulse was pounding in her throat, she was just as interested in the view as he'd been.

Good. Now they'd play.

"Mmm, SEAL fit, indeed," he heard from outside the ring. Ava's scowl said she heard it, too, and didn't like it.

Elijah grinned.

"Ready?" Ava snapped.

"For you? Always."

He didn't drop into fight position. He wasn't about to spar with his wife—ex or otherwise.

Ava, obviously not having the same compunction, shifted her weight, bent her knees and lifted her fists.

Fists. Elijah grinned. *Seriously?*

The first strike wiped his smile away. He yanked his head to the left. Damned if she wouldn't have clipped his nose if his reflexes hadn't kicked in.

He blocked the next strike, wrist to wrist. When she spun around, leg high enough that her foot missed his ear by an inch, he got serious.

Not serious enough to take her down. But serious enough to keep her on her very sexy toes. He matched her, punch for punch, pulling his so they barely skimmed her body.

Uppercut, forearm block. Sidekick with his shin to her waist. Even at 10 percent power, the move sent her flying to the side. To cover it, keeping it looking good for her students, he grabbed her arm and pulled her into a flip. One that she easily twisted to her advantage, sweeping his feet out from under him.

Elijah was grinning again. But this time with pride. She was good. Damned good.

He put her through her paces as they sparred for another five minutes. He'd fought a lot of people, from novice squids to spit-spewing militants. He'd rarely found anyone with moves so clean, precise and targeted. He had a good sixty pounds on her, all of it muscle, but she held her own.

Oh yeah, he thought as he jumped to the side to avoid her backhand fist to the gut. She definitely held her own.

Ava executed an impeccable high kick. This time, instead of letting it slide off his shoulder, Elijah grabbed hold. His hand wrapped around her ankle, angling her higher so she had to shift at the waist to keep her balance.

Tiny drops of sweat beaded her brow and the little tendrils of hair around her face curled. Her breath came faster now. All that was missing were the moans.

He didn't release his hold on her leg. He slid his hand up the taut calf, his fingers teasing the underside of her knee for a second before he wrapped them around her thigh. He was tempted to keep going, but he was aware of their audience.

So he settled for sliding one finger higher, teasing the inside of her thigh. And smiled in satisfaction when she hissed. He used her distraction to sweep her remaining foot out from under her, keeping his grip tight on her leg and the other under the small of her back so when she hit the mat she didn't even bounce.

He followed her, landing on one knee and the opposite fist. She punched out, the heel of her hand coming within an inch of his nose before Elijah's hand snapped up, grabbing hers. To ensure she didn't kick anything important, he wrapped his thigh over both of her legs, holding her in place.

"Draw?" he challenged.

He could see she didn't want to give in. Damned if he didn't find that just as sexy as the sweat-slicked, ripped body pressed against his. As if reading his thoughts, Ava arched. Her eyes like molten chocolate, melting with passion, she stared up at him. Her hips nestled against his, challenging the fit of his cup.

Elijah leaned closer. "Might want to lose the audience," he murmured against her ear.

He felt as much as saw her take a shaky breath and would have taken the time to admire her control if he wasn't fighting to hold on to his own.

"Draw," she decided between clenched teeth.

Eyes locked on hers, he waited a couple more heart-beats and then released her hand. He gave himself the pleasure of another second before sliding her legs free. Their eyes held, hers filled with vulnerability that ripped at his heart. She rolled away and to her feet.

"And that's your demonstration for the day. And proof that the SEALs aren't kidding when they say they're the best."

The rest of her words, her students' questions, they were simply a buzz in the back of his head as Elijah got to his feet. He wasn't winded. He hadn't broken a sweat. But damned if he'd ever put so much effort into a workout.

Feeling numerous eyes on him, he took a moment to give thanks for years of training making his use of a cup automatic, since it shielded most of the evidence of his reaction from her class. *Go, Navy.* Always coming through for him, he thought with a snicker as he swiped a towel over his face.

His snicker died off when he noted that Ava's nipples stood in stark relief against the skimpy fabric of her workout bra. He grabbed her tee off the rope and tossed it her way, considering it a show of immense restraint that he didn't pull it over her head himself.

He might have limited claim but damned if he wanted other men—or women, he was an equal-opportunity ex-husband—staring at her nipples.

Ava didn't seem to care, since she only rolled her eyes at him as she angled out of the ring.

"Class dismissed," she said brightly. "Next time,

we'll get you all in the ring to try a few of your own moves."

There were a few laughs and suggestive remarks shared behind shielded hands, but for the most part, the students simply looked impressed.

Elijah avoided conversation by flipping over the opposite side of the ring and taking up a position next to the door while she wound things up.

He waited as she answered questions, admiring how she reined in the impatience he heard in her voice. He noted the students' admiration, which didn't surprise him, and the respect—which he was ashamed to say did.

He wanted to hurry her along, to grab her and drag her out of the room. But this was her gig and he figured it'd be a dick move to do something to dim that respect he'd noted.

So he shifted from his left foot to his right, then back again. He checked the big clock on the wall, then his body's reaction. Nope, time wasn't putting a damper on his erection. It was still firm, and perfectly happy to stay that way as long as Ava's sexy body was in view.

He wanted her.

He knew she wanted him, too, but she was taking her own sweet time. Another power play, he figured. And a good one, since he was pretty much ready to beg at this point.

Ava HAD NEVER considered herself much of an actress. So she was amazed and proud that she was able to keep her voice upbeat and even as she wound up class. Her expression was even, as if she wasn't using every ounce of energy she had to keep her body from melting into a happy puddle of lust at Elijah's feet.

She wanted to. She wanted him.

For how the hot lust she felt when he touched her. For the needy desire she felt when she looked at him.

She might have been strong enough to fight those, might have been stubborn enough to ignore them.

But the man had respected her enough to face her in the ring. She knew he'd pulled his punches, was pretty sure he wouldn't even consider that a workout. But he'd met her on her level; he'd given her class one hell of a demonstration. And he'd shown respect for her abilities.

That was why she wanted him naked, she assured herself. Because there was nothing sexier than respect.

As she dismissed her students, she cut a sideways glance toward Elijah, noting the rippling strength of his bicep and shoulder as he wiped his face. Mmm, okay, so maybe almost nothing.

She owed him. And she couldn't wait to pay. He was obviously getting tired of waiting, though. His impatience—something she'd rarely seen—was at the point that he was pacing a groove in front of the exit by the time the final students left, shooting curious, amused or lascivious looks over their shoulders as they went.

"Sorry about that," Ava said as she crossed the room, grabbing a towel as she went. "It's an advanced class, and they pay for a full hour. Since our little demonstration was more for my benefit than theirs, I felt like I owed them some extra Q&A time."

"You're a good teacher."

"Whoa." Ava laughed, trying to pretend she wasn't overwhelmed by the compliment. "That's one heck of a thing for a guy to say after being dared into the ring. Especially a guy who could have tossed me down anytime he wanted in there."

"Your ring. Your rules." He shrugged. "And your class. You were showing them some basic combinations. We demonstrated some basic combinations. No big."

No big. Ava blinked.

He'd choreographed their match to align with her lesson. He'd adjusted his own style, tempered his moves, to let her show hers. All the while, he'd pushed her to the edge. To her edge, as if he assumed—not that she needed protecting or indulging—that she could handle being challenged.

Her heart did a long, slow dive.

"Thank you," she said softly, smiling up at him. Relaxed now, she could see the changes on his face. A few more lines creasing his eyes. A furrow etched into his brow that hadn't been there before. But those green eyes were clear, the look in them as familiar to her as her own face.

It was a look of desire, admiration and simple affection. *Oh, God.* She'd missed that so much.

Trying to pull the scattered fragments of her thoughts together, Ava focused on unbanding her hair, combing her fingers through the strands to loosen the braid until the damp tresses flowed like a comfortable blanket over her shoulders.

"You've grown."

She made a show of looking down at her body.

"Most would say I've toned."

"No," he corrected. "You're stronger. Your body

kicks ass, yeah. But you're stronger emotionally. Mentally. I admire that."

Oh, hell. Ava gave up. "Let's go," she said, jerking her chin toward the exit.

"Where're we going?"

"To finish this round."

She'd intended to take it upstairs. To shoot for privacy in a room with a door. And maybe even a lock.

But when Elijah cupped one hand over her butt, squeezing his approval, she lost it. Ava grabbed his hand and yanked him through the next door they came to.

The steam room.

Perfect.

When a quick glance assured her it was empty, she flipped the locks, ensuring privacy. She slapped the buttons on the set of swinging doors and pulled him inside. She'd missed the lights, so the bench-lined room was dim, and the steam was rising. Filling the space. Hot, wet, misty steam.

The second the doors swung shut, he had her back against the wall. The long, hard length of his body slammed into hers, anchoring her there as his fingers dove into her hair.

Ava lifted her chin, managed to suck in one long breath between her teeth before his mouth took hers in huge, hungry bites. She felt as if she were drowning in passion, the power of it washing over her—through her. When his tongue plunged, her body went lax, sagging against the wall as if every muscle had melted in the heat.

It felt so good. He felt so good.

More. Ava's fingers scraped down his arms, reveling in the rounded boulders that were his biceps, rock hard beneath the silk of his skin. She gripped his shoulders, wrapping her leg around his, hooking her ankle behind his thigh.

The wet, pulsating juncture between her legs trembled as she pressed harder against him. Sliding up, then down, then up again.

"More," she breathed against his mouth. "Give me more."

Elijah lifted his head just enough to take in her face, that sexy smile of his playing over his mouth when he saw how hard she was breathing, how much she wanted him.

She knew it put him in the position of power. Ava didn't care. As long as he satisfied the desperate need spiraling in her belly, he could have all the power he wanted.

"How useful is that lock?" he asked, his hand skimming under the tight spandex band of her workout bra.

"Mack has keys. I do. That's it."

Apparently considering that useful enough, Elijah hooked one finger around the band and pulled the damp, sticky fabric over her head in one easy sweep.

Leaving Ava bare from the waist up, and very turned on.

His hands cupped her breasts, thumbs working the nipples as he watched. Steam poured out of the vents now, slicking over her skin so it felt as if he were touching her through water.

Her body felt like liquid. And he was stirring her up. Wet and hot and needy, the feelings, the sensations, they all tangled together in a maelstrom of intensity.

When he leaned down, tracing one bead of steam with his tongue as it dripped down her breast, Ava moaned. When he sucked her nipple into his mouth, she whimpered.

He nipped, teasing the turgid flesh between his teeth while he worked her other nipple, scraping it with his thumbnail before soothing it with the rough pad of his finger.

She pressed tighter against him, the wet heat between her legs demanding release. He angled his thigh higher, offering the pressure she wanted. The release she needed.

Ava let her head rest on the wall, closing her eyes so to better get lost in the sensations.

Her body tightened. The orgasm building, climbing. He pinched, bit. Suckled deep as his hands squeezed.

Ava exploded.

Over and over, waves of pleasure washed through her. So hard, so strong, she almost drowned in them.

Oh, so good.

She didn't know how long she stood there, clitoris throbbing against Elijah's thigh while his fingers soothed gentle circles around her nipples. Calming the storm but not sending it away.

No, she realized as she pried her eyes open. He was keeping her right there on the edge.

Ava took a deep breath, the moist air thick in her lungs as she tried to read his face. But Elijah was too good at masking his feelings.

"Wow," she finally said.

"You like that?"

"Oh yeah. I like it a lot."

"Good." He nodded, then gave her a wicked smile. "Glad it worked for you. But that's it."

Ava blinked. Ignoring the tiny beads of steam dotting her skin, she shook her head. She couldn't have heard right. "What do you mean, that's it?"

"You snuck out of my bed the other day. You refused to discuss what'd happened between us. I'll get you off, sweetheart—it's only fair. But that's it if you're going to keep pushing me away."

"I don't want to push you away. I want you inside me." Angling higher, she rubbed her tongue over his bottom lip, then gave it a good nip. "It's only fair."

"I don't give a damn about right or wrong anymore. I'm not interested in playing fair and couldn't care less about being nice."

Despite the need jangling through her, Ava had to grin. He was so damned cute. Because despite everything he was, deep down, one of the nicest men she knew. And she was about to use that.

"You'd leave me here, like this?" she asked, fluttering her lashes.

"You got off, sweetheart. It's not like I got you all churned up and left you hanging."

Like he was. She could feel the length of his churned-up hardness pressing against her thigh and knew that no cup in the world was strong enough to contain it.

"Mmm, good point." All it took was a slight movement of her shoulders for him to step back. To give her some space. As if she were actually going to leave.

Instead Ava locked her eyes on his as she toed off

her shoes. Her socks, too. She hooked her thumbs in the waistband of her leggings and shimmied free.

"But now I'm naked," she pointed out. "You wouldn't make me go out there naked, would you?"

"You think you can lead me around by my…" Always the gentleman, he changed what she knew he'd been going to say. "Hormones?"

"I think that you got me all hot and bothered, and one little orgasm isn't enough," she challenged.

"You might think that all we've got is sex between us, Ava, but I'll be damned if we're going to have it without respect."

What? Her mouth actually dropped open. "I know you respect me," she said, wondering why they were talking when all it would take was one touch of his hand on her body for her to come again.

"I mean me. You act like I'm just a piece of ass, only here to get you off. If you want this—" he gestured between their bodies "—then we do it right."

Scared of how much he'd want, terrified that she'd give him anything, Ava shook her head. "What's that even mean?"

"Not some long-term commitment," he said, his eyes tightening at her sigh of relief. "But a commitment all the same. We date."

"Date?"

"Like, go places that don't include sex play. We talk to each other. We spend time in nonforeplay events."

"Are you a girl?"

"Are you afraid?"

Hell, yeah. But she was also turned on to the point of tipping into spontaneous orgasm just looking at his body.

As if he knew, Elijah reached down and grasped the fabric of his shirt, yanking it overhead in one swift move.

"Fine," she agreed, ignoring the warnings screaming out in her head.

"It's a deal?" he asked.

"Fine, yeah, it's a deal." After the briefest of hesitations her need to know overcame her need to come again as soon as possible, so Ava asked, "Why does it matter?"

"I'm simply mitigating damage and ensuring that we can both look ourselves in the eyes when this is over." He didn't add "again," but they both heard it. "We both know it's probably a mistake."

"And you don't like making mistakes," Ava said, tossing her head so that her hair tumbled, long and luxurious, over her chest, erotically teasing the tips of her breasts. Sticking to the steam-moistened silk of her skin.

Her nipples ached for more, though. She wanted to beg him to touch her, to taste her. But Ava didn't beg. She preferred to tempt. "Would you really have left me here, Elijah? Could you be satisfied walking away with not getting as good as you gave?"

His eyes locked on her breasts. His fingers clenched and unclenched. But he didn't reach for her. "Depends on the circumstances. And the cost." He tilted his head to one side. "And, of course, the payoff. You going to make it worth my while?"

"I'm going to blow your mind," Ava murmured, running her tongue over her bottom lip and giving a little shiver of delight. "Just as soon as you get naked."

"Blow my mind, huh?"

"Among other things."

A smile, part boyish charm and part seduction, flashed over Elijah's face. God, he was gorgeous.

Ava wished she could get past the passion pounding through her system. It made it hard to think, harder to decide if Elijah was right.

Maybe this was a mistake.

But if it was, she didn't care. Not when he was pulling off his clothes, baring all that gorgeous bare skin.

Ava dropped to her knees in front of him and, before he could say a word, took the huge, rigid length of him between her lips. *Mmm, hard, delicious.*

She warmed her tongue around the velvet head of his penis. Slid it up the shaft. Down again, then sucked hard.

She ran her hands over his butt, cupping the hard muscles before sliding them down his thighs. Over the scars. Along the pain.

He grabbed her hand. "Don't."

She understood his reticence. She'd felt it herself, back when they were married. She hadn't carried scars. She'd carried an extra fifteen pounds. Oh, it had been distributed well enough that she looked pretty good in clothes. But naked? Bared? Every ripple, every bulge, every imperfection. And naked with a man whose body put Greek gods to shame?

There was a reason they'd done most of their love-making in the dark.

So Ava understood. She really did. But that didn't mean she was going to let him think there was a single thing wrong with his body.

Words were worthless. Elijah, he was a man of action. So she'd use action.

She traded. Her hand wrapped around the turgid power of his erection, fingers pulsing, then sliding, pulsing, then sliding. When he groaned, she pressed her mouth to his leg.

"Ava—"

"Shhh."

While her hands soothed the tight muscles in gentle, easy strokes, she ran her tongue over the rippled flesh. Tasted the salty evidence of their game in the ring. Felt the nerves twitch and quiver beneath her mouth.

His cock jerked, warning Ava that playtime was over. She pressed one last kiss to his leg, then rose.

Eyes locked on his, she moved backward until she was pressed against the wall, rivulets of steam dripping down her body.

"Now," she invited. "Do me now."

"Remember the deal," he ordered through clenched teeth.

He'd do it. She knew he'd grab his clothes and walk right out that door. Unless she agreed. She was too desperate to let him.

"Fine," she agreed faintly. "Anything you want."

"As long as I'm here, we're together. We play this out, Ava."

The head of his cock teased her wet lips. Ava tried pressing closer, tried sliding him inside. But Elijah held the controls.

"Fine," she agreed again.

"Yeah?"

He plunged.

"Anything," she promised breathlessly as he drove into her. "I'll give you anything."

With that, she exploded. Pleasure, pain, power, all mingled in an orgasm that sent her flying out of control. Ava didn't know if she screamed. Wasn't even sure she still breathed. All she knew was that she felt good.

Amazingly good.

CHAPTER THIRTEEN

IT HAD BEEN a long time since she'd practiced the fine art of seduction. But Ava figured it was like riding a bike. Once you had the basics down, it was all about embellishments.

The setting. She looked around her freshly cleaned apartment; it offered comfort and privacy. Since the room was always filled with candles, scent and texture, she'd only had to choose the music.

The timing was good, she decided as she glanced out the window. Late afternoon would soon bleed into evening, with Elijah due to arrive just before dusk. A nice, sexy in-between time where anything was possible.

She checked her little kitchenette, where food waited, either marinating or prepped. Everything was good to go for a delicious, homemade dinner.

Now to get herself ready.

She could count on one hand how many times she'd folded herself into the tiny claw-foot tub better suited to a child than an adult of five-ten. But bubbles and hot oil were a part of the seduction ritual, so she folded and soaked in the scent of pomegranate and lily. And dreamed.

After careful consideration, Ava decided that dreaming a little was one of the important basics of seduction.

It elevated it from just being sex. And that, she decided as she slicked the frothy sponge down her leg, was her story and she'd stick to it.

Because she wanted to dream.

Of Elijah. The way his muscles had rippled as he met her in the ring the other day. The feel of his hands on her flesh as they'd sparred. His slick skin, the hard muscles of that gorgeous body. She made her living training, assessing, building hard bodies and wannabe hard bodies. But not one could hold a candle to the pure power of Elijah's.

The man was pure deliciousness. And that was before she even thought about his tight butt and the rigid power between those ripped thighs.

Mmm, Ava breathed in the steamy air, letting her head fall back on the towel she'd bunched behind her neck.

When it came to bedroom skills, Elijah was the master. Not only with his body, although each stroke was a work of art. But those hands. The way he moved his fingers, the way he could tease and torment one second with delicate precision, and the next force her over the edge into an explosion of pleasure.

And his mouth. She'd spent years telling herself that her memories of his kisses were an exaggeration. That he couldn't make her come with just his tongue alone.

Boy had he proved her wrong.

Ava squirmed, the water sloshing high to slap at the edges of the tub.

She wanted to reach down, to relieve the pressure building between her thighs. She was so wound up, so hot and excited, that it would take one dip, maybe two, from her own hand to trigger a nice, bubble-bath-worthy orgasm.

But she resisted.

Because she wanted to let it build. Layer upon layer upon layer of anticipation would add to the fun later.

And she planned to have a *lot* of fun later.

With Elijah.

Smiling, she let herself dream again.

Twenty minutes later the water was cold, the bubbles were gone and Ava was completely turned on.

She rode the mood, reveling in it as she dried off. She coated her skin with lotion until it felt like silk, then slipped into a pair of silk panties. Figuring she might as well continue with the theme, she added a silk slip dress the color of the sky at midnight. It skimmed her bare breasts, teased over her hips to flutter at her knees.

A few dabs of perfume, a few sultry smudges of makeup and a slick of wild cherry lip balm under the gloss. A trick she'd learned in college to add a taste of sweet.

Seductive enough?

Ava stepped back from the bureau mirror, checking her full reflection. *Not bad*, she decided with a glimmer of a smile. Elijah wouldn't know what hit him.

She'd make sure of it.

With taste in mind and a quick glance at the time, Ava got to work on the meal. She had a citrus salad chilling in the fridge. Now it was time to finish the main dish. She'd pulled out chicken pounded to the thickness of cardboard from the bag she'd marinated it in and, with a frown at her dress, tucked a kitchen towel into her neckline in hopes it would work as a modified apron.

After a brief vision of her darling little kitchen going up in flames of protest, she began the frying process. Something she'd avoided for three years of healthy eating. But, she breathed deep, it smelled good.

She tucked each piece of chicken—one small for her and three large for Elijah—into the oven to rest, humming as she continued with preparations. She'd forgotten how fun it was to cook for someone else. Her humming and enjoyment came to an abrupt halt with the knock at the door.

Ava froze. She'd been so worried about doing everything just right, she'd lost track of time.

"No, no, no," she chanted, letting the oven door slam shut as she hurried to the breakfront for the pretty glass dishes. She set them in place, and, ignoring the next knock, hurried over to her meditation corner for a lighter.

She froze at the third knock, halfway between the table and the door. Anticipation was one thing. Rudeness was another.

Ava hurried to the door. "You're early," she said in her throatiest voice as she pulled the door open and posed.

"I am? And I'm obviously underdressed."

Ava rolled her eyes.

"You're not Elijah."

"Talk about stating the obvious," Chloe said with a laugh, angling her head into the room to look past Ava. "Ohh. Seduction time."

Time. Damn. Ava shot a slightly frantic look toward

the clock. Leaving the door open, she hurried back into the room to finish setting the scene. Rich purple candles were centered on the table, so she lit those first, then tossed the lighter to Chloe, who'd followed her inside.

"Since you're here, why don't you light the rest?" Ava hurried back to the kitchen to deal with the frying oil, then pulled out flatware to finish setting the table. Two emerald napkins and a bowl of olives and it was ready.

"Everything looks great." Finished lighting the bank of candles on the breakfront, Chloe sniffed at the delicate spray of freesia spilling from a delicate vase centered on the table. "Smells great, too. Looks peachy."

Peachy? Ava finally slowed enough to give her friend a good look. Her face was clean of makeup, not even a hint of lipstick. She wore a faded black tee that bagged and sagged. Even her dreadlocks seemed to droop.

"What's wrong?"

"Wrong? I'm happy as a clam," Chloe claimed.

"Nothing says clam happy like kitty cats." Ava nodded, gesturing to the flannel sleep pants.

"I'm behind on laundry." Chloe shrugged. "I've been busy. You know, jobs, dogs, bicycles. It's hard to keep track of everything."

Except Chloe was the queen of keeping track of everything.

"Okay," Ava murmured. One eye on Chloe as she tried to figure out what was going on, she kept the other on the stove as she toasted slices of buttered garlic bread on a grilling pan, careful to get the grill marks just so.

"Whatever you're cooking smells good. Is that fried bread? I didn't think you fried food."

"Chunky chimichurri with toast points for a starter,

Milanesa Napolitana is the entrée with my mom's recipe for Berenjena en Escabeche on the side and Tortas
Fritas to finish."

Ava dipped a spoon in the chimichurri sauce, holding it out for her friend to taste. Then she grinned at
Chloe's confused expression.

"A twist on chips and salsa, breaded chicken and
marinated eggplant, doughnuts for dessert."

"Ooh. Mmm, that's good. I guess you've got a major
seduction scene planned for tonight."

"I wouldn't say major."

"You're gonna have to have a whole lot of sex to
ramp your metabolism high enough to process that
many calories, girlfriend." Chloe took a seat on the
couch. "That says major to me."

Hot, calorie-burning sex wasn't major. It was simply
pleasure. Trying to ignore the sudden tension biting at
her spine, Ava focused on spooning the chimichurri into
a vivid polka-dotted turquoise pottery bowl.

There was nothing wrong with enjoying the best sex
she'd ever had with the sexiest man she'd ever known.

"It's no big, Chloe. Good times, nothing else. I don't
believe in fairy-tale endings anymore. That keeps my
emotions safe, keeps me from being stupid."

Didn't it? Ava's fingers trembled as she added the
toasted bread to a platter of crudités.

"Are you sure?"

"Sure?" Frowning over her shoulder, Ava met Chloe's
concerned gaze.

"I'm all for hot sex, wild times and going for the
gusto. But…" Chloe hesitated. She dropped her gaze to
her flannel pants, watching her fingers pleat little kitten

faces. One kitten, then two, then she met Ava's eyes. "You have a history with this guy. A painful history."

"That was then. This is now." She didn't have to see Chloe's exaggerated eye roll to know how lame that sounded. "What we had, it was intense. And I never got over it. Maybe part of the reason was because we have to play this out."

She crossed over to join Chloe on the couch, setting the tray of appetizers on the low trunk, then curling up to tuck one bare foot underneath her.

"I need to get over it this time, Chloe. I don't want to live the rest of my life feeling like there's something missing."

"You think stoking that flame between you until it's so hot it burns out will fix things?" Looking as serious as a woman in kitty cat jammies could, Chloe snagged a carrot stick and gave it a contemplating stare before pointing it at Ava. "Some people think it's dangerous to play with fire."

"Some people are afraid to play at anything that poses a risk." She should know. She'd let fear dictate her every choice for years.

"I saw him today," Chloe told her as she chose a zucchini wedge. "At the gym. He came in looking a little rough."

"Rough?" Ava frowned. Had he strained his leg? She'd thought he was moving fine after their workouts the other day—both public and private, but maybe he'd pulled something? She glanced at the tall, slender chest in the corner. She'd have to choose some manly oils and convince him to lie down for a massage. She'd call it part of the seduction. "Rough in what way?"

"Kinda bummed out, I guess. He seemed okay when he first came in, but then these guys joined him. Big bruisers. They weren't members, so Mack had to clear them in."

Big guys?

Worry she'd thought she'd long ago left behind reached up to grip her guts and tie them into greasy knots. Had Elijah been recalled to duty? Was he gone? No. He'd let her know before he left. But how would he stay safe if he was hurt? If he was on duty, he was in danger. What if this time he was killed?

Her breath racing faster than her panicked thoughts, she wet her lips. "Did you get their names?"

"Mack called one of them Jersey and the other one Gibbs. They both had anchors tattooed on their shoulder. I figured they were Navy buddies of your ex."

Jersey Ambrose and Lonnie Gibbs, Ava realized as the tension ripping through her body eased a little. They'd graduated high school a year ahead of Elijah, and both had joined the Navy. They'd come for dinner a couple of times, but neither had really been part of Elijah's inner circle. Not like the men in Poseidon.

"Sounds like a Navy reunion," she murmured, pretending she didn't care. But her hands twined together, fisting one over the other until they gripped tight against each other.

"I suppose." Chloe shrugged. "Mack said they'd left the Navy. One of them works at the cable company. The other does something with security. From what I overheard, it sounded as if they were going to introduce Elijah to some people."

What was going on? Was Elijah recruiting old Navy

pals for something? Or was he just missing the excitement and wanted someone to talk to about it?

Mack had been there. He'd know what they talked about. Her eyes sliding toward her cell phone, Ava chewed on the inside of her lip.

"One of them, the one called Jersey, he asked your hottie to come talk to some people at the VA. Is that like a club or something?"

"The VA?" Ava wished she could laugh, but the memory of the VA, of the hospital, the loss of Dominic, they were all flashing through her mind like a manic slide show. "He probably just wanted Elijah to talk to a veterans group about the glory and wonder of being a SEAL."

"So your hottie, he's like a rock star?"

"Pretty much," Ava said with a twist of her lips. She shoved her hand through the loose waves of her hair, wishing she could shove the encroaching waves of depression off as easily.

Sex, she reminded herself. This was only about sex. Not about whatever Elijah was going through, not about his career and definitely not about their emotional history or anything that had happened in the past.

"Rock star or not, it's none of my business."

"Aren't you worried about him? The bummed-out part, I mean."

"If I'm sure of anything, it's that Elijah Prescott can take care of himself." After all, she'd spent enough years telling herself that. So often that every once in a while, she almost believed it.

"And you?"

"Me?" Ava did laugh this time, her misery dimming

a little in the face of her friend's sweet concern. "I don't need anyone to take care of me."

Not anymore.

"Are you sure? I mean, do you think you take care of yourself with this guy? The hottie, I mean. He's got intense all over him."

Didn't he just. Needing to recapture her earlier mood—and her justification of the choice to play this out with Elijah—Ava leaned closer and, with her most wicked smile, said, "Intense makes for the best sex."

Chloe laughed. But the worry didn't disappear from her eyes. "And if you fall for him again?"

Ava's smile faded with the taste of bitterness. Her gaze tracked to the small frame by the door.

Falling in love required having a heart. Hers was safely buried next to her baby. "I'm in no danger of that. Believe me." More than ready to change the subject and figuring she'd given Chloe plenty of stalling time, she arched her brow. "So what's up?"

"Up?" Chloe bit off the end of another carrot. Chewed. Bit again. Swallowed. Then shrugged. "I heard from Bones."

Damn. Ava looked at the clock. Was there enough time to call Elijah and delay their date?

"It's no big deal," Chloe offered, still staring at her carrot. "I mean, yeah, it's the first time I've heard from him since he left last spring. But it's not like I've been sitting by the phone or anything."

"I think that phrase has lost something in the age of cell phones," Ava murmured, gesturing to Chloe's only concession to technology, her flip phone.

"Maybe. But I'm fine. I mean, it could be a big deal

if I let it, but I won't." Shoveling her fingers through her dreads, Chloe took a deep breath. "I'm going to take some time off, though. Go to Guerneville, spend some time with my parents. Think things through, you know."

"You're leaving?" Ava sagged into the couch. She felt as if she'd been kicked in the gut.

"I can't keep pretending everything is fine. It's wrong to make believe that I'm happy." Chloe lifted both hands high. "My mom called for a drum circle. It'll be good for me. Some chanting, some meditating. Clarity, you know?"

No, Ava wanted to shout. She didn't know. Pretending was good. Make-believe was great. As long as it was working, why give those up to chase clarity? All clarity got you was pain.

But voicing that might trigger the tears lurking in Chloe's eyes, so Ava clamped her mouth shut and pushed to her feet.

"What are you doing?"

"Calling Elijah to postpone our date."

"No." Chloe dived across the room, grabbing Ava's arm before she could pick up her phone. "I'm packed and I've let all the bosses know. My parents are expecting me before dark. I just wanted to tell you in person."

Seeing the pout forming on Ava's face, Chloe shook her head. "Don't be bummed, okay. I'm doing exactly what you told me to do so many times. I'm getting on with my life." The blonde bit her lip before hesitantly adding, "Don't burn anything down while I'm gone, okay?"

With that and a tight hug, a vow to keep in touch and a promise that she'd be back before the end of the summer, Chloe departed. Leaving Ava to prepare for her night of seduction and worry about burning her life down. Chloe's words rang in her head, dimming the lovely sexual buzz she'd basked in earlier. A part of her still wondered if she should cancel.

Beyond Chloe's concern, she could hear her mother's voice in her head. Lectures on ladylike behavior. Reminders that discretion was more important than valor. Chiding, oh the constant chiding, to be safe, to choose the right path, to be careful. Always freaking careful.

Ava shoved her hands through her hair, tugging a little as if she could pull those words from her head. She hated those words. Hated the paranoid fear that kept her from living beyond the safe little world her parents deemed appropriate. She'd spent years breaking out of that world.

She'd be damned if she'd sink back into it now.

She wanted Elijah.

She wanted to enjoy the moment, without fear, without stressing about what-ifs or worrying about what people thought or what might happen to Elijah.

She knew he was only home for a few weeks—leave was never longer than that. She was going to enjoy these weeks, fear-free.

And if there were a price, whatever it was, she'd pay it later.

With his usual impeccable timing, Elijah knocked on her door. She recognized the rhythm. God, the man had rhythm.

Three short taps, pause, three more.

Focus on the rhythm, she told herself as she hurried

over to open the door. *Focus on the pleasure. Focus on now, dammit.*

It was a lot easier when she saw Elijah standing in her doorway.

"Hey, gorgeous." She skipped the husky voice this time and offered a warm smile. "Hungry?"

"Ava," he murmured. His smile slipped away as Ava skimmed one hand along her hip, up her waist to cup her breast as if offering him a reason to come inside.

His eyes locked on her hand, then on her face. Then Elijah moved in. Through the door, he angled his body to trap hers between him and the wall. He tunneled his fingers into her hair, gripping her head, pinning her exactly where he wanted.

Eyes still watching, his mouth took hers. An intense sweep of his tongue over her lips, demanding entry. Ava gasped. Her body wanted to melt. Her thighs trembled as moisture pooled between them in a hot rush.

One touch, she thought as his tongue swept between her teeth, teasing and tormenting. All Elijah needed was one touch to give her more pleasure than she could feel with anyone else.

To hell with fear, Ava decided as she reached up to grasp his head. The feel of his flesh beneath her fingers, his hair teasing her palms, it was so good. Too good to give up for something as lame as fear.

Slowly, oh so slowly, he pulled his mouth from hers and leaned back to stare into her face.

"Hello." His smile flashed, slow and sexy. "To answer your question, yes."

"What?" She'd asked a question?

"Yes. I am hungry."

Oh. Right. Food. Ava drew a shaky breath, then had to take a couple more because her heart was still racing so fast it sounded like a freight train roaring through her head.

"Come in," she said. As she waved her hand in invitation, she wondered if it was warning ringing in her head or just the echoes of Chloe's nagging.

ELIJAH MOVED THROUGH Ava's place, glancing around with a curiosity that he didn't bother to hide. Cozy, with warmth and a soothing sort of fun, it looked as if a rainbow had settled in to take a nap.

"I like your place. It suits you," he stated as he peered through the beaded curtain separating the sleeping area from her living space. The far wall was covered with sheer curtains shielding a blanket of fairy lights that twinkled like stars. His eyes lingered on the bed. Instead of resting on a frame, it hung on fabric-covered chains from the ceiling like an oversize hammock.

Would it rock, he wondered, in time with their bodies as he drove into her? Would it sway with her sighs as she curled into him in the heady aftermath?

"Suits me?"

Elijah shifted from one foot to the other, trying to ease the stiffness between his legs, and turned his back on the tempting image. Only to find an even more tempting image in the form of Ava. The mightiest temptation he'd ever faced.

Her hair tumbled over bare shoulders and muscled arms. The delicate curve and slender muscles of her body draped in nighttime silk. Her eyes were smoky, her lips wet.

God, he wanted her. But he didn't just want her for the night. Not just for sex—as amazing as the sex was.

He wanted her. Forever.

"Why do you look surprised?" he asked, staying on topic. "You decorated it, didn't you? You must have fixed it up to fit your tastes."

"It's very different from…"

"Our condo?"

Yeah, it was.

Images of glass and gilt, overstuffed furniture too formal for comfort filled his head. Even the kitchen had felt like something out of a fancy magazine, with its designer furniture and crystal glassware. Nothing like her little two-burner stove tucked in its bohemian corner.

"I like this better," he admitted, settling on the couch. Arms stretched along the low back, he sank into the comfort and nodded. "A lot better."

"You do?" Her face creased, she carried a plate of chimichurri and vegetables over to set on the low table in front of them. "Why?"

"That place never felt like you. The you I knew when it was just the two of us," he said, not sure he was explaining it right. "And it definitely wasn't me."

"Oh." Ava contemplated a thin slice of zucchini. "What would have fit you? Blue and white stripes, metal anchors and beer steins from around the world?"

Grinning at the image, Elijah skipped the veggies and went right for the freshly fried tortilla chips.

"I wouldn't say no to the steins." Mouth full of chip and Ava's pseudo-salsa, he let the flavors explode on his tongue, loving the heat, reveling in the spice. "But the rest? I'd be more comfortable in something like this, with all the warmth and color. The sexy comfort."

"Sexy comfort?" She laughed. The surprised delight in her eyes lasted only a moment. "Why didn't you ever say anything?"

Because he'd never thought of it as his place. Sure, he'd lived in it from time to time. He'd paid the expenses. But since Ava had refused to move south, he'd lived most of his life on base, only able to get to Napa on leave or long weekends. He figured that denied him the right to dictate decor, even if he had been so inclined.

"You seemed to like it," was all he said. No point digging at poorly healed wounds. "I did like the art on the walls, however."

Like him, her gaze shifted to the trio of framed charcoals, the only thing he saw in here from their old place. The images—a fairy, a mermaid and a moon goddess—all bore Ava's face. He'd drawn them on their honeymoon, and he was honestly surprised she hadn't ditched them.

"I suppose it seems egocentric to hang drawings of myself on the walls," she murmured.

"Why? Mack has huge framed photos of himself wearing skimpy underwear on his walls. I know guys with pictures on their walls of themselves getting awards, or standing on the field of battle. We surround ourselves with our identity, don't we?" He liked that, even if only in a tiny way, she saw him as a part of her identity.

"I hadn't thought about it like that." She offered him a carrot stick, first swiping it through the spiced black beans she'd creamed into some sort of hummus. Elijah nipped at the tips of her fingers as he took a bite. "You drew me as a fantasy. How would you draw yourself?"

She was his fantasy. But himself? He didn't know how he saw himself any longer.

"I don't know. I drew myself once as Popeye," he admitted with a laugh. "Another time I was He-Man. You know, the cartoon guy."

"The one with long hair?" Ava's smile was pure delight as she skimmed her fingers through his short hair. Longer after ten days of leave, but still nowhere near He-Man length. "I can't imagine you that way. Did you ever grow it out?"

"You're kidding, right? My mother was even more obsessed with hair length than the Navy is."

Smile dimming a bit, Ava seemed to hesitate, then force the words. "How is your mother? And your sisters?"

"Irritated that I'm not around to nag more often."

"They were always gifted at the nagging." They shared a commiseratory look, since overbearing parents had always been something they'd had in common.

The conversation turned to family, a few shared memories and tales of working at Mack's gym. Ava shared dinner along with her debate over buying in as a partner there, with Elijah offering his opinion that she'd kick ass.

By the end of the meal, he was both delighted and frustrated. The food was excellent, the company interesting and fun, keeping him on the edge of laughter one moment, his brain endlessly engaged.

But every time he brought the discussion toward his career, she veered away. He wasn't surprised. She'd always been reluctant to discuss his career. But he recognized the feeling nestled in his stomach alongside the delicious meal as disappointment.

"I saw a couple of old friends," he said, trying again as Ava brought dessert to the table. Tortas Fritas, he noted, his stomach only seconds before full, growling with anticipation. "Jersey and Lon. Do you remember them?"

"Sure. Did you try the dipping sauce? I added spice to the chocolate that I thought would be good with these." She held out a small, cherry-red dish filled with chocolate sauce for him to dip his crispy fried dough into.

"Good," he declared after a taste. "Really good. So, Lon and Jersey and I were talking."

"Did you want more?" Ava interrupted, gesturing with the chocolate.

"Nope. Thanks but I'm full."

"Let me clear this away."

"Can I help?"

"No, thanks, though. I'll just tidy it a little while you relax."

With a brush of her lips over his, she rose, turning on the music so soft rock glided over the room in a gentle beat. As she hurried into the kitchen with the uneaten portion of their dessert she chattered about the meal, about how glad she was he'd enjoyed it, about anything and everything.

Except what he'd been trying to discuss.

It was easy to recognize the familiar irritation scratching at the back of his neck. He'd felt it often enough during their marriage. He'd never pushed back then. Never tried to break down those walls she insisted on. But now he didn't see that there was a lot to lose by giving them a test kick.

When she rejoined him, sufficiently chatted out and looking ready for seduction, Elijah returned her smile. He brushed one hand through the heavy curtain of her hair, sliding it back to bare her throat, to unveil the smooth skin of her shoulder.

"I have more dessert to offer if you're interested in something a little spicier," Ava said, gliding her fingers along his chin, down his throat until she reached his pecs. Combing gently through his chest hair, she briefly rubbed her wet lips over his before leaning against the back of the couch in invitation.

"And if I'd rather talk a bit before diving into dessert?" he asked.

The teasing left her eyes, but her smile stayed in place. "Then I'd distract you."

That was what he thought. But his determination couldn't hold out against the distraction of her finger now teasing his nipples. Elijah shifted, angling himself over her.

"So let me make sure I've got this right." He lifted her arms over her head, bracketing both wrists in one hand as he pressed his hips against hers. "I'm good enough to have sex with, but that's it?"

"Isn't that enough?"

"No talking, no sharing our thoughts, no future?"

"We have now. Right now. Let's enjoy it," she suggested, her tone a hint away from a plea.

He should just shuck his drawers and enjoy. But Elijah couldn't let it go. "You really think you can keep your emotions out of it? That we can sleep together, come together, do each other over and over and over, and you'll feel nothing?"

Arching her back so her nipples lifted in sharp relief against the deep purple silk of her dress, Ava offered a slow smile. "No. I expect to feel a lot of things. Pleasure, delight, excitement, satisfaction. Should I keep going?"

Ava asked the question while licking the sparkles of cinnamon sugar from her thumb, her tongue glistening with temptation.

Elijah's body reacted instantly. He knew where this was going. And he knew how bone-deep stubborn Ava was when she'd made up her mind about something.

If he wanted her, wanted to spend time with her with or without clothes, it'd have to be her way. Or no way at all.

A part of him, the part that was so damned tired of following everyone else's rules, wanted to get up and walk away. Why shouldn't he? He knew the danger of spending time with Ava. She was his Achilles' heel. His soft spot. He'd handed her his heart once already and she'd thrown it back at him.

Free and easy sex? He was a damned SEAL. He could get that anywhere.

Then Ava shifted.

Lifting her chin, she slid him a slumberous look from beneath heavily lashed lids. Her lips appeared wetter, glistening and tempting his mouth to take them. With just the slightest angle of her shoulders, her breasts seemed fuller, tempting his hands to cup them.

He noted how perfectly he fit between her thighs. As if coming home. And damned if he didn't want to come. And, like so many things of late, he'd learned that while he could hold pieces of his life, he couldn't have everything.

He might as well enjoy what he could.

"Just sex?" he murmured.

"You up for it?"

"Babe, I don't think you can handle what I'm up for."

With one strong tug, Ava freed her wrists. She wrapped one hand behind his neck, her fingers teasing his hair where it was growing out of its military sparseness. She slid the other under his shirt, her fingers hot as they scraped their way up his bare chest to tweak his nipple.

It was like an electric shock slamming through his body, right to his erection.

"Show me," she demanded one second before taking his mouth. "Show me that you want me."

CHAPTER FOURTEEN

ELIJAH WONDERED IF there'd ever been a scientific study done to assess how crazy a guy could go on leave.

Because all this inactivity after several days was driving him nuts. Hell, even the activity he was getting—namely, hot sex with his ex—was testing his sanity. He couldn't say he objected to the changes in Ava. She'd always been sexy, but strong and willing to demand a variety of sexual favors?

It was damned appealing. And damned hard to keep in mind that it was only temporary.

Much like the rest of his life at the moment.

Elijah thrummed his fingers on his sketch pad but didn't open it. There was no solace or distraction to be found in those pages. Not since he'd broken the hidden code.

Maybe if Savino, Torres, Lansky or, hell, even Jarrett would return a call he'd at least know what the hell was going on with those numbers. He recognized the series, knew it was a Swiss account. Ramsey's Swiss account. So why the hell wasn't anyone calling to confirm that, filling him in on the status of the operation?

He glanced up as Mack walked into the living room, pausing to give the headless statue a pat on its ceramic ass.

"How's life treating you today?"

"Decent," Elijah said after another contemplative look at his silent cell phone. Five messages out there, and not one person could respond? It was enough to drive a man to drink.

And drink he did. Granted, it was lukewarm coffee, long overdue for the sink drain. But it had a kick.

"That's it? Decent?" Mack rolled his eyes as he dropped into one of the leather chairs flanking the couch Elijah sprawled on. Instead of his usual workout gear, the man was dressed in slacks and a white dress shirt. "Everything you've got going on and you can't do any better than that?"

Decent was better than frustrated, Elijah figured with a shrug.

"You stewing over that meet at the VA?"

"Nah, not stewing. I appreciated Jersey and Lonnie hooking me up. It was a good thing, going in to talk to the veterans, hearing the stories, sharing a few of my own." Sort of like group therapy in tap shoes, since he'd had to dance around facts, details or anything but the basic information about the work he did. Confidentiality didn't end when discharge papers were served.

"You get any ideas about life after the Navy?" Mack asked, his eyes intent.

Only the idea that he didn't see himself fitting into anything appealing. "A few thoughts," was all he said.

"But you and Ava are doing good, right?"

"Sure." *Good.* That was one word for how they were doing. There were a lot of other words that could be said for getting a lot of hot sex with a gorgeous woman, too. *Frustration* shouldn't be one of them.

But *frustration* seemed to be Elijah's word of the week.

He and Ava were having all that sex she'd wanted, and damn it was insanely good. It was like living the best of his old life with her. The laughter, the fun, the pleasure. More pleasure, truth be told, than they'd ever shared before.

She'd found an ease with her body that she hadn't had when they were married. A confidence in its strength, and in its power. She had a firm handle on her life, knew what she liked and had no issue speaking up about it.

Things would be great. If sex was all he wanted.

But she wouldn't talk to him. Not about anything that mattered. Not about the future. And most definitely not about the past. Given that their past drove their relationship, and he had no map to guide his way through his future, that made for some damned frustrating moments.

"Decent is good enough," he finally said, trading his phone for a pencil. He didn't draw, though. He just slid it between his fingers. "How's it going with you? Any big decisions on the gym expansion?"

Nobody's fool, Mack's eyes narrowed. But being a good guy, he didn't call Elijah on the subject change. Instead he launched into a long, rambling description of his plans, the state of the permits and his ideas for the future.

From the sound of it, the whole deal was wearing on Mack's good nature and stressing him out.

Elijah listened with half an ear, the other half of his attention on his phone. No way were they all out on assignment. Was it a group effort, this ignoring him? Was it orders?

And God, how pathetic was this? Giving himself a moment to be grateful that Mack couldn't hear his thoughts, since they'd earn him a smack upside the head from one of those shovel-size hands, no matter how tired his cousin was.

And for good reason. Self-pitying whining was for kids and losers. Elijah tossed the pencil from hand to hand, pulling his focus out of the ugly pit he was spending too much time in and searching for the optimism that'd once been second nature.

He'd almost found it when the doorbell chimed.

"You expecting anyone?" Mack asked, not moving more than to turn his head to the right.

"Nope. Want me to answer it?"

"Nah. My door, I'll get off my ass and answer it." Pushing himself out of the chair with a heavy sigh that said playing businessman was a lot more tiring to him than any amount of intense exercise, the large man lumbered toward the hallway.

With Mack out of sight, Elijah let his head drop back, resting on the cool leather. Was this Nic's way of making the decision easier? Blocking him out? Or was it a challenge, testing Elijah's willingness to push to prove he wanted to remain a part of the team?

He weighed the emptiness in his chest. He'd felt like this before, when Ava had dumped him. It was as if part of him was missing inside. His years of living without her had assured him that no amount of time was going to fill this hole, either.

Thanks to her, he'd learned that he could live with the emptiness. But that didn't mean he wanted to.

Part of his reason for taking leave was to decide if he still had it in him to serve. To assess his own strengths, mostly the strength of his commitment.

But what if they didn't want him to serve?

He was finally coming to the acceptance that he hadn't failed his team. But what if they didn't see it that way? What if the rest of the team thought the same as Jarrett did, that he was too damaged, too lost to handle the job any longer?

Screw that.

He'd been a member of Poseidon for a decade.

His service to the team, to his brothers, the brotherhood, had formed the man he was. A man of strength, of honor. And, dammit, of optimism.

He was a part of the team. He wanted to stay a part of the team.

"Cuz?"

Elijah lifted his head, blinked. Then, with a frown, got to his feet. "Yo," he greeted the men flanking Mack. "What's the deal?"

"Hey there, Rembrandt," Diego said with a grin, tapping a salute to his brow.

"Kitty Cat," Elijah returned, his eyes shifting to his commander. Both men were in civvies, looking chill and comfortable. Nestled just behind Diego was the blonde beauty his teammate was marrying, looking much less chill and a whole lot of uncomfortable. "Hey there, Harper."

"Sorry to do this, Prescott," Savino said, lifting one hand in regret. "But you've just been recalled to duty."

THERE WAS A lot to be said for hot sex on a regular basis, the wild edge of flirtation and simply enjoying life without expectations.

Feeling loose, her muscles singing, Ava strode through

the hard-breathing bodies that filled her classroom, offering encouragement here, a push there. She led her students through a tough, exciting workout, ending with a short cooldown, then hung out for Q&A afterward.

She'd just finished answering a slew of questions on breathing techniques when she noticed Joe talking to Terri, who looked as if she was going to cry.

It hadn't been *that* tough of a workout, so Ava hurried over to see what the problem was.

"What's going on?"

"Just dealing with a membership issue is all," Joe said, his platinum hair gleaming in its pretty, sleek tail. "Her membership badge doesn't cover her for these early classes. I was giving her the down low on upgrading or finding an alternate class."

Upgrading to elite membership, which was another hundred a month. Or taking one of his classes, Ava figured, since he scheduled his classes during afternoon and evening hours so he could hit the biggest segment of the membership. Unlike Ava, who arranged her classes for quality, not quantity.

"You're fine, Terri," Ava said easily, her gaze locked on Joe's as she stepped between them to shield the mortified woman. "I'm sure Joe didn't realize that you were here at my invitation."

"At your—"

"I have the authority to open my classes to anyone I choose, regardless of their membership level," she pointed out, giving a little wave of her hand behind her back. Terri, proving she was as smart as she was determined, took a couple of sidesteps until she was out of Joe's line of sight, then hurried away. "Is there a particular reason you're questioning that authority?"

"Nope. Not questioning it." Putting an easy smile on, he shrugged as if it wasn't a problem. But she could see otherwise in his eyes. "I do think it's a problem when every trainer sets their own rules instead of following a specific gym policy, but that's just my opinion."

"Since it's not Mack's opinion, I don't see that there's an issue." Ava kept her expression friendly. But she waited a long enough beat to get her point across. "Is there?"

"Nope. No issue."

But Ava could see that it was. Joe was the kind of guy who held strong opinions, and if he bought in as partner, ones he'd force on everyone.

Snagging a towel from the shelf, Ava dabbed at the sweat dripping down her cheek as she watched him stride across the gym. Friendly greetings followed him, as did more than one set of lusting looks.

Mack could do worse in partners, but Ava still didn't want the guy for a boss.

Nerves jabbing at her like a stick in the back, she debated calling her mother, giving the trust fund conversation another shot. But any visit with Celeste was bound to touch on dating sooner or later, and since Ava was rolling around naked with her ex, she couldn't in good conscious lie straight to her mother's face.

She'd phone and make that appointment with the bank to discuss a loan. Later. Right now, she had things to do. Or, rather, Elijah to do.

Energized and empowered by more than just a good morning workout, Ava hurried up to Mack's apartment.

Eight thirty. Late by Elijah's standards, but maybe— just maybe—she'd catch him still in bed.

She wondered if she'd ever felt this alive. Not in recent memory, that was certain. She'd love nothing more than to cap off a half hour of yoga, a session of Pilates and a vigorous kickboxing class with a heart-pounding round of sexual calisthenics.

A saucy smile playing over her lips, she inserted the key in the lock and imagined how she'd greet him. With soft kisses, easing him into their lovemaking? Or with wild heat? If he was in the shower, they'd go for water games.

Already damp with anticipation and excitement, Ava pushed open the door and practically danced inside.

And stopped short. *What the hell?*

A woman was curled up on Mack's couch, cuddled under an emerald blanket that Ava knew to be cloud soft and warm. Streaky blond hair fanned over the pillow, framing a face straight out of a magazine. Not only model pretty but society perfect.

Who was she?

Ava knew most of Mack's friends, and she wasn't among them. And she definitely wasn't the type he'd pick up in a bar.

That left Elijah. Was this someone he'd been seeing? Was that what he'd tried to tell her when Ava had shut him down a few nights ago? She hadn't wanted to hear about his current life. She'd insisted that there was nothing between them but this moment.

Despite their agreement, she'd kept things in a strict no commitment mode. Just a little sexy fun. They were both free agents, neither encumbered by expectations or rules or strings.

She gave a low growl. Well to hell with that. Body tight, fight moves choreographing in her mind, Ava stormed across the room. She'd deal with Elijah first, then she'd handle the blonde.

A quick glance showed her the kitchen was empty.

Seething, she headed down the hall. Before she could slam the bedroom door open, a man stepped out.

Her scowl flashed with puzzlement.

That wasn't Elijah. She blinked. "Diego?"

"Quequitos," he said with a wide smile, using the Mexican word for *cupcake* before wrapping her in those huge arms. *"Que pasa?"*

"Estoy confundida," she murmured. And she was, very confused. "What are you doing here? What's going on?"

"I'm here to brighten your day with my awesome company," he said as Elijah came out of the bedroom. Were they having some sort of top secret chat in there?

"You haven't changed," she realized with a laugh. Her hand cupped his cheek for just a moment as she appreciated the Latin perfection of his features.

"Oh, I've changed," he promised, grinning. She could see something in his eyes. The same soul-deep pain she'd seen in Elijah's. But in Diego she also saw acceptance. And, unlike Elijah, a glow of happiness. "I'm engaged."

"No way," Ava said, shooting Elijah a look as if expecting him to deny it. But he simply leaned his shoulder against the door frame and watched, expressionless. "El Gato is getting married? Seriously?"

"As a heart attack," came the response. But it wasn't Diego or Elijah who made the vow. Ava's jaw dropped, her heart shifting just a smidge.

"Nic?"

Ava didn't have time to absorb the shock before she was handed off to another set of strong arms. Nic Savino? Her honorary big brother? The man they'd named Dominic for?

Her heart racing with a combination of delight and fear, Ava pulled back to study his face. Unlike his men, Nic's Italian features showed no sign of wear or woe.

"You don't look a day older," she declared. How fair was that? Four years and not one of these men had aged?

"Ava, I want you to meet Harper. My fiancée."

Her hands still on Nic's arms, Ava glanced down the hall toward Diego.

For a second, her heart sighed because the man looked so incredibly happy. Then her gaze shifted to the blonde from the couch. She was even prettier awake. And very comfortable with the men of Poseidon.

Ava recognized jealousy when it bit at her with its tiny, nipping teeth. Just as she recognized how ridiculous it was for her to lay any claim to the team. She might have been the only woman welcomed in their hallowed circle by virtue of her marriage, but that had been a long time ago. And while Elijah and his friends might be standing in her world again, it wasn't as if she were a part of theirs any longer.

Pretending she didn't feel the digging thorns of grief at a loss she hadn't realized she owned, Ava shifted out of Nic's embrace. Calling on early training, she found her socialite smile and stepped forward to greet the sophisticated blonde.

"Hello, I'm Ava." She offered her hand. "I hope I didn't wake you. I wasn't expecting company. Or—" she glanced at the men "—a reunion."

"I'm sorry to fall asleep on your couch," the woman said as she stepped forward to clasp Ava's hand. "It was a long night."

Curiosity stirred, but Ava stomped it out like a bug. Harper was obviously in on whatever was bothering the men. Whatever it was, it was team related. Something Ava had never been allowed to be part of.

"Then you all must be starving. Let me get you something to eat," she offered the group at large, hiding her feelings behind her best hostess smile.

"Don't worry about it," Nic refused. "We ate."

"Then how about coffee?"

Avoiding everyone's gaze, Ava quickly skirted through the mountainous bodies and down the hall to the kitchen. There she took a second to lean against the counter and try to breathe past the knot in her chest.

She'd missed them. How could she miss something she'd spent so many years telling herself she resented?

"You don't have to serve them. I can make the coffee," Elijah said, his quiet words sneaking up on her.

"But I want to. Unless Mack is around somewhere. You know how he likes playing hostess."

"He cleared out for a while. Said he'd be back later on."

Meaning he knew this was official Poscidon business, too. Tucking that thought away, Ava gestured toward the living room.

"Go visit with your friends. This won't take long." Keeping her back to him, Ava surreptitiously wiped her cheeks. "Why don't you settle everyone in the living room? I'll just be a few minutes here."

They might have eaten, but she knew these men— or she had once. So while the coffee brewed, Ava dug into the back of Mack's pantry for the stash of cookies she knew was hidden there. She found a pretty enamel tray for the plate of cookies, cups, coffee and accompaniments. By the time she'd carefully folded paper napkins into triangles, she finally felt as if she had enough control to face them again.

A half hour later, she could have laughed at herself for worrying. Home, she realized. It was like coming home. The warmth, the acceptance, the familial bond. She hadn't seen these men in four years, but they treated her as if it had been just yesterday. It would be the same with any member of Poseidon, she knew. It was their attachment to Elijah that had brought her into their hallowed circle. But their loyalty, once extended, was forever.

The men of Poseidon were a brotherhood. Closer than brothers, from what she remembered. They'd essentially grown to manhood together, fighting side by side since their early twenties. Everything they'd seen, done, gone through—it only strengthened the bond.

Her eyes met Nic's as she refilled his coffee. Here, she felt guilt. She'd hurt one of his men. Reasons, circumstances, her own pain—the why didn't matter. The bottom line was she'd caused pain to someone Nic cared about. And Nic Savino never forgot a thing like that.

Unable to face that look, Ava excused herself and

hurried back to the kitchen under the pretext of more coffee. Once there, though, she simply stared out the window until she heard the front door open and close, the sound of voices fading.

"They had to go take care of a few things, but Nic asked that you stick around," Elijah said when he came in behind her. "He'd like to talk with you when he gets back."

"What's to talk about?"

"He didn't tell me. I guess we'll both find out."

What if she didn't want to find out? What if she wasn't ready for whatever was going on? Because something was, and it was big. Ava had spent enough time on the periphery of their world to recognize the feeling of something huge about to happen.

"What about you?" she asked. "Does this mean you're leaving?"

"Probably." His eyes searched hers, his expression intense. "But not for long. And not for good."

"Right." She tossed her chin.

A sound in the doorway interrupted Elijah's comeback.

"Elijah? Is my mom here?" A little boy with shaggy chestnut hair and the face of an angel rubbed his eyes. "I can't find her."

"She ran out to pick up a few things, kiddo. You hungry?"

"Starving. Like, I could eat a hippo or something. Except I wouldn't, cuz they're really cool." The boy's blue eyes shone with curiosity when they shifted to Ava. "Hi. I'm Nathan. Who're you?"

"Ava. I'm Ava," she said quietly, melting in the heat

of the emotions burning through her. Her thoughts drained away, leaving her mind buzzing and empty. Her anger sank into a murky puddle. Her heart cried.

From the look on Elijah's face, he saw everything she was feeling.

"I can handle PB&J." Digging through the cupboards, Elijah pulled out ingredients. "Or given that this is Mack's place, almond butter and chutney on a pita. Sound edible?"

The boy grimaced but offered a polite, "Sure, thanks."

Ava couldn't stand it. No child should have to eat that. "Do you like quesadillas?" she heard herself asking. "Vegetables?"

"Yes, ma'am, I like almost all vegetables. Except lima beans cuz they taste like chalk. Quesadillas are good. Way gooder than chutney. Um, what is chutney?" The last was asked in apology to Elijah, who offered a grin and a pat on the shoulder.

"Nothing you want on a sandwich, kid." He shot a careful look at Ava, who pretended to ignore it. She put every ounce of focus she had on making a snack.

She pulled asparagus, mushrooms, zucchini and red peppers from the fridge. Bypassing the Brie and the goat cheese, she went for the softer flavor of Monterey Jack. As Elijah talked about someone called Steve Rogers with the little boy, Ava quickly sautéed the vegetables, adding a dash of spice before spreading the softened pepper over sliced pita bread.

They just chatted along. Obviously they knew each other. How? Where had the boy come from? What was he to Elijah? It didn't matter. She didn't care. She cared only about getting lunch on the table, she told herself as she arranged the vegetables, sprinkled them with cheese.

Her heart pounding loud enough to almost drown out the conversation behind her, she tried to breathe as she slid the plate under the broiler. While the cheese bubbled and browned, she checked the fridge. Blocking the sound of the boy and Elijah laughing, she bypassed the cashew milk in favor of a couple of lemons and sparkling soda.

By the time she slid the pitcher of lemon soda and tidily plated quesadilla to the table, her movements were like a robot's. Automated, emotionless, ice cold. She tried a smile, but it was so stiff it probably looked like it needed oil. With a muttered, "Enjoy," she left the room.

She managed to keep her steps easy and even until she was out of sight. Then she ran. Hurrying into the bathroom, she locked the door behind her to keep Elijah from following.

The boy must be Harper's son. She'd overheard Diego say he was napping in Mack's room, but she hadn't been prepared for the sight of someone so young. She didn't know how long she sat on the edge of the tub bawling her misery out. But it was enough to leave her with a sore throat and swollen eyes. Finally, she sniffed back the last of her tears and scowled at the closed door.

Where was Elijah?

He knew she was upset. Why hadn't he come to check on her? Why hadn't he forced his way in here? He should be here, trying to make her feel better.

But, no. He had other things to do. Other priorities. Always, always other priorities.

Pain, four years rich, oozed through her, coating

her every emotion, seeping into her every thought. Her mind raced with images, memories that dug deep, ripping at her heart.

She thought of the worst time of her life, when she'd sunk into a morass of hideous despair too miserable to be real, and Elijah hadn't been there.

She could see her baby's face so clearly. Porcelain and cold, empty. Gone.

She had the vaguest memory of screaming, screaming, screaming. The baffled sorrow on the EMT's freckled face. The distant regret in the doctor's voice. The tearful sympathy in her parents' arms. But it had taken Elijah three goddamn days to come home. Who knew how long it had taken before he even got the message. He'd been off on one of his secret missions, saving the fucking world.

Yet here he was, there for someone else's little boy.

She burst into guttural sobs of misery, all her shields collapsing. Ava didn't know how long she sat on the edge of the tub, face in her hands, crying like the world was ending. However long it was, it wasn't long enough.

Finally, though, she was empty. And it was time to get back to her life.

The new life she'd built. The one where she was strong and capable and in control. It took her a good five minutes of yoga breathing to reclaim that part of her, and even then she felt as if she were hanging on to it with her fingernails.

But Ava was in control. She stood, splashed cold water on her face, then dug into her duffel for the cosmetics she rarely bothered with.

When she was sure she'd erased all evidence of her

meltdown, Ava pressed one hand against her belly to quiet the nerves jangling there and stepped into the hallway.

Quiet.

Why was it so quiet?

Where the hell was Elijah?

Tiptoeing in case she had to hurry back into hiding, she made her way down the hallway. Nobody in Mack's or Elijah's bedrooms. And the living room appeared empty. She peeked around the corner of the kitchen.

"Hello, Ava." Nic didn't look up, but he lifted one finger in silent command that she wait a second.

A part of her wanted to turn around and leave, just to prove she could. But she couldn't. Even as she rolled her eyes at her own timidity when it came to the power and command of the leader of Poseidon, Ava leaned against the kitchen door frame and sighed.

Whatever he wanted, he'd make sure he got it. So she might as well wait.

AFTER TAKING A moment to save his chosen driving route, along with two alternates, on his tablet, Nic turned his attention to the woman. Always beautiful, she'd grown even lovelier, rocking the buff and toned look just as well as she had her previous pampered appearance. But Ava wasn't any better at hiding her emotions now than she'd been four years ago.

And right now she was an emotional mess.

She'd worked some female magic on her face, so her skin was dewy fresh, the tone even. But makeup couldn't disguise the pain in her eyes or the determined set of her lips.

"Are you going to join me? Or stay poised in the doorway, ready to run?"

"I think I'd rather run," she said honestly. But after another few seconds' debate, she shrugged and joined him at the table. She kept her bag on her lap, though. As if ready to make a break for it.

She cast another cautious look around, but the room was empty other than Nic. "Where's Elijah?"

She didn't ask about the little boy. Not surprising, but her reticence didn't make his job easier. Nic didn't consider that a problem. He never expected easy.

"Recalled to duty." He kept his words easy and light, a sharp contrast to the intensity of his expression.

"And he didn't bother to say goodbye?" With a bitter laugh, Ava snapped her keys off the table, tucking them into the side pocket of her duffel bag.

"He didn't have a choice."

"There's always a choice."

Nic tilted his head to the side, giving her a long, unblinking stare. It only took a few seconds before she stiffened, her chin lifting as she pressed her lips together so they were almost as tight as the set of her shoulders.

"Do you honestly think that? That life's made up of simple choices? A or B? Here or there?" He pursed his lips as he considered that. "I guess that makes it easier to assign blame."

"Check you out, Mr. Marriage Expert. Did you take a course, Nic? Or is that something they teach in leadership training now?"

"You know me. I'm multitalented." His lips twitched at her smart mouth.

"And are you here to use those talents to meddle in one of your men's relationships?"

"Nope. Any relationship conversations are between you and Rembrandt."

"But Elijah isn't here," she reminded him. "Besides, you opened this dialogue. That means you have something to say on the subject. So say it."

Nic debated. He did have something he'd like to say. A few somethings he would have liked to have shared multiple times over the years. But he'd learned long ago to separate himself from his emotions. Feelings were about as useful as wishes. Good enough for kids and special occasions, but in the general day to day, they were a waste of time.

Almost as futile as stepping into the middle of a couple's marital battle. First off, he was too well trained to question the inevitableness of collateral damage. And second, a piece of paper might say differently but as far as Nic was concerned, Ava and Elijah were still just that. A married couple.

He didn't know how big a role he—or rather Poseidon—had played in their split. He couldn't afford to care. But he could—and would—do what he could now to give them a chance to repair that damage. And he had no problem using Operation Fuck Up to do so.

CHAPTER FIFTEEN

HER EYES FOCUSED on her finger as she used it to trace lines through the condensation on her glass for a few moments.

"So? Where is Elijah? And what do you want from me?"

Atta girl. "Rembrandt is doing recon and gathering supplies for a mission." Nic glanced at his watch, calculating how much longer until his men returned. "He'll be leaving in two hours for an undisclosed location until such time as he's recalled to base."

"Two…" The word seemed to stick in her throat. Ava gave him a wide-eyed look of dismay. "He's leaving?"

"He is." Seeing everything he wanted in her expression, Nic stepped into a role he'd never before considered. One that could be terrifyingly close to being termed *matchmaker.* "You'll have about an hour to say your goodbyes, to settle any unfinished business between the two of you."

"Or?" She rolled her eyes at Nic's raised brow. "You left that 'or' hanging there like a flag. What's the rest?"

"Or you can go with him."

Ava's mouth dropped open. It took her a few tries to pull it shut, and even then she shook her head as if she'd heard him wrong. "I'm sorry. Did you say I could go with him? On a mission?" She frowned. "We might not be friends, but I thought we were okay, you and I. Why are you messing with me, Nic?"

"You know, it's a funny thing about friendship. If it's real, the ties are elastic. They stretch and bend, but still bind. It might be four years since we were friendly, but I still consider us friends."

Ava didn't question Nic's assertion that he considered her a friend. She might not know why he'd think that, but she knew the man was brutally honest.

"You'd not only allow me to go on this mission, but you actually want me to take part in it?" she finally said, studying Nic's face carefully. Not that she expected his expression to give anything away. But a girl could always hope. "Why?"

"Rembrandt will be transporting a civilian to a remote location, offering protection and safeguarding until the threat is neutralized. In doing so, he'll have to provide food, care and entertainment since said civilian is a seven-year-old boy." He paused a moment, letting that sink in. And sink it did, as Ava's gut churned and her breath knotted in her chest.

"I figure Rembrandt's got the transport, protection and safeguarding covered. Meals, if nobody is picky, and entertainment is probably in his realm. But the care part? Especially on top of everything else?" Savino shrugged. "It'd serve him well to have a partner. Someone who'd have his back."

"And you think I'd be better than another SEAL?"

"Please." Savino laughed. "We're talking about a kid here. Rembrandt's the best we've got in that regard."

She'd taken a few hits to the chest in her quest for

her black belt, but none had the impact of those words to her heart.

"Wouldn't Diego be better? He's going to be the boy's stepfather."

"Torres is assigned elsewhere, along with Harper, the boy's mother."

Why would they split up mother and son? Ava's heart plummeted. "Are they in danger?"

"Possibly." Savino grimaced and corrected that to, "Probably."

"Why would you include civilians in this? Especially if it'd put at least one of them in probable danger?"

"Harper would be in danger regardless." Nic hesitated, looking as if he was weighing each syllable carefully before he said a word. "She and her son, to a lesser extent, have been targeted by a certain individual. Poseidon is focused on finding this threat and eliminating it. To do that, Torres and Harper will take point on this particular mission. While they do, a team will be assigned to protect the boy."

"You're setting a trap," Ava realized. With Harper as bait. "And this threat? Whatever it is, if it shows up? How am I supposed to be of help there?"

Why was she even asking? Ava rubbed her thumb along her temple, wondering what craziness had taken over that she'd even pretend she was going along with this wild idea.

"There'll be a detail assigned to the perimeter. Rembrandt will have plenty of defensive cover."

Aha. Ava laughed. "So I'm a babysitting assistant?"

"No, of course not." Savino patted her hand. "You're

a better cook. That puts you one up on Rembrandt, making him the assistant and you the expert."

Ava shook her head. "You're crazy," she decided, getting to her feet. It was all she could do not to jump up and run from the room, but she managed to keep her movements easy and smooth. "The last thing Elijah or I need is to be confined together in some remote location. And definitely not with a child."

Oh, God. Her heart ached. Not with a child.

"Before you say no, think about it."

His words stopped her in the doorway. Ava didn't turn around, but she did shoot a questioning look over her shoulder.

"You and Elijah, you're rebuilding something here. Right now the two of you are on equal ground."

Surprised, Ava turned. Arms crossed protectively over her chest—over her weeping heart—she waited to see what else he had to say.

"You've got issues to deal with—this is your chance. You want to know if this thing between you has any hope. This gives you a shot at finding out." Nic leaned back, resting the chair on its back legs and looking for all the world like a man who didn't care in the slightest. Except for the expression in his eyes. Those dark depths spoke of endless compassion. "You walk now, you let Elijah walk? You're finished. Are you ready for that?"

Was she? Ava bit her lip to keep from screaming. She didn't know.

She hadn't been looking for this. Hadn't planned for this. She'd been happily living the second phase of her life while ignoring the existence of the first. It made for a much tidier life, keeping everything on her terms.

Her greatest decision had revolved around the partner-ship with Mack. And really, no matter which way that turned out, the impact on her way of life would have been negligible. Just the way she liked it.

Then Elijah had stormed back into her world. His presence made it impossible for her to remain in her comfort zone, ignoring the past. The soul-deep, gnaw-ing need she had for him made it impossible for her to set parameters around their relationship. Just as it had been impossible to ignore her desperate need for him.

Oh, she'd tried.

With the determination of a woman stubbornly vow-ing to lose weight while keeping her daily fried-food fix, she'd tried.

But as easily as deep-fried grease layered on the pounds, time with Elijah peeled away her safety layers, revealing the depths of the emotions beneath.

God, she wanted him. More, she still loved him.

She didn't know if there was any way they could overcome their past, if there was any way to heal the misery they'd both endured. She wasn't sure she could face the demands she knew Nic was putting in front of her.

But if she'd learned nothing else over the last week and a half, it was that she'd never stopped loving the man she'd married.

She didn't know if that was enough.

But maybe she owed it to herself—and to him—to find out.

Still, she couldn't make any promises.

"I have to check my schedule, see if Mack can cover me. Look into a few things," she said with a wave of her hand to indicate whatever those random things were that could offer her an out if she wanted it. "I'll let you know."

"Good enough." Nic nodded. "You have two hours."

Ava's laugh was a helpless puff of air. "Look at you, Mr. Generosity with the time clock."

"First thing you should have learned about the military, Cupcake. We live by the clock."

"No. The first thing I learned was that nothing matters more than orders. Not family, not life, not loss." With that and the weight of the past dragging behind her, Ava left the room.

He'd answered so many questions. And left her more confused than ever.

ELIJAH HAD WALKED in on the aftermath of bombings that had been more cheerful and welcoming.

His gaze shot between his commander and Ava. Nic's expression, as always, was closed. And Ava's showed only concern—about what, he couldn't guess.

"Where's Nathan?"

"Spending some time with his mom before they split." Elijah angled toward the hallway to watch Ava storm out the front door.

"What'd you say to Ava?" he asked as soon as he heard the door close. "Why does she look so devastated?"

"Not devastated. Perplexed, confused and maybe a little frustrated."

"Nic?"

"I gave her the option to join you on this mission."

"You did what?" Elijah dropped into the chair Ava had vacated so he could sort through his own feelings.

"You're good with kids, Rembrandt, but let's face it—you don't have that mom vibe. Nathan's been through enough already. He'll be out of his element, away from the people he knows. It'd probably go easier on him if he has a little estrogen along to ease the stress."

Elijah cocked one brow.

"So you did this for Nathan's sake? So he doesn't suffer from testosterone overexposure?"

"An overexposure to testosterone has been known to damage boys his age," Nic pointed out seriously.

"Right. And it'll make him go blind, too." Elijah snorted and shook his head. "Dude, what's your game?"

"No game. It's going to be hard enough on the boy already. First there was his kidnapping a few months ago. Now he's going to be separated from his mother and the man he looks on as his father. And we're sending them into what he's likely to think of as a dangerous mission."

"Bait in a trap to lure out a treasonous SOB who doesn't blink at murder with a talent for lies and a proven desire to kidnap his own son?" Elijah put on his pretend-I'm-considering-it face, then rolled his eyes. "Be real. You're sending Diego and Harper to San Francisco, less than an hour away from the most likely place Ramsey is hiding. You've made sure that intel has leaked, not only through official channels but, holy crap, Nic, you put it on social media that they're taking a romantic pre-honeymoon trip. If you take Ramsey's penchant for violence and his obsession with Harper and Nathan, then throw in his hatred for Diego? It's more than dangerous."

"Exactly."

Fingers tapping on the table, Elijah considered his commander's face. There was something Savino wasn't telling him. There usually was, since 90 percent of what the guy did was confidential. But in this case, Elijah had the feeling that it was more. It was personal. Otherwise, he wouldn't ask.

"What's the rest?"

"You mean other than my little ploy to send you and your ex-wife off on a babysitting trip that will either permanently end your relationship or bring you back together?"

"Yeah, other than that."

"Why do you think there's anything else?"

"You'd send me on this mission blind?"

"I could." Looking tired, or rather letting the tired show through the cracks, Savino rubbed his hand over his eyes. "Lansky's tossing red flags."

"What the fuck?" His chair slammed down with a clatter as Elijah shifted forward before he lost his balance. "No way."

"His actions lately have been erratic, his movements furtive."

"You think he's Ramsey's partner?"

"I think someone is tapping Ramsey's funds, funneling the money into various offshore accounts and getting ready for a final sweep before they disappear for good." After a heartbeat, he added, "Whoever is doing this has serious tech skills. Serious enough to bypass the Navy's safeguards, to work around the taps we've set to watch the accounts."

"A lot of people have serious tech skills, including Ramsey himself." Elijah fought the sick feeling in his gut at Savino's words. He'd hated thinking his teammates were looking sideways at him, questioning his loyalty. He hated it just as much that they might be sliding those same looks at someone else on the team. "Nothing you've said points a finger at Lansky."

Savino acknowledged that with a slight inclination of his head. "He's turned secretive, taken to only using his electronics in private instead of setting up in the O Club with his laptop for gameplay. He's been gone more than he's been on base. His entire demeanor has gone through a change since Santa Barbara." Nic stared out the window at the cloudless sky. "We all know he's got a drinking problem. He's had one for years, and it's steadily worsened. But it's changed lately."

"He's drinking even more?" Elijah blew out a heavy breath, trying to comprehend how the man could drink more than MacGyver managed to and actually function.

"No. He's quit drinking. As far as observers can tell, he's quit altogether."

"Quit." *Shit.* Elijah rubbed his thumb and forefinger over his eyes, attempting to ease the sudden pressure throbbing there.

Alcohol and the military went together like peanut butter and jelly. Elijah couldn't remember a time that his friend hadn't drank heavily. Still…

"Everyone's dealt with life choices, life changes since the implosion of Operation Hammerhead," he pointed out. "Myself included."

"True. But I'd be remiss in my duty if I ignored the timing and implication of the choices made by a man under my command."

"Didn't we play this tune already? A couple of months ago, the SEAL team in general and Poseidon in particular were under investigation." Fury pounding in his head like a drum, Elijah shoved out his feet. He slammed his fists into the tabletop and leaned across it. "We were cleared. Why the fuck isn't that good enough? Why are you looking at us again?"

"Us?"

"Aren't you?" Elijah punched the table with enough force to crack the wood, the splinters flying, ricocheting off walls and countertops. "Don't you suspect me? Isn't that why you're all here? You think I had something to do with Ramsey's actions. Isn't that the reason for all the side-eye looks, the ignored phone calls? For keeping me out of the loop?"

Elijah was breathing hard by the last word, his heart racing with pent-up fury.

"Well." Savino gave a slow nod, then smiled. "Glad we got that out in the open. Now the air is clear, and you can move forward without carrying a bunch of garbage you don't need."

Elijah blinked a few times to try to clear the savage beat from his head. But even as it faded enough that he could see past the red haze, it didn't quiet completely. Instead it played out in the background like Muzak. Annoyingly present, but too subtle to fight.

"Was that deliberate?"

Savino simply leaned back, resting one arm across the back of his chair.

"Was what deliberate?"

"Pissing me off. Suggesting that Lansky is under suspicion. Implying that someone in Poseidon could be playing in the dirt with Ramsey."

"I rarely do things by accident, but to clarify, I wasn't suggesting, I was informing you that Lansky's actions are suspicious. I wasn't implying, I was telling you there are more hands than Ramsey's that are dirty. As for pissing you off," Savino said with a shrug. "My friend, you needed to get that off your back. You've already got a monkey living there. It didn't need company."

Elijah's gaze slid toward the hallway.

"You mean Ava?"

"Ava. Dominic." Ignoring Elijah's wince at the mention of his son, Nic continued. "Your divorce. Your loss." He waited a beat. "Your life."

"My life," Elijah ground out. "Mine to deal with or ignore."

"Yep." Nic got to his feet, his moves totally chill as he slid his tablet into his jacket pocket and ran a hand over his closely shorn hair. "Like I said, your monkey, your back. I simply kept another one from taking up residence."

Elijah had to talk himself down from fury to simple frustration. It wouldn't help to react from anger. He knew it. Still, it took chanting that in his head a dozen or so times before he could speak.

Before he could say a word, though, Nic stepped into his space. "Are we friends?"

"Shit."

"As a friend, I've stayed silent while you destroyed yourself over what happened. I stood at your side, never saying a word as you suffered, as you mourned. And if you choose to keep on feeding that particular monkey, I'll still be there by your side." Nic slapped a hand on Elijah's shoulder and squeezed. "But as your commander, I can't consider you in peak condition if you're carrying that other crap. You can't fully function as part of the team if you think your teammates are sliding you the side-eye."

"And if you're sliding it their way?"

"Really?" Nic arched one sharp brow. "Since when do you think I talk to hear the sound of my voice?"

Since never. Savino was known for being a man of few words. So Elijah shoveled the crap out of his head long enough to replay his commander's words.

"You're going to confront Lansky." Just like he would have confronted Elijah if he actually suspected anything. The same confrontation they'd have, Elijah acknowledged, if Savino heard talk he thought Elijah needed to know about.

Because that's what the man did.

He had his men's backs.

"The minute Lansky reports to duty, he and I will be having a chat," Savino confirmed. "After which any pertinent results will be disseminated among the team."

In other words, if Savino determined that Lansky was dirty, he'd let the team know. But if the man was simply having personal issues, they'd remain confidential.

Stepping away from Savino, Elijah shoved both hands through his hair and stared out the window. Sunlight glistened off the treetops, shimmered off the vines visible in the distance. Wine in the making, heated by the sun and cured in the cool evenings.

"I don't know what to think anymore," he admitted quietly. "My head spins out of control too often to ignore. I see things, flashbacks, nonexistent threats, fucking boogeymen. I can't control it. I can't stop it."

"Take this week. Deal with the old baggage—shake off that monkey," Nic advised. "You can't move forward until you do."

"You think dealing with any unresolved feelings between me and Ava, discussing issues we buried with our son, will cure the PTSD?" Elijah scoffed.

"No. But I don't think you can face those horrors and win the fight until you're whole and healed."

With that and a slap on the back, Nic walked out. Leaving Elijah to drown in the screaming silence of his own thoughts.

IF AVA HAD found anything in the last few years, it was the ability to channel everything—frustration, worry, doubts and fears—into physical release. Since sex had been off the table, she used various forms of fitness.

Yoga and Pilates to soothe and balance her thoughts.

Weights and strength training to weigh and consider options.

Taekwondo and kickboxing to release aggressions, work through fears and doubts.

One way or another, by the time she was through with her workout of choice, she was usually dripping sweat, with screaming muscles and a clearer mind. One session rarely gave her answers, but like fitness, it was a cumulative effort.

But right now, as she lay with her back pressed into the weight bench, pushing 110 pounds over her chest again, and again, and again, she desperately needed results.

"Working out some stress?"

Blinking the sting of sweat from her eyes, Ava glanced over. "Working through some decisions," she told Mack.

"Such as?"

"Are you telling me you don't know?" she huffed, the effort of pressing 110 and talking at the same time getting to her. "You've got a houseful of SEALs and all that oozing charm and you haven't got the deets?"

"I know the guys are fighting a bad guy. One who used to wear the face of a friend. I know that nice woman and her little boy are in danger. And I know you can help."

"No," she snapped, dropping the weight bar back on its rack and sitting up to glare at her friend and mentor. "I can't help. There's nothing I can do."

"That's not what I hear."

"Then you heard wrong. Elijah's the one who saves the world. Not me." She just sat there, helpless, doing nothing.

"You're not going with them?"

"Please? What use would I be?" Hadn't she already proven she wasn't cut out for keeping a child safe?

"For God's sake, Ava, they need you. Don't you see? You've turned yourself into a female version of Elijah."

"What a crock." Ava waved the idea away with a flick of her fingers. "That's totally ridiculous."

Mack gave her an intense look. Ava had seen it

plenty of times in her life. More often than not, it made her cave and agree with whatever was said because she was afraid to hear the next painful volley.

But not this time. What'd she spend years building up her strength and endurance for if not to face a few heavy truths?

"Just say it," she finally ordered, her muscles taut.

"Your entire life is a mission, Ava. You're on a quest to prove you don't need anyone, that you aren't the woman you were in the past."

Okay, so maybe she wasn't strong enough to keep the sudden tears from burning her eyes. But not letting them fall had to count for something.

"I'm not." She had to press her lips together for a moment to keep them from trembling, but her voice was strong when she continued. "I'm not the same woman I was. I don't want the same things. I don't need approval and I no longer believe in fairy tales."

She didn't believe in the myth of happily-ever-after.

"No. You channel your dreams now, call them goals as if that makes them more official and less fanciful." Mack gave an exaggerated roll of his eyes. "And you turn those goals into missions, step-by-step plans, each with contingencies in place. You've devoted your life to being the best at what you do, and as a by-product, helping others. To teaching them to face their limits and push past them."

"I sound amazing," she scoffed. "So what's your point?"

"My point is, maybe it's time to give Elijah a real chance. Not just a wild ride." His voice softened. "Maybe it's time to let go of the past and open your heart, Ava."

But an open heart was so easy to break. Ava took a shaky breath. Before she could respond, someone stepped into the room.

"Excuse me."

Ava and Mack turned to the woman in the doorway.

"I'm sorry, but I was hoping for a word with Ava." Looking every inch the lady in her stylish aqua skirt with its full pleats, a silk tank the color of strawberries and a pair of spiked sandals that Ava recognized as Giuseppe Zanotti, Harper Maclean smiled easily. She gave Mack's arm a squeeze when he bussed her cheek on his way out the door.

"Looks like you and Mack got to know each other pretty well," Ava observed, returning to her lifting as she pressed the weight in slow, measured moves. *Up, breathe. Down, breathe.* Three sets, twelve reps.

"He sat with me most of the evening, chatting until I got over my nerves." Harper moved around the small room, sliding her fingers over the various pieces of equipment as if testing the texture.

"I guess someone told him I'm a decorator, so he pretended to need style advice for his apartment. As if he needed advice. His place is great. It suits him, don't you think? Except maybe the headless statue." The pretty blonde wrinkled her nose.

Unable to focus, Ava carefully settled the weight bar back on the rack. Without taking her eyes off Harper, she angled herself into a sitting position.

"You said you wanted to chat," Ava stated, feeling like something the cat dragged in as she wiped a towel over the rivulets of sweat dripping down her cheeks.

"Since you haven't seen my apartment, I doubt it's any sort of decorating advice."

"I'm happy to offer some if you'd like, but you seem like a woman who knows her own style," Harper replied easily. "Mack said you're the one responsible for a lot of the design decisions around the gym here. Did you choose the color scheme at the front desk?"

"Mmm." Having spent years hearing her mother's opinion of her style choices, Ava braced herself.

"It's great." Harper went on to point out the various things she liked, complimenting Ava's design aesthetic for a few minutes while obviously getting her bearings. The woman seemed determined to be friendly and inoffensive. Ava wasn't certain what to make of that.

Since she already had plenty of decisions to make, she decided not to add figuring out Harper's intentions to the list. Instead she gave the woman a steady look. "I don't think you came down here to discuss decorating decisions, or Mack's taste." She dropped onto the weight bench again, this time tucking her legs under her and resting her hands on her knees in meditation pose. "So why don't you tell me what you'd like to know?"

"Mr. Savino—Lieutenant Commander Savino, I mean—he thinks Brandon is going to come after me. He said separating the two of us is the best way to keep Nathan safe, and to hopefully bring Brandon to justice."

"Brandon is Ramsey, right? The one they say committed treason?"

"Yes." Audibly swallowing to get past the knot in her throat, Harper nodded. "He betrayed the team. He faked his death on a mission by causing an explosion and is now in hiding. Living on the money he made selling classified information."

An explosion? Ava's heart stopped. "This man, Ramsey—he caused the explosion that hurt Elijah?" Her vision blurred, the edges misted with black as Ava tried to breathe. Her head filled with the memory of Elijah's nightmares, the tortured sound of the moans that came through his sleep when he was most vulnerable. She could see, without closing her eyes, the vicious scars left by the fire that'd feasted on his flesh.

One of his own men had done that to him? A teammate?

Horror burned in her throat, stung her eyes. She clenched her fists against the urge to hit something. This was the man they were asking her to help stop. And this man was after the pretty woman next to her, and that sweet little boy.

Strength Ava hadn't realized she had surged. "Let's get a drink," she suggested, gesturing to the door. She was desperate for something to cool her throat.

"The gym has a bar?" Harper exclaimed, looking impressed as she glanced around. "Is it like a juice bar? Is there wheatgrass? Nathan would get a kick out of hearing I'd drank something green made of grass."

Harper's easy laugh decimated the last of Ava's reservations. The woman might look like a pampered princess, be set to marry a SEAL and be raising a darling little boy—everything Ava had been once— but she couldn't hold that against her anymore.

Maybe it was the slight difference in ages—Nathan was a couple of years older than her little Dominic would be if he'd lived—but the thought of her son didn't rip at her gut like it usually did. So she was able to smile as she led Harper across the gym.

"More like a smoothie bar and a break room," Ava said as they followed the purple strip of carpet toward the door marked "Staff." "I hope you don't mind."

"Honestly?" Harper's smile flashed, her blue eyes dancing. "I'd be much happier with a bottle of water. The last thing I did to try to impress Nathan that I was a cool mom was go camping. I'm pretty sure I'd hate wheatgrass just as much."

Ava laughed. The nasty tension that had gripped her since she'd walked in to see Harper napping finally dissipated, fading into a surreal calm.

They settled into the relative privacy of the small break room, with its hot-pink walls, framed black-and-white images of Mack competing, and white plastic furniture. They sat together on the narrow couch—one Ava was sure Mack had chosen to keep his staff from enjoying long breaks—each with a bottle of water and the bowl of salted-chocolate almonds between them that Ava had purloined from Chloe's locker.

Harper told her about Nathan's father. The man who'd walked out on her when she was a pregnant teenager. She described his perfidy, his lies, and—although they both knew her information was limited to what Poseidon had allowed her—she filled Ava in on the mission.

"So there will be two teams. One covering Diego and me as we try to draw Brandon out, the other in hiding somewhere that they aren't telling me, protecting Nathan." Harper's smile was a little shaky at the corners when she touched Ava's shoulder. "I'm grateful that you'll be there with Nathan. He loves the guys on the team, but he's used to having a mom around."

Ava had to force herself to breathe around the pain stabbing in her gut at that comment. This wasn't about her, she told herself. It was about national security and bad guys and, more important, the safety of one little boy. "Are you really okay with all of this? Not knowing where Nathan will be? With being bait to catch this guy?" she asked quietly, her eyes locked on her water bottle as she twisted it between her hands. "Are you afraid?"

"I don't like not knowing Nathan's location, but I understand the logic. I don't like being away from him, but I know how Brandon's mind works and agree that he's more likely to come after me, thinking I have his money and can lead him to Nathan. It's a smart plan. Still, Diego's worried. He doesn't say much, but I can tell that there's a lot more going on. More than he's told me. So, yes. I'm afraid." She tilted her head back for a moment, staring at the ceiling as she blinked back tears, then met Ava's gaze with clear eyes. "Brandon's dangerous. He doesn't hesitate to lie, to steal, to betray or to kill. If I can help stop any of that, I have to try."

"He hurt you," Ava said, reaching out to take Harper's hand and give it a squeeze.

"He has to be stopped," Harper stated, staring through the single window into the gym. "He has to pay for what he did. To Diego. To Elijah. To the team, all those people. To the innocents who were hurt because of his actions."

"I can't argue with that. But setting yourself up as bait, Harper? That's dangerous."

Harper rolled the bottle between her palms a couple of times before shrugging. "Sometimes we have to put it on the line, you know? I can't do what Poseidon can. I'm not trained like they are. But I know Brandon. I know he's a bad person and he needs to be brought to justice. I'm willing to do whatever I can to help." Harper wet her lips and gave Ava a beseeching look. "But I can't risk my son. I need to know he's safe."

"Are you asking me for some sort of promise to keep him safe?" She hadn't been able to keep her own son safe—how could she make that kind of promise? "You'd do better to put your trust in Poseidon."

"But you're a mom," Harper said patiently, her eyes fixed on Ava's. The look in them, the overwhelming depths of compassion, told Ava that she knew about Dominic. That she understood the devastation. "They'll do their best. But it's not the same."

Lips pressed tight to keep from crying, Ava thought back to Mack's words, his comparison of her and Elijah. She had a thousand reasons to deny it, and she stood by every one of them. But now, right now?

She knew he was right.

She'd devoted her life to being the best she could be. Elijah was the best at what he did. She knew how to use her body and her mind to set goals, to break them into manageable steps and work toward each one. And she'd use that now.

Because she had a mission. Her mission was to stand by Elijah's side. To help protect Nathan. To make this Ramsey person pay.

For everything.

CHAPTER SIXTEEN

"Wow."

Ava gazed around Nic's trilevel getaway, hoping her jaw wasn't scraping the marble floor. The rich wood inside echoed the forest of pine and fir outside the glistening floor-to-ceiling windows. Beyond the trees she could see Lake Tahoe in all its gorgeous invitation.

"Do you stay in places like this on all of your assignments?" she asked the men surrounding her.

"Hardly." Elijah laughed. "Some digs, Commander. You've done some upgrades."

"You've been here before?" Ava asked.

"Sure, a few years ago we powwowed here." When she tilted her head in question, he explained, "A couple times a year, the team does an off-duty trip. Sometimes it's remote, sometimes it's wild. Nic rented this place once while we showed Reno what kind of damage Poseidon could do."

"Team-building maneuvers," Nic explained, mistaking her frown as confusion.

Gambling in Reno was a team-building maneuver? Something to ponder later, she concluded when her eyes were drawn back to Elijah.

He was different here. He still wore jeans and a tee, just as he had back in Napa. His demeanor was chill, his face scruffed with a sexy hint of a beard and his boots scarred and worn. But he wore an air of power that she'd never seen on him before. His moves were alert, his steps sure. His eyes searched, always watching, assessing. None of them carried weapons, but they spoke in Navy-speak, a sort of shorthand that used gestures as often as words.

Elijah looked to Nic for direction, but the rest looked to him as second-in-command.

Command looked good on him, she decided with a delicate shiver. She watched him give orders with just a word and gesture, sending Rengel and Ward to check the lower floors. Oh, baby, it was so sexy.

"Hey, Nic, can we hike? Are we sleeping inside or camping out? I could sleep in a tent if you guys were with me, right? That'd be safe, wouldn't it?"

She smiled as Nathan, already bouncing around the room with all the pent-up excitement of a kid after four hours in a car, peered out the wall of windows. Tousled hair stuck out every which way from under his ball cap and that gap-toothed smile of his flashed as he asked questions faster than anybody could answer.

Protecting that sweet boy was the reason they were there, she reminded herself. And protect him she would.

She knew she wouldn't be called on to put her martial arts skills to use. But for the first time, she understood what it meant to be willing to. To be ready to defend, to put herself and everything she could muster on the line to protect someone who wasn't her own.

She watched Nathan circle Nic, then Elijah, peppering them with more questions—were there fish in the lake, could they swim, was it cold, who was cooking, were there hot dogs—as if he didn't have a care in the world.

He did, she knew.

Back in Napa she'd watched from the other room as Harper, along with Diego and Nic, had explained why he was separating from his mother for a few days. Had outlined the dangers on a child-safe level.

She remembered the look on Harper's face when she'd described to Ava how her ex had abandoned her and their unborn baby, how his actions had resulted in poor Nathan's kidnapping. His rescue by Diego, Jared and Elijah. Ava's heart sighed as she recalled the expression on Harper's face when she'd explained how Elijah's regular visits and calls had done more to help Nathan's recovery than therapy.

There was no sign of concern, but this little boy was depending on them—all of them, including her—to keep him safe.

Failure, the one that haunted her, didn't matter.

Couldn't matter.

"Everyone pick a room," Nic suggested, gesturing toward the open staircase leading to the third floor. "Settle in—then report in ten."

The men held back, waiting for her to reach the stairs.

"I get first pick?" she realized, tickled at their automatic chivalry.

"Ladies are always first," Nathan told her earnestly. "That's what Diego says. He says a man, a real man, has manners and treats a lady like a queen. Cuz queens are the rulers—did you know that? Like my mom, she rules the house, even when Diego is there."

Rengel snickered. "Gonna have to ride Kitty Cat about that one," he muttered with a grin.

"Your Majesty," Elijah said, his grin just as wide as his friends' as he gestured Ava up the stairs. He followed, waiting until they were out of hearing of the others before sliding his hand along the small of her back. "You looking for a roommate?"

"Only if you're offering." She angled him a sideways smile.

"For you, I'm always offering."

"Then how about this one," she declared, settling on a corner room with a glorious view of the lake and, more important, a huge brocade-covered bed. "We can sleep with the windows open, breathe the pine-scented air and listen to the water below."

"Sounds romantic." Taking his cue from that idea, Elijah stepped behind her, close enough that she felt the heat of his body before he wrapped his arms around her waist. Ava nestled back, her butt wiggling against his groin in a teasing invitation.

The hand on her waist slid under her tee, warm and soothing as he gently rubbed her belly. He cupped her breast with the other, gently squeezing, testing the weight and squeezing again.

Excitement curled hot and needy in her belly as Ava's own fingers curled into her palms, as she forced her hands to stay at her sides instead of grabbing him. There was something erotic about keeping still while being pleasured.

"We only have ten minutes," she reminded him breathlessly.

"Bet I can make you come in five," he whispered before setting out to do just that.

"So WHAT DO you think? A traditional diamond? Bryanna's pretty exotic, maybe she'd rather have a ruby for an engagement ring," Ward mused, frowning at his tablet as he scrolled through the jewelry website pages. "You're the artist, Rembrandt. What do you think suits her?"

Chief Petty Officer Aaron Ward had been hit by love and hit hard. A once dedicated bachelor with no room in his life to commit to more than his team, he'd met Bryanna Radisson a few months back, and that had been it for the big guy. Now he was putting all that dedication toward driving everyone nuts with his talk about his lady, their future and requests for advice.

"Why don't you ask her instead of me, Bulldog? Better yet, ask Ava. She's a woman. She'd know better than I would what her kind likes," Elijah suggested, too busy swabbing down the kitchen to look at sparkly things.

"Really?" Aaron glanced over in surprise. "You want me bringing up engagement rings to the woman you're seeing? Usually that sort of thing is off-limits. It might put ideas in her head, you know."

"Ideas?" Done with the counters, Elijah tossed the sponge in the sink, then leaned back against it with his arms crossed over his chest. "Like what? Marriage ideas?"

"You never know."

As if. He could barely get her to talk about next week, when he returned to active duty. As far as he could tell, getting engaged, getting remarried, they weren't on Ava's radar. But he wasn't about to share that little piece of information.

"Dude, you were at my wedding," Elijah reminded him with a baffled laugh. "You know damned well the marriage idea is always there, spinning around like a category-five hurricane just waiting to land. Even if it wasn't, I'm pretty sure marriage ideas float through any and every woman's mind at least once if they're with a guy and the sex is good."

His fingers tapping on his tablet, Aaron nodded, then waited a beat. "Maybe she's not thinking about it with you because the sex isn't any good," he deadpanned.

Laughing, Elijah dived at him. He'd gotten only a couple of punches in—damned if the Bulldog wasn't aptly named, the guy was as sturdy as a brick wall—when Nic called time-out.

"Gentlemen, let's act like we're still Poseidon and show some dignity," Nic suggested, his face impassive.

The men shifted, their smiles fading as they took their seats. They came to attention as Savino shifted into command mode. He outlined their duties, sketched out the timeline.

"Ward, you and Prescott will continue to monitor electronics. Watch changes at thirteen hundred hours, when Prescott will take Rengel's place on kid watch and Ward, you can take a break while Rengel and I take electronics. Use that time to shop for wedding rings if you have to."

Elijah's lips twitched at Savino's easy sarcasm, but he managed to keep the smirk off his face. No point inviting that sarcasm to aim in his direction.

"Perimeter checks every hour," Savino continued,

issuing orders to each man that'd take them through to the following morning. When he finished, he paused to ask, "Any questions?"

Nada.

Obviously the reaction he'd expected. He nodded and, his signal that they were shifting into work mode, took a seat.

"Rengel has been apprised of the situation, so now I'll bring the two of you up to date," he said, leaning back in the chair. "Operation Fuck Up is about to go critical. As you both know, thanks to Rembrandt, here, we were able to access Ramsey's Swiss account and shut it down."

Nic's smile was as sharp as a blade as he added, "Apparently this pissed him off."

"He reacted?" Elijah straightened, his body hitting full alert. "You're sure it's him this time? Not another fan boy like Adams?"

"According to the intel we've been able to pull, nobody else had access to that account except him. Granted, our intel isn't as tight as I'd like, but I believe it's solid."

It would be tighter if he'd bring Lansky in, let the man work his computer magic. Nobody knew electronics like Lansky. For the first time in the history of their service, Elijah wanted to argue with his commander. He knew what it was like to feel mistrusted. He didn't want any part of sliding a side-eye at one of their own.

But instead of pointing that out, he waited.

Savino finished his briefing, they all wrapped up the discussion. And Elijah still waited. Ward shifted the conversation to honeymoon venues, Nic and Elijah exchanged eye rolls. He kept on waiting.

Until it was just the two of them, him and Nic, in the bright, modern kitchen.

"What's up?" Nic asked, heading to the fridge. He pulled out a soda, held it up. At Elijah's nod, he tossed it to him before grabbing another.

"You're crippling us," Elijah said baldly, rolling the icy can between his palms. "Without Lansky, we're operating at half-mast."

"Perhaps. But if Lansky's the mole, without him we're right and tight."

"Do you honestly think he's dirty?"

When Savino hesitated, Elijah threw the commander's oft-used words back at him. "What does your gut say?"

Savino dropped back into his chair with a sigh.

"My gut says that we could use him. That he's one of us and he'd never screw his brothers." He popped the tab and took a long drink, then shrugged. "But my orders on this mission are specific, as is the allotted crew."

Elijah's fingers tapped the can, but he didn't pop the top. His gaze shifted to the sight just outside their window. Ava was following instructions, keeping Nathan in view.

Orders or not, he trusted Lansky with his life. He'd even trust him over his career. But Nathan's safety? Ava's? Those were too precious to risk. He opened his can, lifted it in a toast and nodded. "To orders."

The cans clicked with a dull thud.

"It's what we do, my friend. We're indoctrinated to push harder, to excel, to win at all costs. But under it all, we follow orders. The chain of command might choke from time to time, but it serves a purpose. And that purpose is higher than our personal preferences. At least, it is if we serve."

Nic was right.

Elijah almost smirked at that, since he didn't think there'd ever been a time that Nic *hadn't* been right. That was why they followed him. That was why he led with such skill.

If they didn't follow orders, they were no better than the treasonous asshole they were trying to capture. He'd bet Ramsey had all sorts of gut feelings to justify his choices.

A man couldn't serve with that kind of thinking. And they were here to serve. To follow orders, in this case, keeping a little boy safe.

That's what it was all about.

Keeping people safe.

Elijah's gaze shifted to the window again.

To Ava laughing as she taught Nathan some basic kicks and punches. She was doing a great job of keeping the kid entertained, making sure he felt safe while distracting him from worrying about a man who wouldn't so much as blink before destroying them. Any of them, including the boy.

"It's not easy putting duty over emotions, is it?" Nic asked quietly. "I suppose that's why so many of us go it alone. You were the bravest of us, marrying Ava. You believed that you could do both. That takes guts."

"Faith is more like it."

"Faith, then. And serious guts."

"I might be the first, but I won't be the last," he

pointed out. "What will happen to Poseidon if one by one we start retiring?"

"Nothing lasts forever, my friend," Nic surmised as he got to his feet. He clapped a hand on Elijah's shoulder before heading out of the room. Before going through the door, he added, "The trick is knowing if you're leaving at the right time, for the right reason. If not, that leaving is going to be hell to live with."

"Wow, Ava. You make really good omelets. Can I have another one? A whole one? With more of that dip stuff on top?"

"Me, too, Ava." Paul Rengel grinned, his dark eyes dancing as he held up his plate, just as licked clean as Nathan's. "The dip stuff was really good."

Laughing, feeling lighter than she had in years, Ava moved to the counter to check the bowl of guacamole she'd made as garnish.

"Two more Spanish omelets coming up," she said, and got to work on breakfast seconds. Since Elijah had already had his before he'd gone outside to walk the perimeter, she didn't worry about running out.

"It's nice of you to cook for us," Nic said, topping off her coffee before taking the pot to the table. "We're used to Chug's cooking, which leaves a lot to be desired."

"Hey," Paul objected with a laugh. "Not saying you're wrong, but hey anyway."

"Why do they call you Chug?" Nathan wondered, planting his elbows on the table and leaning forward with that gap-toothed grin of his. "Are you like a choo-choo train? You know, chug-a-chug, chug-a-chug?"

"I ram through the enemy like a freight train, sure.

But my call sign comes from, um, well…" His face a study of discomfort, Paul shot a pleading look around the table. Obviously bragging about his drinking prowess to a seven-year-old wasn't cool, but he didn't quite know what to say.

Ava grinned as she cooked, waiting to see how they handled it.

"It's the sound he makes when he drinks," Nic said, coming to his rescue.

"What's a call sign?"

"A nickname."

"What's yours?"

"Kahuna," Nic said, sounding a little less amused now.

"That'd be the Big Kahuna," Aaron corrected. "Because he's the boss. I'm Bulldog. Not because I look like one, not with this pretty face. But because I'm stubborn."

"What's Diego called?"

"Kitty Cat."

"El Gato," Nic corrected, ruffling the boy's hair. "It's cat in Spanish. We call him that because he moves with stealth like a cat, and his mom and dad were from Mexico."

"That's really cool. And Elijah is called Rembrandt, right? Cuz he's an artist? He does great drawings. He made one of the Quinjet, with me and Captain America standing in front of it. It's supercool. Mom put it in a frame for me cuz she said it's special."

Ava's smile dimmed a little as Nathan continued. She hadn't realized how close Nathan and Elijah were. He was so good with the boy. Just as he'd been good with—

"You okay?" Nic asked.

Surprised, not sure when he'd joined her at the stove, Ava glanced over.

"Sure. I'm great."

"We really do appreciate the meal. Your cooking is definitely above and beyond."

"It's nice to see my early training coming back so quickly," she said, adding eggs to the sautéing vegetables and giving the pan a shake. "I'm all for healthy eating, but I've got to tell you, it's just not the same making egg-white omelets with spinach puree."

"Eww," Nathan said with a child's refreshing honesty. Trying to shake off the gloom chasing her, Ava laughed.

"I don't burn nearly as many calories as these guys do, so I have to be a little more careful with my calories," she explained as she plated the omelets, one of them boy-size.

"You ever want to move south, we'd line up for training and meals. This grub is way better than sub-grub or anything we'd get in the chow hall."

Move south? Remain connected to Poseidon? In other words, stay with Elijah. Ava didn't know how to respond to that. Not when her heart and her head were screaming one thing, while the little voice—the one steeped in fear—warned another.

"I'm sure you've got some awesome cooks in your area," she demurred. "And I doubt any training I could devise would be on par with yours."

To Ava's relief, the conversation turned to Mack's gym and her work there, to the type of workouts the guys liked best and, of course, Aaron's ode to his new lady love, a pretty brunette named Bryanna that he planned to marry. The way the men bandied about proposal ideas told Ava that they were completely on board with the idea of yet another of their own tying the knot.

She wasn't sure how to take that. She'd never realized these men were so pro-relationship. Not that she'd heard tell of anyone protesting hers when she and Elijah were married, but her mother had warned her time and time again that his friends would split them up. It seemed to her as if they were more focused on keeping them together.

Glad to leave cleanup to the crew, she took her coffee and thoughts out to the wraparound back porch. Glossy wood railings did nothing to obstruct the gorgeous view of the lake through the trees. It was like sitting in an enchanted forest, she decided, leaning back in the cushioned rocking chair.

Gorgeous, peaceful and just a little magical.

She wasn't sure how it'd happened.

She couldn't pinpoint the moment, wasn't even sure if there was a single one or it'd simply been a series of moments all piled together.

But sitting on the wide back porch overlooking the sun rising in a gentle glow over the lake, coffee steaming from the mug in her hand and the sound of a child's laughter in the air, she couldn't deny it.

She was happy.

Snuggling a little deeper into Elijah's flannel shirt, she stretched her feet out in front of her and contemplated the thick wool socks keeping her toes warm in the early morning air.

Happy.

She was happy being here, in Tahoe, in a gorgeous house with a stunning view.

She was happy spending time with Elijah's friends again—his true family, and seeing the teamwork, the shorthand conversations and the bone-deep respect between the men.

She was happy falling asleep in Elijah's arms, sated from the heat of their lovemaking. Waking with his body covering hers with warmth and passion. Talking with him about the little things, even as her mind grappled to accept the big ones.

And she was even happy watching him with Nathan. Seeing the kind of father he would have been. The pain was still there, of course. She finally accepted that it'd never go away. But it wasn't like a knife to her heart any longer. And for that, yes, she was happy.

SHADOWS ENGULFED HIM, smothering the light, smothering hope. He sucked in air, but there was none to be had. Instead it was fire.

Flames surrounded his body, hot and biting and filled with all the furies of hell. They ate into his flesh, ripping and tearing it to the bone. Heat engulfed, roaring with screams of the damned, with warnings of the futility of trying.

But he couldn't give up. He wouldn't go. Not like this.

He called up all his strength to push upright. He couldn't shake off the fire, but he could escape it, dammit. He fought his way through the inferno, running, angling left and then right. *Moving. Keep moving.*

"Elijah!"

His breath came in labored pants. Sweat poured over his skin, cooling, burning. Salvation was close. He knew it. He'd seen it. He just had to find it.

It was up to him.

"Elijah, please. You have to wake up."

His eyes snapped open.

Ava.

He blinked, squeezing his eyes tight against the sweat dripping off his brow. When he opened them, she was still there. Peering down at him in the dusky moonlight, the swathe of hair curtaining her face doing nothing to hide her concerned expression.

Damn.

His fists clenched at his sides.

Damn it all to hell.

"Are you okay?" Her voice trembled almost as much as the hands that were racing over his chest, as if checking for injuries.

"Yeah. Fine."

"Are you sure? Do you need anything? Can I get something? What will help?"

He could use a drink—even ice water. He wouldn't mind a shower to wash away the thick coating of sweat on his skin. And he'd give anything for some fucking privacy so he could pull himself together.

But the look on her face told him he wasn't getting any of that. "I'm fine, Ava. Just a dream. Go back to sleep."

"That wasn't a dream. Dreams don't leave you shaking and moaning in a pool of your own sweat," she said.

Probably not. But it sounded a lot better than flashback, didn't it?

"I'm fine," he said again, tempering his tone as he realized how horrible it must have been for her to be woken like this.

"You're not. You can't be." She pushed into a sitting position and flipped on the bedside light. She used both hands to shove her hair back so she could get a better look at his face.

"Leave it alone."

"Maybe you could talk to Nic, or one of the other guys," she suggested, unable to leave it alone. "You're obviously suffering. I'm sure they won't mind. Should I wake someone?"

"I don't need to talk to anyone," he said dismissively, slapping the light off. As if that would shut her up.

"You need to do something about the nightmares, Elijah. You can't keep suffering through them."

"I've suffered through them for a decade and managed fine. Now I'd like to go back to sleep."

Outraged, Ava flicked the light right back on. Ignoring his groan, she glared. "You never had nightmares before. Not when we were married. This has something to do with that mission, the one that landed you in the hospital. Admit it."

"God." He pulled the pillow over his head.

She pulled it right back off.

He tried a different tact.

"You know, once the sight of a naked woman insisting I stay awake would have been hard to resist. But unless you're offering any sort of kinky sex, I'm going to call this a first and pass."

"Elijah."

"Fine. You want the truth? I did have nightmares

when we were married. Anyone who's fought, who's seen what we see, they revisit it on a regular basis in their sleep. Throw in a few flashbacks to the sight of my son in a coffin and there's plenty of fodder for a tortured psyche. It is what it is."

Her mouth dropped open, but no words came out.

"You had nightmares when we were together? In the same bed, together?" she asked when she found her voice again.

"So?"

"So how could I not know that?"

"Because you didn't want to know, Ava." At her stricken expression, Elijah rubbed his hands over his face. Dropping them, he pushed into a half-sitting position to rest on one elbow and gave her arm a rub. "I didn't want you to know. It was my deal, okay? My problem."

"Your problem?"

Too tired, too worn out from the dream to temper his words, he gave her the honest truth. "Yes, my problem. Because that's how you wanted it. You said that when we were together, you wanted me to focus on our marriage. Not on my career."

"Because hearing about your career terrified me. Most of your life was top secret. I never knew what you were doing, I had no idea where you were half the time. All I knew was that you were in danger."

So she'd said hundreds of times. In that same tone of hurt accusation. He'd always took it on the chin, because that was what a man did. He was trained to do his best, to give his all and to roll with the punches in silence.

But right now, his soul was raw. He simply didn't have the strength to let her words slide.

"Ava, you never wanted to be involved in parts of my career that I *could* share. You wouldn't talk about training, my studies, or travel. You wouldn't even go with me to Hawaii," he reminded her, still baffled by that one. "If you didn't want to be involved with the easy side, why would I assume you wanted to know anything about the dark side?"

"But I'm here," she protested half-heartedly.

"Why, Ava?" he asked, eyes pinned on her face. "Why, exactly, are you here? You still haven't told me why you came along on this little venture."

"I…um…" She glanced at the door as if considering doing something about that, then blew out a breath. "Does it matter?"

Yeah. Oh yeah, it matters. But because it did, because it mattered so damned much, Elijah didn't press. He couldn't. Not when she looked like she was about to cry. "What matters is that you are," he said honestly, sliding his finger along the sweet curve of her cheek. "What matters is that you want to be."

"And if it's a mistake?" she whispered.

He leaned in, nuzzling the soft skin at her throat.

Mmm, she smelled good.

"Babe, it is what it is," he said again, leaning back to watch her face as he slid his hand over the tempting curve of her breast. "But if you're worried about me having dreams, maybe you could try a little distraction."

"Distraction?" she repeated, passion heating her eyes as she slid down onto the mattress. She didn't look pacified by his answer, but she was obviously willing to let it go. Which was all he wanted.

Well, almost all.

"About that kinky sex…"

CHAPTER SEVENTEEN

"You're sure he's moving?"

"Him. Or someone using his credit card." Ward shrugged. "Given that no one's seen Ramsey alive in half a year, your guess is as good as mine who it is. But the card is new, tied to one of the marked bank accounts."

Most of Elijah's attention on the papers Ward had just given him, he listened with half an ear to the conversation floating around the small, well-appointed office Savino had declared HQ.

"What else did you get out of that intercepted transmission?"

"Someone using one of the various email accounts that Lansky uncovered sent a message, he wants an update and is pissed that his funds went missing," Ward surmised. "There's no signature, the message is sent to a dummy account that was shut down within an hour of it being read."

"Well, someone took the bait. The question is, who."

"You want more, ask Rembrandt. Cryptology is his specialty."

"Prescott?" Savino prodded.

Setting his pencil down, Elijah finally looked up to meet his commander's eyes.

"You want the who? If I were a betting man, I'd put it all on this being Ramsey."

"And if you weren't a betting man?"

"I'd put three-quarters of it."

Busy checking the feed from the outside cameras, Rengel laughed.

"Ramsey isn't as smart as he thinks he is. He's not skilled at creating new identities, doesn't know how to go under," Elijah pointed out with a slight sneer. Because while that wasn't a part of standard military training, if the guy was any kind of smart, he'd have figured it out. "He might have bought a fake identity or three, might bounce the transmissions as much as he can, but he's tapping his own accounts for funds."

"And his partner?"

Elijah grabbed the pencil again, tapping it on the table in an attempt to shake off the sick feeling. "I haven't gone through all of this, just the top layer. I need to keep digging, go deeper than a surface look."

"Give me what you've got so far."

"Whoever he's in contact with is good. Superior, in fact. They understand electronics. They have access to quality equipment. And they are playing Ramsey."

Elijah felt like a traitor giving the report. All it needed was Lansky's photo attached to it. From the sick look on the faces around him, he knew the team disliked hearing the information as much as he hated sharing it.

"Keep digging," was all Savino said, though. "In the meantime, can you tell if he's taken the bait? Is he going after Torres?"

Although he'd already memorized them, Elijah

skimmed the decoded emails. "The message says he's heading for Northern California to take back what's his. It isn't specific about where in California or what he's after. He's furious that we found his secret account. Since he's sure we're not smart enough to break his code, he accuses this person of betraying him."

Savino's jaw tightened, the only sign of concern that Ramsey hadn't taken the bait and was coming for Nathan instead. But they all knew that the only way he'd know to come to NorCal was if someone tipped him off.

"Anything else?"

"The message bounced a dozen times between here, Timbuktu and every point in between. The best I can do without better equipment—" namely, the equipment on base where their little secret mission would be exposed "—is that he's emailing someone on the West Coast. California, probably, but possibly Oregon."

"That's good enough."

Enough for Savino to start issuing orders.

Without question, without hesitation, the men moved to obey. Elijah, since he'd been ordered to wait, remained behind.

"Ava's got Nathan?" Savino asked. From where they stood, they could both see the pair practicing tai chi on the upstairs landing. Woman led boy in easy, smooth moves, their steps accompanied by a lot of smiles and the occasional laugh.

"They're secure," Elijah confirmed.

"Send the message."

"Nic." At Savino's look, Elijah grimaced and shifted to attention. "Sir?"

"I know what you're going to say, so don't bother.

You have your orders, Prescott." His face closed, Savino tilted his head toward Elijah's phone. "Follow them."

Elijah took his cell phone off his belt. With quick, easy moves, he typed in the message. But he couldn't bring himself to hit Send.

Ava's laugh, free and light, tumbled down the stairs, quickly followed by Nathan's giggles. The boy's safety was priority. Ava's, too. With the two of them on the line, he had no choice.

So, with a deep breath of regret, he hit Send. And felt like shit as soon as he did.

"We have to know," was all Nic said before walking out of the room.

Yeah, Elijah thought, taking a deep breath.

They had to know.

SITTING ON THE sofa in Nic's plush mountain getaway, her feet curled under her in a position of relaxation while her mind raced, Ava watched Nathan play with his little plastic figures on the floor across from her. Every once in a while, she slid a careful look toward the kitchen.

Although she couldn't hear a word, she could clearly see the men through the closed French door. She could practically feel the intensity hovering in the air like a laser grid. Sharp, defined and dangerous.

As they had the previous day, the four members of Team Poseidon gathered in there for what she supposed was a briefing. Today, they had company. Elijah, Nic, Aaron and Paul had been joined by four other men, the second team, she supposed. She easily recognized Beau Danby and Ty Louden, they hadn't changed much in four years. She was pretty sure the other two were

Mason Powers and Levar Kane, but hadn't got a good enough look at their faces yet to be sure.

They were all armed. They all looked dangerous. Dangerous and ready.

Elijah had warned her the night before that something might go down soon. Like Nic had been when he'd issued the invitation to join them for these few days in Tahoe, Elijah had kept whatever that something was vague.

So she understood why he was prepared and on alert. But there was something else going on.

"Ava, you wanna play? You can be Black Widow." Nathan held up a curvaceous action figure dressed in skintight black. His smile was easy, but like hers, his eyes held worry as they slid to the roomful of men just beyond their hearing.

Wanting to erase that worry, to help him relax, Ava put on an easy smile and joined him on the floor. "Black Widow, that's Natasha, right?"

"Hey, you know Avengers?"

When they came in the form of Chris Evans, Robert Downey Jr., Jeremy Renner and the always luscious Chris Hemsworth? Oh yeah, she knew her superheroes. But she doubted a seven-year-old boy would appreciate the whys behind her interest, so she focused on the figures he had scattered over the rug.

"Captain America, Iron Man, Black Panther, Thor, Hawkeye, Winter Soldier, Scarlet Witch." She tapped each one as she named them, then winked. "Where's Falcon and Hulk?"

"I forgot them at home," he said, wrinkling his nose

in self-condemnation. "They were in the Millennium Falcon with Chewie and Finn."

"I love a crossover universe," she said, checking out Black Widow's mobility as she twisted arms and legs. "So what's the game? Are we fighting bad guys?"

Ava spent the next half hour keeping him distracted while he kept her entertained. Her workouts were the closest she'd ever come to being a tomboy, and Ava was surprised at how easily she fit into the game and at how much fun she had.

Would Dominic have played like this? With full-out imagination and an appreciation for clear uses and clever repartee? Her heart melted a little, but the pain was more sweet than bitter this time.

She and Nathan turned from their play when the door opened. Ava's welcoming smile dimmed a little when she saw it wasn't Elijah. It dimmed a little more when she noticed the look in Paul's eyes. She recognized that look. The warrior look.

She laid a protective hand on Nathan's back.

"What's going on?"

"I'm here to play," Paul said, ignoring her real question. "Rembrandt and the Kahuna are coordinating extraction with the other team."

"Extraction?" Ava glanced at the men gathered around the kitchen table. "That means someone's leaving, right? Who?"

"Not sure yet." Paul dropped to the floor next to Nathan, immediately engaging the boy in a discussion about whose powers were mightier, Iron Man or Cap.

Taking the hint, Ava pushed to her feet. Something was wrong. She wanted to storm into that kitchen and ask Elijah. But she knew he'd deny there was anything going on. He might deny it with a kiss. Maybe seduce her stupid with a kiss that would have her brains leaking out her ears. The same way he'd shut her up last night after his nightmare. But she knew now, as she had then, that something was bothering him.

The thought of that nightmare, the way he'd looked in sleep—teeth gritted, the dripping sweat, the vicious trembling and the smothered moans of pain—made her stomach churn.

Worse than his suffering, Ava couldn't get past the painful truth. Elijah was right. Before, she hadn't wanted to know. She'd wanted to be his wife, but only on her terms. She'd loved him—she'd never believe what she'd felt wasn't love—but she hadn't accepted him. Not the whole of him.

So she'd let him suffer alone.

Unable to stay there stewing, Ava hurried outside.

"Ava?" Aaron asked from his position by the door.

"I just need some air."

She didn't wait for permission, wasn't sure what she'd do if she didn't get it. She had to move. Had to work off this sick feeling of failure. As soon as she was outside, as soon as she breathed in the cool, pine-scented air, the desperate urge to run faded to a mild nagging need. Mild nagging, she could handle.

Remembering the instructions Nic and Elijah had drummed into her, she kept to the path around the house. No farther than twenty feet, never out of sight.

She pulled a small purple flower from a bush, twirling the stem before lifting the bloom to her nose. Breathing deep, she reveled in the sweetness.

Before, she'd been the one refusing to talk about Elijah's career. But now that she was smack-dab in the middle of it, they'd switched roles.

Now he wouldn't talk to her. Not about his feelings. Not about the pain he was going through. Not just in his body or his mind, she realized.

Ava wandered the path around the house, enjoying the view of the wildflowers spearing up through the brush and the feel of the sun dappling through the overhead branches.

She shouldn't be here, a little voice whispered in her head. Every day, every hour, every minute was making it harder to escape.

Harder to want to escape, if she was honest.

As rough as it'd been to cut these strong, valiant men out of her world before, it'd be more painful now. And as painful as it'd been losing Elijah before, this time it would rip her heart to shreds.

Because what she'd thought was love before was a pale ghost of what she felt now.

How was she going to live without him again? How could she recover from another broken heart? This time, there wouldn't be anything left.

"Enjoying the view?"

Ava looked over her shoulder, marveling for a second at the incongruity of Nic Savino dressed down in jeans, a T-shirt and a flannel. But she knew that the loose shirt covered the gun holstered at his back. She'd watched Elijah do the same thing when he dressed that morning, was sure the others were armed, as well.

"It's lovely here," she finally said.

"You're welcome to come back anytime. Maybe you and Rembrandt want to vacation here or something."

"Mmm," was all she said, not able to imagine her and Elijah doing the vacation thing after this. He'd go his way. She'd return to hers.

That was what she'd said she wanted. But now, facing it? It broke her heart. She had an unobstructed view of him through the window. His focus was intense. Head bent, his pencil flew over a sheet of paper. Not drawing, as she was so used to seeing him do. But writing, one hand tracking over the pages he read, the other making notes.

There would be action. Fighting. Injuries. Possibly death. Something Elijah faced every single time he went on a mission, she reminded herself as her breath lodged like a boulder in her chest.

The team hadn't hidden the purpose of this trip. They hadn't sugarcoated the dangers, nor had they treated her as if she had to be protected, like she couldn't handle herself. They—all of them, but most of all Elijah—had shown her nothing but respect.

They'd made her one of them. But she didn't feel worthy of that honor. How could she, when she'd let Elijah down—let them all down, once already?

"So," Nic eventually said. "You gonna stick around this time?"

"I'm here now. How long do you suppose you'll be here?"

"Until the job is done."

"Which means Elijah's here until you're done?"

"He is my left hand."

"And Diego is your right?"

With a shrug and a smile, Nic snagged a broken twig from a low-lying branch.

"I've got a great team."

"Don't you just," she said, watching part of his team run out to the lawn.

There didn't seem to be any rules to their game. It was a rowdy form of keep-away, with the football being thrown from man to man. She noted that each one took care to include Nathan, keeping their throws challenging enough to make him work for it but not so tough that he couldn't keep up.

A small smile fluttered over her lips, but before it could take hold, Elijah ran past, scooping Nathan under his arm instead of the football and running him down the lawn. The men followed, piling on with laughs and challenging shouts.

"They're having fun," she said stiffly when she noticed how closely Nic was watching her.

"Are you?"

"I'm not here for fun, am I?" she sidestepped, not wanting to admit to either of them that she actually was.

"No reason you shouldn't enjoy yourself anyway."

"This?" She waved her hand at the view as if it could encompass her life. "This is just a moment in time."

"Cupcake, they're all moments in time. That's what life is made up of."

"And sometimes moments are all we get."

Nic didn't pretend to not understand.

"He's good without you."

Ava nodded, wishing the words didn't pierce so deep into her heart.

"But he's better with you." He laughed at Ava's

shocked stare. "You're good for him. Being with you gives him a respite, I suppose. A sort of balance."

"Balance," she repeated. Which meant there was something weighing on the other side. From the look on his face, that was exactly where Nic had wanted her thoughts to go. "Does that mean you think he wouldn't need me if he didn't have his commitment to Poseidon and the SEALs weighing on the other side of the scale?"

"Sure he would. I'll bet you'd be happier, too."

"Elijah would never leave the service," she said with a shrug as they continued their meandering trek around the house.

"He's talked about it." At her surprised expresssion, he added, "Recently."

"He'd leave the Navy? The SEALs?" She couldn't wrap her mind around that. "You guys?"

"This deal with Ramsey, the operation going south, it hit Rembrandt hard."

She knew Nic was right. She'd seen the misery in Elijah's eyes. She'd heard the pain in his voice. His heart was hurt. His trust, and his faith, were damaged.

"Given that the two of you are back together, I'd have thought he'd discussed it with you," Nic said with a searching look.

Ava focused on the flowering bushes instead of meeting his gaze. What was she supposed to do? Admit that Elijah had tried to talk to her about it, but she'd been too afraid of delving into his world that she'd distracted him with sex? She thought of the times he'd tried to talk about this career, tried to discuss the guys from the VA. Had he been trying to tell her something?

She'd told herself it was because she wanted to keep

things loose and light, but the reality was she was afraid. Afraid to listen to him talk about the world that'd taken him from her.

Shame trickled down her spine.

Of course, there was all that incredible sex, so it couldn't be completely dismissed as a fail.

But still…

"Elijah is a man of honor, in a team of honorable men. That someone he trusted betrayed that honor has to be hard for him to take," she said quietly, her gaze on the man she loved. "But he wouldn't leave the SEALs because of that."

Would he? Her heart swelled in her chest, hope and fear wrapping around it and squeezing tight. She wished it didn't matter. But it did.

"He could. Right now, he definitely could."

Even as hope rose like the morning sun in her heart, Ava shook her head. "If he did, now especially? His wounds would never heal."

"And that, Cupcake, is why he needs you. You loved him before. But now? Now you understand him. He could use that."

But she didn't want him to need her. Fear grabbed at Ava's throat, choking the words before she could say them. Elijah was one of the strongest men, the most powerful, intelligent, well-trained people in the world. And he needed her? She couldn't help the helpless, how could she help him?

"I shouldn't be here," she murmured. She shouldn't have let things go this far.

"Why are you here?" Nic asked, tossing the words back at her.

Her expression a study of confused frustration, Ava threw her hands in the air. "I don't know. I should know, shouldn't I? I've been really careful to keep firm limits on this thing between us. Yesterday morning I was congratulating myself on how well I was handling it all. On how well I fit in without feeling any emotional commitment. Now? Now I just want to go home."

Nic gave her one of those long looks, the kind that made a person want to squirm and hide their soul. Then he nodded. "That's what I came out to tell you. There's a possibility that our location has been compromised. The second team is leaving in an hour with Nathan. You're going with them."

And just like that, she wanted to stay.

"I thought you'd learned to face fear and live life on your terms. It's a shame." Nic headed toward the front door, but not before tossing over his shoulder, "You and Rembrandt? The two of you could have been perfect together."

"Looks like you're ready to go. It might be a few days before I'm able to follow."

Elijah stared at the tidy stack of suitcases by the door. Ava's a vivid magenta with purple stripes, Nathan's covered in Star Wars characters.

Ava stared at Elijah.

He looked so good. Amazing, even.

Happy. Relaxed. Gorgeous.

As much as she'd like to think it was the lovely surroundings and all that hot sex they were having, she knew better. It wasn't even the joy of spending time with a small boy, although she knew Nathan was part of the reason for his smile.

It was being with his team.

What they were doing weighed on him. Stressed him. But he was still happier with them than he'd been the last couple of weeks without them.

Maybe Nic was right. Maybe she could ask Elijah to leave the Navy.

She'd always been afraid to ask before. She'd been so sure in her mind that he'd choose his career over her that she hadn't been able to face seeing it in reality. But she could ask now. And he'd probably agree.

He'd leave the SEALs. They could be together. Build a life. Make it work.

Because she was too afraid to try to do those things if he stayed with the team. Because she was too terrified to believe that she could heal the wounds that cut so deep into his skin that they tore at his soul.

God, Ava hated herself sometimes.

Pushing a hand through her hair, she shoved that thought and her fears aside and opted for the smart choice. The one she'd picked when she'd agreed to this affair.

To keep it simple. To keep it short.

"I don't think we should see each other again," she said.

"Why?"

She couldn't explain her fear. She wouldn't admit her love. She could only throw her arms in the air.

"I can't deal with this." She waved her hand toward the window. "All this time with Nathan. The memories. The reminders. Reminders of what it costs to be with you."

Elijah scowled, suddenly looking as pissed as she'd ever seen him. "Please, Ava. You act like you're the only one who suffered a loss," he said.

Oh, bad excuse to use, she realized as she took the words like a punch to the gut. "A loss? A loss!" Ava countered hoarsely. "Is that what you call it? Our baby's death was simply a *loss* to you?"

"Did I say simple?" Elijah's set expression didn't change. He didn't soften. "Nothing is simple. Not now. Not then. And running away won't make it so."

Wouldn't it? "I miss him so much," she admitted through trembling lips. She couldn't face Elijah. Not while she was falling apart. But she couldn't leave. She was so miserable, she didn't think her feet would carry her a single step. All she could do was turn away. Stare out the window at the painful reminder in the form of a darling little boy.

She'd left behind the naive princess, Ava Monroe. She'd turned her back on the starry-eyed bride, Ava Prescott. She'd made herself over into a tough, strong woman, dammit.

So why the hell was she crying like a weakling?

She stared through burning eyes as the view out the window blurred like a storm-drenched painting, the colors running together in a painful haze.

"Ava."

"Go away," she muttered.

He didn't of course. Hands pressed against her shoulders, warm and strong. She tried to resist, but couldn't stop him when he turned her to face him. Hating feeling so exposed, so emotionally stripped bare, she shifted, her hair falling around her face, hopefully hiding her features. It was a poor shield, and wouldn't work if he slipped his finger under her chin and lifted her face to his as he had so often in the past. But it was all she had.

Elijah did move his hands off her shoulders, but only to slip them around her back. He pulled her close, snuggling her up against him so her face rested on his chest. She tried to shift away, but he wouldn't let go. She started to pull her head back and order him to let the hell go, but his fingers tangled in her hair, sliding among her scalp in a soothing caress.

With her arms trapped between their bodies, her fingers rested over his heart. The steady beat slowly, surely calmed her. Soothed her. Eased her sobs until all that was left was an exhausted sigh.

Ava didn't know how long they stood there, his fingers running through her hair, his heart throbbing against her ear.

"I lost him, too," Elijah murmured, his words whispering through her hair as softly as his fingers. "I lost my son without even getting to say goodbye. I lost my wife, my family, without ever hearing why."

Ava had been too immersed in her own pain—first wallowing in it, then avoiding it—to care about his.

Not willing to confess that, though, she pressed her lips together. She wished she could ignore the guilt tiptoeing through her conscience, but it wasn't easy. Not when she heard the hurt in his words.

"I should have protected him," she murmured.

"You know better."

She did. Therapy, reading, they all said that there was nothing she could have done. Still, she lifted her eyes to Elijah's and for the first time let him see her anguish.

"I was his mother."

"And I was his father. Do you blame me?"

For the loss of Dominic? "God, no."

"Then how can you blame yourself?"

Watching his face, feeling his pain, Ava finally let go of the knife in her heart with a shaky sigh. "I pushed you away because I felt guilty. Because I couldn't stand to see the blame I was afraid would be in your eyes," she admitted softly, her fingers playing with the fabric of his shirt. "I'm sorry."

"You were hurting terribly, Ava. We both were."

She nodded, then, biting her lip, heard herself blurt out the one question she'd promised herself she wouldn't ask. "Nic said you might be considering leaving the Navy," she heard herself say. Cringing, she wanted to grab the words back but knew he wouldn't let her.

"It's crossed my mind," Elijah said quietly, his gaze locked on her face as if he could see through her eyes and into her brain. "It's something we need to talk about."

"We?"

"Yeah. We. Together, this time."

Her heart raced. Clutching his flannel shirt with shaking fingers, she tried to think of what to say. How to ask. If she should believe.

"Rembrandt."

Elijah and Ava turned their heads to see Nic in the doorway.

"Team's here."

Nic waited long enough for Elijah to nod before stepping back outside, shutting the door behind him with a snap.

"There's a possibility that our location was leaked to Ramsey. To be safe, the second team is taking Nathan out before any possible confrontation." Elijah watched her steadily for a moment, then, breaking her heart, pressed a soft kiss to her forehead. "I'm glad you're going with him. He'll feel better with you there."

"Elijah…" But she didn't know what to say.

Part of her wanted to beg him to fix this, to demand that she commit. If he pushed her, forced the issue, she'd have to figure it out, wouldn't she?

"Go. Go home, spend some time with your family, at the gym, in your world. Think things through." With the gentlest of caresses, just a whisper of the back of his fingers over her cheek, he stepped away.

"I'm not walking away," he told her softly. "I'm not simply giving up. Not again. But I am giving you time."

"Time for what?" she asked, her voice hoarse with tears.

"Time to decide if you can handle a life together."

"I told you a couple of weeks ago, this thing between us is just sex," she said quietly, her words about as solid as a breath of air. "That it wouldn't last longer than your leave."

"Yep. I remember you telling me that." Elijah nodded. "You go ahead and decide if you mean it or not."

And with that and a sweet smile that melted her heart into a puddle of misery, he walked away.

CHAPTER EIGHTEEN

ELIJAH'S PENCIL SCRAPED over the page, leaving loopy swirls and jagged lines. He couldn't draw. Had nothing in his head. But he knew if he looked occupied, nobody would try to talk to him. Or worse, try to make him respond.

He'd said his goodbyes to Ava. He'd heard the extraction team leave. She was gone. Now, sitting in their temporary HQ with his team, he had never felt so alone. So he didn't need to talk about it, didn't want to go see for himself the empty bedroom. He'd deal with all of that later.

Just as he'd deal with their relationship. With convincing her to do whatever it took to give them a chance.

"Target is coming our way. I'm calling in extra backup," Savino stated with a frown. Before Elijah could ask what else was going on, the commander tossed him a comm set. "Rembrandt, you're on the perimeter. Ten minutes."

Perimeter duty, in this case, meant being as visible as possible to distract the target from base. They didn't want Ramsey near the building.

"Time?" Elijah asked, checking his weapons and ammo.

"Estimating one hour," Rengel responded, doing the same.

The team kicked into high gear, Savino checking the progress of Team Two's departure while Rengel, Ward and Elijah readied for the confrontation to come.

Elijah didn't allow himself to think about Ava on her way out of Tahoe, possibly passing Ramsey on the highway. The extraction team was the best. She'd be fine. He focused on the task at hand.

Tension ripped through him as he went through a comm check, as they went through a play-by-play of the mission. Despite the reassurance of his team, Savino and command, in his opinion, the last mission he'd been on, he'd blown. The one before that? He'd been blown to hell. Now it was time to see what he was actually made of.

"I'm heading out." Elijah didn't wait for Nic's agreement before grabbing his MK23, tucking it into his back holster as he bent low to check his ankle holster, then the knife sheathed in the opposite boot. "In position in five."

Which was thirty ahead of schedule. But he wanted another visual of the territory. Time to scope out the best location for taking Ramsey down.

Despite the pressure, the intense thoughts, when he walked out the door, his demeanor was pure, casual ease. His moves were smooth, his expression calm— mellow, even. He looked like an average guy kicking back on vacation. To add to that image, he had a compact sketchbook in hand, the pencil wedged in the spiral binding.

He strolled away from the house, heading east toward the lake. *Nice view*, he decided when he reached the overlook. The delicate play of sunshine through the trees over random patterns in the grass-lined path, but glared with heat when Elijah moved toward the edge. He gauged the fall, the distance to the lake and the number of trees between here and there. A few decent-size boulders, but none big enough to hide a man.

That information committed to memory, he moved on to the next checkpoint. At each one, he checked for civilians, assessed threats, evaluated spider holes.

He took his time, taking a good hour to work his way toward a copse of trees to the far west of the house, off the beaten path with a limited window of visibility. He didn't have to look over his shoulder to know he was being watched.

"Hostile spotted," came Rengel's voice through the tiny comm lodged in Elijah's ear.

"Prescott, you're up."

A quick jerk of his shoulders to shake off any emotions still riding there, and Elijah was ready. He made a show of walking while inspecting the flora, stopping here and there to draw a quick wildlife study.

"Hostile confirmed and on the move."

Hot damn. Elijah couldn't resist smiling. Just a little one.

Because Brandon Ramsey was alive and heading his way.

Anticipation surged, slamming through his system like a pinball ringing all the bells.

"Maintain."

Savino's warning wiped the smile off his face but couldn't dim the glee in his gut. Unprofessional or not, he was looking forward to this little assignment.

Which was probably why Savino had given it to him.

He had to know how badly Elijah wanted to slam his fist into Ramsey's face. That, or kick the guy's balls into his throat. Maybe both.

Enjoying the options, Elijah found his spot. Nathan was long gone, but Ramsey didn't know that. Elijah's assignment was to draw him away, to keep his focus off the cabin. Engage at a distance, employ intelligence measures to extract information, ensure the safety of any civilians.

Backup would get here when it got here. Until then, he was on his own. *Not a problem*, Elijah decided with a grim set of his chin. He had a score to settle and some scores—especially blood scores—were better settled one on one.

He made a show of searching for the right tree trunk, taking his time settling in for a view. He flipped his sketch pad open, pulled his pencil free.

And drew a quick little image of Ramsey with a knife in his gut, a stake through his heart and a grinning vulture eating out his eye. Gruesome but satisfying.

He added prison bars around it to the sound of pebbles sliding down the hill, leaves rustling.

"Oughta watch your six, Rembrandt."

Elijah didn't bother faking surprise. He was done playing Ramsey's game.

"Please," he murmured, not bothering to look up from his sketch. "I heard your attempt at stealth two minutes before you got here."

"You're so full of shit, Prescott. You Poseidon guys like to pretend you're so damned better than everyone else, but all you're good at is lying. Mostly to yourselves."

"So says the Pinocchio of lies." After sketching in a few electrical wires to the bars for good measure, he nodded with satisfaction. Then, and only then, did he glance up at the liar. His eyes widened as he got a good look at the other man's appearance.

Ramsey had always come across as a poster boy for Prince Charming. Blond hair and blue eyes, he'd had the all-American looks of a movie star. A perfect glistening white smile, chiseled features and charming demeanor.

There wasn't much charming about the man's looks now.

Shoulder-length hair was in disarray, partially concealing the puckered scar bisecting his sculpted features. It wasn't a fire scar, Elijah noted, not bothering to hide his inspection. Seemed more like the guy had taken a piece of shrapnel to the face. It was petty, but Elijah didn't bother hiding his smile.

"Looks like that mission took a piece out of you, too," he observed. He leaned back against the tree, his flannel shirt a barrier between him and the rough bark, and tapped his pencil on his knee. "Bet it's rough, shaving around that scar."

"You're trying to psych me out. It won't work."

"Why would I do that? You think I've got a grudge to settle or something? That'd make this personal."

"It's always personal."

"And that's why you were never as good a SEAL as you thought you were. You couldn't get your ego out of the way and give the mission your all."

Ramsey's lips tightened, his fist clenching until knuckles showed white.

Direct hit.

"I hear you've been looking for me," was all he said.

"Not me," Elijah shot back with an easy shrug. "I'm on vacation, dude. Besides, I thought the official word was that your ass had been burned to ash."

"We both know how worthless anything official is."

"Do we?"

Making sure Ramsey could see both his hands, Elijah used his pencil to tap out a casual beat across his notebook cover.

"Red tape, protocol, politics," the other man muttered. "All official bullshit organized by fat, lazy, self-aggrandizing assholes with one eye on their retirement and the other on whatever ass they're kissing."

"Sounds like you're harboring a little bitterness toward the Navy."

"Aren't you? Isn't the Navy the reason why you spent two months in a hospital? Isn't the Navy the reason you lost your wife? Your kid? You and me, Prescott, the Navy fucked us both over the same."

Seriously? Fury flamed behind Elijah's eyes in a vicious flash. This motherfucker blew him up, and he blamed the Navy? The man abandoned his girlfriend, walked away from his unborn child, and he had the balls to compare that to the death of Elijah's son?

Adrenaline surged, his body tightening in readiness to attack. His breath was fire in his throat, his heart thundering in his ears.

Focus, he ordered himself. *Focus on the mission.*

Because as soon as the mission was complete, he could kick this fucker's ass.

"Some would say that fire you set was the reason I was in the hospital," Elijah ground out, working to keep his smile in place. "You remember that fire, don't you? The one you used to escape after stealing a top secret weapons formula."

"Just doing my job." With a hint of his old charm, Ramsey smiled and gave a boyish shrug.

Elijah took the confirmation with the same mindset he'd take a bullet from an enemy. As the cost of war. Ramsey hadn't accidentally set him on fire. The bastard had blown him to hell because he wanted his tracks covered.

"Your job bites," Elijah pointed out. "I hope you're getting paid damned well for destroying your life."

"You recording this conversation, Rembrandt?"

"What'd be the point of that? Official word is that you're ash, remember? And I'm not the vendetta type."

"Yeah, but you're the loyal type. Like, to your exclusive little club of assholes."

Bingo. The key to Ramsey's actions, the one that would throw his ass in a cage. Resisting the urge to tell the guy that he was little more than a pimple to those assholes, Elijah followed the playbook. The one Savino had outlined when he'd given him this assignment.

He smiled. He lifted both hands in the air. And he pretended he could be bought.

"Loyal, sure. To my friends. I thought you were a friend once, Ramsey."

Ice-blue eyes sparked with suspicion as Ramsey leaned against his own tree. "A friend? Sure, why not." Ramsey laughed, the sound cold and bitter. "Like Adams was a friend. But you took him down."

"First, Adams was a douche. It was irritating as hell the way he followed you around like a lovesick puppy."

Watching Ramsey's face, Elijah saw the flash of satisfaction and thought, score one. "Second, he went off the reservation, my friend. Kidnapping a kid? That's ugly business."

"My kid." The claim was made with about as much emotion as calling dibs on a doughnut.

"Which is why Adams grabbed him. To lure you out. You shoulda smacked that puppy on the nose with a rolled-up paper, Ramsey." Elijah shook his head in disgust. "He was a total failure."

"Maybe," Ramsey said with a smirk. "Or maybe he was part of your plan to lure me out?"

"You think? I guess Torres, Lansky and I are like, what? The killer strike force? Because it was just the three of us there rescuing that kid."

He wasn't giving anything away with that news. The mission report had been in those transmissions he'd decoded. So someone was keeping Ramsey in the loop. It was his job to use that loop to tie this asshole in a nice, tidy bowline knot.

"Torres leading the way, I suppose."

The way he spit the bitter words out like they were poison told Elijah he'd gotten word that Diego and Harper were a happy couple.

"Actually, Lansky cracked the location," Elijah said. Was Lansky his informant? Elijah didn't want to believe that his Poseidon brother was dirty. But wants didn't factor in here. Facts did. "He seemed almost as disappointed as Adams was that you didn't show."

"If you think I'd walk into a trap like that you're as delusional as Lansky."

"Lansky's delusional?"

Ramsey shrugged as if to say, sure. But Elijah could see the caginess in his eyes. He'd said it before, the guy might have been a decent Special Operative but he was crap as a criminal mastermind.

He wanted Elijah to think Lansky was dirty. Whether because he hoped to out the guy or to set him up was the question.

"You got my messages?" Ramsey asked after a prolonged silence. "The pictures, the notes and texts?"

"Was that you?" Pulling out his best fake surprised look, Elijah shook his head. "I'd have figured love notes were a little lame to be your style, dude."

"Reminders."

"Of?"

"Of what matters. Of what doesn't. Of what a waste it is to try to please masters who don't give a fuck about us." Fury shimmered off Ramsey's declaration. His voice rose with each sentence, each word bit off through clenched teeth. "How many times did you bust your ass in training? Put your life on the line during a mission? Take fire for worthless, unappreciative assholes? And for what? Our lousy pay? For fucking anonymity?"

Flames practically spewed from his lips as he spat that last bit out at Elijah's feet. Ramsey paced as if there was too much fury in his gut to stand still.

Elijah could relate. Because he could, he wasn't sure how long he'd be able to hold back the urge to pound on Ramsey's face. He tried to calculate the time since he'd dispatched the message, how long it'd take Savino to deploy. But he couldn't count seconds when his mind was racing through the past.

"You knew the rules when you signed up to play,"

he pointed out, pushing to his feet. He forced himself to keep it casual, though. Instead of posturing, he continued to lean against the tree, digging the heel of one boot into the bark. The only sign of agitation he allowed was to tap the sketch pad against his thigh. He used the beat to help shake off some of the anger—or at least to channel it since nothing seemed to be putting a dent in the wall of fury surrounding him.

"So you're saying you're okay with it?" Ramsey gave a pitying shake of his head. "I thought better of you, man."

"You thought I'd play your game? Is that what this is all about? You're looking for an inside man?"

Something flashed in Ramsey's eyes. And that something told Elijah that he already had his inside man. Not that he'd be averse to gathering a few extra, but he was set. For what was the question.

"Wouldn't hurt," was all Ramsey said, though. "You should consider it. Some decent money, a chance at a real retirement. The kind that includes sun-drenched beaches, a fat cushion of cash and all your body parts. Hell of a better deal than you'll get in the Navy."

"Now there's an offer," Elijah managed to say. "Is that what's going on? You're recruiting?"

"You think I'm the only one involved?" Ramsey gave a bitter laugh, "Orders are orders, my man. I was simply seeding the ground, waiting to see what grew."

"That's why you left the number for your Swiss account in my possessions?"

"A precaution," Ramsey corrected. "You know as well as I that being prepared is key to a successful mission. So is having a backup."

So Ramsey wanted to make sure that he had a backup in case he fried his brains. He hadn't left it in his own possessions because his dirty pals would have found it. So he'd used Elijah.

Again.

"Why're you here?" he asked, wanting to know who'd tipped Ramsey to their location. "And more to the point, how'd you track me?"

"I figure a guy with your skills, you know who froze my funds. That, and like I already said. You're an idiot if you think I'm the only one involved. So maybe that someone is interested in you. Interested enough to know you're burned out and might like some new friends," Ramsey taunted with a laugh. "I follow orders, I get rewarded. A lot better system than the crap pay and lack of recognition in the SEALs."

Someone higher up, Elijah realized. It would take authority to get even a hint of respect out of Ramsey. And that was a combination of respect and fear in his voice. Who would have that kind of power? More important, what reward?

Those were questions for Savino to ask, he knew. Still, he was so pissed, it took him two tries to trigger the button with his toe. He had to take another slow, surreptitious breath to calm the fury before he could continue. But all in all, not a bad job for a man who couldn't dance a step, he decided as he knocked out the *all clear* message in a few taps.

"If preparation is the first rule, having a solid team is the second," Elijah pointed out. "And while I might work with an asshole like you if so ordered, I'd never play on your team, Ramsey. I don't play with losers."

Before Ramsey could respond with the fist he'd lifted, there was a rustle in the bushes to their right. Both he and Elijah went on alert.

Damn. Savino had moved a lot faster than he'd expected. Elijah shifted his weight.

The moment Ramsey turned his head toward the noise, he moved. A quick dive forward, sidekick to the head and a satisfying right cross to that pretty-boy face.

Ramsey tried to kick out but Elijah swept his feet out from under him. Both men hit the dirt with a thud. Elijah smiled through the pain as his knuckles split on Ramsey's teeth. The guy's nose broke with a crack and a spray of blood, spattering them both as they hit the ground.

It felt damned good to sink his fist over and over into the other man's face. This might be the first time Elijah had ever been tempted to laugh aloud during a fight.

Before Ramsey could react, before he got more than that one punch, Elijah had him on his stomach, arm wrenched high between his shoulder blades as he dug his knee into the small of the traitor's back.

Ramsey reared back, his head smacking into Elijah's face. Stars exploded, pain flashing. Barely resisting the temptation to grab the guy's hair and use it to slam his head into the ground a few—or few dozen—times, Elijah shook it off. Blood spurted from his nose, spattering his shirt.

"You need some help, Rembrandt?" said a calm voice. "Or you gonna mop up that blood with his head?"

Elijah looked over his shoulder, blinking to clear the spots from his vision until Lansky swam into view.

"Yo," he greeted him, swiping his tongue along the side of his mouth where his lip had split. "How's it going?"

"Not bad." Lansky sauntered closer, stopping two feet away. "You should have followed up with a knee to the balls, though. If anyone deserves to have his nuts kicked in, it's this guy."

"Ain't that the truth," Elijah said with a laugh, angling himself so Lansky could step in and restrain the prisoner.

"I'll make you pay, you sonovabitch," Ramsey said as Lansky hauled him to his feet, his words muffled by dirt and blood. He turned his glare on his captor just long enough to identify him, then shot a killing look at Elijah. "You won't get away with this."

"Pretty sure I just did," Elijah shot back, leaning back on his heels and swiping the back of his hand over his own cut lip. He eyed the speckle of blood, compared it to the flood gushing over Ramsey's face and risked the pain of splitting his lip wider as he grinned. "Pretty sure I kicked your ass, dude."

"You can't hold me. You can't stop me. Do you have any idea who the fuck I am, you idiot? What the hell I can do to you?"

"Oh yeah." Elijah pushed to his feet, the scars on his leg pulling tight as he straightened. "I know exactly what you can do."

Ignoring Savino as his commander stepped through the trees, Elijah strode forward until he was right there in Ramsey's face. With Lansky holding his arms behind him, the man couldn't move, so he was left with baring his teeth and glaring.

"You're the guy who turned your back on your brothers. The man who betrayed your team, your rank, your country. You're a lying SOB who ran out on your own kid. You're the lying motherfucker who left me to burn while you ran away like the weasel you are."

"Prescott."

Elijah blinked, then when that didn't clear the blood from his eyes, sucked in a deep breath and blinked again.

"Lansky, you want to secure this trash," Savino ordered, whipping out a zip tie and watching, stone-faced, while his men wrapped the guy's hands together behind his back. "Lieutenant Brandon Ramsey, you'll be escorted back to base, where you'll stand trial for treason. Do you have anything to say for yourself?"

"Fuck you."

Savino nodded.

"That's what I figured. Men." He gestured for Lansky to release him to the waiting SEALs.

"We've got this," Ward said, snagging one arm while Rengel grabbed the other. "We'll lock him up in the transport."

Fighting like the crazed lunatic he was, Ramsey resisted all the way.

"You'll pay," he screamed as Rengel and Ward hauled his kicking, swearing ass through the woods. "I'll make sure of it."

"Dude is a total cliché." Shaking his head, Elijah gave Savino a sardonic smile. "You'd think he'd take a little more pride in his big exit."

"Given that he never thought he'd be caught, I guess he didn't have anything prepared," Lansky said. "Guys like that are crap at improv."

"Guys like you are aces at it, though," Savino said, clearly still prepared for confrontation as he stood, feet planted and arms crossed, staring at Lansky.

"Can't deny I've got a quick brain," Lansky replied. His grin fell away as his eyes traveled from Savino's set expression to Elijah's closed one and back again. "My quick brain is telling me right now that there's an issue. Other than the loser they just hauled away."

Taking his cue from Savino, Elijah stayed silent. But, man, it was killing him. He wanted his friend cleared. He wanted his team cleared. And he wanted this mission finished so he could get back to Napa and settle life with Ava.

"Am I the issue?" Lansky asked, chin stiff as he stared at his commanding officer.

"Prescott?"

Elijah knew the prompt wasn't for an explanation, but to bring them both up to date. "Key information was disbursed among specific personnel with the goal of ascertaining the intelligence leak. Lieutenant Lansky's information was not shared in any way, shape or form. Added to that, specifics shared by the hostile indicate that the leak is a higher ranking officer, one in a position of authority."

Savino's expression didn't change, but Elijah could see his body stiffen. Lansky, on the other hand, turned an interesting shade of purple.

"You thought I was working with that scumbag?" Lansky said.

"Not me," Elijah claimed, throwing his hands in the air.

"Your behavior over the last couple of months was questionable. Your actions suspicious." Savino stood, arms clasped behind his back as he stared coldly at the man under his command. "Given the delicacy of the situation, and the fact that one of our own already betrayed us, you've been looked at carefully."

"And now?"

"And now that Rembrandt cleared you, you can tag along to the extraction point while you explain what the hell's been going on."

"Yes, sir." Lansky seemed to sag in place, the tension simply dropping away as he took a deep breath. Then, shaking it off with his usual verve, he tried a smile. It was a little edgy, but it was there.

"And what about Ramsey?" Elijah asked. "Do we have enough on him?"

"We have enough to try him." Savino stared down the ravaged path, evidence of Ramsey's reluctant departure evident in the deep grooves in the dirt and damage to the surrounding underbrush. He slanted an arch look at Elijah. "You'll have to live it all over again. You up for that?"

"I live it all over again every time I close my eyes," Elijah admitted with a sigh. Then he realized the heavy weight of horror that had anchored him to those memories was missing. Like the scars, like his past, what had happened was a part of him now. And he could finally accept that nothing was going to change that.

"What happened, happened. It was crap—it hurt a lot of people. But at least reliving it in court, we can get some use out of it."

After a long second and a longer inspection of Elijah's face, Savino nodded. "There ya go."

Together the three of them hit the path, heading in the direction that Ramsey had been hauled.

"So what's the deal?" Elijah asked, giving Jared a sidelong inspection. The guy looked good. Lighter, a little easier than usual.

"So, well, yeah." Jared cleared his throat, jerked his shoulders a couple of times, then took a breath. "I realized recently that I might have a drinking problem."

"Noooo," Elijah and Nic said together, as mocking as mocking could be.

"Right. Whatever." Jared laughed. "I can handle it. I can live with it and do my job and be excellent. But it was affecting other things."

"The woman?" Elijah realized. "The Greek goddess?"

"Yeah. Andi didn't want anything to do with me. She hated what I do, and she called me a lush. At first, I figured fine. A woman's a woman, right?"

"Unless she's the right woman."

"Exactly. So I pushed it, I asked her to give it a chance. She didn't want anything to do with a guy in the Special Ops, who lived on the edge of lies, but I was able to talk her around on that. You know, serving the country, saving lives, that sort of thing." Angling through a break in the trees, the other men nodded. That sort of thing did tend to turn the tide. "But she had another issue. She insisted that I get cleaned up. Get sober. All the way sober."

Elijah's snort was drowned out by the sound of Nic's laugh. Then they realized he was serious.

"You're sober?"

"I joined AA, started going to the meetings." His eyes locked on his feet, Jared kicked the dirt a little and shrugged. "At first it was just for her. Then, after a while, it seemed the right thing to do. For her. For me. For the team."

"Good man," Nic said, slapping him on the shoulder.

"If you need anything, we're here for you," Elijah added.

As they continued their trip through the woods and Jared filled them in on his AA adventures and the world according to Andi, a calm filled Elijah. A sense of mellow contentment seeped in, filling the holes left by bitterness and anger.

It was done. It was all done. He'd brought down Ramsey. Cleared his name. Sure, the trial was yet to come, but it was secondary. Primary was that the brotherhood knew he was innocent—and now, thanks to Savino, he'd achieved that.

"You'll need to report for duty Monday."

"Duty?" Elijah frowned, but didn't say anything else. Since Savino didn't, either, he knew his commander understood.

Elijah might not be going back. He'd testify. He'd complete Operation Fuck Up. But his time in service?

He puffed out a long breath, trying to unknot the tangle of thoughts speeding through his head.

Serving again? That was a hard decision to make. He'd have to give up Ava. He didn't know if they had a chance, if they had a future. But he did know that the only shot they'd get at one was if they didn't repeat the same mistakes they'd made in the past.

Which meant they couldn't live 90 percent of their lives apart and expect to be a couple. He didn't want to be torn like that again, one foot in both worlds. Always feeling as if a piece of him was always missing, waiting and longing on the other side.

They couldn't survive Ava hating his career. Hating what made him who he was. He didn't know if he could change, but he was willing to try. Especially now that he knew he was more than a SEAL. More than part of the brotherhood.

Bottom line? He couldn't survive without giving them a shot. As long as Ava was willing to give him one. Which meant the decision wasn't so hard after all.

"I'm going to need an extension on my leave. I can't report on Monday," he told Savino quietly. "I have to go back to Napa. I have to settle things with Ava."

"You and Cupcake are back together?" Jared asked with a smile and a congratulatory slap on the back.

"I don't know what we are. That's what I have to figure out."

"And if being back together means leaving the Navy?" Nic asked, his tone as neutral as Switzerland.

"What? No way..." Jared stopped in his tracks, his boots kicking up a cloud of dust as he stared at Elijah. "Seriously?"

Elijah and Nic stopped with him, the three of them shaded by tall trees on one side and the view of the lake glistening on the other. The scent of the forest surrounded them as Elijah faced his friends.

"I didn't give my marriage one hundred percent before, and I lost Ava. I want her back. I want it to work this time. That means making a choice."

"And you're choosing her." Like Nic, there was no judgment in Jared's tone. Just understanding.

"I love her. She deserves to be put first."

And that was that.

There was no remorse in his heart, except for the regret of leaving his friends. But he could see it in the other men's eyes. Because they were friends, there was nothing to be sorry for. Savino understood. The others would, too.

"You'll be the first to walk away from Poseidon," Savino said as they stopped on the edge of the clearing. The path to the left led to the cabin, nestled in a gentle copse of trees. The right led to the transport and Ramsey.

"I'll always value my time serving with you, the honor of being a part of the brotherhood," Elijah murmured. "You, the team, you've made me who I am. But me and Ava. I have to give us a fair shot."

"And that's what makes you an honorable man. Whatever happens, whether you're serving or not, we're tied by more than duty. We're tied by blood, by sweat, by vows. The brotherhood holds true," Savino said.

"Damn," Jared breathed, swiping a fake tear from his cheek. "Did you practice that speech? It was pretty sweet."

"Kiss ass, MacGyver," Nic said, laughing. "Let's go make sure Ramsey is secured and on his way. Then we'll head back to the cabin. You have a report to make and Rembrandt here has some issues to settle."

CHAPTER NINETEEN

AVA PACED FROM one end of the kitchen to the other, stopping every few steps to look out the window.

Something was going on.

Ty Loudon, Beau Danby, Mason Powers and Levar Kane made up what Nic called the second team. They'd arrived two hours ago, a couple of them offering a brief hello and Powers a friendly wave before they'd joined the kitchen powwow.

Ten minutes after that Elijah had told her goodbye, so Ava had missed whatever happened next, what with being busy sobbing her heart out. It wasn't until Nic found her curled up on her bed, staring at the wall, that she'd realized that whatever their mission was, it was under way.

"Time to go, Cupcake," he'd told her.

"Go?"

"You and Nathan are to be escorted to a safe location where he'll be met by his mother."

"And Elijah?"

Elijah was through talking with her. Nic's expression hadn't changed, but she'd seen it in his eyes.

"He indicated that your goodbyes were said."

She'd lain there for a moment. Then, terrified but

unable to convince herself to change her mind, she'd shaken her head. "I'm waiting here."

"No, Ava. You're leaving with Nathan in ten minutes."

"No, Nic. I'm not. I'm waiting here for Elijah."

He'd stared, long and hard, then asked one word. "Okay. But why?"

Ava still didn't know. Nic had let her sidestep the question then had let her stay, but she knew she couldn't dance around it for long. Not once Elijah was back. Maybe she just wanted to finish their discussion now, instead of later, she considered as she paced.

Then she overheard Aaron tell Nic that the hostile was spotted, a new target was in sight. Nic had stepped out of the kitchen just long enough to give her a hard look.

"Things are going down in a different direction than planned. I don't have time to get you out of here. If I did, I'd be shorthanded." His face was set, but she could see the worry in his eyes. "There's a man on the door. You stay inside. If you step outside this building, you'll be stepping into the line of fire. That means you stay indoors, you stay under wraps and you keep away from the windows."

"Okay." Ava swallowed hard. She'd never seen him look so tense.

"I shouldn't have let you stay," he muttered, looking as if he were going to send her packing despite the possibility of being a man short and out of time.

But Ava had left Elijah too many times in the past. She couldn't now. She just couldn't. "You can trust me,

Nic," she promised. "I'll stay here, I'll follow directions. I won't endanger your mission."

After a long look, first at her and then at his watch, he nodded. "One step out that door before I return, and you'll be putting our lives in danger," Nic said, one hand on the doorknob, the other on the gun at his hip. "Including Prescott."

"I'll wait here," she said, chin high as she bit her lip to keep from screaming at him to protect Elijah.

An excruciating half hour had passed since then, and she wasn't sure how much longer she could bottle those screams. She paced. She fidgeted. She sat, tapped her foot, then jumped up again. She paced to the far end of the living room, carefully peering out the window. Nothing but nature.

She paced to the other end to stare out the window by the kitchen entrance. She could see the detached garage flanked by a pair of benches, a few squirrels scampering around, and a whole lot of emptiness.

God. What were they doing out there? How long did she have to wait to find out?

Ava pressed her fingers against her eyes, trying to relieve the pressure building behind her brain. What was Elijah going to say when he saw she hadn't left? Worse, when he realized she still hadn't made any decisions about their relationship. What did she do now?

She wanted air. She wanted sound. She was tempted to turn on the radio, but was afraid to miss hearing anything important. Like, maybe a bird sending up a signal on Elijah's status.

Rolling her eyes at herself, Ava puffed out a breath and tried to massage the tension out of her stomach. But it was knotted too tight. She wanted air. She wanted to go outside, but she'd promised Nic she wouldn't.

Yoga, she decided. She'd do yoga. It was that, or start pulling her hair out, one yank at a time.

Already dressed in loose-fitting capri pants, she tucked her tank top into the waistband, slipped out of her shoes and took a deep breath. She put all her thoughts toward centering herself as she moved through the series of vinyasa poses, flowing from one stance to the next on each breath.

"Peace," she breathed in dolphin pose. *Be at peace.*

Plank to downward facing dog.

Center, faith, confidence.

Cobra to twisting lunge.

Center, faith, love.

Arrow lunge to triangle to interlock warrior.

Center, faith, Elijah.

Pigeon pose, hold, to savasana.

Ava lay flat on the floor, eyes closed as her breath released, the last of the pent-up fear releasing with it. There, she breathed, a smile sliding over her face. She'd found her center. Now she could figure out the rest.

Opening her eyes, Ava pushed into a handstand, this time from joy, then flipped out to her feet. A second to be sure of her balance and she was ready.

Snapping up the bottle of water she'd left on a nearby table, Ava offered a finger wave to Powers, the SEAL Elijah always called Flipper, who stood guard just outside the door, giving her a what-the-hell-are-you-doing look.

She was getting past the fear, she realized. She'd spent years learning to control her body, to be strong

This was why. Now she could do that thinking Elijah had asked of her.

Preferring movement as often as possible, she continued to pace, sipping water and debating her options. Would it make her life happy if she and Elijah were back together, with him still serving in Special Ops? Off on death-defying missions, risking everything for something he'd never be able to tell her about.

Would her life be happier if they were together and he stayed in the military, but downgraded so he wasn't always off on those dangerous, body-scarring missions?

Or would everything be peachy keen if he left altogether, moved up to Napa and got a normal job, the kind that had him home at the dinner table each night? She wrinkled her nose as she tried to imagine year after year of that, the two of them kicking back after a meal, their feet up on the couch. She could easily see them rolling around naked on the couch, but not the rest.

Elijah wasn't made for normal. It was a total waste of what made him so special. And the bottom line was, she wanted Elijah.

So the question wasn't whether she could live with him. It was whether she could live without him.

Feeling actually ready to make a welcome-home feast for the men now that she wasn't afraid she'd burn the place down, Ava turned toward the kitchen.

And frowned. Where was Powers? He'd been right there, standing outside the door just a minute ago.

Eyes narrowed, she moved toward the wall of windows and the door. Before she'd gone two steps, there was a crash in the kitchen. Like glass shattering or a dish hitting the floor.

"What the—"

A stranger stepped out of the kitchen.

Ava didn't consider herself overly sensitive, but she swore, like body odor wafting off a burly guy dripping sweat, she could actually feel the evil emanating from him.

"Excuse me, I'm just passing through," said the man. His blond hair was longer now, his face scarred and beaten but still pretty enough that she recognized him as Brandon Ramsey from the briefing photo Nic had shared. "I'm here for my son."

Thank God, Ava took a moment to breathe, grateful for Nic's foresight in sending Nathan away.

"I'm the only one here," she lied. At least she hoped it was a lie. Wasn't Powers out there somewhere? Trying to keep her moves casual, Ava took a step closer to the window. When he didn't stop her, she took one more. And couldn't stop her gasp.

From this angle, all she could see was the foot of a man lying on the ground. And blood.

"Where's the boy?" Ramsey demanded, his hand resting on the butt of the gun holstered at his hip. Had he used that on Powers? Had he hurt the man? Ava tried to breathe through the panic. Or worse?

"There's nobody here," she repeated, saying it for herself now. Because she needed to hear it. Needed to accept that right now, for this moment, she was on her own.

"Don't fuck with me, lady," he growled, his gaze cold as it swept the room. "Do you have any idea who I am?"

"I'm pretty sure you're that Ramsey guy, right? I've heard a lot about you," she said, putting on her best so cialite smile. Her guts might be quaking, but she knew how to keep that to herself. Since she had a feeling her life might depend on it right now, she figured subtlety was a hell of a lot smarter than admitting her fear. "You're the guy who's irritating Nic and his Poseidon team."

"Nic, is it?" His face twisting into a sneer made all the uglier by the scar bisecting it, the man angled himself against the wall so he could peer out the window.

With his attention outside, Ava tried a step toward the kitchen. If she could get in there, she'd have a better chance of escape. Or if nothing else, at finding a weapon more powerful than a piece of fancy bric-a-brac.

Weapon, she mentally scoffed at herself. As if she had a chance against this guy? He might be scum, but he was a SEAL. Special Ops trained.

She'd done no more than shift her weight before his eyes locked on her again.

"So you're, what? Savino's girlfriend? I didn't realize the all-powerful Kahuna went for pretty little pieces of fluff."

That did it. The terror that'd been sliding its greasy tentacles through her system froze. *Piece of fluff?* She was a goddamn black belt, fit as hell and now—thanks to his misogynistic dismissal—she was pissed.

A dear little boy's life had been threatened because of this man. Harper, who was one of the sweetest women Ava had ever met, was suffering because of him. He'd damaged the team's reputation. He'd dishonored his commission. He'd betrayed their country.

And he'd hurt Elijah. Left him to burn in flames created to hide treason. He'd put nightmares in his head, doubts and questions that didn't belong.

So yeah, Ava decided. She could handle him.

"Where's my son?" Ramsey demanded, aiming the gun her way before gesturing with it toward the stairs. "Is he up there? Who's with him?"

"Your son?"

"Don't play stupid, sweetheart. Savino wouldn't allow you to be here without some basic intel. I figure you're the babysitter, right? Entertain the kid during the day, the men at night."

"Did you just equate me to a hooker?"

"And if I did?"

"You'll need to apologize."

"Or what? You can't take me on." He dismissed her with a laugh that held just enough charm for her to see what Harper had fallen for all those years ago.

"You don't think so?" Making each step casual, she walked over to the couch and sat on the arm closest to the kitchen. Lifting a pillow, she fluffed it with a couple of casual shakes, then set it back down. And flashed him a friendly smile. "Isn't there something in the SEAL handbook that warns about underestimating an enemy?"

"Get real. A pretty little thing like you? You're hardly an enemy," he snapped. And, as she'd hoped, remembering that his actual enemies were nearby, he shifted his attention out the window again. "So why don't you sit down, shut up and focus on looking pretty."

Ava used his distraction to slip her cell phone out of the back pocket of her jeans, keeping it between her hip and the pillow. Her eyes on the man across the room.

she toggled the sound with her thumb, hopefully putting it on Silent. Moving solely by feel and memory, she swiped it on, hit Message and rubbed her thumb over the top of the screen to open the last person she'd texted.

Elijah.

One word, four letters. Heart racing, she typed them as fast as she could, freezing between the L and the P when Ramsey checked her position. As soon as he returned his gaze to the window, she risked a quick glance to make sure she was begging the right contact for help, then hit Send.

And let her phone slide down between the cushions.

Then, worried because she hadn't shut off the vibrate function and didn't want to be sitting next to a buzzing pillow, she got to her feet and took another step toward the kitchen.

"Where do you think you're going?"

"Me? Nowhere important. I'm just a piece of fluff," she reminded him in a cutting tone. "Remember? I'm no threat."

"You're quickly becoming a pain in the ass, though." Another glance out the window, then he angled toward Ava with his gun still shoulder high, pointed at the ceiling. "Where's my son?"

"No idea."

"Try again." With an easy move that told her he had no compunction about following through, Ramsey pointed the gun at her head.

Her gaze shifted from his face to the gun and back again. She knew nothing about weapons. Had no clue what make or model that was. All she knew was that the best-case scenario was a whole lot of pain if he shot her.

Without thinking, she dropped, spun, kicked high. Her aim true, her foot clipped his wrist, sent the weapon flying. Before he could react, she flipped backward, landing a good foot out of his reach with fists high.

"You should have stuck with sitting down and shutting up, sweetheart." He dropped into a fighter's crouch, his scarred face ugly. "You really think you can take me on?"

"Sure, why not," she said, shifting into attack stance. "I've fought guys bigger than you. A couple of women, too."

She could tell by the tightening of his lips that the insult hit its target.

Besides, she didn't have to win. She just had to stall the idiot until Elijah rescued her.

"Yo, Lansky? Does this mean I can have your Drank My Way around the World tee?" Elijah asked Jared, stepping over the log barrier between the forest and the road.

The air was warmer here, electrical even, as they made their way to the transport van.

They only made it a foot before Savino threw out one hand to halt their steps. Elijah got it a second later. The scent of blood.

Shit.

Smiles disappeared, ease shifted to awareness as all three men instantly flipped into fight mode. Bodies tensed, muscles alert, they split without a word.

Lansky flanked the van to the left, snagging a tire iron as he went. Gun held low, Elijah took right. Arm-ing himself, Savino went right up the middle. They didn't go more than a foot before they saw men down.

Sprawled in the dirt next to the van, Rengel and Ward were hit. Elijah growled. And that fucker Ramsey was nowhere in sight.

"How bad are they?" Leaping forward, Lansky dropped the tire iron to lift Rengel's wrist. Checked his pulse. Savino rushed to Ward.

Covering them, Elijah secured the area. Then he got to work.

"Ramsey did this? How the hell did he get loose from two armed SEALs?" Lansky ground out, catching the first-aid kit Savino tossed at him.

"He had help," Elijah declared, kneeling in the dirt to study the tracks. "One person, he was waiting here with Ramsey's vehicle. The men walked into an ambush."

A groan interrupted his inspection. Elijah jumped to his feet, hurried back to the van just as Ward opened his eyes.

"Report," Savino demanded. "Where's Ramsey?"

"Played us. Someone waiting. Shot Rengel just as we rounded the vehicle." Ward closed his eyes, swallowing a gasp as Lansky pressed a wadded cloth against the gash on his head. "Didn't see the accomplice, hit me on the back of the head. Rengel. Where's Chug? He okay?"

"Chill," Lansky ordered, checking Ward's pupils. "Rengel's going to be fine."

"Flesh wound." Finishing the field dressing on Rengel's shoulder, Savino leaned back on his heels. He did a quick scan, then looked at Elijah, frowning when he noted the gun in his hand. "Ramsey's vehicle is gone?"

"Vehicle is. He's not."

He and Lansky rose, both of them looking around as Ward pushed himself into a sitting position.

"What d'you see?"

"Ramsey's partner isn't much on loyalty. As far as I can tell, he provided the jump, then ditched our boy."

"Who the hell is this guy working with? Fucker's got the loyalty of an alley cat," Lansky noted, half his attention on his phone where he was signaling for medical backup.

"One partner?" Eyes narrowed, Savino surveyed the track marks just as Elijah had. "What do you mean, he ditched Ramsey?"

"Car tracks." Elijah pointed.

"Footsteps from both sides." He gestured. "Only one set getting back inside."

He checked again, wiped a bead of sweat off his forehead with the back of one hand, then gestured with his gun toward the woods.

"Fresh footsteps, leading out of the scuffle and going that a'way," Elijah said, jerking his chin toward a tight copse of trees. "Unless he changes trajectory, he's heading for the cabin."

"Damn." Savino turned away, tapping his comm. "Powers. Come in Powers." After a long second, he clenched his teeth and tried again. "Powers, report."

"You think they overtook the second team?" Elijah asked, a small seed of panic unfurling in his belly. But reality kept that seed from taking root. There were four men escorting Ava and Nathan, all on full alert. No way they'd been overpowered. "I thought they already checked in."

"The team confirmed they'd made the checkpoint,"

Savino acknowledged, trying one more time to raise Powers while Lansky finished treating the other men's wounds.

Rengel was still out but breathing evenly, so he turned his attention to the cut on Ward's head.

"Secure the injured." With that and a rare expression of panic on his face, Savino dove into the back of the van. Elijah and Lansky exchanged baffled looks as the man unlocked the munitions storage and started strapping on weapons. It was only when he started tossing extras their way that Elijah asked.

"What the hell?"

"Ava's at the cabin. Powers is with her and he's not answering his comm."

"Go," Ward said, swiping at the blood dripping off his chin at the same time he slid the gun out of his ankle holster. "I'll cover Rengel."

Ava? Panic ripped through him like vicious shards of lightning. "What the hell are you talking about?" Elijah yelled as he ran, full out, toward the cabin. He didn't worry about stealth as he tore over the blanket of pine needles, leaping logs and boulders as panic fueled his steps. "Ava left," he ground out as he ran. "She and Nathan were escorted out of here at two-hundred-hours."

"Nathan was escorted," Savino said, keeping pace with Elijah as Lansky brought up the rear. "Ava refused. Powers stayed behind."

Elijah grabbed his silenced cell phone from his back pocket, but before he could call her, check on her, he saw the text message flash over his screen.

Help.

It could only mean one thing. "Ramsey's there. He's got Ava."

That's all he said. All he had to say. As one, he and his teammates flew through the forest.

A million questions raced, faster than his steps, but Elijah didn't bother voicing them. He'd get answers later. All that mattered right now was reaching Ava.

They didn't slow until they reached the break in trees, then moving in concert, they again spread out. Lansky to the left, Elijah to the right and Savino straight up the middle.

Noting no movement, they slowly began canvassing the perimeter. Elijah rounded the trees to the right just as Lansky came around left while Savino crawled down the roofline like a lizard.

Savino lifted a finger.

Lansky froze. Despite the desperate need raging through him to storm the house and find Ava, Elijah forced himself to do the same.

Hands gripping the gutters, Savino slowly inched his eyes over the edge to check the porch. His expression, as unfathomable as ever, froze as he lifted his gaze to meet Elijah's.

The world stopped. It simply iced over as Elijah felt terror for the first time in his life. Without thinking, he started to run toward the house. When Savino slashed his hand through the air, training halted his steps, but only for a second. Savino slashed again, this time with a jab of his finger.

Sucking air through his teeth, his vision blurred by fury, Elijah froze. Sonovabitch. Ava was in there. Ramsey must be in there. He had to save her.

His eyes met Savino's.

Even yards away, he could see the intensity in his commander's gaze. The authority. For over a decade, Elijah had unquestionably followed that authority. Had trusted the man.

After two hard breaths, he accepted that if he wanted to save the woman he loved, his best chance was to follow that pattern.

To listen to Savino. To treat this as an op and do his fucking job. He gave himself another half second to rein in control, then gave Savino a nod. He slid a side glance at Lansky, who tapped a finger to his brow to signal he was ready.

Their comms were active, but until they'd assessed the situation, they couldn't risk being overheard. So they worked with hand signals.

Savino circled his finger, indicating that Lansky go around to the front of the house. The man gave Elijah a reassuring look before he angled through the trees, and on Savino's command, ran across the clearing in a low crouch. Eyes locked on Savino, Elijah waited for the signal, then made the same run toward the east side of the house.

Crouched low to stay out of view, they moved as one for the secluded visibility of the kitchen door, each checking their weapons as they moved.

"Ava?" Elijah mouthed.

"Unsecured," Savino signed.

"Anything from Powers?" Lansky asked, his voice just above a whisper as he yanked a length of wire from the back of his belt. He wasn't on duty, so unlike Elijah and Savino, he didn't carry a gun. But like them, he was trained to improvise.

"He's down."

"Ramsey?"

"In the living room with Ava." He checked his weapon, then tilted his head toward the window he'd jimmied open. "On three."

One. Elijah stretched his head to the left, then to the right.

Two. Elijah crouched low.

Three. Savino slid the window high. Hands on the frame, Elijah rolled inside with an overhead flip.

He landed silently on his feet with his gun in one hand, knife in the other, both aimed at Ramsey.

And blinked.

Because Ava was keeping the treasonous bastard too distracted to notice three SEALs bursting in.

Holy shit. She was going hand to hand with the guy. She was losing, but damned if she wasn't making him work for it.

"I was chatting with Harper," Ava said breathlessly, her leg sweeping out in a hook kick that barely missed Ramsey's belly. "Gotta say, I wasn't surprised to hear that all it takes is a straw to give you a blow job."

Elijah might have laughed if he wasn't in shock. Ramsey didn't think that insult was funny, though.

Flushing beet red, the man roared and charged. Before Elijah could shoot, Ava grabbed hold and shifted her weight, flipping the man over her shoulder. The former SEAL went crashing into a table, wood exploding into splinters.

The men rushed in. Lansky took over the ass kicking, going hand to hand to take Ramsey down.

And Elijah grabbed Ava.

"Oh my God," he breathed, pulling her into his arms. "What the hell were you doing?"

"Waiting for you. I knew you'd come. I knew you'd save me. You love me. You'd never let anything happen if you could help it." She kept babbling, her words moving so fast they ran over the top of each other. Her fists clenched the back of Elijah's shirt, her sobs breathless as reaction set in.

"You kicked ass, babe," Elijah assured her, his own heart racing as he ran one hand down her hair, the other wrapping tight enough to hold her to him forever. "You're amazing. I do love you. I'll always be here. Never let anything happen. Anything you want."

Maybe he was babbling a little, too.

"You definitely kicked ass," Lansky agreed. "Guess we're going to have to change your name to Cupcake Kick Ass."

Ava's laugh was breathless as she turned her head, still resting against Elijah's chest, and met Jared's eyes.

"I think I owe Nic a new table," Ava mumbled, burrowing deeper into Elijah's arms. She was trembling so hard, the tears shook off her face to soak his shirt.

"Looks like Ava managed to protect herself just fine," Lansky concluded, slamming his fist into Ramsey's face one more time for good measure before flipping him onto his stomach and wrapping the wires around his wrists tight enough to draw blood.

"Why the hell did she have to?" Elijah ground out,

glaring at his commander over Ava's head. "I thought Powers was covering her."

His face looking like it was carved in ice, Savino glanced out the window before answering. "He was."

"And?"

"And he's dead."

CHAPTER TWENTY

A BUGLE WAILED its mournful call as taps floated over the gentle sweep of grass, winding through trees and offering comfort to the people gathered, heads bowed, around the grave of Chief Warrant Officer Mason Powers, Navy SEAL and the first member of Poseidon to fall.

The morning sunlight gleaming over Arlington's majesty honored the fallen, as did the Admiral's words as Cree paid tribute to the loss.

Ava wondered if she'd ever seen anything as bittersweetly beautiful. Her gaze traveled from face to face, noting the identical expressions of stoic duty on the faces of the men she'd once known so well.

Diego, his dark eyes filled with banked fury, stood next to Aaron Ward, who while not refusing the white sling on his arm, had insisted on leaving his crutches behind. Lansky, Loudon, Rengel, Davidson, Kane and Brandt stood at attention to their left. To their right stood Nic Savino, his eyes shaded by glasses, his head bowed with pain.

And Elijah.

Ava's heart wept at the sight of him there, glorious in dress whites as he spoke about his friend, about his sacrifice.

Knowing she'd break at any second, Ava tore her gaze away. Her eyes skimmed Mason's family, most of whom she'd never met but recognized from photos shared long ago. Harper stood, chin high and tears trailing down her cheeks, with one arm wrapped around Nathan. Ava didn't question the boy's presence. She might have once, but she knew better now. When sacrifices were made, it was important to acknowledge them. And Nathan needed to know.

On the other side of Nathan was a curvaceous woman with an exotic air. Lansky's Greek goddess, Ava realized. The one he'd turned his life around for. Like Harper, she had one hand on Nathan's shoulder but her eyes were locked on her man.

Would it be enough? Ava wondered. Would Jared's role in all this help her see the importance of what he did, of who he was? Or would they push her further away?

Not wanting to think about that, especially since it hit much too close to home, Ava continued scanning the cemetery. Her eyes landed on a woman standing in the distance, just beyond the farthest mourner. She was slight, maybe five-five in her seriously kick-ass high heels, but she exuded a serious power that offset her small stature. Like most of the civilians, she wore black. The short skirt and fitted jacket were edged in leather, its gleam matching her short sweep of hair. Huge, round sunglasses shielded her face. The sharp edge of her jaw held enough anger to make Ava wonder who she was.

She stopped wondering when Nic caught her attention as he stepped to the front of the crowd.

"Warrant Officer Mason Powers was a man of honor,

of duty and of sacrifice. But more, he was a friend. The type of friend who was always there to listen, to talk through problems or to simply hang out over a beer. Or, in Mason's case, a twelve-pack." A hint of a smile ghosted over Nic's lips before he continued. "We called him Flipper. Not because he swam like a dolphin, although he was unmatched in the water. But because he could flip any situation to its bright side. No matter how bad things looked, Mason found a silver lining."

Nic's eyes shifted from the crowd to rest on the flag-draped casket.

"The world is already darker without him. Because there is no silver lining to the loss of an officer of his caliber. Mason Powers gave his life in service of his country, in service of his team. Today we honor our loss. We will forever honor his memory."

Ava watched the honor guard as they took position, guns at the ready.

The men came to attention. Perfectly aligned, shoulder to shoulder. Poseidon in front, SEALs in the next row, servicemen after them. As one, they saluted.

Shots rang out as seven guns fired.

Once. Twice. Thrice.

A time-honored custom that brought tears to Ava's eyes. She sniffled, lifting her chin as she tried to keep them from falling. Others weren't as concerned with hiding emotion; loud sobs sounded behind her. She wished there were words she could say, some comfort to offer.

But she knew from experience that nothing could dim the pain of death's goodbye.

The ceremony ended shortly thereafter with the reverently folded flag cradled on Mason's mother's lap. Knowing Elijah needed time with his men, not ready to share her own thoughts with anyone else, Ava walked across the lawn to a shaded bench.

"Are you okay?" Harper asked when she'd made her way over to sit by Ava. The pretty blonde slid a pair of oversize sunglasses on before laying her hand on Ava's.

"I am. A part of me feels like this is the first time I've sat, the first time I've been able to think, since those horrible events at the cabin three days ago."

"You took down Brandon." Just a hint of wicked in her laugh, Harper gave Ava's hand a squeeze before letting go. "Someone mentioned a reference to his dick being the size of a straw?"

Heat burned Ava's cheeks. That sort of talk was fine in the gym and in a fight, but she could practically hear her mother's horrified voice in her head, bemoaning that a lady shouldn't even know such words. And Harper was a lady, through and through.

But when Ava slid a sidelong look at the elegant woman next to her, she could only laugh. "I guess I did say something like that," she acknowledged, still smiling.

"Maybe it's tacky but I think that's my favorite part of this whole debacle. Beyond the pain of watching Diego deal with losing one of his men. More than gratitude that Brandon is finally caught, finally going to be brought to justice." Harper lifted her face to the gentle sun and gave a deep, heartfelt sigh of relief. "Those are all overwhelming. But through it all, I keep thinking that you took him on. You fought him. And you insulted his penis."

"I didn't really fight him. I know my limits," Ava said, brushing at the hair that'd come loose from her French braid. "I just kept him distracted until the team arrived."

"You trusted that they would?"

"I never doubted that Elijah, that his team, would come to the rescue." Eyes tracking him as he stood at the graveside, Ava knew that was one thing she'd never question again. Elijah would always be there for her. As long as she wanted him.

She remembered that faith.

Everything else—Powers's death, Ramsey's attack, his arrest, they were a blur. She vaguely remembered the cabin being swarmed by military types as Elijah had taken her upstairs to rest. She'd been happy enough having Lansky, the resident medic, give her a once-over but Elijah had insisted on a doctor visit before they were all swept onto a military plane last night to fly east to Virginia.

She'd tried to talk to Elijah. But other than heartfelt sympathy for his loss, she hadn't been able to find words to express her feelings. A part of her, still in shock over everything that'd happened, had welcomed the respite.

But the time for respite was over. Now it was time for answers. And speaking of…

"Are she and Jared a couple?" Ava gestured toward the dark-haired beauty with her arm around Nathan.

"I don't know. I think they care about each other. A lot. But even though she's trying, Andi can't seem to get past Jared's career. I can relate to her fears, but…"

"But you love Diego too much to let them stop you from being together," Ava finished for her. At Harper's stare, she shrugged. "I used to tell myself that, too. That love would overcome fear."

"Did it?"

"No." Smiling a little at Harper's scowl, Ava tilted her head to acknowledge the woman's frustration. "But believing in myself did. Believing that I'm strong enough to live with the reality of what he does, who he is."

She gestured to the cemetery, the lush green carpet dotted with the painful truth of that reality. All around them was evidence of the cost involved in serving one's country. A cost that, for so long, Ava had thought she couldn't handle.

"Those are the beliefs that matter. Those, and being confident of the life I've built, of my ability to maintain it. Those things? They drown out the fear. And they give me faith that I can handle whatever Elijah's career brings." Then, realizing she was starting to sound like an evangelist, she wrinkled her nose and added, "And, of course, I don't want to give up the great sex."

"God forbid," Harper agreed with a laugh. It faded into a soft smile as her gaze found Diego, who'd lifted a woebegone Nathan into his arms. "I've been sure that I could handle whatever comes with Diego and me. But I have to admit, your words make me feel even better."

"And your friend?" Ava wondered, watching Jared's face as he stared after the exotic woman making her way alone toward the parking lot.

"I suppose time will tell. And speaking of." Harper checked her watch, then leaned over to brush a kiss on Ava's cheek. "It's time for me to go. I hope we'll see each other soon, Ava."

"Count on it," Ava promised, giving her new friend a hug back before the blonde left to join her family.

As soon as Harper left, Elijah angled away from the uniformed crowd, his steps heavy as he crossed to join Ava. Rather than sit, he stood next to the bench, watching the crowd slowly disperse.

Ava didn't know what to say. Wasn't sure what words she could offer that would soothe the misery she saw on his face. But she'd closed herself off to his grief once before.

She couldn't do it again.

"I wish there were words that helped. Something I could say that would comfort you." She watched as Mason's mother was led away, still sobbing and nearly bent in half as she cradled the flag. "I know there aren't. But I do wish otherwise."

"It helps simply knowing you're here. That you care enough to be."

When Elijah rested a hand on her shoulder, she reached up to squeeze it.

"I used to think this was impossible."

"Dying?" she asked, although she knew that's not what he meant.

"Dying at the hands of an enemy, I accepted that." Elijah's jaw stiffened, his eyes bitter as they scanned the endless sea of graves. "Dying at the hand of a friend? Never."

"But he was the enemy," she pointed out quietly. In heels, her eyes were level with Elijah's. And she had a feeling this was going to be an eye-to-eye type of conversation. "He might have worn the face of a friend, might have worn the uniform of a brother. But he was just as much your enemy as those terrorists you faced on the field of battle."

"Right up until he said otherwise, I was sure that fire was an accident," Elijah murmured, his eyes on the people still gathered around the grave. "I'd accepted his deceit, his dishonesty and even his treason. But to deliberately hurt a brother in arms?"

He shook his head, but he couldn't shake off the pain. It was right there, etched on his face. Ava moved closer and, after a brief hesitation, wrapped her arm around his waist. Once she'd have figured he didn't want or need her support. Now she didn't care. He was getting it anyway.

Elijah's arms wound around her, gripping tight as if she were a lifeline. Ava's heart swelled, the last fortified wall disintegrating as she accepted that he did need her. And that she was strong enough to be there for him.

"I never wanted to see you here, in a place like this."

Ava leaned back to study Elijah's face. "Because you didn't think I was strong enough to handle it?"

"Maybe." His lips twisted; then he stepped around so his back was to the grave, his face toward hers. "You are now. Strong enough, I mean. But I still don't want you to ever have to do this again."

Ava's belly took a slow dive into her pretty black stilettos.

She knew what was coming.

And she was ready for it.

ELIJAH WATCHED HIS team slowly disperse. Among them, they carried grief, pain and anger. He knew, because those emotions ran through him, too.

Seething in many of the men was a thirst for revenge, the desire for answers, a need for justice. He wanted all of those, he needed to play his part in bringing them to fruition.

But he'd learned his priorities.

"Ava, we need to talk." After sliding his hand down the heavy rope of her hair, he pulled back enough to see her face.

"Here? Now?" Brow arched, she shot a look around the cemetery.

Where better, he wondered, to discuss the death of dreams? But a little distance wouldn't hurt, so he rubbed his hand down her arm before reaching for her hand and leading her along the path, away from the crowd.

He stopped when they'd reached the next set of benches, this one by a mausoleum so white it reflected sunlight with a blinding glare.

"I love you," he said, twisting his finger through one of the flyaway locks of hair drifting around Ava's face. "We made mistakes before, but loving each other wasn't one of them."

"I love you, too." Her smile was as soft as sunrise, filled with joy and hope, with promise. "I never stopped. Even when I wanted to."

"But you did want to."

Elijah shook his head before she could respond. "What we have, Ava, it's special. It's important. Too important to throw away again. I want us to be together. To have a life together. So I'm going to—"

Her fingers on his mouth stopped his words, halted the declaration he'd been practicing in his head for the past four days.

"No."

Nonplussed, he wrapped his hand around hers, lowered it to his chest.

"What?" He shook his head with a scowl. "I didn't even say anything and you're telling me no?"

"You're going to offer to leave Poseidon. That you'll leave the SEALs, leave the Navy altogether. For me."

"For us." He lifted their entwined hands to his lips, pressing a soft kiss over her knuckle. "So we can build a life together."

"You can't give up who you are, what you are. Not if we want this life together to work."

"Who I am, what I do, it put you in danger." Elijah had faced some gut-wrenching things in his life. But letting Savino haul Ramsey out of that cabin instead of beating the man into a bloody pulp was one of the hardest.

"No. You protected me." She shook her head before he could protest. "I'm the one who chose to go to the cabin. I'm the one who convinced Nic to let me stay after you told me to go. And Ramsey's the one who made the hideous choices he did. You? You're the one who rescued me, remember?"

"You were doing a damned good job of rescuing yourself."

"I couldn't have held him off. But I had to try. In part, because, well, what else was I going to do? Hide under the couch?" She gave a shaky laugh. "But mostly because I wanted to be worthy of you, Elijah. Worthy of the heroism you show every day."

Fighting off embarrassment, he shook his head.

"You devote your life to protecting others. To serv-

ing your country. To being the best. I always understood that intellectually. But this week, I finally came
to understand what it means."

"How so?"

"I went along to help protect a little boy. I fought a
treasonous ass-hat because I wouldn't—couldn't—back
down to his threat. It would have been easier to play the
weak-girl card, found a way to bullshit my way out of
the situation," she admitted. "But I had to stand up to
him. Otherwise, you could have been hurt. Otherwise
more people could have been hurt."

Voice breaking, her gaze shifted over his shoulder
to the graveside, where a brave man had just been laid
to rest. She bit her lip when it trembled, then gave a
brave lift of her chin.

"That's what you do. That's who you are. Mack told
me once that we're a lot alike, you and I. That's when I
realized that if we are, it's because I've tried to follow
your footsteps."

"Say what?"

He was all for equal opportunity, and Ava was definitely an ass kicker. But he shuddered at the idea of her
joining the Navy.

"I watched you push to be the best. Physically and
mentally, you always push yourself. And you live by a
code, one you're true to regardless of what others might
think about it." Shifting a little in his arms, she laid one
hand on his heart. "Honestly? That used to intimidate
me. But over the last few years, without realizing it, I
used you as my guide. I worked to live up to my own
code. I pushed myself. I embraced life. And I grew up."

"You've always been amazing to me," he said.

"And that's just one of the reasons why you're my hero." Laughing a little when Elijah's cheeks flushed, Ava brushed a soft kiss over his lips. "That's why I want to build that life with you, Elijah. I hope—and I'm starting to believe—that I'm finally worthy of you."

"You humble me," he murmured, overwhelmed by the intensity of his feelings.

"You're the strongest man I know." Ava lifted her free hand to cup his cheek. "And I'm finally strong enough to appreciate your strength. And to live with it."

He shook his head, not sure how to take those words. He wanted face value. Desperately. But to have all of his dreams handed to him, and love, too? It seemed impossible.

"You're serious? You really want me to remain in the Navy, in the SEALs. To continue serving with Poseidon," he confirmed.

"I do."

His chest tightened at the phrase, sure she didn't mean it to bring back memories of their wedding.

"And you'll continue to live in Napa, train others to be bad asses and go into partnership with Mack?"

His brain raced over the calendar, trying to calculate how often he'd be able to get back to see her. He wanted to believe he could have it all, but other than a few work-related-stress issues in the form of nightmares and flashbacks, nothing in his life had led him toward delusions.

"No. Actually, I was thinking I'd like to spend a little time living by the beach. A warmer climate would suit me—don't you think?"

His heart leaped. "You'd move to San Diego?"

"I was hoping for Coronado, actually." Sliding her sunglasses off, she tucked them into her pocket, staring at him with those huge brown eyes. Gaze locked on his, she smiled. "If you want me to, that is."

"You want to move south?" Reining in the part of him that wanted to agree before she changed her mind, Elijah forced himself to slow down. To make sure.

"I want to become a Navy wife. I want to follow you, wherever you're stationed. Whether that's Coronado, Hawaii, Dubai or Timbuktu." She shrugged so her breasts rubbed against his chest in teasing promise. As if that wasn't temptation, she wet her lips and smiled. "I'll follow you around the world, Elijah. And you'll make it worth my while."

"You bet I will," he agreed, his eyes locked on her mouth. Those full lips, the delicious hint of tongue. Then he blinked and shook his head, wishing it was as easy to shake off the spell of desire. "Did you want to open your own gym? If you prefer, I'll bet Mack would like the idea of opening a second location instead of expanding his current one."

"If I owned something, even if I was a partner, I'd be tied down. Stuck," she said. "The main reason I wanted to go into partnership with Mack was because I was afraid."

Elijah couldn't quite decode that connection. "You wanted to invest a large amount of money and take on a huge responsibility because you were afraid? Of what?" He'd learned the meaning of fear over the last few months, but still didn't see how it applied in this situation. But he knew, having screwed it all up once, to get any questions or doubts out in the open with Ava instead of hoping they'd fix themselves.

"Of things changing," she explained. "Mack might have brought in a partner that I didn't like, or one that I didn't get along with, or even someone who wanted to change things in ways I wasn't comfortable with."

Pushing at the wisps of hair dancing around her face, Ava wrinkled her nose. "That makes me sound like a wimp, doesn't it?"

"It makes you sound like a woman who knows what she wants and how she prefers things," he corrected.

"I've decided to stop letting fear guide my decisions," she said, her fingers tiptoeing up his chest, then sliding along the sides of his neck. "Instead I'm opting for hope."

"Yeah?" He scooped her closer, his hands resting in the sweet curve of her butt. "And just what is it that you hope for?"

"Us."

"In Southern California?" he confirmed.

"I'm hoping that I can find some coaching or teaching jobs in a gym in Coronado. Harper already said she wanted to train with me."

"She liked the idea of you kicking her ex's ass."

"Exactly," Ava said with a laugh, her hands sliding along his arms.

"Or I could do massage, work at a spa or a yoga studio. It just depends on what feels right when I get there. The only thing that matters is that this time, I follow you. That I'm there for you."

God.

Overcome, Elijah rested his forehead against hers

breathing in the gentle scent of green grass and the heady perfume that was Ava's alone.

"You're sure?"

"Positive," she said softly, leaning back so her gaze could roam over his face like a caress. "I want to live there with you. So we can build a life together."

"You want to rebuild what we had?"

"No. I want to build a new life. One based on trust and faith and—"

"Hope," he interrupted as it sank in. He really was getting all his dreams handed to him.

The ability to push beyond fear, to live strong and achieve greatness. He could do that now, knowing he'd moved past the nightmares, beyond the doubts.

His career, specializing in a field in which he excelled, one he loved and appreciated all the more now that he'd seen what it meant in his life. He could continue with it, grow with it, protect it.

And the only woman he loved.

Eyes locked on Ava's, he leaned down, but before he took her mouth, he forced himself to stop.

And ask.

"Children?"

Elijah knew he could live without them. Nothing and nobody could ever take Dominic's place in his life or in his heart. But he wanted the parameters clear, and he wanted to make sure Ava knew he wasn't expecting more than she wanted to give.

"I'd like three," she said softly, her hands framing his face now as she smiled that gorgeous smile of hers. The one that lit up his heart. "We have our angel, so let's see about two more."

And there it was. Everything he'd ever wanted in life.

Elijah's heart felt too big for his chest, hope and joy swelling huge as he stared into the face of the one woman he wanted to spend his life with.

Gone was the feeling of having his life adrift like a rudderless boat tossed about on a storm-swept sea. He'd found his North Star. As long as he had her, he'd always find his way.

"I love you, Ava."

"I love you, too," she said just before she lifted her mouth to his. "Forever this time."

* * * * *

Navy SEAL Nic Savino has a score to settle—but one woman is standing in his way...
Look for CALL TO REDEMPTION by
New York Times *bestselling author Tawny Weber,*
another TEAM POSEIDON *story,*
on sale in November 2017.

SPECIAL EXCERPT FROM

*Read on for a sneak peek at CALL TO REDEMPTION
an exciting new **TEAM POSEIDON** novel from*
New York Times *bestselling author Tawny Weber!*

"Lieutenant Commander Dominic Savino, you stand accused of conduct unbecoming an officer, disobeying orders and complicity in treason."

The voice boomed like a cannon, its roar a vivid contrast to the courtroom's silence. As he stood at attention on the stand, the sound ricocheted down Nic's spine like a piece of shrapnel, ripping and tearing.

"Commander, do you understand these charges?"

Understand? Nic had a solid understanding of the fact that he'd been framed, that he was the fall guy for some treasonous son of a bitch.

Yeah.

He understood that.

That and everything that came with the charges leveled against him. Court martial. Prison time. The end of his career. The loss of his freedom. The destruction of his team. Fury rose, rolling like waves that crested higher with each heartbeat.

But none of that was evident on his face. Neither awareness nor fury were allowed to show.

"Affirmative."

"How do you plead?"

Nic's gaze didn't shift left, didn't move right. His deadeye stare was aimed straight ahead, focused on the rippling glory of the American flag hanging over the courtroom's double doors.

He replayed the accusation. He thought back over the previous year's events.

An operation gone horribly wrong that'd resulted in life-threatening injuries to one team member and the supposed death of another.

The realization that a SEAL, a man sworn to serve his country, would steal classified information to sell to the highest bidder, put his teammates' lives in peril and fake his death—all for money. The shocking acceptance that the same man would target a young child and a defenseless woman, and kill a fellow SEAL.

And now the emotional train wreck of watching his team be targeted by an asshole with an agenda, who was determined to ignore the fact that Poseidon was being framed by a traitorous sociopath with psychotic tendencies.

Ignoring the tight knot in his gut, he gave Lieutenant Thomas a look cold enough to freeze the man's innards and, in a clear voice, stated, "Not guilty."

Thomas's eyes narrowed; his lips tightened. Why the man should flash frustration was baffling. Nic filed the look away to decipher later.

For now, he simply let his stare intimidate until the lieutenant turned away. But not before Nic caught the line between his brows twitching.

For the first time since he'd walked into the courtroom that morning, the tension tying his intestines in knots loosened.

He was innocent.

His team was clean.

No matter what information the lieutenant and his crew thought they'd brought to the table over the course of this trial, Nic knew that none of them had done anything illegal, against orders or in any way traitorous.

But now?

Nic watched as Thomas exchanged frowns with the lieutenant commander seated at the prosecutors' table.

Now? He had hope. More, he had faith that he'd not only be vindicated, but that he'd keep his command, his team and, dammit, that they'd nail the real traitor before this was over.

He glanced toward the gallery. His team spanned the first row. Ten men in uniform, each one wearing a look of implacable determination. Each one radiating strength and dedication. And, yes, each one looking equally pissed at the insult they knew they'd been served.

Nic's gaze shifted to the right, toward the woman sitting just behind the prosecution.

Beneath an edgy fringe of bangs, a pair of huge gold eyes stared back at him. In those molten depths he saw two things. Strength and challenge.

How had he gotten this far in life without her?

And what the hell was he going to do now that he'd found her? Nic had risked something that many people—including himself—had come to believe didn't exist.

His heart.

Because he'd lost it to the woman who was about to destroy his life.

Will treason and scandal tear Nic and Darby apart?

Find out what happens next in CALL TO REDEMPTION
by New York Times bestselling author Tawny Weber!

Available November 2017 wherever HQN books and ebooks are sold.

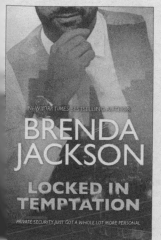

The *Killer Instinct* series from *New York Times* bestselling author

CYNTHIA EDEN

continues as an FBI profiler tracks a case that resurrects ghosts from his past.

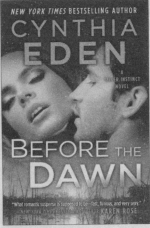

Ex-SEAL Tucker Frost knows that the world is full of evil. He saw it in the face of his own brother, Mason Frost, a cold, methodical, sadistic killer. A killer Tucker put down with his own hands in order to save Mason's final victim—Dawn Alexander, the only girl who got away from the infamous "Iceman."

It's Tucker's up-close-and-personal experience with evil that's made him perfect for Samantha Dark's experimental profiling division in the FBI. Samantha wants agents who have personal ties with killers, who have unique insights into the minds of monsters. And when women start turning up murdered with the same MO used by the Iceman, Tucker is sent back to Louisiana to investigate.

The last person he expects to see is his ex-lover, Dawn. Ten full years have passed since the night that Tucker faced down his brother…and since he last saw Dawn. But the dark need still burns just as hot between Tucker and Dawn. As they grapple with a desire that never died, they must also face the shared shadow from their pasts. Both Tucker and Dawn have the same question—has Mason Frost come back from the dead to hunt again? And this time, will he succeed in killing the victim who got away?

Available July 25

Order your copy today!

www.HQNBooks.com

PHCE3